I0691325

UNTO THE LAST SEED

BY
CRAIG LEONARD SR.

Copyright © 2015 by Craig Leonard Sr.

All rights reserved.

Book design by Craig Leonard Sr.

No part of this book may be reproduced in any form or
by any electronic or mechanical means including information storage
and retrieval systems, without permission in writing
from the author. The only exception is by a reviewer,
who may quote short excerpts in a review.

Craig Leonard Sr. Books are available for order
through Ingram Press Catalogues

Craig Leonard Sr.
Visit my website at www.craigleonardsr.com

Printed in the United States of America
First Printing: November 2015
Published by Sojourn Publishing, LLC

ISBN: 978-1-62747-180-0
Ebook ISBN: 978-1-62747-181-7

DEDICATION

This book is dedicated to Adam and Thelma (Sis) Leonard, my parents. My earliest memories in life are those on shrimp and oyster boats, hunting, fishing, floundering and throwing a cast net. I've eaten at the finest restaurants across the world and have never eaten a finer meal than at my mother's table. Under my father's guidance, I've learned the true meaning of what it means to be Cajun.

ACKNOWLEDGEMENTS

There are many people who helped with the final outcome of my novel. I thank Marinda and Donald Johnfroe for the endless times you came to my rescue and moral support. I thank Heather, Holly, T-Craig and Sissy, for their kind and uplifting words on every phone call- (I can always count on you guys. You've never let me down!) I especially thank Dr. Bill Scaggs for his editing expertise and pushing me forward. I thank you Glenda for tirelessly putting up with me and my sometimes snappy tone during the editing process–you are loved!! Last but not least–Thank you, to all my friends and relatives for all the encouraging words and show of support. With people like you all around me, I know I am Loved!! With all that is in me THANK YOU!!

CHAPTER 1

Hand in hand, Eric and Olivia Cameaux walked with their young daughters Teresa and Toni along the banks of a muddy South Louisiana bayou, held in check by its low-lying levees; the bayou, barely wider than a stone's throw, snaked its way lazily southward. Giant oak trees bearded with Spanish moss dominated both levees while the bayou's clouded waters tumbled below. Unexpectedly a thick, dark fog rolled in upon them. Without warning Eric suddenly released Olivia's hand; instantly the impenetrable mist consumed him. Disoriented and terrified, she groped for him in the darkness, clutching only emptiness for her effort.

Through the fog Olivia heard Eric call for help, but it was impossible to determine the direction of his cries. His words were unintelligible, distorted by the rising winds that suddenly began whipping around them. Teresa and Toni clung to her, their escalating screams blending into an unquenchable shrillness.

In her mind, Olivia screamed Eric's name, but no sound escaped her lips. Finally, she vaguely sensed that Eric's continuing cries came from the opposite side of the bayou. Though still not understanding his messages, there was no doubt he needed her. But for what? She searched frantically for some means of assistance, but she and the girls stood alone and helpless. Frustrated but determined, Olivia knew she had but one choice: She tore free from her children and dove into the

dark, forbidding bayou. The water seemed calm despite the raging winds. As she began swimming toward the direction of Eric's voice, however, Teresa and Toni begged her to return. Torn between her husband's muffled cries and her daughters' piercing wails, Olivia paused only momentarily before turning, intending to swim back to her children. But, hearing renewed calls from Eric, she turned back to seek him, only to discover that his cries had been consumed by deafening peals of crashing, rolling thunder.

Stinging pellets of icy rain assaulted her, and jagged streaks of lightning sizzled and smoked the blackness. Suddenly the waters began churning, and in the lightning's eerie glow, Olivia saw four silhouetted shadows in the direction of Eric's cries. Men, perhaps – yet she couldn't be certain. The shadows elongated, reaching toward her. The chill of water and rain reached into her being. Confusion gave way to terror. The grasping shadows darkened. Olivia stared into darkness and felt an overpowering sense of evil.

Her maternal instinct took control, and her only thoughts were for the safety of her children. Yet as she tried swimming toward them, the water around her had become like molasses. Although she struggled and thrashed, the bayou clutched her; progress was impossible. She could no longer see Teresa and Toni on the shore; they, too, had vanished before her eyes. In panic she screamed repeatedly calling out to both the girls and Eric. Suddenly, a dark silence gripped her raw vocal cords—her voice was gone.

And then, Olivia Awakened.

Daybreak was shrouded in pre-dawn frost when Olivia Cameaux awoke with her heart pounding and her trembling body drenched in sweat. She reached through the darkness to touch Eric's arm.

A wave of relief swept over her as his stirring reassured her he was still sleeping peacefully. "Thank God, it was only a dream," Olivia sighed as she took a deep breath and slowly swung her legs off her side of the bed. She rarely dreamed, especially one so realistic. She knew she'd get no more sleep until she'd assured herself that Teresa and Toni were equally safe and secure, and this she did.

Shivering as she returned to bed, Olivia saw that Eric had awakened, and she snuggled close to him to be sheltered and warmed

in his comforting embrace. As always, his strong arms enfolded her and she whispered an oft-spoken prayer of blessing and protection upon her family.

Eric and Jon Cameaux had been eagerly looking forward to the next few days of their guys-only duck hunt, for what had begun as just an occasional getaway had turned into a yearly tradition. The two brothers and their first cousin Derrick would drop whatever their work and family demanded and slip away for a week of hunting, fishing and relaxing. It wasn't always easy to get away. Dr. Eric, at thirty-two, had a full, busy schedule of seeing patients five days a week in his general practice. On the home front Olivia was the girl of Eric's dreams. Five-foot-eight inches tall, slender, dark shoulder-length hair and even darker eyes that complemented her olive complexion, Olivia stayed in great shape. She wasn't gorgeous in the New York sense, nevertheless her beauty and intelligence held the heart of her husband. Olivia, five-year-old Teresa and three-year-old Toni were the driving forces behind Eric's life. At first Olivia had resented the all-guys week. Later she came to terms with Eric's need for a change of pace and renewal. He was a good husband and father, never complaining of being too tired to help even after a long day of seeing patients. Eric seemed to understand that Olivia's days of caring for their two small children were every bit as demanding as his own. After six years of marriage, both Eric and Olivia knew their relationship was not only very special, but also very strong. Now she no longer felt threatened by the annual getaway. In fact, she was happy for him.

If Eric appeared the epitome of maturity and responsibility, thirty-year-old Jon Cameaux seemed the exact opposite. Jon claimed he had no intention of marrying and settling down any time soon. After attending two years of college, he decided that too much education wasn't good for the soul. Convinced he needed to broaden his horizons, Jon had joined the Navy at the age of twenty. After eight years the call of home overwhelmed the thrill of adventure, and this sailor decided not to re-enlist; instead, he accepted an offer from his father Ben to join the family business. Reflecting on this life-altering decision and his past two years in the business, Jon never doubted that he had made the right choice. Even knowing that most people still

thought of him as immature and irresponsible, especially compared to Eric, didn't concern him – not that it really mattered to him what other people thought. Besides, he might just prove them all wrong someday.

Cameaux Fish and Shrimp Company, located along Bayou Lafourche in Golden Meadow, Louisiana, bought seafood from local fishermen and shipped it to processing plants in Alabama and Florida. It had been a family business for nearly fifty years, having been established by Ben's father, Olidore Cameaux, whom everyone called Pappy.

Despite his earlier lack of direction, Jon found something he really enjoyed. As a young boy, he worked in the family business and hated it. Back then he could see no future in smelly seafood. Now he could see a business that would someday be his. This venture, both rewarding and serving an important role in the community, would be his responsibility to carry through to the next generation. Reuniting with his family, reconnecting with his community, brought Jon "Home." He and Eric were more than just brothers; they were best friends. Jon's being away for a while only strengthened the bond between them.

The time set for leaving for the camp had been Friday; however, Eric and Jon decided Monday that they would leave a day earlier. The brutal winter brought temperatures dipping below freezing three days in a row. Jon thought that perhaps some of the water pipes at the camp could have burst and he wanted to fix any problem ASAP. Eric contacted Derrick in Mississippi to let him know of their rescheduled plans and tried to get him to join them a day earlier, but Derrick stuck with the original plan of leaving on Friday.

CHAPTER 2

Early Tuesday morning Jon went to Bayou Hardware and Supply co. to buy the pipe fittings he thought they might need. Though Bayou Hardware had everything he needed for pipe repairs, that wasn't the only reason he did business there. Working in the store office was Julie Brasseaux, the daughter of Hilton Brasseaux, who owned the business. Julie and Jon dated a few times in the past month and had really enjoyed each other's company. Since their first date neither one had dated anyone else. Jon wouldn't admit it just yet, but Julie certainly had captured a part of his heart.

Without making it too obvious, he quickly looked straight to the rear of the store. Through the large plate-glass window he could see a lady working with a computer, but it wasn't Julie. Then from the corner of his eye he saw Mr. Hilton coming toward him, calling out in a loud, friendly voice, "Jon, how are you?"

"Oh, I'm just fine, Sir, how about you?"

Grinning, Mr. Hilton answered, "Well Jon, it don't pay to complain. No one listens anyway. What can I do for you?"

"I just need some pipe fittings, Mr. Hilton."

"Okay, follow me. We ought to have exactly what you need." Mr. Hilton led Jon down an aisle to the plumbing section. Every chance he could, he continued scanning the store in search of Julie, but finally shook his head in frustration, convinced that bad timing was his

problem. Glancing over his shoulder as they reached the fittings section, Mr. Hilton said, "Jon, if you call out what you want, I'll gather it up for you."

"Yes, Sir, let's start with half-inch couplings and tees."

As both men worked on the list, they were unaware that someone else had noticed Jon's entering the store. In the sporting-goods section stood an old man wearing camouflage coveralls and a pair of hip boots turned down to just below his knees. From under his hunting cap, which was completely encircled by an unbroken string of mallard curl feathers, a shock of straight white hair flowed down to his shoulders. His creased face suggested his age to be at least sixty very hard years. His dark, leathery skin revealed a life of exposure to the sun and hard work. Where his face exposed his age, though, his physique did not. Every muscle over his six-foot frame was taut and behind this mask of age stood a man of power and resolve. The penetrating stare of his dark, deep-set eyes, his most haunting feature, could leave people feeling uneasy and unclean. Only the resolute could maintain eye contact for long. When he caught sight of Jon, the old Cajun focused his venomous gaze on him.

When Mr. Hilton led Jon down the aisle with the pipe fittings; the old man followed down an adjacent isle. He stopped even with Jon, but neither man could see the other because of the high shelving. Then, leaning closer, the old man listened with interest to everything Jon and Mr. Hilton said.

"That should fix me up, Mr. Hilton. Put this on the Cameaux account, please."

Curious, Mr. Hilton asked, "Ya'll got some busted lines at the shrimp shed, Jon?"

"No, Sir, Eric and I are going to the camp Thursday morning. I just thought we might have a couple busted water lines with all the cold weather we had lately."

"Oh yeah, Julie was tellin' me you boys were goin' huntin' this weekend."

"That's right. I think it'll be a good weekend. The ducks are really coming in, according to a few folks I've talked to."

Smiling, Mr. Hilton replied, "That's what I've heard too. Listen, Jon, I know someone who would love to see you. Why don't you wait right here while I get her?"

"Yes, Sir," said Jon with more enthusiasm than he intended.

Now, unnoticed by anyone else in the store, the old man who followed Jon and listened so intently to his conversation with Mr. Hilton quietly made his way back to the sporting-goods department where a young clerk asked, "Yes, Sir, can I help you?"

Looking squarely at the clerk, the old man replied in a steely voice, "Gimme a case of 12-gauge 00 buckshot."

"Yes Sir," he replied and promptly disappeared through a curtained door leading to a storage room. The old man slowly glanced over his shoulder; he spotted Jon again and transfixed a chilling glare on the young Cameaux. As the clerk emerged from behind the curtain, the old man turned quickly to face him.

"Can I get you anything else, Sir?"

The old man's hesitant response and probing stare lasted just a little too long for the young man's comfort. "No!" came the curt response.

Quickly, the clerk rang up the charge. "That comes to $72.25."

The old man threw a hundred dollar bill on the counter and watched closely as the change was counted. He scooped up the money and the case of buckshot and walked to the front door. He paused for one last glance at Jon, who was still waiting for Julie.

"Cameaux fool," he muttered as he turned and walked out of the store.

Jon, meanwhile, remained unaware of the strange old man and was simply trying to calm that unfamiliar fluttering feeling in his stomach. As he double-checked his list of needed supplies, he heard that sweet voice.

"Hi, Jon, Dad said you were out here."

Smiling, he answered, "Hi Julie. Hope your dad didn't bother you. I know you're busy." He wondered whether she felt as foolishly nervous as he did.

"Oh, I'm never too busy to talk to you." Before he could respond, she continued, "Besides, no matter how busy we are, I leave at five sharp."

"Well, what about supper tonight?"

Hesitating, Julie smiled. "I've already been asked to supper tonight, Jon." His mouth opened slightly, and his color changed in spite of his best effort. "Dad's boiling crawfish. Can you make it?"

Relief flooded his face, as both of them started laughing. Jon bowed his head and said "I would be honored, Lovely Lady. What time would you like me there?"

"How about seven?"

Walking closer to Julie, he lightly touched her arm as he spoke. "Sounds good to me, I look forward to spending the evening with you and your family. You know we should talk after dinner about our future."

Those words caught Julie a little off guard. Of course she wanted this handsome man in her future. As though to confirm her thoughts, Jon leaned closer till his lips lightly met hers. It was the first time they kissed each other and she thought her knees would buckle. Just as she started to press forward, Jon withdrew, smiling. "See you tonight, gotta go and finish my to-do list."

"OK," was her only response as she took a deep breath and watched him walk away. Julie smiled, hoping their relationship would develop into something permanent. She was certainly planning to do everything she could to make that happen.

CHAPTER 3

By mid-morning Thursday Eric and Jon were busy loading all the provisions onto their skiff. They were almost finished when Jon asked, "Olivia and the girls coming down to see us off, Breaux?"

"Of course, they should be here any time now. What about you, Little Brother?"

"What do you mean?"

Laughing, Eric teased, "Don't give me that dumb look. You know what I mean. Is Miss Julie coming to see you off?"

"Oh," said Jon casually, "we said our good-byes last night."

Ribbing Jon, Eric dug a little deeper. "You mean you're telling me you went out with Julie Tuesday and Wednesday night?" Well, looks to me like you just might be changing that Navy ring in for a wedding ring in the not-too-distant future."

"Don't read too much into that, Breaux!"

Eric smiled, "Oh, I don't think I'm doing that at all."

Looking up, Jon saw Olivia, Teresa and Toni, along with his father Ben, coming down the wharf and said, "Thank you, Lord, for small favors."

Overhearing him, Olivia asked, "And what favors would that be, Jon?"

"Any that'll change this conversation! Hi Olivia, hey muskrats!"

Teresa and Toni waved excitedly to their Uncle Jon; then Ben spoke, "Now remember boys, Derrick should get to Golden Meadow about dinner time tomorrow. Course, he'll want to spend some time with your grandpa first. So about one o'clock, I'll pick Derrick up from Pappy's house and bring him here. He'll take the small skiff to the camp."

"Sure Dad that reminds me," said Eric. "I put two five-gallon cans of oil-mixed fuel in the small skiff. Do you think we'll have enough to last the week?"

Ben hesitated but a second, then responded, "I tell you what, Valdore Gisclair's runnin' a short trap line in our swamp about a mile an a piece past the camp on Bayou Raphael. I told him about your huntin' trip, an he says he'll stop by an say hello. I'm sure if you run short of something, he wouldn't mind to get it for you."

"Got ya, Dad, I look forward to seeing Mr. Gisclair." This time Eric couldn't hide his smile because he knew Valdore's visit would be Ben's way of watching over them,

The elder Cameaux then turned his attention to his youngest son and granddaughters. This was the perfect time for Olivia as she walked up close to Eric and asked, "Are you sure Derrick doesn't mind helping us with the house plans? I just don't want to impose on him."

"Impose on Derrick?" said Eric, with an amused look on his face. "Honey, when I told him about our plans to build a new home, he said it was about time I moved you and the girls into something decent. Then he told me, not asked but told me, to send him all the details we want so he could get started. He's as excited about this as we are. What could I say, but thanks?"

"I just wanted to make sure," said Olivia.

Quietly walking up to stand between her mother and father, Teresa reached up and grabbed her mother's hand. Eric reached down and gently scooped up his older daughter in his arms. "Are you going to take care of Mommy while Daddy's gone?"

"Uh-huh," answered Teresa, nodding her head affirmatively before laying it gently against his chest.

Toni, not wanting to be left out, immediately ran shouting, "Me too, Daddy! I'll take care of Mommy for you!"

Kneeling down with Teresa still in one arm, Eric smiled and also picked up his younger daughter, saying to each of them, "Daddy loves you very, very much, and I'm counting on both of you to take care of Mommy. Now, give me a big kiss and a big bear hug." As the girls smothered their father with affection, Eric laughed, "Wow, that's some good sugar! Now hug your Uncle Jon goodbye." As soon as Eric let them down, they scrambled forward.

Obviously touched, but also eager to get their venture under way, Jon quickly climbed out of the skiff and onto the wharf to receive his nieces' affections. Eric turned to Olivia and they embraced tightly. Olivia whispered, "Eric, come home safely to me."

Thinking her words sounded more like a plea, he assured her, "Baby, we're just going hunting. We've done this a thousand times. We'll be fine. I love you." For some strange reason, though, her words echoed in his mind and her eyes revealed such deep concern that he felt uneasy.

Watching all the good-byes and smiling, Ben said, "Boys, you better be on your way."

Eric and Jon bid their father farewell and quickly climbed into the skiff. At the controls as usual, Jon started the engine and then shouted above the noise. "Pop, sure wish you were coming with us."

"Me, too son, maybe next year," replied Ben in a steady voice. Since his wife Emily died of cancer two years before, Ben had a difficult time regaining that light Cajun spirit for which he had always been known. Ben didn't want to dampen the excitement of the boys' hunting trip. The boys loved and respected their father and would give him whatever time he needed to regain the joy lost to his heart.

"Bye, Daddy! Bye, Uncle Jon!" yelled Teresa and Toni. Both men waved and blew kisses to the girls. Then Eric blew a special kiss to Olivia, and she warmly returned the affectionate gesture.

Jon slowly moved the skiff away from the dock. Once clear, he pushed the throttle forward, and the Miss Teresa came alive. Surging forward, the men had to find a hand-hold to steady themselves for a moment while the skiff settled on her speed. At eighteen feet in length and sporting a hundred-fifty horse power Cruiser out-board on her

stern, the Miss Teresa was quick and light, a perfect combination for maneuvering through the bayous and bays of South Louisiana.

As Eric looked back toward the diminishing figures on the dock, he gave one last exaggerated wave. In response Olivia raised her hand and suddenly thought of her dream of a few nights ago; a cold chill made the hair on the back of her neck stand out. Stunned by that unexpected, crude sensation, she gathered the girls and without a word hurried them off the dock, followed closely by Ben.

CHAPTER 4

After heading in a southerly direction for half a mile, Jon had turned due east off Bayou Lafourche onto Yankee Canal. Glancing toward Eric with a sly look on his face, Jon pointed toward the ice chest. Eric grinned, reached down, and opened to reveal an assortment of iced beverages. "Well, what'll it be, Little Brother? We have Coke, 7-Up, grape juice. . . ."

Jon cut in with a quick "How abooooout beer?"

"Thought you'd never ask," laughed Eric as he picked up two beers, handing one to Jon and opening the other.

The Yankee Canal was so named after the Yankee farmers many years ago who tried unsuccessfully to farm the area by building a series of levees and draining the swamp. It had failed because the levees were unable to hold back the surrounding waters long enough to produce a crop. What these outsiders hadn't known was that in a normal year, Louisiana experiences more rainfall than any other state in the nation. Add to that the usual annual Gulf hurricanes, and the Yankee farmers finally realized what Cajuns from times past already knew: You eat with a grateful heart whatever shrimp, crabs and oysters the bayous and the lakes give you, and then you harvest whatever crops of coon, mink, alligator and crawfish the swamps allow you, but you must never demand this land to give you the unnatural.

13

Yankee Canal was one of the main arteries connecting Bayou Lafourche with the eastern marshlands and swamps, but there were no road signs to direct sojourners to turn here or to exit one mile. A wrong turn out here could be hazardous to one's health, but that wasn't a problem for Eric, Jon or Derrick. They had been weaned in this South Louisiana "paradise." Now, as the brothers made their way through the canal, Jon eased up on the throttle as the water lilies thickened. Both men's attention was transfixed on their surroundings. Enormous alligators sliced through the water ahead of them while herons and egrets used their long necks as spears to catch minnows along the water's edge. Ducks and geese in abundance flew high overhead noisily searching for just the right feeding ponds. On either side of the canal, ancient oaks and huge weeping willows stood tall and proud like mighty sentinels guarding a magical watery kingdom. Thick vegetation under the ancient trees afforded protection to rabbits, coons, bobcats, deer and even an occasional black bear. Old timers swore there were even stranger creatures slithering in these swamps.

After an hour and a half they came to the end of Yankee Canal. Jon turned the *Miss* Teresa north into Bayou Chienne and followed it for an additional two miles before making the final turn. From the time they turned off Bayou Chienne, they were in what Cajuns called the Cameaux Swamp. Belonging to the Cameaux family, these five thousand acres were considered one of the richest wildlife habitats in North America. Straight ahead in the distance, not more than a mile away, Eric and Jon could see a portion of the clearing where the family camp was located. They were proud of their little haven. Designed by Derrick, the camp house was practical and convenient. Facing the bayou in front of the camp, the tiny wharf extended twenty-five feet from the bank of the levee. Hovering a foot above this levee was the catwalk, which extended from the wharf to the camp's screened porch. As they approached the wharf, Jon pulled back on the throttle and initiated his docking maneuver. As they drew within a few feet of the wharf, Eric noticed that the porch's screened door was slightly ajar, a door which was normally always kept locked. They knew that occasionally a trapper or hunter caught in stormy weather would seek shelter in the camp. Usually though, that person would tell the family

what happened and that would be the end of that. Neither Eric nor Jon was aware of anyone who had sought shelter lately.

Jon guided the *Miss Teresa* to the wharf and put her starboard side in line with the mooring bits. As the skiff gently touched the wharf, Eric grabbed the bow line, climbed onto the dock and quickly tied first the bow, then the stern. After turning off the motor, Jon threw Eric the first of two duffel bags containing their clothes, and then Eric caught hold of Jon's arm to help his younger brother out of the skiff. On the way up Jon said, "You know, Eric, it wouldn't take much for me to move out here and live."

"Sure, Jon, and on those lonesome summer nights, maybe you could find a cold female gator to cuddle with."

Laughing Jon answered, "Hey, Breaux, I didn't think of that! Did I ever tell you about the time I went on shore-leave in Dubai . . . . . ."

Eric, sorry that he had spurred Jon into telling another of his overseas exploits, picked up the duffel bags and proceeded to nudge him up the catwalk toward the camp. Soon both men were laughing as they approached the screened porch. That laughter quickly faded though, as Jon, still walking just one step in front of Eric, glanced up and was startled to see a man standing at the screened door. The intruder held a shotgun pointed directly at them, and at that same instant two other men, one from the left and one from the right sides of the camp, came running toward them with shotguns raised as well. Both brothers stopped short; without hearing a word of explanation, they stood in silent horror at the sight of three shotguns aimed directly at them. Just as Eric opened his mouth to speak, the deafening explosion of shotgun blasts suddenly broke the moment of confused silence. The force of the impact lifted and violently thrust Jon backward into Eric, sending both men crashing to the catwalk. With his last breath, as he lay there atop his brother, Jon whispered, "Eric, Eric. . . . "

Eric was stunned. Surely this wasn't happening! Then another round of shotgun blasts brought reality into focus: Eric felt the sting on both the right and left sides of his body. His right arm and hand were shattered; that very hand that was once used to heal other people's broken bones had now been shredded beyond repair. He was only vaguely aware of the multiple pellets of buckshot that had violated his lungs. He was dying.

Although it was difficult for him to breathe, with all the strength left in his body he raised his head from the catwalk to look directly into the cold, vacant eyes of his murderers. He could see three figures standing at his feet. When they looked to their left in the direction of a thicket, Eric also rolled his eyes in that direction to watch a fourth man walking toward him. As the figure approached, he saw an elderly man wearing camouflage coveralls and hip-boots turned down to just below the knees. As he felt his life ebbing away, no longer able to hold up his head, he slowly lowered it onto the catwalk, but never closed his eyes. Within moments the old man stood over him and peered down in cold, contented silence. Eric couldn't see the face clearly; all he could focus on was what looked like a mass of feathers around the old man's head. Straining painfully to somehow sharpen his blurred vision, he and his enemy met eye to eye and Eric recognized him. Like venom-soaked steel darts of pure malicious evil, the old man's eyes seemed to bore into the very depths of Eric's soul. His thin, tight lips contorted and twisted his mouth into what might be described as a self-satisfied smirk. Then Jon's murderer threw back his head and cackled loud, coarse, cruel laughter of perverse pleasure.

Though too late, Eric now realized that his grandfather Pappy had been right. Lost in the echoes of that chorus of wicked laughter – for now the other three men had joined their elder in his malignant mirth – Eric whispered, "Rabeaux."

The old man bent forward until his face was just inches from Eric's face and hissed, "Now I done kill two more damn Cameaux!" Then he spat in Eric's face before rising to walk away. As Eric slipped away, his fading consciousness softly played the familiar voices of two little girls crying, "We love you, Daddy. Don't worry; we'll take care of Mommy. We love you." Tears ran from the corners of his eyes as darkness closed in. Almost as if from some other dimension, it seemed that he could see Olivia standing on the opposite side of some nameless bayou, holding tightly to their daughters and whispering again and again, "I love you, Eric." Barely noticeable, Eric's lips moved, "I love you, Olivia. . . ."

CHAPTER 5

At thirty-three, Derrick Cameaux was a very successful, well-respected Mississippi businessman. Owner of Magnolia State Construction Company, Inc., he had built quite a reputation in the building industry. Like his cousins Eric and Jon, he was born and reared in the small South Louisiana town of Golden Meadow, an un-Cajun name for a very Cajun place.

Derrick's new home and company were located in Meridian, Mississippi, a growing city in the eastern mid-section of the state just nineteen miles from the Alabama state line. It had taken him ten years to build his company to its current status, the second-largest construction company in the state, a fact which made him a wealthy man.

In spite of his riches, Derrick felt loneliness in his life that money couldn't fill. He was beginning to realize this, especially at the end of the day when he came home to an empty house. Of course, there were plenty of young ladies willing to change Derrick's bachelor status – and not just because of his money. At six-foot-three and two hundred pounds in a well-conditioned body not to mention his near shoulder-length dark curly hair and even darker eyes Derrick was considered a "catch." He was handsome by any definition and though he dated on occasion, he never felt that tingle or throbbing heartbeat people talked about when falling in love. That's not to say that a beautiful woman

17

couldn't arouse his natural male instincts; it's just that none of them held his attention for very long.

Derrick's work schedule stood as another barrier to Derrick's love life; fifteen-hour days were not uncommon and many weekends were no different. He loved his work, and the only days he ever really allowed himself away from it were spent hunting, his true love. Thus, it actually wasn't hard to see why he came home to an empty house each day. There was little time for anything else in his world.

Perhaps the one thing Derrick wouldn't miss or put off to another day was the annual duck hunt with Eric and Jon. Regardless of everything else, he made sure his schedule remained opened for that hunt and wouldn't miss it for anything.

Derrick's company had a reputation not only for treating their employees fairly, but was also highly respected in the business community. Everyone knew that Magnolia State reflected the character of its owner, but only Derrick knew that Magnolia State was a direct reflection of his entire Cajun upbringing, and credit for that could only go to one man, his grandfather Pappy. Everything Derrick stood for – honesty, integrity, character and everything else Derrick was – he learned from this patriarch of the Cameaux family. Derrick's inner soul was solid. Never a day passed that he didn't think of his Louisiana hometown and his family living there. Though now surrounded by his new friends in Mississippi, he still longed for the sights and smells of the bayou state.

Tuesday and Wednesday found Derrick gathering and packing his hunting gear and provisions. He took his time to assess all the necessary equipment he would carry with him. The first item loaded in his Jeep was his weapon of choice, a 12-gauge Winchester pump model 1100 shotgun, which his now-deceased father Louis gave him when he was nine years old. It was a treasure so valuable that it felt like family, and every time he picked it up, his vivid memories took him back to those days as that nine-year-old boy. Derrick felt his father's trust in him to respect and handle with confidence so powerful a weapon, a trust he would never betray. Now even as an adult many years after his father's death, Derrick still had great respect for this weapon, and his confidence in his ability to use it had never been

higher. Along with the shotgun, he also packed his 7mm hand gun which he always carried on hunting trips, especially in the swamps of his home state where the cottonmouth moccasins grew bigger than a man's arm and twice as long.

The last weapon he packed was his Bowie knife. The personal and up-close nature of using this knife got Derrick's adrenaline flowing.

On Thursday night, Derrick was packed and ready to go. It had been a long week, but each day had brought him closer to going home and had heightened his excitement because he looked forward to seeing his family and old friends in Golden Meadow. As he laid his head on his pillow, he thought of the possibility of permanently returning one day to the state he loved so dearly. As his eyes grew heavy, he also thought of Eric and Jon and of the good times the three had growing up in South Louisiana.

Everyone at some point in the course of a life can pinpoint a day or an event that surpasses all others in changing his direction. For Derrick Cameaux, however, neither that one day nor that one event occurred in his own lifetime, but more than a hundred years earlier. Furthermore, though presently unaware of that eventful day which *then* had nothing to do with him personally; the *now* of today's timing was an entirely different matter.

CHAPTER 6

At sixty-eight, Valdore Gisclair was one of a remnant of Cajuns to make a living solely from the swamps and marshlands. He trapped, crawfished and worked his oysters in fall and winter; in spring and summer he harvested shrimp, fish and crabs. He raised his family solely on the sometimes uncertain income gained from the bayous of South Louisiana. Nevertheless, Valdore knew there was no other job that would have given him more pleasure than reaping the bounty the land afforded.

His three sons and one daughter, now all grown and married, opted for more stable and higher paying work in the oil industry. Valdore always felt a slight sadness when he thought of his ancestors who made their livings on the bayou because he knew that he would be the last in his line to do the same.

One area most prolific for Valdore's trapping endeavors was the Cameaux swamp owned by the Cameaux family. Lifelong friends, the Cameaux and Gisclair families always worked together for their common survival.

Leaving the Cameaux docks at 4:30 a.m., Valdore tried to find some protection from the cold behind the small windshield in front of his skiff's steering column. Turning east on Yankee Canal and, away from the lights of Golden Meadow, it took him a few moments for his eyes to adjust to the darkness. As he maneuvered through the water,

his thoughts were on the trapping season thus far. He was well pleased with the trapping line he chose this year, for the nutria and muskrat populations were booming; and if the prices held up, he should have an excellent year.

Valdore smiled as he thought of his grandson's scheduled trip with him tomorrow. Lane was only 10 years old, but already showing considerable interest in the swamps and marshlands. Valdore always enjoyed his grandson's inquisitive mind and encouraged his questions. In fact, on the last trip, Lane delighted his grandfather when he asked about the differences between swamps and marshlands, to which Valdore explained that Golden Meadow stood at the dividing line between fresh-water swamps to the north and salt-water marshlands to the south. He explained that in the swamps there were more varieties of vegetation, such as cat-tails, burreed, elephant's-ear and many varieties of flowering plants and beautiful irises. The mineral-rich, black "gumbo mud" of the swamplands grew huge cypress, willow and oak trees. Palmetto provided cover to a number of animals, while sweet-smelling honeysuckle vines and thick blackberry bushes intertwined to form an almost impenetrable living wall.

In contrast, Valdore explained that the marsh to the south had its vast expanses of salt water grass and endless bayous, bays and lakes. Along with the barrier islands, the marsh provided a first line of defense against hurricanes and Gulf storms. He also explained that these marshlands were his prime shrimping, oystering and fishing areas. Lane hung on every word his grandfather said, and his genuine interest gave Valdore hope for the future. Valdore's daydreaming brought him to the final turn into the Cameaux swamp.

Dawn was turning the darkness to lighter shades of gray; already Valdore could see flocks of cranes and ducks flying low overhead. When he spotted the Cameaux wharf in the distance, he assumed the Cameaux boys were already in their duck blinds. He planned to stop to say hello on his return trip from passing his traps, figuring the boys would be back at the camp by then.

Valdore slowed the skiff so that his wake wouldn't beat the Cameaux skiff against the wharf. As he approached the campsite, he noticed something dark lying on the catwalk. That didn't seem too out

of place, but what really caught his attention was the open screen door. With all the mosquitoes and small animals in the area, he knew the boys wouldn't have gone off without closing that door. As he contemplated whether or not to go on past the camp to his traps, he just couldn't shake the feeling that something wasn't right. Deciding to check things out, he edged his skiff to the opposite side of the wharf from the *Miss Teresa*. As he tied his skiff to the wharf, he strained to see what was lying on the catwalk. It was still not light enough to see clearly, and his being at a lower elevation than the catwalk didn't help matters either.

"Now I have to get out the damn boat!" lamented Valdore, knowing he would have to climb out of his skiff to get a better look. As he stood up on the wharf, his eyes were fixed on the dark objects heaped just ahead. Slowly he made his way up the catwalk, "Why," he thought, "would the boys clutter the cat. . . . "Bon Dieu! Good God!" cried Valdore, stopping dead in his tracks. He couldn't move. His heart pounded in his chest; his hands started to shake, and a cold, cold, chill swept his body as he realized that what he had assumed to be mere clutter was, in reality, two bodies. Instantly he knew the two bodies in front of him were the Cameaux boys. True, he hadn't seen the faces yet, but he knew it had to be them.

Taking a step back, Valdore went to his knees and put his hands to his face in disbelief. "Quoi faire? Why, why?" he moaned out loud. Then fear gripped him as his sharp gaze scanned the immediate camp area just in case whoever did this unimaginable act of carnage were still around, but seeing and hearing nothing, he quickly realized he was alone. Rising, he walked the last few feet to the bodies. Blood was everywhere. When he bent over to touch the faces of both Eric and Jon, their skin felt cold, reinforcing his thought that the murderers were long gone. He couldn't believe his eyes as he gazed at the splintered wood and the shredded bodies. He whispered, "Shotgun attack."

Valdore then looked at the camp. He could see that not only was the screened door open, but the main camp door as well. Cautiously, he made his way inside. It clearly had been pillaged; all dresser

drawers and cabinet doors had been opened and their contents scattered on the floor. "Looks like the boys stumbled upon thieves."

Shaking his head sadly at the waste and already dreading having to tell Ben and Pappy, Valdore walked back to the bodies. So far it didn't look as if they had been disturbed by animals, but that wouldn't last long in this swamp and for that reason, he decided to load them onto his skiff to take to their father and grandfather. He would leave everything else as he had found it. He just hoped he could handle the bodies because both Eric and Jon were big men.

Kneeling and reaching down for Jon's body first, he gently slid his hands under the lifeless shoulders and was about to lift when he noticed something shining on what was left of Jon's upper chest. Removing his hands from under the body, Valdore slowly opened Jon's coat a bit more and saw two bloody, ring-encircled, severed fingers. Valdore turned away and vomited. "Why would anyone do such a hideous thing!" Physically weakening by the minute, he knew if he didn't hurry, he wouldn't be able to move the boys at all, so he gathered his remaining strength. Taking an old sweat rag from his coat pocket, he carefully removed the two rings from the bloody fingers, wrapped them in the rag, and pushed them deeply into his back pocket. Next, he gently placed the two severed fingers in one of Jon's coat pockets.

Then, as quickly as possible, Valdore loaded the bodies onto the fantail of his skiff and wrapped each one in a piece of canvas. As if in a daze, he untied from the wharf, pointed the bow of his skiff in the direction of Golden Meadow, pushed the throttle forward, and sped toward the Cameaux docks.

Ben Cameaux and his men had been at work since around 6:00 a.m. re-icing yesterday's catch of fish. By 8:15 they had one refrigerated truck loaded and were half-way finished with the second. Because business was slow this time of the year, it was buying and selling of fish and crawfish that kept the doors open and the employees working.

Marco Doucet had worked at the Cameaux shed for the past ten years and the first thing every morning as part of his job he washed the wharf, which surrounded the shed on three sides. Using a pressure

hose, he'd blast away the smelly fish scales and other fish parts which clung to the wooden deck from the previous day's transactions. This kept the flies and odor down to a minimum, and though it wasn't an especially appealing job, Marco did it with pride. He had just stretched out his hose and was about to turn on the water when he heard the sound of a boat engine in the distance.

Looking toward the mouth of the Yankee Canal, he recognized Valdore Gisclair's trapping skiff as it came roaring out of the canal and made a hard turn starboard onto Bayou Lafourche. For a second, Marco didn't think he would make the turn successfully, but watched as Valdore raced straight for the wharf where he stood. Startled, Marco threw down the hose and ran to the door of the shed, yelling, "Mr. Valdore's comin' in! I think he's in trouble!" All the men, including Ben, hurried out the door and onto the wharf. One man asked, "What's on the skiff's fantail?" Getting closer by the second, Valdore didn't let up on the throttle until he was within two hundred feet of the wharf.

"Looks like sometin' wrap in two pieces of canvas," said Marco.

Valdore, now within fifty feet of the wharf and gliding slowly closer, could contain himself no longer. With tears streaming down his face, he stood with his arms outstretched and cried, "BEN! MAY GOD AVENGE THE BLOOD OF THE CAMEAUX FAMILY! FOR THE DEVIL HIMSELF HAVE COME AGAINST YOU!!"

"What?" was Ben's only response. Then, in an uncontrollable reflex, he raised his hands to cover his ears. He tried to block out Valdore's words, but it was too late. With those fateful words echoing in his head, he understood that it was his boys wrapped in that canvas on the fantail of the skiff. Slowly lowering his hands, the words faded and he heard no more; darkness flooded in from all sides while an awful pain seized his chest.

25

CHAPTER 7

Derrick switched from I-59 South to I-10 West just north of Slidell. With this, traffic grew even heavier once he crossed Lake Pontchartrain. Finally seeing the skyline of the Crescent City, he spotted the Super Dome and remembered the days his parents and other relatives had taken him, Eric and Jon to Saints' football games.

As Derrick crossed the Mississippi River on the high, shaky, narrow Huey P. Long Bridge, he smiled to himself when he noticed the death grip he held on the steering wheel. As a young boy, he had always closed his eyes during that dreaded crossing. And even now that still seemed to him the best way to handle this old bridge. Once on the West Bank of the river, he quickly left the city behind. Heading west on US 90, Derrick now traveled on the familiar ground of low, wet terrain. Clusters of giant cypress trees casting ominous shadows over forbidden places grudgingly gave way to even denser thickets of live oaks caped with Spanish moss. Everywhere the swamps seemed on the verge of reclaiming all dry ground. His excitement was building; as a matter of fact, he could barely contain this feeling every time he came home. He popped in a CD of his favorite Cajun artist, Wade Bernard, and the Cajun in him came alive. When he crossed Bayou Lafourche, he turned off U.S. 90 onto La. 1 South. He could almost taste Pappy's seafood gumbo.

27

The last conversation he had with Pappy, a week earlier, was a bit mysterious, with the older Cameaux saying they needed to talk. Derrick couldn't imagine what Pappy needed to talk about, but he knew his curiosity would soon be satisfied because he was almost home. Pappy lived on the west side of the bayou in the heart of Golden Meadow.

An hour later as he approached Pappy's house, he was surprised to see so many cars parked in the area. "Somebody must be having a crawfish boil," he thought. Soon he could see three police cars parked on the side of the road. Not only police cars, though, he also noticed a pontoon helicopter tied up to a small wharf in the bayou across from Pappy's house. Coming within sight of his grandfather's property, he realized that most of the cars were parked in Pappy's yard. "What's going on?" he wondered aloud. Derrick then saw someone waving at him from in front of Pappy's driveway. His cousin Ray Calliou directed him to a parking spot. Rolling down his window as he parked his Jeep, he asked, "What's going on, Ray?"

Walking up to Derrick's door, Ray didn't say a word, nor was he smiling. Derrick unhooked his seatbelt and stepped out of the Jeep. As the two men faced each other, Derrick demanded, "What is it?"

"Derrick – been waiting for you, bad news!"

"Did something happen to Pappy?"

"No,. . . not Pappy," said Ray with tears in his eyes. "It's Eric and Jon. They're dead!"

The answer caught Derrick off-guard and didn't make any sense; perhaps Ray hadn't meant what he had said. Derrick blurted, "What do you mean? Dead, Ray? That can't be." But Ray's face said it all. He looked hard into Ray's still moist eyes, and tears began rolling down his tanned cheeks as he realized that Ray was, indeed, telling the truth. All he could say was, "Both of them, Ray? God, why? What happened?"

"Why don't we sit down, Derrick."

"No, just tell me what happened!"

"Well, earlier today Valdore Gisclair brought Eric's and Jon's bodies back from the camp, Looks like they were murdered."

"Murdered!" exclaimed Derrick, his sorrow suddenly exploded into anger.

28

"Looks that way, they were found on the catwalk leading up to the camp. They never even made it inside. Mr. Gisclair seems to think they walked up on burglars. He said they never had a chance, said their shotguns were still in the skiff, so they were unarmed."

"How were they killed?"

"Mr. Valdore said it was buckshot and a lot of it. Said it was a real awful sight. The coroner's doing autopsies."

"Pappy and Uncle Ben – where are they?" asked Derrick, again brushing away tears.

"Uncle Ben's in the hospital. He collapsed with a heart attack when he heard the news. Pappy's inside, he's taking it about as well as anyone can. The sheriff's inside too. He's already sent his investigating team to the camp, and he's going there himself in a few minutes."

"What about Olivia and the girls?"

"They're at Olivia's mama's house. I haven't seen them yet."

Derrick suddenly buried his face in both hands and gave in to the grief that was overwhelming him. Not since his parent's deaths had he felt such pain and sorrow. Eric and Jon had been closer than brothers to him and it was like losing a part of himself. Struggling to regained his composure and, barely above a whisper, he asked, "Who killed them?"

"We don't know, we haven't heard a thing."

"I gotta see Pappy now."

"Come on, he's inside."

The two men walked in silence toward the house. Before reaching the door, they could hear women's voices in both English and French wailing. Derrick entered first. As soon as the mourners saw him, he was surrounded by friends and relatives who were expressing their sympathy and relief that he hadn't left a day earlier with Eric and Jon. The scene was one of bitter weeping, but he refused to be drawn into their despair and asked with an even voice, "Where's Pappy?"

"He's in the kitchen with Sheriff Lebeouf," Ray said.

Derrick excused himself and made his way through the mourners and down a long, narrow hallway to where he saw a light shining through a doorway to his right. As he walked through the entrance, he saw the sheriff and Pappy seated at the table. The two men stood when they saw him. Sheriff Lebeouf quickly extended his hand to Derrick. "Sorry about your cousins."

Pappy made his way from around the table and firmly embraced Derrick, whispering in heavy Cajun English, "Good to see you, Son."

"Are you doin' okay, Pappy?"

"Yeah, Derrick, I want you to go with the sheriff to the camp. Think you can do that?"

"Sure, Pappy."

Sheriff Lebeouf said softly, "I'll be waiting for you in the living room. Take your time. I need to make a couple of calls before we leave. We'll use the pontoon helicopter to take us to the camp."

"I'll be with you in just a few minutes," answered Derrick.

As soon as the sheriff had left the room, Pappy told him to sit down and immediately the old Cajun set a cup before him and poured steaming, strong black coffee. With no sugar or cream to mask the taste, he took a sip. Pappy then poured himself a cup and sat opposite Derrick at the table. He watched his grandfather closely as the old Cajun took a deep breath and sighed. His upper lip quivered slightly as he stared deeply into the black brew. Though Pappy seldom showed his feelings, today Derrick could feel his pain and would not be the first to break the silence.

Pappy, the patriarch of the Cameaux family, was an imposing figure when Derrick was a young boy. The once handsome face, now leathered and creased with lines of age, told a story of too many sorrowful events for one life. Lately, even his usually thick dark brown hair seemed to whiten with every passing day. Pappy's one steadfast feature, his hazel eyes, remained bright and alert. Although still in good shape, it was obvious the old man was beginning to feel his seventy-five years.

After a few moments he said, "The sheriff's been kind enough to fill me in on what he knows so far about the murders. But, between you an me, I think this is gonna be way ova the sheriff's head. So if you would, go with him an be my eyes. Look around the camp an ax plenty questions. Bring me back all you can."

"I'll do that. Anything else?"

"Yeah, from now on, watch yourself."

Derrick wasn't sure what Pappy meant. Knowing that he was a complex man of few words, Derrick had learned long ago that when his grandfather spoke, there was often more there than the words spoken. Derrick also recognized that there would be time later for a more involved conversation; thus, he turned his attention to Ben. "Pappy, how's Uncle Ben?"

"I'm gonna see him after you leave. It don't look good, but he's a strong man. He'll make it. It's you I'm worried for."

"I'll be just fine. Don't worry."

"Remember when I told you on the phone I want to talk to you sometime on your trip?"

"I remember. We were going to talk before I left for the camp."

"Well, after the funerals. You an me, we talk. Now, Son, you better go with the sheriff." Both men got up from the table, and then Pappy came around to Derrick and laid his big hands on his shoulders, just as he had done so many times when Derrick was a boy. "After your trip with the sheriff, promise me you won't go back to the swamp again till we have that talk."

Derrick assured him, "Okay".

"Bon, see you when you get back."

Derrick and Pappy walked back into the living room, which was still filled with people. Sheriff Lebeouf clicked off his cell phone, and motioned for Derrick to follow him. Both men made their way from the house and walked side by side toward the helicopter. The sheriff spoke first, though rather hesitantly. "I just called the coroner. He hadn't started the autopsies, but sure enough, he agreed with Mr. Gisclair's assessment and said it was the worst shotgun attack he's seen. I tell you, Derrick, this is strange. I have a hunch or two, but can't seem to make any sense of it all."

Derrick stopped. "Well, who would have done something like that? Don't you have any ideas?"

Stopping also, the sheriff hesitated before replying. "We don't know yet, but we'll find them. You can bet on that."

Boarding the helicopter, Derrick had a sick feeling in his stomach, which had nothing to do with the ride. What had begun as a day of pleasant expectations had turned into a horrid nightmare.

CHAPTER 8

B efore making their descent, Derrick looked out the window at the Cameaux Swamp below. Certain that he was gazing at a Louisiana as it must have been before man had ever set foot here, he saw the familiar islets blanketed with thickets of blackberry bushes, palmetto, oak and willow trees. Consuming every inch of solid ground, these in turn were surrounded by giant cypress trees draped in Spanish moss and standing so tall in the shallow waters that their resulting canopy made seeing the water below difficult. Straining forward to peer into the occasional slits in the dark canopy, Derrick recoiled slightly as the sun's rays found just the right angle to bounce light squarely into his eyes. These islets and the dense cypress canopy also frequently gave way to pockets of calm uncluttered ponds, some only a few feet wide while others stretched more than half a mile. Over these open spaces Derrick squinted into the glittering light dancing atop the still bodies of water destined soon to disappear under the next clusters of islets and cypress trees. The only observable sign of wildlife was the constant movement of birds, the majority of which were ducks of every kind. Everywhere over this Cameaux Swamp, these flocks flew busily in search of prime feeding sites. "Such a deceptively peaceful place," he thought, reflecting on the numerous tragedies that had struck these south Louisiana wetlands and on the many people who had perished as victims of the elements.

As they descended Derrick could see the Cameaux campsite just ahead. Four skiffs were tied up to the tiny wharf, and at least a dozen sheriff's deputies roamed the area beside the camp. Guided by an officer giving hand signals, the chopper pilot landed close to the western edge of the camp clearing.

Leaving the chopper, Derrick and the sheriff were met by Lt. Frank Autin, who greeted them with a somber face and a rather grave "Hi Sheriff," and a nod toward Derrick.

"Frank, this is Derrick Cameaux. He's the victims' cousin." As Derrick and Lt. Autin exchanged a handshake, the Sheriff asked, "What you got so far, Frank?"

Pointing toward the catwalk, he replied, "That's where the victims were shot. We're retrieving the buckshot from that area now. We've also found some footprints so we're taking casts."

"How many shooters?"

"Looks like at least three so far."

"Is Mr. Gisclair still with you?"

"Yes Sir, he's inside the camp. He's been real helpful."

Derrick impatiently interjected, "Don't you have any idea who did this – and why?"

Deputy Autin replied, "Not yet, but it looks like a burglary. The camp was ransacked pretty good. My guess is that your cousins walked up at the wrong time. Of course, there is a small problem with that theory."

"What's that?" asked Derrick.

"Well, it looks like the victims were shot at least eight to ten times. To me, that means that all the burglars had shotguns and used them. I find that odd." Derrick stiffened and clenched his fist.

"Yeah, they didn't want to leave any witnesses," said the sheriff as he walked toward the camp. Derrick walked near the spot where Eric and Jon had been killed. Considering all the blood that had been shed, he hoped his cousins didn't suffer much before the end. He actually gave wide birth to the death area, approaching instead two officers making casts of some footprints. He noticed that the prints looked like those made from rubber boots, and in this country, that usually meant hip boots.

"Derrick, would you come up here?" called the sheriff from the door of the porch. As he made his way up to the door, Sheriff Lebeouf asked, "Would you look in here and tell us if anything is missing?"

As soon as he walked through the door of the camp, Valdore met him. "Derrick, I'm sorry what happen to your cousins. The Devil himself was here. If I would have got here soona, maybe things –"

Derrick shook his hand, "Mr. Valdore, I'm glad you weren't here earlier. I thank you for what you did for the family, but I don't think you could have stopped this." Derrick looked over Valdore's shoulder at the mess inside the camp. "Whoever they were," he said as much to himself as anyone else, "they did a good job of wrecking the place."

"See anything missing?" asked the sheriff.

"Nothing yet," answered Derrick, "it'll take a while just to sift through all the debris."

"Well, I'll leave you here to look around then. I'll be outside if you need me. Mr. Gisclair, will you come with me? I need to ask you a few more questions."

Actually thankful to be left alone, Derrick fought to keep his mounting emotions under control. Seeing an overturned sofa with its underside ripped did suggest that the intruders were looking for money. In addition, all the cabinet doors were standing open, dishes and utensils strewn everywhere. When he walked into one of the bedrooms, he found that the mattress had been overturned and dresser drawers had been pulled out and emptied in a heap on the floor. He checked the other three bedrooms, finding them all the same. Walking back into the large living room, he was overwhelmed with memories of all the good times he and the rest of the family had at this camp. Thankfully, he noticed that none of the dozens of pictures that covered the walls had been damaged. To Derrick, these were the most valuable items in the camp, especially the photos of his mother and father. Surveying the gallery of past hunts, he realized that one was in fact missing. The most recent photo of himself, Eric and Jon, taken three years ago, was nowhere to be found though he searched everywhere. Derrick was puzzled; he thought to himself that Ben or one of the boys must have taken it home. "That's all it could be," he reasoned aloud.

As far as he could tell, nothing from the camp was missing. Whatever the thieves were looking for, it didn't appear they had found it. "Ambush," he said to himself reflectively. In fact, the more he thought about it, he realized that it seemed more like an ambush than anything else – a well-planned execution, not surprised thieves frightened by the thought of being caught red-handed.

Derrick made his way out of the camp and walked toward the wharf where the *Miss Teresa* and a number of the parish water patrol boats were tied. He peered down into the familiar small skiff, having a difficult time seeing the flooring with all the provisions Eric and Jon had brought with them. Looking toward the bow, he saw both Erick's and Jon's shotguns still lying neatly side by side in their carrying cases. Even if he had not already been suspicious, that fact alone made him wonder, "What kind of thief would leave such valuables behind? Even at half price, these shotguns are worth hundreds of dollars." Yet, nothing's touched in the skiff, nothing at all. "Some robbery," mused Derrick, "very strange."

He walked back to the spot where his cousins had been killed. There Sheriff Lebeouf and Lt. Autin were talking to Valdore and though Derrick wasn't paying much attention, something Valdore mentioned about fingers caught his attention. Lightly laying his hand on Valdore's shoulder, he interrupted, "Excuse me, Mr. Valdore. What were you saying about fingers?"

Valdore looked first at Derrick and then at Sheriff Lebeouf, but no one uttered a word until the sheriff finally spoke. "Derrick, I thought you knew."

"Knew what?"

The sheriff slowly replied, "The boys had their ring fingers cut off – with the rings still in place. Valdore removed the rings and put the fingers in Jon's coat pocket."

Derrick looked at the blood on the catwalk, then back to the sheriff in disbelief. "That doesn't sound like thieves to me!" The more details he learned, the more bizarre things got. "Tell me, Sheriff, have you ever seen thieves leave behind a boatload of goods? Fact is, I can't find anything missing anywhere!" Derrick snapped.

The sheriff replied, "People on drugs nowadays will do anything, Derrick. Sometimes cash is all they're looking for, not stuff that has to be fenced. Hell, they might not even remember tomorrow what they did today."

"Something's just not right here," said Derrick.

Lt. Autin added, "That's why we're gathering up all the evidence we can. We'll try and make some kind of sense of all this and then arrest someone."

Derrick didn't reply, only staring at the bloody catwalk, shaking his head and repeatedly mumbling, "Just doesn't add up, doesn't add up . . ."

Sheriff Lebeouf asked, "You 'bout ready to go, Derrick?"

"I'm ready," he answered, in disgust.

"Frank, you got a couple of men staying the night?" asked the sheriff.

"Yes Sir, LeConte and Akins. The rest of us will leave. Tomorrow I'll bring back another team, and we'll conduct a wider search of the area."

"Okay, just don't stay much longer today, it'll be dark soon."

"Yes, Sir"

At that moment Sheriff Lebeouf turned to Valdore. "Mr. Gisclair, would you like to ride back with me?"

"No, I don't trust those steel horseflies. Too daindruss."

Both the sheriff and Derrick thanked and shook hands with Valdore. Derrick shook Lt. Autin's hand as well and said, "It was good to meet you Frank."

"Good to meet you too, Derrick. Wish it were under better circumstances."

Derrick nodded and turned to walk away but not before Valdore caught his arm. "I almost forgot to give you this." He quickly pulled his old sweat rag form his back pocket, carefully opened it and placed into Derrick's hand Eric's and Jon's rings. Derrick stared at them a few seconds before putting them into his pocket. An unnerving shiver passed through him.

During the flight back to Golden Meadow, Derrick contemplated just how close he had come to death. When Eric had called him earlier

in the week to try to convince him to come a day early, he had almost agreed. If not for his pre-arranged work schedule, he would have been there with Eric and Jon. He wondered what the killers would have cut off him since he didn't wear a ring. As he looked down at his hands, he wondered, "What was it they were really after? The rings, or was it the ring fingers? And why would they want either one?" Then it dawned on him: they could have sold the rings, yet they didn't take them. "No damn way was this a robbery," he thought, more convinced now than ever. "This whole thing was just to make some kind of statement, but why."

At the end of the flight, Derrick walked the sheriff to his car. "Mr. Valdore gave me the rings. Won't you need them as evidence?"

"To be honest, I'm not sure. Valdore moved the bodies and the rings. I'll ask the DA. If we need them, I'll let you know."

"Well, Sheriff, thanks for all your work and letting me go with you to the camp."

"Listen, Derrick, we'll catch these killers. I'm sorry for the loss to your family. I'll keep in touch." The two men shook hands, and then the sheriff drove off, leaving only Derrick's Jeep parked in the once-crowded yard. It was late afternoon and the sun was casting long shadows as he walked slowly to the Jeep to get his duffel bag. He knew that now he'd be spending time with his grandfather, much more than he originally intended. Somehow the thought appealed to him, in spite of the awful circumstances.

CHAPTER 9

As he entered the house, Pappy's sister Aunt Camellia greeted him. A kind and caring woman, she always looked the same to Derrick because time had been so gentle with her. Her plump body and sweet red-cheeked face naturally beckoned the needy to her bosom for comfort, and she was always the first to assist and the last to leave. He loved her dearly. "Oh, Derrick, my Cherie, I'm glad to see you back. Pappy an Ray went to the hospital to check on Ben. Now, I got some gumbo ready, so you wash your hands an sit down while I catch you a bowl."

Dutifully, Derrick washed his hands as his aunt instructed and smiled to himself as he thought that she was almost as bossy as his housekeeper, Mrs. Magee. He sat at the table as Aunt Camellia set before him a huge bowl of that seafood gumbo Pappy promised him. Knowing the way Pappy seasoned his gumbos, he added only a pinch of file', but dared not add another drop of hot sauce. He hadn't eaten all day and he was starved. As always, the gumbo was delicious. Each spoonful brought a delectable combination of different seafood flavors to his taste buds, and he ate every bit put before him. He even ate a big piece of his aunt's famous custard pie, insisting afterward, "You're the best, Aunt Camellia, that was all delicious! Thanks."

"There's plenty more in the pot."

"No thanks. I couldn't eat another bite." Derrick asked, "Aunt Camellia, have you heard any word on the funeral arrangements?"

"Your Pappy said the burials would be Monday morning if the autopsy work was done."

"What about Olivia and the girls? Have you heard anything about how they're doing?"

"I spoke to Olivia's mama and she told me the doctor gave Olivia a shot to help her sleep. The girls don't understand what's going on, but they been axin' questions about their daddy."

Noticing the pile of dishes his aunt was working on, Derrick said, "Thanks, Aunt Camellia. I'll help you with this mess."

"No! No!" she protested. "I can handle this kitchen. You go sit yourself down an rest, an I don't want no argument from you."

Derrick smiled at his aunt and left the kitchen, going straight to his old room to unpack his clothes. As he entered, he felt the weight of the day and wished he could unload it as easily as his duffel bag. While putting his socks into the dresser drawer, he noticed a stack of pictures under some of his old tee shirts. His heart warmed as he realized that Pappy left almost everything in his room just as he had always remembered it all those years ago when he was growing up there. Especially untouched was anything Pappy had thought was personal or private to his grandson. "Thanks, Pappy," Derrick whispered as he pulled the pictures out, sat on the bed, and went through the stack one by one. Most were of long-ago family celebrations. One photo that especially caught his eye was a high-school picture of Olivia, the very first one she had ever given him. For a brief moment he wondered what happened to all her other pictures; as he thought of those innocent days when they first met, he knew he had been a fool to have ever let her go. At least Eric had better sense and married her. He shook his head sadly as he thought of how everything had turned out, especially now. There were also pictures of his mom and dad. "Such a handsome couple," thought Derrick as he allowed himself to drift into the vague, though happy, memories of his early childhood before his parents' deaths. He was still looking at the pictures and deeply lost in thought when he heard the front door open. He quickly returned the

pictures to the drawer and walked into the living room to greet Pappy and Ray, who were returning from the hospital.

"Derrick, did you eat something?" asked Pappy.

"I ate too much. How's Uncle Ben?"

Ray answered, "The doctor said the next few days should tell a lot. It was a bad heart attack."

Pappy added, "He's had a rough time, Derrick. Tomorrow Rays' gonna bring me to the funeral home to make the final arrangements for the boys."

"Pappy, I'll be glad to go and. . . ."

"No, no, no, I know you would go, but it's my place to do this. Now if you boys excuse me, I better get some rest. Ray, I see you first thing in the morning, six o'clock sharp."

"Okay, Pappy," answered Ray watching the old man disappear down the hallway.

As Ray walked toward the door to leave, he said, "Derrick, I'm sorry I had to greet you the way I did earlier today."

"Someone had to do it and I'm glad it was you, Ray."

"Well, I'll see you tomorrow. Good night."

"Good night Ray and thanks again," answered Derrick closing the door after his cousin. Walking to the kitchen he found his Aunt still at work and startled her when he said, "I'm going out for a ride, Aunt Camellia, don't wait up for me." She started to protest but thought better of it and simply said, "Do what you have to, son."

The night was cold and dark. At first, Derrick just drove his Jeep around Golden Meadow, not looking for anything in particular; then, shortly before midnight, he pulled into the Cameaux Shrimp Shed parking lot. He got out of the Jeep and walked down the poorly lit wharf where he stopped at the skiff he was supposed to have taken to the camp. He just stood there staring at the skiff he knew so well, feeling weak and useless. Both feelings were unfamiliar to him. Then, without warning a great sense of grief overwhelmed him, causing him to lean against one of the old pilings and weep bitterly for Eric and Jon. Peering out into the dark cold emptiness of the night, he knew he was looking at the very depths of his soul. Tears ran freely down his face and sobs rocked every inch of his body, forcing him to cling

41

tightly to the piling lest he fall to the deck of the wharf. He asked question after question of himself, but had no answers. The loneliness he felt was almost too much to bear. Eric and Jon were dead, but not just dead – murdered! Memories flooded his mind of his childhood when he, Eric and Jon were growing up on this bayou, good memories of fun times and endless laughter. Eric had always been the smartest; he was the cautious one who never did anything without careful thought. Jon, on the other hand, always operated on the impulse of whatever felt right and, thus, usually acted before thinking. As different as they were, though, both were kind-hearted men known for their generosity and easy-going manners and never at odds with each other or anyone else. Trembling and unable to control his emotions, Derrick shouted into the night, "Why are they dead? Why?" His only answer was the echo of his questions reverberating around the dark emptiness. Now, seemingly without any fortitude or desire to subdue his grief, his weeping turned into loud, wailing cries of sorrow.

His very soul had been forever branded by an indelible iron, and something had happened to Derrick that night. At his darkest moment, from the deepest recesses of his grief, the first sign of a different emotion had been implanted – vengeance. Unexpectedly, a cool breeze swept across his face as though to wipe away his tears and to restore his composure. Though his grief was still present, he was vitally aware that he was alive and there were people depending on him. He would not let them down.

CHAPTER 10

D errick awoke early Monday morning to the faint rumble of thunder. It had been three days since the murders. The clock by his bed read 5 a. m.; that meant Pappy was up and ready to start the day. In fact, at that very moment, he heard his grandfather in the kitchen, and knew he was making his first cup of coffee. Derrick remembered fondly the many mornings awakening in this old house to the smell of strong blended coffee with chicory and the sounds of Cajun music on the radio. This morning, however, as well as the past two mornings, no music had awakened Derrick, only the smell of coffee. There would be no music or television in this house for at least one year. That was the traditional time of mourning for a loved one in many Cajun homes, and Pappy was as traditional as they came.

Perhaps the worst day, at least for Derrick, would be today; burial services for Eric and Jon had been scheduled for ten o'clock at Our Lady of the Bayou Catholic Church in Golden Meadow. With Olivia's consent, Pappy had made all the arrangements, including those for the boys to be buried in the Cameaux family cemetery. Derrick's heart ached as he thought of his Uncle Ben, who would not be able to attend the funeral. True to her nature, Aunt Camellia had insisted on staying at the hospital with him. Pappy and Derrick left the house at 8:45 and headed for the funeral home. At 9:30 the caskets were loaded into hearses and taken to the church. Derrick expected a large crowd at the

43

church, and he wasn't disappointed as virtually the whole town showed up. The crowd was a marvelous testimony to the lives of Eric and Jon; they were truly loved and would be missed by many.

As the caskets were brought to the front of the church, Derrick walked close to Pappy in case he needed assistance. They sat with Olivia and the girls in the second pew. Derrick reached over and held Olivia's hand as he said, "I think the whole town turned out to show their support and pay their respect." That brought fresh tears to her eyes as well as a smile to her face.

It was an appropriate service; the priest had kind words to say about both young men. The overwhelming show of love and support for Olivia and the girls was touching and genuine.

At the small plot of ground known as the Cameaux Cemetery, the crowd gathered and watched as the caskets were placed in tombs above ground. The two burial plots chosen by Pappy were centrally located among the neat rows of fifty or so existing whitewashed tombs in the area of the cemetery where the old Cajun would one day be buried himself. Pappy held up fairly well until Eric's two little girls followed their mother's lead by walking up to the casket and touching it. Pappy's knees gave way and Derrick had to physically support his grandfather to prevent his collapsing. Pappy asked, "Take me home, son." He could no longer stand the pain. With Ray's help, he placed Pappy in his Jeep and the two of them drove away. Ray stayed with Olivia.

It was a short drive, just two streets from the cemetery to Pappy's house. Once inside Derrick helped him to bed.

"Call me if you need anything Pappy."

"I will son, I will." The exhausted old Cameaux slept the rest of the day and all that night. Derrick checked on him almost every hour until midnight, when the day finally also caught up to him. Just as he lay down to sleep, the rain began falling. He was glad it hadn't rained on the funeral, and he was relieved that the day was over. Perhaps now the healing could begin.

The next morning Pappy was up early at his usual five o'clock. Derrick neither heard Pappy nor smelled coffee. Aunt Camellia woke him a couple of hours later for breakfast. "Seven o'clock!" he

exclaimed to himself as he looked at his watch. "I haven't slept this late in years!" He hadn't intended for Pappy to be up without him. Quickly dressing and walking into the kitchen, he asked, "Aunt Camellia how's Uncle Ben? I didn't hear you come in last night."

"He's doing a little more better this morning. I stayed up with him all night. Fact is, I just got in an hour ago."

"Where's Pappy?"

"It just stopped raining, so he went for a walk in his orchard," answered his aunt as she set a plate of Cajun lost bread and syrup before him.

"Aunt Camellia, I appreciate all you've done for Pappy and me."

"It's the least I can do. I'm afraid I'll be gone home tomorrow. I got a doctor's appointment."

"I hope it's nothing serious."

"Oh no, just my usual check-up."

Just then the back door opened and in walked Pappy obviously wet but of good cheer, "Well, looks like it start to rain again."

His sister chided him good-naturedly, "Then you better get yourself inside, or you'll catch something."

"Like a little rain's gonna hurt me," he grumbled. Then smiling and winking at Camellia, he teased Derrick, "About time you get up, Cityboy."

Derrick was relieved to see Pappy smile, and he joked back. "Don't know what's wrong with me. Why, every now and again, I'll just waste half the day sleeping till six or six-thirty!"

"Or seven," chimed in Aunt Camellia, pouring Pappy a cup of coffee. All three laughed, and Derrick mentioned that Aunt Camellia would soon be leaving them.

Pappy said, "Yep, the ole gal gotta get her rest."

Aunt Camellia laughed and looked directly at Pappy. "An just who you are to call someone ole, ole man?" She was the only person Derrick had ever known who could get the last word in on Pappy.

Chuckling and holding up both hands as if to signal surrender, Pappy then looked at Derrick and asked, "Son, you got something plan this morning?"

"Nothing I can't put off. What's up?"

Pappy hesitated a few seconds and then answered, "Well, it's time for that talk, Son. It's raining, but I want for you an me to take a little ride in your Jeep."

"I'm ready whenever you are, Pappy."

Derrick, watching as his grandfather quickly drank the last of his coffee, saw the look that passed between Pappy and Aunt Camellia for just a split second before his grandfather pushed back his chair and stood up. "Looks like it might be a little nippy. I'll get our coats."

As soon as he had left the kitchen, Aunt Camellia asked, "Have enough to eat?"

"Yes Ma'am."

Derrick could see her face redden and knew something was bothering her. Picking up his coffee cup and plate, she whispered, "Derrick, you a grown man. Whatever Pappy tells you, remember you have your own life to live. Do what's best for you."

"What do you mean?"

"Just remember what I tell you, you understand later."

Whatever it was that his grandfather knew, Aunt Camellia knew it too. Hearing Pappy coming down the hall, she put her finger to her lips. When Pappy entered the kitchen he handed Derrick his coat and asked, "You ready?"

"Yes, Sir. I'm ready."

Pappy turned toward Camellia. "Sista, can't tell you when we'll be back."

Smiling at both of them she said, "Just be careful on those wet roads. I'm gonna be staying with Ben most of tonight, but tomorrow I'm gonna head home."

"Thanks again, Aunt Camellia," said Derrick as he gave her an affectionate hug. "I don't know what we'd have done without you."

"Yeah, ole gal, the boy's right again. Thanks for everything."

"Oh, you two!" It's not as if I'll be gone far or for very long. I'll be back soon. Now, hurry before this weather gets even more bad." Then, as the men were leaving the kitchen, she quietly reminded Derrick, "Don't forget what I told you." He smiled and nodded to allay her obvious concerns.

They walked from the house into the driving rain and then hurried to the Jeep. Once inside Derrick asked, "where to?"

"Cheniere Caminada."

"You mean right before Grand Isle?"

Pappy answered a bit sharply, "You know another Cheniere Caminada?"

"No, Sir," sighed Derrick, backing out of the driveway.

As they headed south on La. Hwy 1, Derrick glanced at his grandfather and could tell he was deep in thought and whatever was on his mind was serious business. After driving several miles through a fierce thunderstorm without saying a word, Derrick asked, "Pappy, can you at least give me a hint about all this?"

"It's raining!"

Derrick waited for Pappy to continue, but the old man didn't say another word. Finally Derrick asked, "What? It's raining – that's the hint?"

Pappy just gave Derrick "the look."

"What a strange man," thought Derrick, and as the drive continued, the conversation became even stranger when Pappy finally spoke again.

"Sure was alota people at the funeral."

"Sure was."

"Derrick?"

"Sir?"

"You like living in Missippi better than here?"

"Well, I wouldn't say I like it better. It's just where I've ended up."

"I understand."

Derrick caught himself just before thinking aloud, "How could you understand when I don't understand myself?" The rain finally stopped and the rest of the ride was filled with more small talk.

Cheniere Caminada, thirty miles south of Golden Meadow, was located on the western end of Caminada Bay. The only road leading to Grand Isle passed through this tiny settlement. As Derrick neared the small fishing village, Pappy told him to slow down and park on the side of the road in front of an old cemetery. As directed, Derrick pulled off the road and was waiting for further instructions when

Pappy opened his door and stepped from the Jeep. Looking at Derrick, he said, "Come with me."

Derrick turned the engine off and quickly climbed from the Jeep. A misty, cool drizzle was falling; Derrick was glad Pappy thought to bring their coats. He quickened his step to catch up with the spry old Cajun, whom he followed to the very back of the cemetery where there stood a huge, ancient oak tree. Pappy stopped under its thick, sprawling branches and looked upward.

"Derrick, this oak have been standing here for more than two hundred years. This oak stands as a silent witness to all I'm gonna tell you. All that comes out of my mouth, this oak lived to see. Now, what do you know about the hurricane of 1893?"

Derrick shrugged his shoulders and thought for a moment before answering, "Just that it was a bad one that killed some people."

Looking down, Pappy shook his head in disgust. "Then, Son, you don't know nothing about this hurricane. What I'm gonna tell you, you best remember. Eric didn't listen an now he's dead. Maybe, an I do mean maybe, if you listen to me, you can live a long life. If you do like Eric, you'll be a dead man, too."

CHAPTER 11

"**D**errick, I'm gonna speak in French so I don't make no mistake, if that's good with you?" Taking a notebook from his coat pocket, Pappy continued, "Here, take this an write down everything in English. It's past time we have a written record."

Derrick realized how serious Pappy was in telling the story accurately. The old man could speak English fairly well, with the exception of the occasional mispronunciations and the shortcuts he took. However, if he wanted to tell it in French for the sake of accuracy, that was fine with Derrick. "Whichever way you feel most comfortable, Pappy."

"Merci, Son." Derrick was one of a dwindling number of younger Cajuns who was fluent in both English and Cajun French, easily able to both speak and translate each language. As Pappy began, Derrick listened intently, mentally translating and then recording in English each word his grandfather spoke in his native Cajun language.

"On October 1, 1893, Cheniere Caminada was the largest community on the Louisiana Gulf Coast, with about fifteen hundred people living here. Add to that another five hundred or more people living on other islands and small levees in the area, and you can see that it was a prosperous community for its time. Among those people were my grandparents and their family of four boys and three girls. Many others also had large families, so inevitably the adults felt the

49

time had come to build a school. It was a close-knit community and everyone joined in this effort. Some gave building materials; others donated money, but most gave the only thing they could – their labor and skills to build this schoolhouse. It was a project which brought the people even closer together, and they felt a great sense of pride because the school would give their community a certain legitimacy that some felt was lacking. The new school would bring Cheniere Caminada a new reputation, one of being a hometown, not just a commercial fishing village, which it certainly was. After much hard work, the school was completed on September 28, 1893, and was to open the following Monday, October 2. The new teacher, Miss Andrea Palket, had arrived Saturday, and everyone was excited and looking forward with great anticipation to the opening of their first school. Most of the children had no formal education of any kind.

"Life back then was far different from what it is now. People in those days didn't make much money, but no one went hungry. They had food in abundance, and more importantly, they had each other. I can't stress enough how close these people were to one another. Back then, seeing a neighbor needing help to build his house, you gave him that help. When you needed help working your oyster beds or building a skiff, people were there to lend you a hand. You wouldn't charge your neighbors and friends for your help, as so many do today.

"Life was good and people seemed to be more civil and decent to each other back then. That's not to say they didn't have problems. After all, some of these people were descendants of Jean Lafitte's privateers, and a zeal for adventure would occasionally land someone in trouble. There wasn't any official law to keep the peace, so it was up to the men to set boundaries and limitations on acceptable behavior. If a man, or in some cases a family, couldn't get along with the rest of the community, they were asked to leave on their own. If they wouldn't, the community then would drive them out, but that was done only in extreme and rare cases. One such rare case was the Beto Rabeaux family. They were caught stealing more than once, and there was even talk that they once murdered a visitor from New Orleans. This murder couldn't be proved, or someone would have been hanged for that crime. But, by October 1, 1893, the leaders of Cheniere had

enough of this unruly Rabeaux family and were going to ask them or force them to leave, whichever it took. One of those community leaders was my grandfather Jerasine Cameaux. Before the Rabeaux family could be dealt with, however, something terrible happened which forever changed the lives of the poor souls of Cheniere Caminada.

"There had been a few severe hurricanes to hit the Louisiana coast before October 1, 1893. Some people on Cheniere had even experienced hurricanes before, but that had been years earlier and the destruction, for the most part, had been minimal. Most people in '93 were well aware of the dangers of living so close to the Gulf, but like people today, they had been lulled into a false sense of safety. Perhaps they believed that a bad storm was little more than a strong wind to be tolerated and then life would continue as normal. My father Augustine, who was thirteen at the time, often said later that most people had been confident their homes could withstand anything the Gulf could throw at them. They were wrong, so very, very wrong.

"By Sunday morning, October 1, the old timers knew a storm was fast approaching. Some of the younger men who were too young to have ever experienced a real hurricane laughed and made fun of the old timers. After all, they reasoned, bad thunderstorms were a part of life in South Louisiana. But by late afternoon, I guarantee you, even the bravest of the brave looked to the sky in fear. All the livestock headed for the highest land they could find, and the birds flew overhead by the thousands in a mad rush inland. Their flurry of activity foretold of the approaching winds, which from early morning had been steadily increasing from the southeast.

"The increasing winds produced swelling tides and rising coastal water levels which were already swirling and surging in angry, foaming whitecaps. My father Augustine helped my grandfather tie his two small skiffs to the pilings of their camp as the water rose ever higher and higher. They even brought two pirogues inside the camp to be used as a last-resort means of escape. Then, after my grandfather had all seven of his kids huddle in the middle of the kitchen floor with my grandmother Lovenia, he covered them with a feather mattress.

"The counterclockwise winds of the hurricane first touched Cheniere about 5:00 p.m. What people had thought was hurricane winds before then were just a prelude to the horror yet to come. Those southeast winds increased by the minute until the continual roar of that wind and rain pounding against the camp was deafening. The children became hysterical, for no matter how hard they pressed their tiny hands to their ears, they could still hear the howl of the great beast which was upon them. The winds would not let up. The water added its deadly force to the fray. The raging currents and relentless winds soon began consuming the community. Camp after camp yielded to the storm, each crushed by the growing waves, winds and debris. The human contents of the camps were cast into utter darkness and death.

"Women screamed to save their children. Even the strongest men cried out for mercy. The children, oh the children, how they pleaded and cried out for their mamas and papas to save them. In the distance, ever so faint above the wind, the remaining living could hear the ringing of the church bell, perhaps a demonic toll for each victim claimed."

"Most of the camps had been built three, four, or some like my grandfather Jerasine's, six feet off the ground. It didn't matter how high you were, though, because this storm was determined to kill all. By 9:00 pm, two feet of water stood inside my grandfather's camp, and it was rising - higher by the minute. Back then, camps were humble dwellings, nowhere near the luxurious buildings you see going up today. Most of these earlier camps had no ceilings, and when you stood in the middle of one of them and looked straight up, you would see the underside of the roof. They used the rafters as storage space, much as we do today with our attics; then, whenever they wanted to store something or retrieve it, all they had to do was to reach up through the rafters and put it up or pull it down. My grandfather's camp was like that; when the water came inside, he just lifted my grandmother and his children, including my father, one at a time through the rafters and into the attic space. Before he joined his family, he tied the two pirogues together with a long piece of rope and then pushed both of them out the back door. He then secured the loose end of the rope to the family's big black iron stove. All this time, his oldest

daughter Alicia was screaming for him to hurry. The relentless attacks of both water and winds shook the camp, making it sway and jerk in an odd, unpredictable fashion. This naturally made it very difficult, if not impossible, for the family to stand on the slender rafters.

"Finally my grandfather Jerasine joined his family, but he knew what was soon to come. He worked his way to my grandmother's side and told her how much he loved her. My father Augustine later said that she was such a beautiful woman and that on that fateful night she was wearing a tiny gold necklace that my grandfather had worked all summer to buy. Besides her wedding ring, he said it was the only jewelry she owned. My father also said she was holding his youngest sister Franny close to her breast and that the child hardly cried, so confident was she that her mother could protect her. The rest of the children held tightly to each other for life. My grandfather Jerasine told everyone that if the camp collapsed, they should swim to the pirogues trailing downwind. His final desperate act to save his family was to open the double attic doors at the rear of the camp.

"No sooner had my grandfather spoken these words than the camp was violently jolted again and again by tremendous waves. Seven-year-old Bernice lost her balance, fell through the rafters, and was swept away as her screams pierced the thick night air. The waves and wind crashed against the camp, this time knocking out a main outside wall. The roof shifted back and forth above their heads, unable to stand without the support of that missing wall. In another instant, the roof and entire camp came crashing down. Panic gripped everyone, and baby Franny was ripped from my grandmother's breast by the rushing current. My grandfather tried to save as many children as possible by diving and carrying them to the surface, but the splintered wood and debris from the camp made it impossible to reach everyone.

"As my father Augustine gasped for air, one final wave tore into the ruins and swept the remains of the camp away. He later said that above the roar and howl of the storm, he heard my grandmother as she cried, 'My children, my children, where are you, my children!!' He also said it was the last time he ever heard or saw his mother alive.

"My grandfather Jerasine pulled my father and two of his other sons to one of the pirogues. They all hung on for dear life, sometimes

53

swallowing sickening amounts of salt water and choking. Throughout the horrid night the screams of the living melded with the howl of the demonic wind. The watery hands of the strong currents ceaselessly tried to drown everyone. My father thought he could no longer hold on to the pirogue. He used to say that, to his surprise, he was at the point where death didn't seem so bad or frightening. Pain permeated his body, especially his arms and hands, and he just knew he couldn't hold on any longer. Then, he sensed that the wind seemed to be dropping. He said that he really thought he was hallucinating, losing his mind just before death would take him. But no, in a short while the wind quit blowing and the rain stopped completely. A calmness that seemed almost as frightening as everything that had preceded it gradually settled over the land. There were no screams; in fact, no one even said a word for a few minutes. Then my grandfather Jerasine told my father and his other sons to swim for a huge oak tree not twenty fee away. My father said he tried to tell him that he didn't think he could make it, but my grandfather insisted that he must live. He always said he would never forget my grandfather's words to him: 'If for nothing else, my son, you must live to help find your mother and the rest of our family.'

"My father swore that he never could remember how he got to that tree. Immediately my grandfather made the boys climb higher and higher in the tree until they were well out of the water. Then with their belts, he tied his sons' arms to a big branch so they wouldn't be blown away. Next my grandfather told them that the second half of the storm was about to begin and that they must hold on. My father declared that the second half of the storm was every bit as fierce as the first half, but he said that the tree they were in held its ground. He also said that one of the worst things about the whole storm was that throughout the night, they kept calling out to their missing family members, but no one called back.

"For what seemed like an eternity, that beast of a hurricane tried to destroy what few remained alive. By 3:00 a.m., only after having satisfied its appetite for carnage, the dark menace moved further inland. The winds gradually died down to a gentle breeze, the torrential rains stopped, and it seemed that almost instantly the flood waters began to recede as though ashamed of the role it had been

54

forced to play in the mass destruction. The water fled the land quickly, once again seeking the bays and bayous of its natural habitation.

"By daybreak, all the water was gone. Looking from their vantage point high in the top of that tree, daylight brought to them an awful sight. Scattered in every direction as far as they could see, the ground was littered with bodies entangled in debris. They could also see a few other survivors both in treetops and clinging to makeshift rafts. At full light, my grandfather Jerasine began climbing down from the tree; he was soon followed by his three remaining sons. Just as my father was climbing down, he heard my grandfather cry aloud. He said that when he looked down, he saw his oldest sister Alicia hanging from a branch of a nearby tree by her long, beautiful hair.

"The great moan that rose from the living that Monday morning was heartbreaking. Almost every family had lost someone, and in many families, everyone had perished. Naturally the search for their family members started right away. Two hundred feet west of the oak tree that had sheltered him, my father found the body of little Franny in the arms of father's younger brother Octave, as the two had somehow come together in their final moments of life. Mr. Armonde Baramoure later brought little Bernice's body, which had drifted a quarter mile inland. The search for my grandmother continued, but without success that first day. Father said he and his brothers began digging graves right away for their sisters and brother, but that these burials actually weren't completed until well into the night.

CHAPTER 12

"By the next day, Tuesday, October 3, the men who were left had no choice but to dig huge pits and put the bodies into common graves. Everyone was in shock; barely any words were spoken as the work continued hour after hour. On Tuesday afternoon the body of the school teacher Miss Andrea Palket was found. The children had never gotten to learn from the teacher who had never gotten to teach in a school that had never seen a student. The next day my grandfather was with a burial detail that came upon something which would change the lives of many for generations to come."

Pappy then looked Derrick straight in the eye as he said, "Son, these changes I'm talking about are the reason we're here today in this cemetery sitting here under this ole oak. These changes have touched every Cameaux since my grandpa Jerasine, including me, and now they're going to touch your life too."

"How could that day so long ago affect my life today?" Derrick asked, but Pappy raised his hand to stop more questions and continued his story.

"My grandfather and the men with him came upon a ridge of trees about a half mile inland. There they saw a man, a woman and three boys robbing from the dead. It was Beto Rabeaux and his family, and the men of the search party immediately seized all of them. In the pockets of Beto Rabeaux they found jewelry of every description,

57

including a handful of wedding bands. They had cut the swollen fingers from the corpses to get the gold rings. When they searched Beto's shirt pocket, they found my grandmother's gold chain. Seeing that, my grandfather grabbed Beto by the throat and made him tell where my grandmother's body was located. Beto pointed to a body not fifty feet away.

"My grandfather Jerasine rushed to my grandmother's body, and when he got to her, he cried aloud. Not only was her gold chain missing, but her ring finger had also been severed and her wedding band stolen. My grandfather almost went insane. He couldn't imagine the women he loved, the mother of his children, having been so violated in death as she was. This desecration of the dead was just too much for all these distraught men to handle. Had the dead not been through enough? It was these men, with my grandfather in the lead, who marched the Rabeaux family to what was left of Cheniere, where all the rest of the survivors were told of what the Rabeaux family had done. Someone asked what should be done to them, and my grandfather answered that Beto Rabeaux should die. Many wanted to kill the whole family, but through the pleading of the priest Father Doucet, the three Rabeaux boys and their mother were spared.

"Beto fought and cursed as they took him to an oak tree and brought his family to watch the execution. They tied the thief's hands and feet; then my grandfather threw a rope across a low limb of the oak tree. He tied one end to Beto's neck and five men grabbed the other end. When my grandfather asked whether he wanted to say anything before they hanged him, Beto spat on him and then, looking at his three sons, challenged them: 'May a curse be on the Cameaux family! Avenge my death, my sons! Wipe out the Cameaux name! Tell your children and your children's children I will not rest till they destroy the name of Cameaux—even Unto The Last Seed!'

"When Beto quit talking, my grandfather looked to the men holding the end of the rope and said, 'Hang him!' They pulled Beto Rabeaux up until his feet no longer touched the ground. After they had tied off the rope, he kicked and jerked a few minutes and then just hung there lifeless. His family never once cried out. My father, who had also witnessed the hanging, said that the Rabeaux stared with unblinking eyes at Jerasine.

"The few men and women who had survived the storm then kicked the Rabeaux family out of the community, and their name has been loathed ever since. At first, they hung around the edges of the community for a few days; then they were gone. A long time later it was learned that they had moved into the swamps east of Golden Meadow."

Derrick suddenly stopped writing as he realized the implication of the story and its connection to his cousins' murders. The idea that some act of desecrating the dead over a hundred years ago could have such deadly consequences to his family today was absurd. He had serious questions for his grandfather, questions that couldn't wait any longer. So when Pappy began to continue the story, Derrick interrupted. "Are you telling me that the Rabeaux family killed Eric and Jon?"

The unexpected question naturally broke Pappy's train of thought, but he hesitated only a moment before answering reluctantly. "Yes, it was them. That's what I'm saying."

Derrick immediately shot back at his grandfather, "Why didn't you tell the sheriff?"

Pappy was visible upset by this question and answered harshly, "Listen to me, Derrick Cameaux, an listen real good. No sheriff is ever gonna stop this curse on our family! So, Sheriff Lebeouf won't never know, not from me, an not even you gonna tell him what I told you here today."

"Why not? I don't understand."

"Because no sheriff or deputy in Lafourche Parish can even come close to catching Ludvick Rabeaux. Maybe they could catch one Rabeaux, maybe even two, but Ludvick Rabeaux won't never be caught. The Rabeaux have been at this deadly game too long to be caught by some pretty dressed sheriff."

"Wait a minute. So you're telling me someone actually took that fool Beto Rabeaux seriously?"

Pappy was clearly frustrated with Derrick's attempt to make sense of it all. "Son, I want you to stop thinking with your head an start

59

thinking with your heart! The reason I brought you here to this place is because it's here it all started! This tree we stand under today is the very tree my grandfather Jerasine Cameaux hung Beto Rabeaux on! The very same tree! What I'm telling you is that not one male Cameaux or one male Rabeaux have died a natural death in over a hundred years! We been in a war ever since 1893!"

"Pappy, why did you say every male Cameaux?"

In the heat of their conversation Pappy revealed more than intended at that moment. The old Cajun's countenance suddenly changed to one of deep sorrow. Always intending to tell Derrick the truth about his parents' deaths, he just couldn't bring himself to say the words. Now, with the deaths of Eric and Jon, he had to tell his grandson everything; he had no choice. Both men looked at each other with intensity as Derrick waited with dread Pappy's next words. "What I told you already, Son, is shocking an will take time to sink in. What I'm about to tell you now will hurt you an I'm sorry. The Rabeaux murdered your momma and poppa. They were really after your papa, but taking your mama out was pure lagniappe. You know, sorta like the icing on the cake for them, that little something extra to twist the knife in our guts."

Derrick turned from his grandfather, closed his eyes and cried out, "No! You told me they had died in a car wreck!" Derrick faced the marsh that surrounded the cemetery, trying to make some sense of the senseless. Finally he turned once more toward Pappy and asked, "Why didn't you tell me all this before?"

"I thought that I could save you boys from all this."

"Well it didn't work, did it!"

In a low, tired voice Pappy answered, "Come here an sit on this bench." Derrick obeyed, walking slowly toward the rickety old bench under the tree. He sat in stunned silence. The old Cajun stood just feet away. Then, in a calm voice Pappy said, "When you papa an Ben was jus young men, they ran trap lines in our swamp. They would save four or five days' catch an then deliver the load to me. Everything was going good, an they work almost the whole season without nothing bad happening. Then one day while they were on their way to make a delivery, a boat carrying three Rabeaux cut them off. They force the

boat you papa was steering to beach itself on a levee. The next pass the Rabeaux boys made was with shotguns blasting away at you papa an Ben. Both you papa an Ben was wounded, but that didn't stop them pulling out their own shotguns and return fire. Two of the Rabeaux boys was killed. It was self-defense, Son, plain an simple. The Rabeaux boys wanted to do the dirty work of their papa Ludvick."

Pausing only long enough to catch his breath, Pappy continued, "Derrick, I have fought this family all my life. Long ago I had to kill a few members of that Rabeaux family myself. They killed my father and his brothers; they killed my only brother an even five cousins for helping us. On an on it went. They killed us, an then we killed them. Now, their family an ours are down to almost nuttin'."

Derrick interrupted, "Well, how was not telling me, Eric and Jon supposed to help us?"

"Let me finish. For a long time after you papa an Ben had that run-in with the Rabeaux, nothing happen. You papa married you mama an Ben married Emily. Things was good an getting better. Like I said before, over the years the Rabeaux killed us an we killed them back. I was determine to stop the madness, Derrick. I just wanted a safe life for my grandchildren. I never wanted any of you involve with this."

"Yes," said Derrick, "go on."

Now taking a deep breath, Pappy walked to the bench where Derrick was sitting and sat next to him. "Like I said, for a long time there was peace. Your mama an papa had you. Den Eric an Jon was born to Ben an Emily. Your mama an papa loved each other very much, Derrick. The only thing they loved more was you. Almost every weekend they would go to the camp to fish or hunt or just pass a good time. Most of the time you was right there with them, but thank God you didn't go with them the weekend they was killed."

"I remember," said Derrick. "I was working at the shed with Eric and Jon. We were saving our money to buy a motor for that old skiff Uncle Ben gave us."

"That's right, an it's a lucky thing you did stay or you would've died with your mama an papa. I always told you they died in a wreck coming back from the camp. That much is true, but they didn't die on

the road to the house. Ludvick Rabeaux somehow found out they was at the camp. He set up a ambush halfway down Yankee Canal."

Derrick again interrupted Pappy. "You've told me some awful things here today, especially the part about Mom and Dad being killed by this Ludvick Rabeaux." Then, without another word he suddenly got up and began walking back to his Jeep.

Pappy called out, "Derrick, you papa would want you to hear the rest. It will help explain your cousins' killing."

Derrick stopped, paused and walked slowly back to Pappy, but now leaned against the huge oak rather than again sit beside his grandfather.

Watching Derrick out of the corner of his eye, Pappy looked down and continued, "The Rabeaux tied a narrow cable cross Yankee Canal. One end tied to a big willow tree, but the other end they held in their hands till they saw you papa an mama coming down the canal. Then they tied the loose end to a oak tree. The cable was hanging about four feet above the water. You papa was traveling at full speed, almost 45 mph. They didn't never know what hit them. That cable threw them out of the boat an into the water; the coroner said they died instant before they ever even touch the water."

"How do you know it was the Rabeaux?" asked Derrick.

"A friend of mines saw them in the area just before it all happen." Then Pappy looked away, as if he were again reliving the anguish.

Derrick knew that there was more. "What else, Pappy?"

Slowly and in a very low voice Pappy said, "Both you mama an papa had their ring fingers cut off an their rings was missing. Those filthy Rabeaux paddle to the middle of that canal to get their bodies an do their dirty work so we'd know it was them. Then they threw you papa an mama back in the water an disappeared before they were seen by the people that did fine the bodies. Officially it was said they hit a log or something else, but I saw where the cable marked the tree an boot prints all round both trees. Derrick, I knew then that something had to change or this madness would continue on to you, Eric an Jon. So, I decided not to avenge the deaths of your mama an papa. I wanted them to be the last Cameaux to die in this evil cycle. I let Ludvick know that, as far as I was concern, the war between our families would

be put to rest with my son an his wife. Your Uncle Ben wanted to avenge his brother's death, but I forbid him. I never heard nothing back from Ludvick, but for twenty-three years there has been peace until now. That's why I axed you if you like living in Missippi. I want for you to go back there an never come back to this bayou no more."

"What about Olivia and the girls?"

"Remember that Beto Rabeaux said that he wanted the Cameaux name wiped out? Well, never was there a woman killed till your mama's death, and that was only because she was with your papa, as I said before. I don't think Olivia an the girls are in any danger, but you, Derrick, are now the last in the Cameaux line. Now you're the only one that can carry on the Cameaux name. Derrick, you're the last seed! Ludvick wants you dead. That's why you must leave the bayou an never come back!"

Derrick looked down, but didn't reply. He wondered, Does the missing picture mean I'm next? He decided not to worry his grandfather further by mentioning the missing photograph, but he did have one more question for him. "You said Eric knew about the Rabeaux. What did he say about them, and what was his reaction to all they've done?"

"He said he wasn't worried, said times an people were more civilized today. He dismissed the warning."

Derrick looked away from Pappy and somberly said, "I won't dismiss the warning and I'm sorry Eric did. Let's go, Pappy. It's getting late." He couldn't help breathing a sigh of relief when his grandfather agreed.

As they walked back through the cemetery to the Jeep, Derrick noticed the many headstones that listed the death date as October 1, 1893. "Pappy, do you have any idea just how many people died during that hurricane of 1893?"

"Well, that beast of a hurricane killed at least eight hundred souls, and they are lyin' under you feet, Son, in mostly unmarked graves."

"Yes, beast of a hurricane," Derrick thought, But this time, the beast wasn't strong wind and high water; this time the beast bore a man's name—RABEAUX!

CHAPTER 13

Nestled on a small levee deep in the swamp, some ten miles east of the Cameaux Swamp, stands an off-square black box of old cypress planks overlapped with black roofing paper. Smaller than a two-car garage, the one-room shack serves as refuge from the elements for the Rabeaux men during the winter trapping season. Built some forty years earlier by Ludvick Rabeaux, the camp had looked uninhabitable even from the day of its completion. Rays of sunlight and swarms of mosquitoes filtered through the decayed palmetto roof, which needed replacing years ago.

The camp rested on four two-foot high cypress stumps, with a noticeable sag in the framing between the stumps. Facing a shallow-watered bayou, a single door and a single window serviced the old shack, inadequate though they were. The camp seemed a cruel joke played on nature's lush paradise. The giant cypress trees in the shallow waters surrounding the camp and the beautiful oak trees dripping Spanish moss somehow seemed determined to hide the eyesore. A litter-strewn campsite surrounded the run-down camp, which appeared abandoned, except for the irreverent, boisterous laughter echoing from inside the tar-paper walls.

Around a square, three-plank-topped table sat four men. As night overtook the camp each evening, these men felt safe around this dimly lighted table, and tonight food was being served by Victor Rabeaux,

65

the only living son of Ludvick. He prepared rail meat with rue, a frequent meal here, since at least one or two of the flightless birds got caught each day in the steel traps intended for nutria and muskrat. The brown rails, which were about the size of small chickens, commonly ran the shallow water's edge in search of minnows and insects; it was their particular misfortune to end up in the Rabeaux cooking pot.

As always, the first to be served was the leader of the family. A man of few words, Ludvick ruled his pack with unquestionable authority. Though he spoke crude, slang Cajun English often difficult to understand, behind this twisted tongue worked the mind of a genius. For more than fifty years, Ludvick had led his family's war with the Cameaux family, often callously sending his own brothers or even his own sons to their deaths.

After serving his father, Victor then served himself and finally his own sons, twenty-five-year-old Mato and twenty-year-old Toby. These two young men had matured under the oppressive hand of their grandfather Ludvick. And now, under the dim light of the kerosene lantern hanging above the table, all four men were busy with the task of consuming as much food as their bellies could hold. Ludvick, or Gramps, as the others called him, spit out a leg bone on the floor and called out to his younger grandson Toby, "Pass that wine, Boy!"

Toby picked up the gallon jug of homemade blackberry wine and started to pour some into Ludvick's cup when the old man cursed. "Stupid, I said pass me that wine. I can fill my own damn cup." Toby said nothing, but quickly set the jug down in front of Ludvick.

Victor's older son Mato naturally began laughing and ribbing his younger brother. "Toby, you just a dumb-ass, just like Gramps said!"

Toby, clearly not seeing any humor in all this, answered, "Mato, you the stupid one in the family. A coon got more brains than you!" As usual any words spoken to degrade or insult prompted all four men to erupt in a chorus of laughter.

Then as suddenly as it began, the laughter stopped when Ludvick hit the table and commanded, "Shut up! I want to say something!" The hush was immediate. Each man looked toward Ludvick. "Not none of you boys – Victor, Mato an Toby—not none of you gonna win no smarts contest in this lifetime, but you all did good this time. We

handle those Cameaux boys just like I plan. My grandpa Beto Rabeaux is smiling in his grave." Ludvick lifted his tin cup and continued, "Let's make a toast." As each man obediently lifted his cup to the center of the table, Ludvick proclaimed, "To the long life of the Rabeaux family!" Loud cheers rang out around the table as their smiling, greasy faces reflected the dim light above them.

Ludvick's brief bout with satisfaction didn't last long; his face soon resumed its normal expressionless glare, and he continued in his coarse voice. "I want for each you boys to listen to me an listen good." Victor and his two sons automatically fixed their eyes on Ludvick as he reminded them, "For all the good done that Thursday, there's still a job to finish. Those two Cameaux boys Eric an Jon, they was Ben Cameaux's only boys, an he's not gonna have no more sons. We stop that line of the Cameaux family, but like I said, the job is not finish. I thought the other boy Derrick would be there too, but he wasn't. If he would have been, then we could have finish off that whole damn family for sure!"

Interrupting his grandfather Mato asked, "Isn't one ole Cameaux man still living?"

"That's right, stupid!" answered the patriarch sharply. "But that old man is older than me an he for sure won't have no more sons." Ludvick then scanned the faces around the table and asked, "Do you know what that leaves?" A puzzled look came over the faces of his offspring prompting him to answer his own question: "That means only one Cameaux boy left to kill – Derrick Cameaux, he's the last seed. An, after we kill him, then my grandpa Beto can rest in peace."

Toby pleaded, "Gramps, tell us again why we got to kill all them Cameaux men!"

Ludvick stared at Toby and asked, "How ole you are, Boy?"

Toby answered, "Gramps, you know how old me an Mato are."

"That's right an for twenty years I been telling you the same damn thing!"

Mato cut in, "Aw, Gramps, we know why we killing them. We jus like the way you tell it."

Having had his pride pumped a bit, Ludvick quickly drained the last swallow of wine and refilled his cup. He glared coldly at Mato and

Toby, commanding their full attention with his stare. "Okay, it's been awhile, so I'll tell you again. My grandpa Beto an his family lived around Cheniere Caminada. One day a big hurricane blew in an wreck the place an kill a bunch of people. My grandpa, because he was smarter than all the other men, saved his whole family. The Cameaux family was living there too, but they almost all died in that hurricane. Well, my grandpa was a good man. He was helping to bury all those dead peoples when that damn Jerasine Cameaux accuse him of stealing from the dead, like it was a big crime! What the hell the dead gonna do with gold or anything else? Jerasine was jealous of my grandpa an he got some peoples together an told a bunch of lies on Beto. Before they hung him, my grandpa made the Rabeaux family promise to kill out the Cameaux family name, an that's what we been doing ever since. The Cameaux done us wrong, so now they pay."

Victor growled, "I hate those Cameaux, an I want to kill them all with my bare hands! An when we done kill that last Cameaux boy, then I'm gonna kill Ben Cameaux an his old papa as the extra bonus. I don't never forget that Ben killed my brothers."

"Is he the one that killed you brothers?" asked Mato as if hearing this for the first time.

Without giving Victor time to respond, again Ludvick slammed his fist on the table and cut in. "Over the past one hundred years, many men died between the Rabeaux an the Cameaux families! Now, finally we got the chance to end it all with this Mississippi Cameaux!" He arose abruptly from the table as he recalled Pappy's offer of peace after he killed the old Cameaux's son and daughter-in-law. "That foolish ole man," mumbled Ludvick to himself, "there won't never be no peace till all the Cameaux is dead an buried!" After leaving the table, he went straight to his bunk, only to be followed without a word by the rest of the Rabeaux family. They left behind their filthy table. Once again tiny, as well as not so tiny, night creatures would have their fill from the scraps left behind.

After a few minutes in the still, quiet darkness Toby asked, "How we gonna kill that last Cameaux boy?"

Ludvick answered, "I live a long time to kill that last Cameaux. When the time's right, I got ways to end his life that you don't never

dream. I want the Cameaux to suffer a little more before the end comes. Now shut up an go to sleep."

Toby didn't say another word; in fact, he always obeyed his grandfather without question. It hadn't taken many of Ludvick's beatings for him, as a young boy, to understand his place in the Rabeaux clan. Now both Toby and Mato were as Ludvick had cultivated them. In the background Toby could hear a rush of activity on the table of half-empty plates. The sounds of pitched battles for tiny scraps of food eased his mind to sleep, just as it usually did to end another typical day for the Rabeaux.

CHAPTER 14

D errick awoke early on Saturday morning, but as usual Pappy was already up. Walking into the kitchen, he was greeted by a pan of biscuits and a fresh pot of coffee which the elder Cameaux had prepared earlier. Pulling back the curtain of the window next to the kitchen table, he spotted Pappy working his garden. Hoe in hand to remove the beginnings of unwanted weeds, the elder Cameaux stood between a row of okra and Creole tomatoes.

Derrick watched as Pappy wiped the sweat from his brow. Under his breath he whispered, "If I have half the energy you have when I get old, I'll be happy." With a slight smile on his face, Derrick thought of the Rabeaux. If it were up to them, he would never make it to his next birthday, much less live to be an old man. Suddenly the piercing truth of this sobering thought quickly banished any trace of that smile, slight or otherwise.

Buttering his biscuits and pouring his first cup of coffee, Derrick reflected on the past four months since the murders of Eric and John – four months, as well, since Pappy had told him about the Cameaux family history at Cheniere Caminada. Derrick had returned to Mississippi a few times after the funerals to resume running his company, but came home to Golden Meadow every weekend, despite Pappy's determined protests.

During these past four months, he communicated often with Sheriff Lebeouf and Lt. Autin. They kept him informed of the progress or lack of the investigation. In fact, the last time he had spoken to Sheriff Lebeouf, the lawman had told him that it was possible they would never catch the murderers. "You just don't know how right you are, Sheriff," Derrick had wanted to say.

Slowly drinking his coffee on this Saturday morning, Derrick couldn't lie to himself. It wasn't just loyalty to Pappy keeping him quiet. He wanted vengeance. Thoughts of the Rabeaux family fired his anger. He kept his cool by observing and following Pappy's example. Derrick knew Pappy was hurting, yet the old man never let it show; his daily activities continued as though nothing had happened. In fact, the only sign of his grandfather's grief was the absence of his laughter and lighthearted conversation. Pappy also became uncharacteristically nostalgic and overly protective of all family members, especially his only remaining grandson. Finishing his breakfast, Derrick wandered outside where Pappy tended his herb garden. The stoic old Cajun looked up as he approached and asked, "What's on you mind for today, Son?"

"I thought I'd visit Olivia and the girls. Wanna come?"

"I'd like to, but I gotta get some more work done in the garden before the next rain. Tell my great-granddaughters I'll see them tomorrow sometimes."

"I can stay and help you with the garden and visit later," offered Derrick.

Pappy protested, "No, Son, everything is in good shape here. You go on. Will you be back for dinna?"

"I was hoping to take the girls and Olivia out for some burgers or something."

"Good, you do that. I'll visit Ben at the shed."

"I think it's great that Uncle Ben's getting back to work."

"Yeah, well, the doctor said that one more heart attack like this last one could kill him. I want to make sure he's doing what the doctor told him an nothing more."

"Pappy, does Uncle Ben know it was the Rabeaux that killed Eric and Jon?"

"He knows. He said he was gonna kill every last one of them."

"Uncle Ben's going through some tough times, but he's not in any shape to go hunting the Rabeaux."

"Well, Derrick, like you pop, Ben would do anything I ax him under normal situations. But as you know, this is not normal times. When he was in the hospital, he said he want to get better for only one reason and that was to kill every damn Rabeaux that cross his path. I thought maybe once he got better he would see what a fool idea that was, but he still feels the same."

"We can't let him try anything like that, Pappy."

"Don't worry. I don't plan on letting nothing happening to him, or you. Now you better let me finish up here before the day gets away from me. Have a good visit with Olivia an the girls, Son."

Derrick knew he was being dismissed by Pappy. The subject was still just too tough for the old man at this time. As he turned to leave, he said, "Don't work too hard, and tell Uncle Ben I hope he's feeling better."

On the way to the Jeep, Derrick realized that this conversation with his grandfather had bothered him.

He never really knew what was on Pappy's mind or what he'd do next. "What did Pappy mean when he had said that he didn't plan on letting anything happen to Ben or me?" Derrick wondered and then shook his head knowingly as he mumbled under his breath, "Well, whatever it is, I damn sure know I'm not gonna like it."

CHAPTER 15

Teresa and Toni had awakened their mother early that Saturday with the sounds of cartoons on the TV. As she lay in bed, Olivia remembered how Eric had told everyone in his office that he could hardly wait for Saturdays to watch his favorite cartoons with his little girls. She fought back tears as she thought of what a special time it always had been for them to enjoy each other's company. Now the girls watched alone.

Olivia awoke every morning with Eric on her mind. She wouldn't cry in front of the girls anymore, as she had done at first when uncontrollable emotions flowed at will. Now she could sense when a good cry was coming on, and she would quietly go into another room to grieve her loss. Both Teresa and Toni missed their father and still asked time and time again whether he was ever coming home. Olivia also had heard whimpering in their room late at night and knew that they were slowly coming to the realization that their daddy would never return. Their little hearts had been deeply scarred by Eric's death; however, she also knew that a scar was a sign of healing. And healing her little family was exactly what Olivia had silently promised Eric she would do.

Pushing all other thoughts aside, she hurriedly donned her robe and walked into the living room where she was greeted by a cheerful chorus of "Good morning, Mommy."

75

"Good morning girls. Goodness, you two are up mighty early! Ready for breakfast?"

"Yes Ma'am," shouted Teresa, "I want cereal and chocolate milk!"

"I want cereal and chocolate milk too!" echoed Toni.

"Okay. That's two big bowls of Nutty Crunch cereal. Let's see, do you young ladies also want coffee with that?" teased Olivia while pretending to write their breakfast orders on the palm of her hand.

"Yuk!" answered Toni, with a sour look on her face.

"Mom! We don't drink coffee with cereal and chocolate milk!" protested Teresa.

"Oh well, I guess you're right. They don't really go together. Two bowls of Nutty Crunch cereal then and hold the coffee. Coming right up, ladies," chirped Olivia in their favorite high-pitched waitress voice. Clapping their hands in approval and dissolving into laughter, both little girls quickly resumed watching their cartoons. It pleased Olivia to see the girls laughing; she was relieved to know that she could still make them laugh, despite the fact that the antics were no longer spontaneous and effortless. She really had to work at it now, and she couldn't help wondering whether it would ever be natural and easy again.

She fixed the breakfast and allowed the girls to sit on the floor in front of the TV to eat. Next she made herself a couple of pieces of toast and a cup of coffee and sat down at the kitchen table, which was covered with piles of envelopes and papers. "Well, I see that you're all still here," she whispered with resignation. She wanted to close her eyes and just shove them aside, but she took a deep breath and slowly forced herself to filter through the previously untouched bank statements, bills and life-insurance policies.

True to his maturity and wisdom well beyond his years, Eric had planned well for their future. "Just in case the unthinkable happens," he had always insisted. Well, the unthinkable had happened.

Her most immediate concern had to be wisely managing the proceeds from the insurance. Panic almost overwhelmed her until she thought of Derrick. He would know what to do; she could ask him for help. In fact, she wondered why she hadn't thought of it sooner because she certainly didn't know how they would have made it this

far without his help. It was obvious the girls loved Derrick. Thoughts of how he always fussed over them and of how naturally they always called him Uncle Derrick made her smile. Olivia allowed her mind to wander as she remembered Eric's first approach to her after she and Derrick had gone their separate ways. "Olivia," he said with conviction, "I'm not as stupid as my cousin. Would you consider a date with me?" She had accepted. "And the rest is history," she whispered.

Whether it was her melancholy mood or some deeply buried subconscious longing, Olivia found herself drifting into a different world of memories from which she made no attempt to escape. She was even allowing her mind to vividly replay intimate scenes and images of Derrick, whom she hadn't thought of in a romantic way since she married Eric. With that particular thought, Olivia suddenly turned beet red, sitting right there alone at her own table in her own house, with no one else watching her. "How stupid, Olivia!" she exclaimed. Upset that she would even be thinking of Derrick, much less thinking of him in such a way, she quickly restacked the now scattered insurance paperwork and bills and hurried to check on the girls.

Since Teresa and Toni were still watching TV, she occupied herself with going to their room to lay out their clothes for the day before going to her own room to get dressed. Then as she entered the bedroom she had shared with Eric, an awful sense of guilt overwhelmed her because of her memories of Derrick. Had her thoughts of Derrick been a betrayal of Eric? She had never before even remotely imagined living with anyone but Eric; furthermore, she had never ever wanted anyone else, but now he was gone.

The abrupt ringing of the phone suddenly jolted her enough to regain control of her fragile emotions, but just barely. When it became obvious that the girls weren't going to answer the phone downstairs, she slowly began making her way to her bedside table.

When she managed to reach the phone, it quit ringing. Feeling relieved, she sighed, put on an old shirt and a pair of cut-off jeans. Work was what she needed to fill her mind, and work she did, reminding herself again that she knew better than to allow herself to

dwell on Eric too much. "It always makes you a basket-case even after four months! Now get busy!" she whispered.

By mid-morning Olivia was dusting and cleaning her whole house as if her very life depended upon it. And perhaps, in a way, it did. In fact, so involved in her work was she that she didn't even hear the knock at the front door. She was startled when Teresa came running and announced, "Uncle Derrick's in the living room. He said he tried to call."

At first Olivia was in a minor panic, but she quickly told Teresa to tell him that she would come out in a minute. It was obviously too late to change into something more presentable, but as she glanced in the vanity mirror hanging in the hall bathroom, she ran her hand through her disarrayed hair in an attempt to restore some order. She momentarily wondered whether she should put on some make-up, then realized how silly, "After all," she thought, "there's no reason to make a big fuss. It's just Derrick. . . ."

When Olivia entered the living room, she noticed Toni curled up in Derrick's lap, listening intently as he read to her one of her favorite stories. Looking up at her, he smiled. "Good morning, hope I didn't bother you. I tried to call, but there was no answer. So I thought I'd better come on over to check on you and the girls."

"Oh, no, I was just catching up on some cleaning I've been putting off for a long time," replied Olivia, ignoring the reference to the phone call.

"Well, I could come back later. I don't want to interrupt your work."

"No need, Derrick. I didn't stop anything that can't wait until another time!" With that, she sank comfortably into the big chair across the living area from Derrick and Toni.

Casually, Derrick said, "I was wondering what you and the girls had planned for lunch. Thought maybe you just might like to get out and eat a burger or some pizza."

Instantly, the two little girls were determined to make up their mother's mind by begging, "Please, Mommy, pretty please!"

Neither she nor the girls ventured out much since Eric's funeral. "That sounds like a good idea. Besides, I've got a few questions I'd like to ask you about some business matters."

"Fine," replied Derrick. "Now, what will it be, girls, pizza or burgers?"

"Pizza!!"

Olivia laughed and playfully covered her ears with both hands. "Okay now, calm down or Uncle Derrick just might change his mind. I've got your clothes out on your bed, so hurry and get dressed."

With another excited, yet not nearly as loud, chorus of "Yes Ma'm!" both of them scurried away without another word.

Laughing, Derrick observed, "They're a ball of energy! How do you ever keep up with them?" Joining in his laughter, Olivia just shrugged her shoulders as he continued, "Liv, I know I should have tried calling you again, but for some strange reason I just thought it would be fun to surprise the girls."

Derrick's calling her Liv immediately caught her attention, for only Derrick had ever called her that. She quickly glanced down to avert his eyes before answering softly. "Derrick, you really don't have to do this, I already know how much you love the girls and care about them. Besides, you've already done so much and you've been very helpful in so many ways, but I know you have a business and a life to get back to in Mississippi. The girls and I will be all right. Please don't worry or neglect your own responsibilities for us. I promise you, we'll make it just fine."

When Olivia looked up and saw a faint hurt look cross his face, she knew immediately she had said the wrong thing. Before she could apologize, he responded in a low voice tinged with emotion. "Olivia, you know how much I loved Eric. If things were the other way around, he would do this for my family. Besides, I can honestly say I have a great time with the girls. I never thought I'd enjoy young kids so much."

Smiling Olivia said, "You know, I believe you really do enjoy the girls. I know I certainly never thought I'd ever envision you reading to a three-year-old!"

Grinning, Derrick said, "I do beg your pardon Madam. I hereby declare to you that I do happen to love kids, especially your two beautiful daughters!"

"I know you love the girls, I can't tell you what that means to me."

For a moment, neither one said a word. Then, without fanfare or a hint of his intention, Derrick nonchalantly announced, "Liv, I've decided to move back to Golden Meadow –permanently."

Clearly surprised, Olivia fumbled over her next words. "Derrick, why? What about your business and your house? Have you told Pappy about this?"

"You're the first person I've mentioned it to. I haven't even worked out all the details, but I've already made up my mind to do it."

"Derrick, I think that's great! Do you mind if I ask why you're moving back now?"

At that moment Teresa and Toni skipped into the room, obviously very much ready for pizza. Derrick just grinned and whispered, "Later."

Nodding, Olivia agreed and then excused herself. "I'll change and freshen up a bit before we go. I won't be long, if Uncle Derrick can hold down the fort till I get back."

"Oh, Mommy! But we're ready now! Please, please hurry!" came another instantaneous chorus of little voices.

"I promise!" Olivia assured them all as she backed from the room just before turning quickly to run up the stairs.

Derrick smiled at the girls and boasted, "Have no fear. I'll guard the fort from being overrun by these little heathens." Though clearly disappointed by what to them was an unexpected delay, Toni smiled broadly at Derrick asking him to finish reading to her while Teresa watched TV.

Olivia applied her make-up and changed her clothes in record time. "Eric would have been proud of me," she thought. "Of course, Derrick doesn't know the difference." Hurrying downstairs and entering the living room she asked, "My car or yours?"

"If it's all the same to you, let's go in my Jeep."

"That's fine. Is everybody ready?" As the girls ran ahead to the door amid shouts of joy, Olivia whispered to Derrick, "I really appreciate this. The girls needed to get out. This is perfect!"

He didn't make eye contact with her when he answered, "It's not just the girls I'm concerned about." She was pleased that he felt

concern for her. She'd known all along that he was a man of compassion.

Derrick opened the rear door of the Jeep and the girls climbed in eagerly. He opened the door for Olivia, who smiled and said, "Thank you, Mr. Cameaux."

"My pleasure, Madam."

The short trip to the pizza place was both pleasant and relaxing. As they drove along the bayou the girls were fascinated by the water skiers trying to perform tricks, though often without success. Not only were people enjoying the water, but the warm summer also brought many outside activities to the small town. They noticed more than one family hosting the traditional shrimp boil where dozens of family and friends gathered in their yards for great food, fun, and fellowship. Seeing all the familiar sights, Derrick again felt that inevitable Cajun heritage stirring his blood and felt convinced he made the right decision to move back.

Within a few minutes, he drove into the parking lot of Aunt Audrey's Pizza. Once inside, Olivia asked the waitress for a table next to the rear door, which opened to a small play area the girls had always enjoyed previously. Derrick left the ordering to Olivia.

During the meal, laughter and a light-hearted mood were the rule of the table. When they finished eating, the girls were ready for the playground; Teresa even said that she wanted to do some tricks her daddy had taught her. When they left, tears ran freely down Olivia's cheeks. She asked Derrick to excuse her as she rose from the table and hurried to the ladies' room.

Derrick shifted in his chair. The words "I'm insensitive" crossed his mind. He whispered, "Why couldn't I have just left her to grieve in peace?" When she returned a few minutes later, she apologized for what she called her lack of control. They both smiled as they realized that no harm had been done and that they were both trying hard to restore life to some form of normalcy.

Eager to again lighten the mood, Olivia directed the conversation back to what he had told her earlier. "Tell me, Derrick, why are you moving back?"

Taking a few seconds to answer, he worded his thoughts carefully. "Well, actually I've been thinking about moving back for about a year. Until Eric and Jon's deaths, it was just an idea."

"What did Eric and Jon's deaths have to do with your decision?"

"Well, it made me realize for sure that my future and destiny are here. I can't help thinking that if I had done this years ago, I would have traveled with them that day and maybe things would have been different."

"No, Derrick, you wouldn't have made any difference. You would have been killed just like Eric and Jon. If anyone should feel guilty, it's me."

"Liv, the events that took Eric's life had nothing to do with you, and there is absolutely nothing you could have done to prevent it."

"No, I think I could have prevented it!" she said sternly with a far-away look in her eyes. She took a deep breath. "You see, Derrick, a few days before they left, I had a dream – a nightmare, actually – that something terrible would happen to Eric. But I never told him about it. And, Derrick, that something terrible did happen! If only I—"

"What kind of dream?" he interrupted.

Olivia paused for a moment, took a drink of water and sighed. Somehow she knew she had to tell someone. "I dreamed that Eric had disappeared in a thick, dark fog as he and the girls and I were walking along a lonely bayou. Though I searched everywhere, I never saw him again. And when I finally heard him calling me, I realized he was across the bayou. I tried to swim to him but the girls began calling me back to their side of the bayou. As I turned to them, Eric again called me and begged for my help. I was torn between them. When I turned back toward him the second time, I saw four dark figures of God knows what. Honestly, Derrick, I couldn't tell whether they were even human. Oh, Derrick, if I had only warned him." Olivia began sobbing quietly again, clearly unable to continue. Derrick slowly reached across the table and gently grasped her hand.

He was uncomfortably surprised by the accuracy of her dream. "Liv, there's nothing any of us could have done to prevent what happened."

Nodding her head, she wiped tears from her eyes and asked, "Derrick, do you think the murderers will ever be brought to justice? You know I've never hated anyone in my whole life, but I hate whoever killed my husband!"

Hesitating only slightly, Derrick answered, "I know, and I hate them too, Liv, and yes, I do think they'll be brought to justice." He dared not reveal any of the information he had about the Rabeaux, hoping in time he would settle the situation so Olivia and the girls need never know the painful truth of Eric's murder.

The rest of their lunch outing went well enough. It was a good step in the healing process for all of them.

As he left her house later that day he had no doubt he would avenge the deaths of his family. He felt, however, in no hurry to carry out his plan. First he would settle his business in Mississippi; there would be plenty of time later to exact judgment.

CHAPTER 16

As Pappy entered Cameaux Shrimp Shed, he headed straight to Ben's office. To say he was concerned for his son's health would be putting it mildly; from Ben's point of view, Pappy fussed over him too much. However, even Ben could not deny that he wasn't recovering as the doctors thought he would after his heart attack. Nevertheless, Pappy's concern for Ben's health wasn't his main concern for this visit.

Pappy knocked sharply on the office door and walked right in, just as he had always done. Ben was standing next to a filing cabinet when his father entered. "Hey, Pop, what brings you here today?"

"No special reason. I just come by to see how you doing."

"I'm getting stronger by the day," lied Ben.

"The doctor said you shouldn't be back here at work so soon. You should take it easy. Take a trip an relax."

"Pop, let's sit down. Can I get you a cup of coffee?"

The elder Cameaux took his seat and said, "I think I'd like a cup." Ben walked over to an old coffee pot next to the door and poured Pappy a cup. Handing it to his father, he sat down in his chair behind the desk, hoping his father hadn't noticed what a physical effort even that small gesture extracted from him.

"How's business?" Pappy asked, deliberately ignoring what his still-keen eyes had seen.

85

"Slow right now, but it'll pick up. The next trawling season's not far off."

"What kinda season you think it will be?"

"Well, a good one, according to some test drags. Of course, that could change by opening day of the season. You know that yourself."

"That's true," said Pappy, nodding in agreement. Pappy never changed the expression on his face; he just continued sipping his coffee. When he was finally ready to talk, he firmly set the cup on Ben's desk and said in a calm, even voice, "Ben, you too sick to go after Ludvick an his boys. He'll kill you an you know that!"

This discussion had been long overdue and both men were going to speak their minds. Ben looked right into his father's eyes and said, "No, Pop, my death's already happen! I died when my boys died! All that's left is to bury this old failing body you see before you! But before it fails completely, I'm going to do my best to kill, not only Ludvick, but all the damn Rabeaux! We should have done that a long time ago!"

Pappy's cool, calm voice quickly became defensive and challenging. "Go ahead an say it. It's my fault! If I would have let you do what you want to twenty years ago, none of this mess would have happen!"

"I'm not saying that, Pop, an I don't think it's your fault. I know you were trying to protect the boys. All I'm saying is that we, the Cameaux family, have been trying to live in peace while the Rabeaux family has but one purpose in life and that's to kill every last one of us. We're the foolish ones, Pop. We're the ones who think people should forgive an forget an live in peace, but that only works when all the sides agree. If we would have worked as hard at solving this problem as the Rabeaux did to killing us, then long ago this war would have been settled."

Ben tried to keep his emotions in check but his blood churned with anger as he slammed his fist on his desk. "We had the advantage the day Julien an me killed those two Rabeaux brothers! Then there was only Ludvick, Victor and Victor's two young boys left! But we let that advantage slip away, an you know, Ludvick doesn't never want no peace! The only reason we never heard nothing from them is that

Ludvick was just waiting for those boys to grow up to help him! Now they're grown men! That bastard Ludvick killed Eric and Jon, an you know Derrick is next! They'll never stop till Derrick's dead, or I kill them first!"

Pappy couldn't contain himself, "Ben, I'm your dad! I always done what I thought was in the family's best interest, an now I'm gonna give you some advice. Don't you go out looking for Ludvick Rabeaux. You just not strong enough yet, an you don't have no business running around in no swamps! BON DIEU! I don't want to bury no more son! Do you hear me, Ben?" When there was no response, Pappy sighed and continued. "Believe me, Ludvick Rabeaux won't never get away with this! He'll pay dearly for all he's done, but not by you an not by Derrick. You must promise me you won't go after the Rabeaux!"

Ben and Pappy stared deeply into each other's eyes. With each passing moment, the heavy silence between them grew almost deafening. Finally Ben voiced the obvious. "Pop, you know I love you, but you also know I can't say what you want me to say."

Pappy shook his head, took a deep breath, got up and walked toward the door. With his hand on the doorknob, he stopped and turned toward Ben. "Your two granddaughters need you now more than ever. Just think about that." Pivoting abruptly, he walked out the door, slamming it behind him without a second look.

Ben sat still, looking out the window at the rows of boats tied up to the Cameaux docks. He surely hadn't wanted to hurt Pappy, but the Rabeaux must pay with their lives and he resolved to collect that debt himself.

CHAPTER 17

After leaving Olivia's house, Derrick stopped to see his old high-school buddy Scott Armont, who had always been one of his best friends. Scott began playing the guitar when he and Derrick were only freshmen. He was so talented that by the time he had finished high school, his career as a Cajun singer and band leader was a foregone conclusion.

Derrick knew his friend was home because in a huge garage just off the driveway he could see the bus Scott and his band used for traveling. Just like old times, Derrick blew the horn a couple of times and Scott hurried out the door even before Derrick could get out of his Jeep.

Scott greeted him with a big grin. "Man, it's been a long time!" How're you doing?"

"Good Scott, real good; you're right, it's been awhile, you old gator!"

When Scott's wife Pam walked out the front door and saw Derrick, her smile said it all. "Well, Scott, you just gonna keep him out here all afternoon? Bring that stranger inside! Come on, you bring him in right now!" she chided while hurrying out to meet him. She and Derrick held each other at arm's length momentarily to exclaim the mutual "Wow!"

"Pam, you're just as pretty today as you were in high school," Derrick said with a smile.

Scott laughed. "Will you listen to him? You haven't lost your touch, Breaux. Still hittin' on every female you meet."

"Well," said Pam, "no one else has said I'm pretty in such a long, long time." Then, with a toss of her hand in mock defiance of her husband she continued, "Derrick's a gentlemen. You could learn a lot from him."

Still laughing, Scott declared, "Yeah, right, but nothing I could use as a married man!"

"Be nice, honey!" said Pam with a stern voice. Turning her full attention toward Derrick she declared, "This is your lucky day Mr. Cameaux!"

"And why is it my lucky day?" asked an apprehensive Derrick.

Pam held tight to Derrick's arm as she led him through the front door and into the dimly lit den. It took him a couple seconds for his eyes to adjust before he realized there was a woman standing in the middle of the room. Teasing, Pam asked, "Derrick, do you remember this young lady?"

Instantly, the amazed look on his face was matched by the woman's obvious surprise. "Bonnie Sladder?".

"Derrick Cameaux, is that you?"

As Derrick and Bonnie embraced, a flood of memories engulfed each of them. They had dated in high school for a short time.

Finally releasing their embrace, Bonnie looked over her shoulder at Pam to complain. "If I'd known Derrick Cameaux was going to be here, I'd have at least put on something nice. I can't believe you brought me over here in these faded, paint-splattered shorts! But I sure wouldn't miss seeing Derrick for the world, paint-splattered shorts or not!"

Laughing, Scott said, "Man, I had nothing to do with this."

Pam scolded Scott, "Now just let things happen the way they happen!" Then turning her attention to Derrick she explained, "Bonnie was kind enough to accept my invite to help me with painting the kids' bedroom. Her car is on the blink so I picked her up."

It was certainly a pleasant surprise for Derrick to see Bonnie Sladder. He couldn't believe how beautiful she had become. Her hair was the same light blonde he remembered, except that now it was styled in a shorter, more sophisticated cut. Derrick's appreciative gaze

confirmed that the years had only improved her notable figure, a feature not in the least minimized by those faded, paint-spattered short-shorts. An outstanding athlete in high school, she was definitely a head-turner. At the first opportunity, Derrick stole a quick glance at Bonnie's hand for a wedding band and didn't see one.

Pam, ever the match-maker and never lacking good old-fashioned nerve, asked, "Doesn't she look great, Derrick?"

Before he could answer, however, Bonnie laughed and said, "Oh no, you don't! Don't you dare sit there and put words in Derrick's mouth!"

Derrick said the only thing he could: "Well, you do look great, Bonnie."

Bonnie purred in her low, sweet voice, "Thanks, Derrick, that means a lot to me." He was certain his ears were red, and if at that moment he could have disappeared into thin air, he would have immediately done so.

Laughing at the two of them, Scott coaxed, "Hey, you two, cut it out. You might give Pam the idea our honeymoon is over with all that mushy talk."

"Honey Buns," said Pam, looking at Scott intensely, "I can't remember the last time you said I looked great or that I was beautiful."

"Awe, Baby, you're the most beautiful woman in the world and you know you always look great to me." Scott interrupted her, barely able to contain his laughter.

"Talk about mushy," declared Derrick, "you two are insane!"

"Yeah, crazy in love with each other, right, Pam my baby?" cooed Scott as he leaned over to kiss her cheek and nibble her ear.

Deliberately ignoring his attempts to say something nice, Pam turned instead to Derrick and Bonnie. "Would you two like something to drink? I've made a fresh pot of tea." When they accepted her offer, she motioned for Scott to help her in the kitchen. Though he pretended to protest, he followed her willingly, still kidding her all the way. Just as they rounded the corner to the kitchen, Derrick and Bonnie clearly heard Pam exclaim, "Oh my goodness, Scott! Can't you ever be serious? After all, we do have company of sorts!" Looking at each other at the same time and laughing, Bonnie and Derrick nodded in

approval of the warm, affectionate relationship enjoyed by their friends.

Derrick said, "I'm sorry we had to meet again under such circumstances."

Evidently, she hadn't noticed or was just purposely overlooking any sense of his awkwardness. Her reaction to him brought back memories of their high-school days when she would always take his hand and look deeply into his eyes before speaking. He now felt his heart pound a little harder as Bonnie reached for his hand. She always had known how to flirt with the best of them, which was the main reason he had broken up with her so many years ago. She treated all men the same, and he doubted she was any different today. Oh yes, he knew better than to fall for her enticements, but he was spellbound. As Bonnie looked intently at him and held his hand firmly in her own, he could feel the heat from her body rush up his arm. He was helpless to resist. In a silky-smooth voice she whispered, "I'd love to see you under any circumstances, Derrick. Now tell me what's been happening in your life." Derrick knew he was being seduced by the best.

He sighed and shrugged his shoulders. "Well, tell you the truth, Bonnie, things were going great till a few months ago."

With a sad look on her face Bonnie said, "Oh, yes, that's right, I heard about your cousins. That's terrible, I'm so sorry."

"Yes, it is terrible," said Derrick solemnly, "but we'll survive."

"I'm sure you will. How's your grandfather?"

"Oh, Pappy's as hard-headed as ever but you know, Bonnie, he sure thought a lot of you. I can't wait to tell him I saw you today."

"Oh, please do tell him hello for me and how sorry I am about Eric and Jon."

Yes, Bonnie had been a one-time girlfriend, and regardless of how disconcerting it might be to him, sitting next to her now brought back feelings he thought had been long buried. Derrick knew he never would or could love her as a husband should love a wife. She stirred him; this much was true, but the stirrings were purely physical.

Pam and Scott soon returned with iced tea, chips and dip. The four spent the rest of the afternoon laughing and reminiscing as well as playfully arguing and teasing about some of those so-called "convenient

memory" lapses that often are actually better left undisturbed. In spite of the sometimes embarrassing revelations, it was all about old times. Derrick welcomed the respite since smiling faces and light talk had so obviously been missing from his life during the previous few months.

Nearing supper time Bonnie glanced at her watch and mentioned that she really should be getting home, and almost as if on cue, Pam casually responded, "Wow, such a long day and I'm so tired, Derrick would you mind dropping Bonnie off on your way home? That is, unless we can talk you two into staying for supper rather than spending the rest of the evening at Bonnie's!"

"Pam!" exclaimed Bonnie in mock disbelief.

Even Scott looked at his wife and was about to come to his friend's rescue when Derrick surprised himself as well as the rest of them, except for Bonnie who just smiled unconcerned. "I would be more than happy to drive Bonnie home."

"Man, are you sure?" Scott questioned.

"No problem," Derrick assured him, to which Scott rolled his eyes.

As they stood, Derrick asked with exaggerated drawl, "Are you ready now, Fine Lady, to leave the company of these fine folks?"

"Absolutely!" answered Bonnie.

"Well, then, I guess we'd better be on our way. All kidding aside, thanks for the hospitality; you're the best friends ever. "

"We'll finish painting the room later," Bonnie said to Pam.

"No big deal; you two have fun!"

CHAPTER 18

When they reached the Jeep, Derrick opened the passenger door for Bonnie. She smiled as she remembered how gentlemanly he was. In fact, she couldn't help thinking of him as an example of what all men should be. Reaching the main highway he asked, "Which way, young lady?"

"Oh, that's right, you don't even know where I live. Well, several years ago I bought an old wood frame house down Cedar Street."

As Derrick headed in that direction, he thought it a good time to ask, "Bonnie weren't you married or something?"

Without hesitation Bonnie answered, "That's right, only it was more like the 'or something.' "I was married to a jerk from Texas, but it didn't last long. Then I married a jerk from Nevada, and that didn't last either. Guess that makes me a two-time loser, and the way I look at it, I get only one more shot at this marriage thing. What about you?"

"No way, you know me. I couldn't stand being tied down."

"Take it from me, Derrick, this whole marriage bit isn't what it's made out to be. I've about decided the next time I find someone I really like, why, I'll just live with him first to see if we can get along for more than a month."

Derrick smiled and asked, "Well, did it ever occur to you to marry a jerk from Louisiana? Seems you'd have more in common with a

95

Cajun boy. Then if it didn't work out, at least you couldn't say you didn't have the best, right?"

That brought the smile back to Bonnie's face as she laughed, "Derrick Cameaux, if you're not the typical 'not conceited, just convinced Cajun,' I don't know who is!"

As Derrick turned onto Cedar Street, Bonnie pointed to the second house on the right and invited him in for a drink. Seeing no harm, and really not quite ready to go home yet, Derrick accepted and parked in the driveway next to Bonnie's ancient Beetle.

Bonnie led the way and as she unlocked the door, said, "Please excuse the mess. Make yourself comfortable while I get something cool for us."

Derrick sat on the sofa no more than a minute when his newly activated conscience unexpectedly assaulted him. Rubbing his hands together and taking a deep breath were the first visible signs of his uneasiness with the situation. Bonnie returned with a chilled bottle of wine and two glasses, and she stood before him, smiling directly into his eyes as she set the glasses on the coffee table. Smiling, she slowly and deliberately poured the wine with the enticing expertise of the well-practiced. "Let's make a toast, shall we?"

"Sure, what shall we toast?"

"Well," continued Bonnie as she sat next to him on the sofa and raised her glass, "let's toast to our friendship."

Nodding, he smiled and raised his glass to meet hers. Derrick quickly asked, "So, Bonnie, what brought you back to Golden Meadow?"

In her low sultry voice she answered, "Derrick I really don't want to talk about me!"

She still doesn't miss a beat, thought Derrick. It was undeniable that this was the precise moment they both knew further words were unnecessary. When Bonnie had first sat next to him, there had been room for another person to sit between them. However, as their conversation had continued, that space somehow closed until Derrick could both feel and hear her breathing as vividly as his own. He wasn't quite sure who had kissed who first; all he knew was that after a while, no one was talking and things were proceeding at hurricane speed. In

fact, their passions were about to explode when Derrick's body tensed at the unexpected and surprising thought of Olivia. Just as quickly, Bonnie stopped kissing him and looked into his eyes.

With disappointment clearly on her face, she asked, "What's wrong?" He couldn't answer; he didn't know how to answer. Undaunted, Bonnie continued, "I know you're not married. I also thought you weren't seeing anyone, but maybe I was wrong. Do you love someone, Derrick?

"What is this—some woman's intuition thing?" asked Derrick, wishing he were almost any other place at that very moment, or that Bonnie was. However, she didn't move away from him, and he knew he could say the right words at that moment and finish what they had started. Instead, he surprised them both by the unexpected demeanor and tone by which he now totally shattered not only the mood, but also any hopes either of them might have had of kindling a romance. "You're right. I do love someone very dearly. I'm only just now coming to understand how much."

"Does she know?" asked Bonnie.

"No, and I don't intend her to ever find out," he answered with an unmistakable sadness as he moved away from Bonnie. "I'd better be going now. I'm sure Pappy must be wondering what happened to me."

She touched his arm to halt him, whispering, "Well, in that case, we could just finish what we started at least this once." Ice water thrown directly in her beautiful, radiant face couldn't have spoken more forcefully than the incredulous look on Derrick's face. "Just kidding," she mumbled as she stood up before he could say anything.

As he also rose to his feet, she quickly kissed him gently on the cheek before he could protest, but not before she felt him stiffen his resolve against her. Then, without a backward glance or another word, Derrick turned and walked out the door.

Much to his surprise, that evening had sealed for Derrick once and for all the fact that Olivia was the one and only woman for him. Thanks to Bonnie, he could see that clearly. For the first time in his life, Derrick was in love, albeit a love he had vowed never to reveal.

97

CHAPTER 19

Since returning from his talk with Ben, Pappy paced the floor, waiting for Derrick. No one knew the Rabeaux as he did and now, to make matters worse, things were advancing much more quickly than he anticipated. He knew it would be only a matter of time until they tried to kill his grandson; the worst part was that Derrick seemed so oblivious. Suddenly thinking he heard something outside, Pappy looked out the window, but saw nothing. He had warned Derrick not to come back to Golden Meadow. "The boy should just go to Mississippi an get on with his life," grumbled Pappy to himself. "Where can that boy be?" Finally his frustration drove him to call Olivia, but that only compounded his fears when she told him Derrick had left hours earlier.

Now almost sick with worry, Pappy was about to go looking for Derrick when he heard a vehicle pull into the driveway. He opened the curtain just wide enough to see that it was, indeed, the Jeep, and a feeling of relief swept over him. However, as soon as he felt that relief, it was replaced with anger, an unsettling anger directed toward his beloved grandson who seemed so completely deaf to the danger that surrounded him.

Entering the house Derrick began speaking to his grandfather even before Pappy had a chance to scold him. "Oh good, Pappy, I'm glad you're still up so I can tell you I've decided to go to Mississippi tomorrow morning and start the process of selling my company. I plan to move back here with you." Even though he never looked at Pappy as

99

he spoke, he felt an icy silence and his grandfather's glaring stare and knew his news was not received well. What he didn't know, however, was the churning turmoil boiling inside the outwardly calm old Cajun.

"Didn't I tell you that you will be killed if you stay here! Bon Dieu, Boy! Have you lost your mind?"

Derrick hadn't anticipated his grandfather's stinging rebuke. Masking his own feelings, he turned to face Pappy squarely and answered with determination, "I'm moving back here because I want to move back."

With his anger no longer concealed, Pappy exploded, "I told you, Derrick Cameaux! You betta listen to me!"

Not wanting to argue with his grandfather, Derrick simply replied, "I'm a grown man, and I've decided to handle the Rabeaux situation on my own terms."

"You a grown man, Derrick, yes, but believe me; they'll still kill you, Boy. You think you can handle the Rabeaux, but it'll be out of your hands! I promise you that. Now, tell me, is this decision final?"

Without hesitation Derrick answered, "I've made up my mind, Pappy." It was actually just as well that he didn't quite catch all the words in the old Cajun's mumbled response as his grandfather turned and walked angrily from the living room.

"Hard headed cooyon! Now I got two stupid decisions to fix!" Pappy exclaimed as he entered his bedroom, and he knew exactly what he had to do. He was the head of the family. The responsibility for his family's safety was his alone and he felt it was his fault that they suffered as they did. With Ben and Derrick each set on fighting the Rabeaux single-handedly, he had little choice but to be the one to deliver the deadly blow to his family's enemies. He would take his time and prepare well, but sometime before Ben could fully recover and Derrick's return from Mississippi, he'd do whatever necessary to kill the Rabeaux.

Early the next morning Derrick awoke to the smell of smoked bacon, homemade biscuits, grits and fried eggs. Pappy had fixed him a large breakfast to see him on his way; neither man mentioned the previous night's sharp words. However, Derrick did

think it odd that Pappy would so easily give up trying to persuade him not to move back to Louisiana.

As he was leaving, Pappy kissed him on the forehead and assured him that he loved him. That, in itself, wasn't unusual; Pappy had always greeted and seen him off with such affection. However, what caught Derrick's attention was the disturbingly unmistakable sense of the finality of the kiss, as though it were the last farewell.

Late that afternoon Pappy sat on the back steps looking over his garden. As usual, the days were hot and humid, and the summer garden showed signs of stress, especially since the rains fell only in sporadic intervals this time of the year. Pappy had often marveled at how differently plants and people lived their lives and yet in some ways, how similar their life patterns were. He thought of Eric and Jon, two young men in their prime capable of producing much great fruit; cut down long before their full potential could be reached. Then he thought of himself, an old man withering away, long past his prime and no longer productive. "What a waste in both cases!" he grumbled. He stared at the rows of vegetable, but saw nothing; the scenery was all in his mind. Why hadn't he been cut down? Gladly he would have traded places with Jon and Eric. "The ole pass away to leave the young to carry on. God never intend for the young to perish before the ole. If only I taught my grandsons about the Rabeaux they might be alive today. Now, if only Derrick would stay away, but he's no coward; he's coming back to hunt the Rabeaux. That's why I must get to them first. I'm just a ole man withering away. Maybe, before I go, I can take a few weeds with me." That would leave room for Derrick to blossom an grow ole. Pappy was an old man, much older than Ludvick. His body no longer looked or felt strong, but he had a clear mind and a strong heart. He had killed Rabeaux before; in fact, no one had decimated them more than he, but that had been many years earlier. Once more the blood of his enemies must be spilled! Uncertain whether nature were sanctioning or condemning his vendetta, Pappy heard the distant rumble of an approaching thunderstorm. He knew rain must come if the young plants had any chance to blossom and grow; he was also well aware that a severe storm could destroy tender plants not yet strong or deeply rooted enough to survive its fury. With a shrug, the tough old man dismissed Mother Nature's foreshadowing what might lie ahead. It was time for him to leave. Time to carry the storm to Ludvick!

CHAPTER 20

L udvick Rabeaux had sent his grandsons Mato and Toby to run a new crab line in South Caminada Bay while he and Victor ran a line just to the northeast in Barataria Bay. It was only the second time Ludvick split up his family. Two winters earlier, he allowed Victor and Toby to run a trap line not far from the Cameaux Swamp while he and Mato ran one further east. After a month apart, the four had joined forces once again to compare successes. Ludvick - counted Victor and Toby's money, and thinking that there should have been more, accused the two of stealing. Never mind that Victor and Toby had made more money than he and Mato; Ludvick reasoned that more was expected because they were in a better, more productive area. Proclaiming their untrustworthiness, Ludvick swore an oath never to split up again, just so he could keep an eye on them.

That's why it came as a shock to the boys when the controlling old patriarch told them to run a new crab line in Caminada Bay. Neither boy thought it safe or wise to remind their grandfather of his oath two years earlier. Of course Ludvick, as always, gave them specific instructions. First, set this new crab line far enough away from the town of Caminada so as not to be seen from land. Second, once they had passed their own line, they were to scout for other crab lines not belonging to them. Ludvick expected them to check these traps as well, being careful to collect all crabs without detection. Third, sell

103

their catch in Caminada, leave as soon as they had been paid. Fourth, under no circumstances, ever go into any Bar. Last, but most importantly, they were not to spend a penny on anything but fuel!

That had been three weeks ago, and Mato and Toby had done everything exactly as Ludvick had instructed. Tomorrow all four men were scheduled to meet at the camp on Bayou Castete. Thus far, to their credit, during this last day on their own the two Rabeaux boys worked hard picking up their crab line and storing the crab cages on the stern of their skiff. It was dusk as they headed back toward the dead-end canal where they had found an abandoned oil well; nothing was left but a few pilings, which were perfect for tying up the Rabeaux skiff, and it was here, far off the normal fishing grounds, that Mato and Toby had spent every night after each day's work. After tying up their skiff, Toby could tell that something was eating at his older brother. As usual, it wasn't long until Mato complained. "For three damn weeks we been sleeping in this canal getting our ass eat up by mosquitoes!"

"So, what's new about that?" asked Toby offhandedly.

Mato yelled, "I tell you what the hell's different, Pisshead! Not two miles from here there's beer and women! You know what a woman is, Pisshead? Well, they got some women there you can lick on an get all the sugar you can eat! An they just waiting for us to lick on them, and here us cooyons sit not doing a damn thing but getting eat alive by a million mosquitoes! I say we just get up from here an go get us a woman!"

But Toby wasn't about to let Mato ruin their first chance to show Ludvick they could handle a job on their own. "Stupid, don't you never remember what Gramps said? Stay out the Bars! Dumbass!"

Mato took a deep breath and continued, "An whose gonna tell? How he's gonna know? I'm not gonna tell, an if you tell, I break your neck! So, what you say we get us a woman an have some fun?"

"I say no! It's a dumb idea, one I expect from a dumbass like you!" Toby's response to his older brother was honest but not very wise.

Mato snapped, a reaction not at all unusual for the huge, hulking elder brother. Leaping over a crab trap that separated the two, Mato suddenly flew headlong into Toby. Caught off guard, Toby fell hard to

the deck of the skiff, with Mato heavy on top of him with his big right hand raised in a clenched fist, taking dead aim at Toby's head. Seeing his brother's intention, Toby quickly moved his head just in time to miss the blow, and Mato's hand went crashing to the deck. The painful look on Mato's face was instantly replaced with rage—he would not be denied again! He grabbed Toby's neck with his left hand and swung again at his little brother's head; this time his fist found its mark. Again and again, the big man pounded his fist into his brother's face until the blood flowed freely from Toby's eyes, nose and mouth.

As had so often happened before, again Toby was being victimized. The two brothers had always fought, but this time Toby really feared Mato would kill him. In all previous scrapes, either Victor or Ludvick had stopped the fight before any serious damage had been done, but this time no one was around to stop Mato. He was out of control: the harder he hit Toby, the angrier he became. In fact, in his insane rage he was actually choking Toby with his left hand while beating him with his right, and after a while, even that didn't seem punishment enough. Suddenly, to Toby's horror, he saw Mato reach for his long Bowie knife, fortunately catching sight of the weapon just as the day's final glimmer of sunlight bounced off the shining blade.

Convinced that he would soon die, Toby seized his opportunity when he realized that at that moment Mato lifted the blade, he had also loosened his grip on his neck long enough to allow a trace of air into lungs. Barely able to breathe, Toby gasped the one word he could manage: "Bar." That's all he said, but it was enough.

The crazed look in Mato's eyes subsided as he heard Toby's almost inaudible word. Once again he eased his grip on Toby's neck long enough to allow a small flow of air into his brother's lungs. Then, still on top of him, he demanded, "You saying you want to go for a beer in that Bar at Caminada?"

Still gasping for air, Toby sputtered, "An maybe we can find us a woman."

"You not saying that just so I let you up, are you?"

In a hoarse whisper Toby said, "No, I think we deserve a beer. What you say?"

"Well, if you insist, I better go with you an make sure you don't get in no trouble," reasoned Mato, without a trace of remorse over beating his brother almost to death. "You better get clean up. You can't go to no honky-tonk looking like that." Finally he slowly got off Toby and even helped him up after he had carefully put the Bowie knife back into its sheath. Then reaching into a plastic five-gallon bucket, he pulled out a dirty rag and a bottle of hot sauce.

"What you gonna do with that?" asked Toby.

"Well, Stupid, I'm gonna clean those cuts on your face. That's what I'm gonna do."

"I never seen no one put no hot sauce on a cut before. You sure about that?" asked Toby with a noticeable look of concern.

"I seen Gramps do this plenty of time on Ole Blue," Mato assured him as he removed the rusty top of the hot sauce bottle.

"But Ole Blue's a dog. An besides, I think Gramps just liked to hear Ole Blue hollar."

"What, you think you better than Ole Blue? Now sit yourself down and be still!"

Toby, not wanting to re-aggravate Mato and realizing that he was too weak to resist him anyway, obediently sat down before his older brother. Mato grabbed hold of Toby's face and looked at the wounds. Most were minor cuts, but one under the right eye could have used at least four stitches. Concentrating on the large cut, Mato slowly picked up the bottle of hot sauce. Although Toby couldn't move his head because of Mato's tight grip, he still could see the bottle of hot sauce coming near his face, and he began squirming despite his best intentions. Automatically tightening his grip, Mato looked Toby in the eye and said in a stern voice, "Don't you move or I'm gonna have to sit on you to do this!"

Seeing the big grin cross Mato's face proved to Toby that the following would be most unpleasant. His eyes grew bigger as he watched his brother very carefully place his left index finger above the cut and his left thumb below the cut. He closed his eyes, unable to watch what would happen next. Mato spread his fingers, making the wound under Toby's eye open wide, lifted the bottle of hot sauce, and poured the liquid fire into the wound.

106

In his life Toby had been stabbed with an ice pick, bitten by an alligator, run over by not one, but two boats, and he had even lost small parts of his fingers in fur traps; but never in his life did he experience pain as he did now. His face felt as if it were literally on fire; instinctively he jumped to his feet, picking up his brother in the process. When Mato tried to hold him down, Toby tossed him aside effortlessly, surprising both of them. Clawing his face and screaming as loudly as any man could scream, Toby jumped overboard.

Mato immediately leaned over the side of the skiff, but he saw only a big rush of air bubbles where Toby had entered the water. With a shrug, he waited and watched for what seemed like minutes for the youngest Rabeaux to surface. Contrary to what one might expect, the expression on his face wasn't one of concern for his brother, but rather one of confusion. After all, he had never seen Toby act that way before. "Cooyon! Stupid!" he grumbled to himself. "Now how you think that hot sauce gonna do you some good! It's not gonna do no good in the water!" Of course Mato had no intention of jumping in after Toby. In fact, if the cooyon didn't come up soon, he would just go to the Bar by himself. He certainly had no intention of missing his last opportunity for a fling before having to report to Ludvick.

As soon as Toby hit the salt water, the many smaller cuts began stinging his face, but that was a small price to pay compared to the fire caused by the hot sauce. Holding his breath and gritting his teeth in defiance of even more pain, he scrubbed at the large wound until all the hot sauce had been removed. And though this did bring some relief, it also made his face feel like a piece of raw meat caught in a meat grinder. Then, becoming aware of the mounting pressure in his chest, Toby suddenly realized just how far under the muddy water he had gone. The darkness was complete; his feet rested on the muddy bottom; and at that moment of stark reality, his priorities shifted drastically. He pushed off the soft bottom and strained for the surface.

Mato, still scanning the water but not nearly as patiently, finally noticed a dark object swimming toward the surface. "Bout time!" he mumbled as he watched Toby break the surface, gasp for air, and gesture obscenely in his direction.

Toby yelled, "You son of a bitch! French whore! Bastard!"

Mato grinned, shrugging his shoulders again as if he were completely oblivious to the stream of profanity his victim hurled at him. When Toby extended his hand to Mato to be helped out of the water, the bully stood there smiling broadly and folded his huge arms across his chest. "Now, if that don't beat all. First you cuss me an now you think I ought to pick you up! Well, I'm gonna pull you out this time, but never do no fool thing like that again, or I'll just let you stay there!"

With that callous ultimatum, Mato unceremoniously hauled him up over the side of the skiff and dumped him in a heap on the deck. As Toby squinted up at the mass of muscle towering over him, he demanded bravely, "What that hell you do to me, Stupid?"

"Cooyon! I probably saved you fool life! Like I told you, that's the way Gramps helps Ole Blue when he gets all cut up. But, now that I think about it, Ole Blue usually ends up in the bayou, too." Then with a casual wave as if to dismiss the whole situation, he looked critically at his brother's ravaged face and declared emphatically, "Well, looks like all the bleeding stop. Now, put you on some dry clothes an let's go get that beer!" Still in no shape to argue or to resist his brother, Toby slowly managed to remove his wet dirty clothes and put on some dry dirty ones. With eager anticipation Mato started the engine, untied the skiff, and steered them out of the canal into Caminada Bay.

After having completely forgotten his fight with Toby, Mato began singing his favorite old Cajun tunes. Even when he forgot the words, he improvised, never missing a beat, for nothing would deter him from what he was certain would be good times ahead. Smiling as he sang, he revealed a mouth full of dead teeth embedded in a crater of an uncertain brown color mixed with black.

The fact that it was now night and difficult to see was no problem for Mato, he saw what he needed—the distant lights of Caminada. He navigated toward the southeast end of the town where the tiny Bar stood and looking at Toby, he grinned. "Got the money?"

Toby reached down into the same bucket that stored the hot sauce and pulled out an old glass jar full of bills. "How much we gonna need?"

Mato thought for a moment and then suggested, "Each a fifty ought to do it." Toby didn't like it one bit. His grandfather Ludvick would know for sure if they spent anywhere near that kind of money, but he didn't say a word of protest. He had learned his lesson.

As they approached the quiet fishing village, Mato eased the skiff into a narrow slip and tied up to the first piling of a long wharf. He automatically turned the skiff around to put the bow facing away from land; Ludvick taught these boys well. Both knew that before this night was over, they just might have to make a quick get-away if things happened to get a little out of hand, as was often the case with them. This little Bar on the edge of the bay was accustomed to rowdy, unruly oilfield roughnecks, roustabouts and riggers; nevertheless, the two Rabeaux boys could teach everyone a new lesson in abnormal behavior.

After tying up the skiff, they jumped onto the wharf and walked toward the Bar not two hundred feet away. Toby was looking forward to drinking beer, whiskey or anything else that would ease the constant pounding in his head after Mato's beating. As he watched his older brother walk in front of him, he knew that he could never let Mato put him in that kind of danger again. Although he never came that close to killing him before, Toby knew that unless he himself prevented it, it could easily happen again. Suddenly remembering the Bowie knife Mato was caring, he suggested, "You know, they just might not let us in if they see that knife you got."

Mato stopped, placed his right hand over the knife and began gently stroking it while deciding what to do. He never went anywhere without his knife, and though sometimes people gave him strange looks, no one ever questioned his carrying it. This time, though, he pulled his shirt tail out of his pants to let it hang freely over the knife. Next, just for good measure, he hiked his pants up a little higher, further concealing the long blade. Grinning at Toby, he then asked, "Now, how do I look?"

Toby was convinced that Mato was undoubtedly the ugliest man he had ever seen, and normally he would have said so; however, after what had happened earlier he said, "You look like a French

109

gentlemen." Mato raised his head a little higher and again walked on ahead of his younger brother.

As they neared the front door of the Bar, their spirits soared with the sounds of loud music and laughter. Mato turned to Toby, winked and boasted, "I hear women an I'm gonna get me one tonight!" Nodding in agreement, Toby quickly circled around Mato, reached the door first, and jerked it open. A thin billow of cigarette and cigar smoke rushed out to greet them as the Rabeaux brothers disappeared into the dimly lit bar.

CHAPTER 21

Pappy had traveled to Caminada in one of his smaller skiffs. Taking his time, the old Cajun cautiously explored the many bays and bayous along the way. He watched dozens of crab fishermen going about their tasks, generally oblivious to his passing. But for good measure, whenever he came close to one of them he stayed low in his seat so as not to be recognized. He also frequently scanned the waters with a pair of binoculars in search of the Rabeaux, but saw nothing.

It had been two days since he left Golden Meadow, and now he was nearing the small fishing village of Caminada, the very same Caminada totally devastated by that mighty hurricane so long ago. And it wasn't by mistake that he was approaching Caminada so late in the day; he had keen memories of Ludvick and Victor's occasional visits to a small bar on the water's edge. The Rabeaux shunned people for the most part; however, they liked strong drink and easy women, features gladly provided for the right price in small dingy Bars catering to fishermen and oilfield workers away from homes and families. Just such a bar operated here on the water's edge of Caminada.

Pappy tied his skiff to a lone piling a few feet from shore. The day was now spent and if nothing happened during the night, he would get an early start in the morning. He was far enough away from the Bar so

that his searching eyes wouldn't arouse suspicion yet close enough to see clearly the front door and all those who entered.

With the night now almost totally upon them, many fishermen had tied up in the numerous slips along the shoreline and were making their way to the small bar.

After nightfall, no one else approached the bar by way of the bay; however, a narrow clamshell road connected the tiny bar with the rest of Caminada, and a few men in vehicles had stopped by for drinks.

Although two long hours had passed since Pappy had set up his lookout position, he wasn't ready to call it a night. "At least the breeze from the Gulf keeps the damn mosquitoes away," he grumbled. Well aware of only an outside chance that Ludvick would show up on this night, he figured it was as good a place as any to look for his old nemesis.

Nearly an hour had now passed since the last men had entered the bar. Tiring now and almost ready to settle down for the night, Pappy quickly changed his mind when he heard the faint sound of a skiff approaching from the bay. His eyes strained to see the skiff as it emerged from the darkness, watching closely as it was tied to the last piling leading out of the main slip. Soon two men climbed out and although he couldn't make out their faces, he did hear them say something about a knife. He continued watching as they stood there, but couldn't figure out what they were doing. When they finally walked on, he tried his best but was still unable to see their faces very clearly. One thing he had determined was that the two weren't Ludvick and Victor, yet something about their manner tagged them as pure Rabeaux. He decided they could be Mato and Toby, both of whom he had seen a few years earlier at a shrimp shed in Leeville. To his advantage, neither young man knew him then, nor would they recognize him now.

Pappy waited patiently for the two men to enter the bar; then he quickly untied his skiff and pushed away from the piling. After drifting the few feet to land, he tied up at an old stump and made his way to the skiff belonging to the two men. "Let's see you up close, boys," whispered Pappy to himself. As he got closer, he recognized the skiff as one of the Rabeauxs', an old one Ludvick had used many years ago.

To be sure though, Pappy made his way to the small Bar, stopping along the bay side next to a half-opened window. He crouched beside the opening, staying well out of sight while scanning the crowded room. At first he saw no one he recognized; then, at a table near the entrance he noticed two men who caught his attention. True, it had been several years since he had seen the Rabeaux boys, but here they were, no mistake about it. "Bastard Rabeaux!" sounded Pappy through clenched teeth. Pappy would have recognized those characteristic Rabeaux features no matter how long it had been.

After seeing what he wanted, he eased away from the window and made his way back to his skiff. He returned to his original secluded location, tying up to the piling away from the land so that he could see the Rabeaux boys when they left the bar. While waiting, the old Cameaux pulled out the long leather case containing his shotgun. He would keep it close to his side.

All thought of sleeping this night left him, as eager anticipation mounted within. He would follow these Rabeaux boys to his main target: Ludvick. "Just like the ole days again!"

A sudden cool breeze licked the back of Pappy's neck, too cool for a hot summer night in South Louisiana. Was this a sign? Was his own time approaching? Nothing could weaken his resolve or deter him from his intention. On the contrary, deep inside he actually looked forward to this final confrontation.

In time the breeze slacked a bit and the mosquitoes thickened in a swarm encircling him. His old tough, leathery skin presented a challenge to the tiny blood-sucking creatures, but they never gave up the fight. In much the same way, this stubborn old Cajun would never give up the fight now that the enemy was within his reach. Only occasionally did his gaze leave the door of the tiny bar. The old bloodhound of the swamp was once again on the trail of the Rabeaux.

CHAPTER 22

As soon as they walked through the door, Toby headed straight for the long bar on the opposite end of the room, but Mato caught him by the arm, motioning to a vacant table close to the door. Just as the brothers were seated, a waitress appeared at their table. "What'll it be, boys?"

"First, what's your name?" Toby asked boldly.

Gloria had seen these types before; treat them a little special and they leave good tips. "My name is Gloria, Good lookin'. You want two beers?"

Toby and Mato glanced at each other in awe. No more than a handful of women had ever spoken to either of the Rabeaux boys.

"Yeah, two beers," answered Toby with a grin.

Gloria gave the boys a big smile. "Be right back, Sugar."

As soon as she left, the stunned Toby turned to Mato. "Hey, Breaux, you know, I think she likes me."

But Mato simply looked at Toby with a puzzled look and insisted, "Don't be stupid. She just using you to get to me!"

When Gloria returned with their beers, she also brought a small ashtray full of salted peanuts. "There you go, Gentlemen. Anything else I can do for you?"

With a broad smile revealing his pitted teeth, Mato answered, "Honey, keep the beer an yourself comin'."

"Sure will, Sugar."

Both brothers drank like bottomless pits. They kept Gloria busy and with every trip she made to their table, they grew bolder. At first they tried to get her to take a boat ride with them, to which she politely refused. Then Mato casually began touching her butt every time she made the mistake of standing too near him. Now, Gloria was thirty years old and no stranger to drunk men. She really wasn't very attractive, and she certainly had never been called pretty; yet to Mato and Toby, she was a queen. After almost two hours of drinking one beer after another and feeling no pain, the two brothers began directing their full attention to Gloria and her queenly body.

On one of her trips to replenish their beers, the bartender Fredrick expressed his concerns about the two rowdy young men, but Gloria assured him she could handle the situation. Her first opportunity to prove her ability presented itself on her very next trip to the Rabeaux table. By this time Mato was drunk enough to get really friendly and he wasted no time, not only touching, but also awkwardly fondling her. Gloria hadn't minded the nasty talk and crude jokes Mato and Toby had thrown her way; she was conditioned to that. However, when Mato began squeezing her like a bag of oranges at the grocery store, she thought things just might get a little out of control, and she quickly tried to push his groping hands away.

Mato wasn't about to let this beautiful flower slip through his fingers, and he grabbed Gloria's arm and pulled her to his lap. Before she could even utter a protest, he opened his mouth and kissed her, his tongue probing so deeply that he accomplished something no one else had ever done before: He made her gag with revulsion. Mato, however, mistaking her gagging for a sign of enjoyment, plunged his tongue even deeper into her mouth.

It was now decision time for Gloria. She never objected to making a little side-cash by selling her body; in fact, that's how she earned most of her money. This time, though, she had to convince herself that she could tolerate anything for a few minutes to earn a few bucks because this ape trying to lick her tonsils was absolutely the most repulsive human she had ever met. On the other hand, she also felt that if she didn't do something very quickly, she could get hurt. She had

two options: She could call for help which certainly would result in a big fight, or she give in, earn a little money and just call this a very bad night. She chose that option. Therefore, pulling herself free from the suction of Mato's lips, Gloria gasped, "Okay, okay, Honey, come with me and I'll show you a good time, but it'll cost you!"

Encouraged, Mato still held tightly to Gloria's arm, but let her stand. Then, with a big grin on his face he looked at Toby, obviously pleased with himself. "Where we gonna go?" he asked loudly.

Pointing to the rear of the bar with her free hand and trying to quiet him by putting her finger against her lips, she whispered, "I have a little room in the back."

"Lead the way," responded Mato, still holding her arm. As they made their way through the crowded room and passed the bar, the concerned Fredrick shook his head, desperately trying to alert her to change her mind with this one. Obviously choosing to ignore him, she managed a frail smile to signal that everything was okay, a smile which in a very short while Mato would certainly erase.

Toby couldn't believe what he was seeing. There was actually a woman who would take her clothes off and let Mato—yes, even Mato—have his way with her. "Well, that can't be," mumbled a shocked Toby. "That woman is playing with an even thinner deck than Mato!"

After entering a small room, no bigger than a walk-in closet, Mato shut the door and leaned against it. Under a dim light which hung overhead, Gloria turned to face him, and the look in his eyes told her instantly that she made the wrong choice. She frantically began trying to call the whole thing off when, not totally unexpected, the big man struck her. Because he hadn't a clue as to how to treat a lady, he dealt with her as he did everyone else—with violence. In fact, he hit her so hard on the left side of her head that the force flung her like a rag doll the short distance to the dirty makeshift bed. Stunned, but not unconscious, Gloria buried her face in the lumpy pillow and covered her head with both hands. Her left ear bled profusely and she could hear nothing, which actually alarmed her even more than the searing pain. Now convinced that this ordeal would definitely be much more than just a bad night, she actually feared for her life. Meanwhile, just as a hungry gator eyes its prey, Mato now stood over Gloria, his mouth

117

watering in his eagerness to consume her. Then completely unable to control his fiery passion, he ripped her clothes from her trembling body and, for the first time since she had been assaulted as a young girl, the seasoned barmaid was reduced to tears.

Fredrick was accustomed to seeing his girlfriend Gloria take strange men to the back room, but this big Cajun looked like trouble to him. Although he kept looking toward the back room for any sign that she might need him, he could hear nothing above the loud music.

Finally, after what seemed like an hour to Fredrick but was in fact no more than fifteen minutes, the door of the little room opened and out strolled Mato, but there was no sign of Gloria. "Well, at least he don't take too long," Toby muttered under his breath, "but where's the girl?" He was nervous. True, he hoped that Mato wouldn't be long; in fact, he had even hoped he would also get his turn. Now he was watching a peacock-strutting Mato ambling back toward the table. As Mato neared the table, he let out a bone-chilling Cajun yell of victory. The loud music continued to play, but all the conversation in the bar ceased at once, and everyone stared at the big Rabeaux. Fredrick's heart skipped a beat as he dropped the glass he was holding and ran toward the back room. Gloria, badly beaten, bleeding and clutching a dirty sheet to hide her nakedness, met him at the door to the little room and collapsed in his arms. Another man came to her aid, and Fredrick lost control of his senses. He ran back to the bar, picked up a billy club, and pushed his way through the crowd of men hovering around the bar.

Toby saw not only the bartender coming toward them, but two other men rushing their way as well. He had just enough time to turn Mato around before the men reached them. Furious with Toby for interrupting his celebration, Mato was about to punch him when something hard hit him hard on the side of his head, sending him crashing to the floor where he stayed but a split second before jumping to his feet to help Toby fight off two attackers.

When Mato threw one of the men into another table, fights erupted everywhere in the bar. The big Rabeaux couldn't be stopped; his power and fighting ability were more than any in the bar could handle. Big men, little men, all men fell before his fury. When Toby realized

that things were really getting out of hand, he called out above the noise, "Mato, let's get outta here!"

As the fighting raged around them, Mato nodded to Toby and both men ran for the door but not before Fredrick cut them off, blocking their escape. Holding his billy club poised for attack, Fredrick stood his ground. Like a cornered animal, Mato's instincts took over, and in an instant his Bowie knife was out of its sheath. Fredrick swung his club at the elder Rabeaux's head, but this time Mato caught the weapon in mid-air with his left hand. Without hesitation, Mato plunged the long-bladed knife to its hilt into the bartender's soft belly. With a look of surprise on his face, Fredrick fell motionless at Mato's feet.

"Come on!" shouted Toby. Without a backward glance, the two Rabeaux raced through the door, leaving Fredrick the bartender dying on the filthy floor. Toby reached the skiff first and immediately started the engine; Mato was right behind him. Toby hastily navigated the skiff away from the slip and out into the bay. Finally looking back at the fading Bar door, they were relieved to see that no one had followed them. Toby headed straight for the dead-end canal.

Pappy heard the bar fight and had little doubt who started it. In fact, he wasn't at all surprised when the two Rabeaux came running from the Bar to make their getaway. He laid low in his own skiff, not wanting to be detected, but he need not have been so cautious; the brothers were in such a hurry that they were thinking of nothing more than a quick getaway. As they had pulled away from Caminada, Pappy was also ready and pursued them in his own skiff. He kept the Rabeaux skiff just out of sight as he followed the trail of white foam they left in their wake. When it was no longer clearly visible, he would increase his speed somewhat so that he could once more pick up their trail. It was delicate work to follow in nearly total darkness.

Once away from Caminada and apparently away from danger, Toby reduced his speed, completely unaware that Pappy trailed them. Both Rabeaux men could think of little more than getting a good night's rest. Toby's head was hurting again from the beating Mato had given him earlier, and Mato's head hurt even more from being hit by Fredrick's billy club. As Pappy continued his close pursuit for the next

119

forty-five minutes in a northwesterly direction, he realized they were headed for the western shore of the bay.

As Toby approached the shoreline, he missed the mouth of the canal by a few yards. When he realized he was off course, he maneuvered his skiff in a circular pattern and headed straight back for the opening. Unaware of this move by Toby until the Rabeaux skiff was bearing down on a collision course with his own Pappy saw what was about to happen and turned his skiff hard to port. So sharp was the turn, in fact, that his skiff momentarily went airborne and almost capsized; instead, it fell hard to the water throwing the old Cajun forcefully to the deck. Though a bit disoriented, Pappy managed to reach the throttle and pull it back, reducing his speed. He looked toward the stern of his skiff just in time to see the shadowy Rabeaux skiff enter the canal. If Mato and Toby had been looking in his direction, they would have spotted him, but both were too busy keeping the mouth of the canal as the focus of their attention to even notice the near collision.

With most of his life spent in this marsh, Pappy knew well that the Rabeaux had entered a dead-end canal. So he just sat in his skiff, in no hurry to pursue. Within seconds, as expected, they had vanished from sight and sound. Staring into the darkness he knew he couldn't kill all the Rabeaux men; he didn't think he'd ever have that much luck, but he would make sure that his first shot was leveled at Ludvick. Then, whatever happened next he would be prepared—even if it cost him his life.

CHAPTER 23

P appy carefully guided his skiff to the mouth of the canal and turned the engine off so that his forward momentum would carry the skiff silently into the canal itself. He stood behind the steering wheel and with his ear to the wind listened intently. He could hear the low hum of the Rabeaux engine about half a mile down the canal. When the sound of their engine stopped, he immediately picked up his paddle and inched his small skiff through the darkness toward them.

As soon as they had tied up to the abandoned well, Mato and Toby wasted little time unrolling their bedding and finding comfortable spots on the deck of their skiff. Normally they would have spread their mosquito net overhead, but the full effects of the long day plus the many beers commanded them to sleep. Yawning and rubbing the side of his head where the billy club had left its mark, Mato still just couldn't resist needling his brother with his boasting proclamation: "Whooooo, Man, what a woman! I got all I wanted an give her more than she ever got before!" His words however, were wasted on Toby since the younger Rabeaux was already sound asleep. Yawning again, Mato shrugged his shoulders at his brother's silence, turned over, and also fell asleep. Completely oblivious to all else around them, as well as to the situation they created in the Bar, neither Mato nor Toby gave a second thought to the bartender they left dying on the Bar floor.

121

It took Pappy nearly an hour to reach the end of the canal. He could sense the Rabeaux nearby and stopped paddling, letting his skiff drift slowly forward. His shotgun ready and resting on his lap, he now peered into the darkness, straining to see his foe. A slight smile played at the corners of his mouth as this reminded him of his younger days.

The silence was eerie and unsettling; he could even hear his own breathing. As unnerving as this situation might have been for any other man, Pappy was steady, his movements, deliberate. Ever closer he drifted toward the end of the canal until finally, even through the darkness, he could detect the vague dark outline of a skiff. Though barely distinguishable at first, as he drifted closer, he recognized the skiff used earlier by the young Rabeaux men. He carefully scanned the darkness for Ludvick's skiff, but found no other. Disappointment crossed his face. He searched again the edges of the marsh all the way to the very end of the canal itself, but to no avail; Ludvick wasn't there. A gentle breeze from the Gulf helped carry him even closer to the Rabeaux skiff now, and he had to make a quick decision. Should he confront the two Rabeaux boys or paddle away? He settled on confronting the young Rabeaux.

Mato and Toby were sleeping soundly, so soundly that long before he even made contact with the Rabeaux skiff, Pappy could hear them snoring. He moved in closer, and when he was within twenty feet of them he positioned his own skiff so that the two would meet broadside. He then removed his paddle from the water and set it down beside his seat. The momentum from his paddling, assisted by the wind, carried him the last few feet to the sleeping boys. Now within ten feet and with his shotgun in his hands, Pappy stood up so that he could see directly into their old skiff. He brought the shotgun to his shoulder and with his right index finger depressed the shotgun's safety switch, making it ready to fire. As the gap between the two skiffs disappeared they met with a gentle bump, Pappy could see the bodily outlines of the two men sleeping under blankets. Standing there a few awkward seconds listening to their snoring, Pappy hoped that the young men would cooperate. He would hate having to kill them before they had told him where Ludvick was hiding. He then lowered the shotgun from his shoulder and used it to nudge the figure closest to him, whispering in a calm voice, "Rabeaux, wake up."

Mato felt the nudge, but assumed that it was only Toby's moving next to him. However, when he felt another jab at his back, this time much harder than the first, he jerked himself upright, squinting in an effort to get his bearings. Still groggy, but never allowing a lack of alertness to hinder his loose, untamed tongue, he demanded loudly, "What the hell?" And as he threw off his blanket, he kicked Toby for waking him so early.

Now Toby, with his head still pounding, angrily shouted, "Why you kick me, Mato?"

Mato, still dazed shouted, "Why, I kick you, Pisshead? Why you wake me for?"

"Now boys, don't take it out on each other," urged Pappy in a rather amused tone. Mato and Toby stared dumbfounded, at the dark figure standing not more than three feet from Mato. "Don't move or you're dead," commanded Pappy in a steely voice.

"What you want?" asked Mato indignantly.

"Where's Ludvick?" Pappy demanded.

"Who are you?" spat Mato.

Without hesitation Pappy replied, "Olidore Cameaux!"

Mato gasped, "Olidore Cameaux?"

"What?" asked Toby, completely confused by the whole ordeal.

"That's Olidore Cameaux himself," said Mato.

"So, you boys heard of me. Where's Ludvick?" Pappy demanded of them again.

"What makes you think we gonna tell you where Gramps is at?" replied a cocky Mato.

In a forceful voice Pappy answered, "I tell you quick what makes me think you tell me. It's all I can do right now, not to kill you, an if you don't tell where Ludvick is, I'll just let my shotgun say good-bye to you right here. You understand, Fonchock? Then we see just how smart you really are, not how smart you think you are."

Both Mato and Toby were in a crouched position looking up toward Pappy, with Toby slightly to Mato's right. Pappy had the shotgun pointed directly at Mato's chest, but neither Pappy nor Toby noticed Mato's hand as he slowly drew his Bowie knife from its sheath.

"What you want wit Gramps?" asked Toby sullenly.

Pappy's eyes shifted to Toby as he answered the question. Mato knew that if he were to do something, it would have to be soon. One advantage he had was that it was still quite dark; and while shapes were distinguishable, detailed sight was impossible.

"Don't act stupid with me, Rabeaux. I'm here to settle once an for all our family differences," answered Pappy determinedly.

Mato was ready.

"I think Gramps would like that," laughed Toby disrespectfully.

"Laugh while you can, Rabe—"

Mato suddenly lunged forward, catching Pappy completely by surprise. Although in the dim light he had seen something flash in Mato's hand, Pappy had squeezed the trigger of the shotgun a split second too late. Mato knocked the barrel to his right just as the blast lit up the darkness. A slight gasp could be heard for just an instant as the buckshot all but decapitated Toby. Then before Pappy could regain control of the shotgun, Mato swung his blade in the direction of the old man's dark figure, hitting him with great force across his lower chest. Instantly Pappy dropped his shotgun and clutched at his wound. He took an involuntary step backward, lost his balance, and fell into the water. Frantically, Mato cranked the engine and cut the ropes which had held the skiff to the old oil well. He pushed the throttle forward and turned the steering wheel hard to starboard, almost capsizing the Cameaux skiff.

Meanwhile, the injured Pappy was trying desperately to swim to the surface. Finally he broke through the water just in time to see the Rabeaux skiff about to run him over. He used both hands to push away from the oncoming skiff's hull, trying to prevent being struck by the propeller. Down went his body, but not before he felt a tear at his right arm where the propeller had hit him just below the right elbow. He could hear the bone breaking as though someone had snapped a twig from a tree. He could also hear the Rabeaux skiff making its escape as he drifted, for what seemed like minutes, downward toward the bottom of the canal. He was disoriented and not fully aware of where he was until his feet settled into the muddy bottom of the canal. Instinctively he pushed off, and with his good arm, swam for the surface once more. As he was slowly regaining his senses, he had begun to feel not only a

throbbing pain in his right arm, but also a burning sensation in his lower chest just above his stomach. With his good arm he kept reaching upward again and again, clawing at the water, not sure he was making any progress until he hit the hard bottom of his skiff. As best he could, he grabbed the side of his skiff and pulled his head out of the water, sucking in water with the precious air he craved.

Once the painful choking and coughing had subsided and his lungs had cleared, he assessed his condition and quickly realized the seriousness of his wounds. His right arm was hanging limply at his side, and the wound to his chest was long, deep, and bleeding profusely. Still holding with his good arm to the side of his skiff, he knew it was impossible to climb aboard, so he slowly kicked his feet to steer the skiff to shore. His head began to spin from the loss of blood, and the water was cold; he thought of just giving up and ending it all right there, but he couldn't bring himself to let go of the skiff. He kept paddling with his feet, pushing his body to its limit and beyond. Then he said aloud, "Fight! Fight till the end!" One thing was certain, though; if he didn't get out of the water soon, it would be the end, regardless of what he wanted. In facing the likelihood that his life was ebbing away, Pappy knew that Derrick would have to face the young Rabeaux he had failed to kill; but worst of all, Ludvick was still alive.

By now Mato had cleared the mouth of the canal and was headed north. He had yelled at Toby to get up, but had gotten no response; he then kicked at his little brother, who was still lying at his feet. "Get up, Pisshead, an help me see where I'm going."

Finally Mato realized that something was seriously wrong with his brother. He reached down under the steering column and brought out a flashlight, pointing the weak beam of light at Toby's feet and working his way toward his head. As he brought the beam of light over the length of Toby's body, he noticed that blood was everywhere, and when the light reached what was left of Toby's head, Mato didn't even recognize him. He quickly turned the light off and looked straight out to sea; his only thought was the fear that his grandfather would find out about their visit to the Bar.

CHAPTER 24

"Come on, Pappy, pick up the phone," insisted an impatient Derrick. He had tried to reach him all that Saturday morning, but had received no answer. He dialed Olivia's number, relieved that Teresa answered on the second ring.

"Teresa, it's Uncle Derrick."

"Hi, Uncle Derrick, when you coming back to see us?"

"Maybe tomorrow, hon, have you seen Pappy?"

"Nope."

"Is your mommy around?"

"Yes, you want to talk to her?"

"If she's not too busy."

Without another word, Teresa put the receiver down and ran from the room to find her mother who answered a few seconds later. "Hi, Derrick, where are you?"

"I'm at home in Meridian, Liv. How are things going?"

"Some better. When are you coming back?"

"I was planning on tomorrow, but I've been trying to call Pappy all morning and can't seem to get him. Have you seen him today?"

"I haven't seen him in a few days now. He came over, I believe, on Wednesday to tell us he was going on a fishing trip with some old friends. Said he'd call when he got back. Didn't he tell you?" asked Olivia surprised.

127

Derrick didn't want to worry her but Pappy had always told him where he was going if the trip would take longer than a day. "No, he didn't."

"Hmmm, if I remember correctly, he said he might be back by the weekend, and today's Saturday. So, maybe he'll be back this afternoon."

"I sure hope so," answered a worried Derrick.

"Anything wrong, Derrick?"

"No, not at all, I just wanted to tell him about my plans to come home tomorrow."

"Well, if he comes in today, I'll certainly tell him you called."

Derrick was careful not to alarm Olivia with his next question. "Thanks, Liv. By the way, do you remember if Pappy said where he was going fishing or who he was going with?"

"No, he only said old friends and that he'd just have to be going wherever necessary to get the big ones. In fact, now that I think about it, he really was rather vague about the details."

"Well, Liv, if you see him, would you just tell him to call me on my cell phone?"

"Sure, you think Pappy's all right?" asked a now concerned Olivia.

"Of course, he probably told me a week or so ago he was going. I've just been so busy lately that I can't even remember things that happened ten minutes ago. Look, I'll take you and the girls out for another pizza when I get in, okay?"

"Sounds good to me."

"See you tomorrow then. Kiss the girls for me."

"I will, and you have a safe trip. Bye for now," said Olivia, happy that he had called and delighted over the prospect of another outing, but very uncomfortable about Pappy.

As soon as he was off the phone with Olivia, Derrick called the shrimp shed as fast as he could. Pappy had always let him know where he was going; he wondered why, this time, he hadn't called. He recognized the deep Cajun voice of Marco Doucet as he answered with the familiar, "Cameaux Shrimp Shed."

"Marco, it's Derrick. Is Ben around?"

"Just a second, Derrick."

If anyone knew where Pappy was, it would be Ben. Derrick was anxious; he didn't like the thoughts that were storming his mind. Thankfully after only a few seconds, Ben answered.

"Uncle Ben, where's Pappy?"

"He's out fishing with some of his ole buddies. Didn't he tell you? He left Wednesday. He came by here and picked up the old skiff."

"And just who were these buddies and where were they going fishing, Uncle Ben?"

Ben was caught completely off guard by Derrick's question. The more he thought about it the more worried he became. "Well, I'm not sure." Completely at ease with his father's seemingly innocent trip until now, the truth suddenly hit Ben like a ton of bricks. "Good God, Derrick! He's gone after the Rabeaux!"

"Uncle Ben, stay calm, you have any idea where he might be?'

Trying his best to stay composed Ben answered, "As a matter of fact, he did say he would try his luck in the southeast marshes. Course, that could mean anywhere from Bayou Lafourche to the mouth of the Mississippi River!"

"Uncle Ben, you'd better call the sheriff!"

"I will!"

"I'm leaving right now. Hold a skiff for me."

"The *Miss Teresa* will be tied up where she normally is when you get here."

"Uncle Ben," Derrick's voice almost faltered, "we've got to find him before Ludvick does!"

"I know," agreed Ben as he hung up the phone. He then turned to the men nearest him and shouted, "Pappy's in danger and needs help!"

The word quickly spread to all the employees of the shed and everyone sprang into action. Then Ben called virtually every fisherman he knew for help, as well as sending out the distress signal over his marine band radio to any within hearing range. Within two hours of Derrick's call, dozens of vessels were pouring out of the Cameaux Docks searching for Pappy. Ben had also called Sheriff Lebeouf, who had ordered all available patrol boats, two seaplanes and his pontoon helicopter to aid in the search. Almost every man involved in the search knew Pappy personally; he was well-like and respected by all.

Given the time, they would search every bayou, canal, bay, lake and pond if necessary. However, time wasn't on their side; even a thousand boats couldn't cover that vast area in a month. They would need a lot of luck.

Ben contacted Olivia and told her what they were doing. She took the girls to her mother's house and went to the shrimp shed to help by answering phone calls and monitoring the marine radio for updated information from the skiffs in the marsh. In the middle of the shed Ben erected a huge map of the areas to be covered, and together with the sheriff, directed the search in a coordinated effort.

Derrick arrived in Golden Meadow late that Saturday afternoon and headed straight for the shrimp shed where Ben was waiting for him. "Uncle Ben, I want to take the *Miss Teresa* out to look for Pappy!"

"Son, I know you do, but it's late in the day. I need your help here to keep track of all the people in the marsh. Just stay with me for the rest of today. Tomorrow you can get an early start. I need you, Son." It was hard to argue with Ben's wisdom, and rationale. Derrick's shoulders slumped a little, and his enthusiasm turned to a more somber reality as he answered, "Okay, Uncle Ben, I'll help here the rest of the day."

Ben took him into the shed where Derrick immediately turned his attention to the map Ben set up and was soon filled in on the progress of the search up to that point. People were busy coming and going; women from the community brought food and drinks. The sheriff even stayed at the shed, coordinating his seaplanes and helicopters from that base. Impressed and deeply touched by such responsive support. Derrick asked, "How many people are involved in this search anyway, Sheriff Lebeouf?"

"About fifty boats, two seaplanes and a chopper."

"What about tomorrow?"

"I've contacted the Coast Guard, and the sheriff of Jefferson Parish, and he'll send us all the help he can spare," answered the sheriff.

"Good, I have a feeling we'll need all the help we can get," replied a worried Derrick.

The sheriff knew and respected the relationship between Derrick and his grandfather, "Look, Derrick, we'll probably find Pappy fishing on some big lake, just like he said. And when he sees all the fuss we've made trying to find him, well, I don't have to tell you what he'll say to that."

"I hope you're right, Sheriff," said Olivia as she and Ben walked up just in time to overhear.

Derrick's face lit up when he saw her and he asked, "Liv, where did you come from?"

"I axed her here. I knew she'd want to help," said Ben.

Looking at Derrick, Olivia asked, "What time will you be leaving in the morning?"

"Think I'll leave around 4:30 a.m."

Aware that the *Miss Teresa* didn't have a marine radio, Ben reminded Derrick, "Before you leave, pick up a portable radio in my office. You know your cell phone won't work out there. That way, we can stay in touch and I can tell you the progress of the search throughout the day."

It was now late in the day, and an hour after dark the Sheriff called off the search until daybreak Sunday. Most of the smaller skiffs returned to the dock, but some of the larger ones just dropped anchor in one of the shallow bays and spent the night in the marsh. Sheriff Lebeouf left the shed around 9:00 p.m.; Olivia left about an hour later. Derrick and Ben spent the night in Ben's office. Both men wanted to stand by the radio in case something developed during the night. Derrick spread an old piece of canvas on the floor as his bedding and used a life preserver as a pillow; Ben lay down on the sofa. The two men were physically and emotionally drained, and Derrick was especially concerned that this ordeal could trigger another heart attack for his uncle.

As they lay there in the darkness, neither man said a word for a time. Both were running the events of the past few days through their minds, trying to think of any hint that Pappy might have left as to his whereabouts. Finally, Derrick posed the question that bothered him all day. "Uncle Ben, if Pappy was so determined to hunt Ludvick Rabeaux, why didn't he take any help?"

131

Ben thought for a moment before answering. "Your Pappy's a special kind of man. In the old days when he was a young man, both the Rabeaux and the Cameaux families had other families in this war. My grandfather always took help from the families who were our allies. I have to tell you, Derrick, too many young men on both sides died awful deaths. The Rabeaux are merciless in their killing. Any opportunity they had of killing one of us they took, and the way they killed was almost always with a shotgun. Most of the young men that were killed died instantly, but a few of the wounded suffered terribly before the end came. Back fifty years ago it was a real battlefield around here. We finally killed so many Rabeaux that they just retreated into the marshes and swamps, and from there they've fought a type of guerrilla war ever since. I call it ambush and murder. You see, Derrick, Pappy remembers those old days. So, since he took charge of the family, he never asked anyone to help him fight the Rabeaux."

"Well, what about the Rabeaux women? What are they like?"

"Now, that's an interesting story. Far as I know, there hasn't been no official marriage in that family in more than a hundred years."

"What?" asked Derrick, "Why not?"

"That's right, the Rabeaux men don't marry their women, they just like to have their fun with them, but they won't marry. Victor lived awhile with a woman many years ago, and she birthed him two sons. Some distant relatives of the Rabeaux who knew about her claimed she wasn't nothing but a wild woman."

"What kind of wild?"

"People say a crazy kind of woman. They say she needed help, but never got none," answered Ben matter-of-factly.

"What happened to her?"

"Ludvick took her out in the swamp and killed her just like you'd kill a rabid dog."

"It's hard to understand a people so cruel. Aren't we all the same? I mean, aren't we all Cajun?" reasoned Derrick.

"We might all be Cajun, but we're not all the same. To the outside world, Cajuns are just people who cook great food and know how to

have a good time. I don't have to tell you how wrong that is. There's always a few who go contrary to the rest in all cultures.

"How did this whole feuding between us survive all these years? I know how it started. Pappy told me that much, but I can't figure out why or how it could still be going on today."

Without hesitation Ben answered, "Hatred, Derrick, hatred. That's all I can think of. Hatred, not on the part of our family, but hatred by the Rabeaux. They're demonic, Derrick. I have never seen or heard one act of kindness from any Rabeaux. Do you know that since the great hurricane hit Caminada, not one girl was ever birthed in that family? You want to know why? Cause they just kill every girl baby the second she comes out the mother. They just want boys in that family."

"That's insane!" exclaimed Derrick.

Ben agreed. "Yeah, that's why Pappy's out there now. He's trying to end it so we don't have to." Neither man said another word, but both knew that Pappy was in desperate trouble.

Derrick was confident that he had plans for dealing with the Rabeaux, but that had been before today. Now he just felt he was being played like a stringed instrument: Pluck him one way, and he made a certain tone; pluck him another, and he produced an entirely different sound. What Derrick was starting to comprehend was that the expert musician playing him was a grand master of manipulation and if he didn't play Ludvick's game to win, he would lose – both the battle and his life.

CHAPTER 25

M ato arrived at the camp on Bayou Castete earlier than expected; to his relief, Ludvick and Victor weren't there yet. He wrapped Toby's body in a blanket and laid it in the hot sun on the wharf, where flies immediately began to swarm. Then suddenly remembering the money in Toby's pocket, he quickly retrieved and returned it to the money jar; the money in his own pocket would remain where it was. Now, pacing nervously back and forth on the wharf and pounding his right fist into his left hand, Mato strained to formulate a plausible story for his father and grandfather. To help clarify his thought, he finally spoke aloud, "I'll just tell them how me an Toby was attacked by a lota men for the money. I killed three of them an run the rest off, but not before one of them killed Toby. I try to save Toby, but it was too late." After a few trial runs, Mato was pleased with his story and was sure Ludvick and Victor would buy it. He would also be sure to give the money he and Toby had made to Ludvick before his grandfather asked about it. Satisfied that he had things under control, Mato went inside the camp. Still very tired and hung over from all the drinking the night before, he stretched out on a cot for a little rest, but soon fell into a deep sleep.

Ludvick and Victor timed their arrival at the camp on Bayou Castete for about noon. Even as they traveled all morning, for some reason he couldn't quite put his finger on, Ludvick felt that things just

weren't quite right. He knew well that it was risky to separate his family; but after all, it was time for Toby and Mato to prove they were men. So he convinced himself that his nagging, apprehensive doubts were exaggerated, and turned his thoughts to more important matters at hand. Soon he would plan the death of Derrick Cameaux; then he would find his grandsons some women to bear him great-grandsons. It was time, in Ludvick's opinion, for him to expand the Rabeaux bloodline and to make sure this expansion would occur threat-free of extinction at the hands of his mortal enemy. Proud of the fact that he killed more Cameaux than any of his ancestors, now, of the three Cameaux men still left alive, only Derrick was of any real concern to him. "Kill Derrick," he thought with satisfaction, "an then all my ancestors can rest in peace."

Now nearing the campsite, Ludvick kept a sharp eye focused on his surroundings; years of fighting in these marshlands had taught him to always expect the unexpected. The campsite was still a half-mile away when he saw the skiff tied up to the tiny wharf. He knew it was the one the boys had used because of the crab traps piled high on the stern. As he got closer he also noticed the object on the wharf and immediately knew it meant that one of his grandsons was dead. Without revealing emotion of any kind, he simply looked at Victor. "Looks like you got a dead son." Making absolutely no reply, Victor put aside the nets he had been mending and walked to the front of the skiff. He stood silent and expressionless, staring fixedly at the bundle lying on the wharf. Though not quite as cold as Ludvick, Victor also uttered no word of grief; he just shook his head in disbelief. Then as soon as their skiff had been secured to the piling, Ludvick climbed onto the wharf and unwrapped the body. Though unrecognizable because of the shotgun blast to the head, they both knew it was Toby by the size of the body and the clothes he was wearing.

Roused from his sleep by the noises outside, Mato stumbled to the door of the camp to see the two men standing over Toby's body. He quickly grabbed the jar of money as planned and leaving the door ajar in his haste, walked out of the camp toward his grandfather. Ludvick's eyes were set on Toby, however; he didn't even look up as Mato

approached. Instead, in a steely, barely audible voice he demanded, "What happen to your brother?"

Ignoring the question, Mato instead extended his hand with the jar of money clenched tightly in his fist. "Me an Toby, we have done real good. Made plenty money."

Ludvick made no move for the jar, but rather demanded once more, this time with even more edge to his voice, "What happen to you brother?"

Mato, instantly recognizing that all-too familiar tone, knew that now was the time to tell the bogus story. "A lota men try to ambush us an steal the money, but I wouldn't never give it to them. I killed three of them an then the others run away, but not before one of them killed Toby."

Without a word, Ludvick then walked right past Mato and headed straight for an old wood pile they always used as a source for cooking fuel. Before walking back to his grandson, he casually bent down to pick up an old ax handle that was missing the steel head. Mato was wondering if his grandfather had believed his story. However, the closer he got to him with the ax handle, the less likely it seemed that the story had come across as truth. No other man or beast did Mato fear, but one—and that was Ludvick. He instinctively blurted out, "What you gonna do, Gramps?"

"Cover you brother with the blanket," ordered Ludvick. Mato knew better than to bend down so close to his grandfather, but he had little choice. He reached for the blanket, but hadn't quite touched it when Ludvick lunged forward with the ax handle raised high. Mato heard the thump even before he felt it; Ludvick had hit just below his shoulder blades, knocking him to his knees. Gasping for air, he never saw the boot until it had crashed into his nose, sending blood flying everywhere and him rolling to the edge of the wharf. Coldly watching him groan in pain, Ludvick calmly walked to Mato's side and kicked him in the stomach, producing violent spasms of pain ricocheting throughout his grandson's quivering body. Ludvick's eyes held the look of a predator that would not be denied its prey, and through tightly clenched teeth he once again demanded, "What happen to you brother?"

137

Mato rolled onto his back, trying desperately to catch his breath so he could answer, but he was too slow in replying. Ludvick didn't wait. With lightning speed, he again struck him hard with the ax handle, this time across the chest. Again Mato groaned in pain; he started to reach for his knife to kill Ludvick, but was still lucid enough to comprehend that he was in no position or condition to win. Ludvick had him just where he wanted him. Thus, with a big gasp for breath, Mato finally managed to whisper, "Okay, okay."

"Sit up," ordered Ludvick.

Victor watched passively as his father questioned his son. And though seething with resentment, he remembered the many times he received such beatings from Ludvick. Therefore, he didn't offer any assistance to his son, lest he be next in line for more of the same.

Despite having been nearly physically disabled by his grandfather's blows, Mato clenched his teeth and finally manage to raise himself on one elbow. Without question, this was clearly the most severe beating Ludvick had ever inflicted on him, and there was little doubt in his mind that Ludvick would kill him if he didn't tell at least part of the truth.

"I said sit up, you stupid fool! Don't you never learn, Cooyon! You need some more help?"

Mato knew full well that his grandfather's idea of help was not an extended hand of comforting physical aid. He took several deep breaths and strained to push himself into a more upright position, fearful all the while that his painful slowness would again trigger Ludvick's fierce anger. Finally, in words barely audible, he tried again: "Toby an me was in a pipeline canal tied up to this ole well. We been there all week. Then the last night a man come to kill us an steal the money, but—"

Ludvick immediately crouched down in front of him, staring into his frightened eyes and interrupting his story with his icy ultimatum: "Start with the Bar, Fonchock!"

Mato was startled. How could Ludvick know about the Bar? Quickly, Mato told a somewhat altered version of what had actually happened. "Yeah, Gramps, me an Toby, we went to the Bar cause he want a drink. You know how Toby is when he gets something in his

thick head. I try to talk him outta that dumb idea, but he don't never listen. It was either go with him to the Bar, or beat him up to make him stay away. So I went with him just to keep him outta trouble. Toby, he drunk plenty, just like a fish, but me, I just got me a woman."

Ludvick simply stared even more deeply into the eyes and face of his grandson, reading him through and through. He knew Mato was still lying to cover himself, at least as far as the part about Toby's being the one who had insisted on going to the bar. He would let that part slide for now, though, because he figured he'd finally convinced Mato that it was in his best interest to tell the core of the truth. Thus, he nodded and again listened intently as Mato continued. "We left the bar way before daylight. I guess that's when he followed us."

"He – who's he?" asked Ludvick.

Mato broke eye contact with Ludvick as he answered, "Olidore Cameaux." Hearing the name was a shock, but Ludvick's mouth opened only slightly as a sign of surprise.

When Victor heard the name, though, he immediately yelled, "Mato, you let that ole bastard kill your brother?"

"Shut up, fool!" Ludvick shouted at Victor. Then he turned back to Mato. "Finish telling me what happen."

"That ole man must be a ghost. We never heard him coming. Then he just appear an pull a shotgun on us," said Mato.

"What did he say?" asked Ludvick.

Pointing a finger at Ludvick, Mato readily replied, "He want you."

"What else?"

Mato answered, "I told him we don't know where you at. He said he can help me remember. Then, but for no reason, he shot Toby in the head. So I jump him fast an killed him with my knife."

Immediately Ludvick raised the ax handle, ready to again assault the helpless Mato. "You killed him, Boy? You sure? Don't you lie to me! I'll beat you dead if you lie again!"

Mato frantically answered, "I cut him good an he fall in the water! Then I don't see him no more, so I start the motor an come here. I'm sure I killed that ole man, Gramps!"

With his left hand Ludvick suddenly grabbed Mato by the shirt collar, his hands only inches from Mato's throat. "All my life I been

139

trying to kill that man, an you expect me to think you killed him?!" Ludvick spat on the wharf next to Mato and continued, "A thousand men like you can't kill that ole Cameaux!"

Ludvick finally released Mato and stood up. Glaring first at Toby's body, then directing his piercing gaze upon Victor, he directed as if he were speaking of an animal rather than his own flesh and blood, "Bury your son." Looking at each other as if they had been waiting for those orders, Mato somehow managed to struggle to his feet to help Victor carry Toby's body a few hundred feet east of the camp along the narrow levee. They laid his body in what little shade they could find and set to work. Before they could dig the grave, however, they first had to clear the thick vegetation which had enveloped every inch of dry land. And how Mato was even partially able to do his share was a feat in itself.

Ludvick offered no help; instead, he walked to the edge of the camp clearing and stared at the endless marshland surrounding him. He was deep in thought, carefully replaying all that had happened. He hadn't figured on Pappy's coming after him. Until now the threat from the oldest Cameaux seemingly had all but vanished as age had caught up with him. Perhaps Mato had killed him, but Ludvick doubted it. Either way, his main target was still Derrick Cameaux.

When Mato and Victor finished burying Toby's body, no words were spoken over the grave. No one hung his head in silent memory, and no one shed a tear. There were no flowers left at the grave site to celebrate the passing from one life to another, and no marker was placed at either the head or foot to mark a final resting place of a loved one. As a matter of fact, in a few months the thick vegetation would reclaim the small clearing, completely covering any and all evidence of this day's activities.

Toby Rabeaux had been known to only a handful of people. His short life had left no lasting mark on the land, and even his memory would fade to nothing in a short time.

As Victor and Mato returned to the campsite, Ludvick ordered them to remove the crab traps from the skiffs and hide them. Later that night, when the three men were finishing the meal Victor had cooked, Ludvick laid out part of his plan for dealing with the

Cameaux. "In the morning, Victor, you an Mato take all the food from this camp an load it in my skiff. Don't forget the kerosene lanterns."

"You expecting more trouble?" asked Victor.

"Yeah, an I don't want none here, this camp's not a good place to hide. There's too much open space in this salt-water marsh. I want you an Mato to go to the trappin' camp on Bayou Bernard. Wait for me there."

"Where you going?" asked Victor.

Ludvick didn't like to answer so many questions and was becoming irritated with Victor's probing. Nevertheless, because it was more important to Ludvick that Victor and Mato carry out his orders without fouling up, he replied curtly, "I'm gonna get a close look at what's happening at the Cameaux shed an fine out if Olidore is dead like Mato said. Maybe I even pick up supplies if I can. Now, anymore stupid questions to ax me?"

"When we gonna kill the rest of them Cameaux?" blurted Mato, still obviously in severe pain from his broken nose and swollen, lacerated face.

At Mato's outburst, Ludvick did something neither Victor nor Mato could remember happening in recent times: he smiled. Not that it was much of a smile, though, and it quickly vanished as he replied, "It's good that you wanna kill these men. You just do what I say an you get your chance."

Mato tried to sleep that night, but with great difficulty because of the extreme pain that wracked his entire body. Actually, he didn't realize how fortunate he was to be alive. Not only had he barely escaped death through the vicious beating Ludvick had inflicted upon him, but very few Rabeaux had ever crossed paths with Pappy Cameaux and lived to tell of it. Finally, through sheer exhaustion and the heavy stresses of this dreadful day, the big Rabeaux slipped fitfully into a restless sleep of sorts. His last thoughts, however, weren't of Toby's lying in a fresh grave or even of his eventually getting even with Ludvick. No, his last thoughts were on Derrick Cameaux and the pleasure he would reap from killing him. Then, just before his heavy lids finally dropped over his bloodshot eyes, he also thought briefly of the barmaid Gloria. She gave him something he had never known before, and it was something he wanted to try again.

CHAPTER 26

Derrick and Ben were up and drinking coffee by four o'clock that Sunday morning; Pappy was still missing. Though the radio had been silent all night, neither man had gotten much sleep. As he sipped his coffee, Derrick traced in his mind that area he would cover in his search for Pappy. He tried desperately to remember anything Pappy said that might hint where he should search, but had no success.

Within a few minutes he asked Ben to step into the office to look at the map with him and pointed out the area he was planning to search. "I'm thinking of going east on Yankee Canal and then heading south on Bayou Juno. That's a long way north of Caminada, but I figure with all the activity in the south, I should cover a different area."

Ben thought for a moment before replying, "I directed a couple of bigger boats into that area late yesterday afternoon. They'll have to stay pretty much in the deep water bayous. That leaves a lot of smaller, shallower areas uncovered. I think you have the right idea. Concentrate your search in the small bays an tranauses."

Derrick looked at his watch, noting that it was now half past four. "Well, Uncle Ben, I'd better get started."

As Derrick took a step toward the docks the side door of the shed swung open. Derrick's heart raced, while Ben was noticeably startled. "You two look surprised to see me," said Olivia, holding the portable radio securely in both hands.

Derrick answered, "You're up early, Olivia. You didn't have to come down so early."

"Well, you said you were leaving at four thirty, didn't you?" Derrick nodded as he realized that Olivia wasn't handing him the radio. "Well, we'd better get started then!"

"Now, wait a minute," countered Derrick. "I don't think this is such a good idea."

"Four eyes are better than two. Right, Dad?" asked Olivia, encouraging Ben's help.

Ben thought for a moment and then answered hesitantly, "Well, I guess it's all right."

"Ben, you know there's no telling what we'll run into out there," reasoned Derrick.

"Derrick, I'm going with you. So come on," said Olivia, turning abruptly and walking out of the shed without a backward look.

He immediately opened his mouth to protest again, but said nothing when Ben put his hand on his shoulder and whispered, "Let her go with you, Derrick. After all, she's part of this too."

Derrick still wasn't sure about it, though. Finding Pappy was going to be hard enough, without adding the responsibility for Olivia's safety to the equation. However, it was obvious she had made up her mind, and he couldn't waste more time trying to change it. He had mixed emotions as he walked toward the *Miss Teresa* and noticed Olivia loading a small ice chest and two full grocery bags into the skiff. His first and rather irritated reaction was that this wasn't a joy ride to a picnic, and he was just about to say so when Olivia explained. "When we find Pappy, he might be hungry. So I brought something for him to eat."

Derrick hadn't even thought of that. At least, he hadn't made a fool of himself by opening his mouth too soon. "That's a great idea, ready to go?"

"Waiting on you," she said as she climbed into the skiff ahead of him.

Derrick climbed aboard and sat behind the controls. As soon as he had started the engine, he automatically headed for the stern of the skiff to untie the rear line, but Olivia had beaten him to it. "Hey, you'd make a good deck hand," he said in surprise.

Olivia, however, offered neither a verbal response nor eye contact. In fact, as soon as she untied the stern line, she pulled out the two-way radio and was busy calling Ben. "Radio check, Pop. Got a copy, over?"

Ben answered almost immediately, "Read you loud and clear."

"Good. We'll keep you posted on our progress."

"Roger, I'll do the same. Be careful out there,"

Derrick reached forward from his seat to untie the bow line, as Olivia moved in to the seat next to him. Within seconds they sped away. She leaned toward him so she could be heard over the engine noise, and with a serious look on her face, asked, "What area will we search?" He was pleasantly surprised to see that she wasn't along just for the ride; she was obviously determined to be as much help as possible.

"I thought we'd search some of the smaller bays and bayous off Yankee Canal," answered Derrick; Olivia nodded her approval.

They traveled several miles without saying a word. Both scanned the darkness as the warm glow of daybreak became faintly visible on the horizon. And, when the crest of the sun finally broke the horizon, the whole of nature seemed to struggle desperately to hold its nighttime dominion over the swamp. But ever so slowly the sun unfurled its rays, steadily gaining its mounting advantage until the last of the night was in full retreat. Olivia couldn't help but look skyward as great flocks of birds took flight in joyous chatter. Both herons and cranes stroked their wings majestically in the cool dawn to reach proper heights over the pristine swamp; then they flattened their wings to glide on the unseen wind, gracefully swinging their long necks slowly from side to side in search of just the right shallow bay or bayou. Birds by the thousands rose and fell in unison as numerous flocks repeatedly filled the morning sky. Shrill, songs and calls erupted from so many birds that they could be heard clearly, even above the roar of the skiff's engine. The sound was one of disorder, but the great flocks moved in perfect harmony.

Their arrival at the first area Derrick wanted to cover was right on time, meaning full light so that they could begin the search immediately. He pulled back on the throttle until the *Miss Teresa* barely moved forward. Then, pointing to an opening in the south bank of the canal, he explained, "This cut will take us to a series of small

145

bays. Many times, as a kid, Pappy would take me fishing in this area. Just maybe we'll find him here."

"How far south does it go?" asked Olivia.

"Not very far, maybe a couple miles." He turned the skiff to starboard and maneuvered her straight through the narrow cut in the levee, almost touching the thick vegetation on either side. This passage ran about twenty-five feet, then opened into a small bay. The vegetation on the levee that separated the canal and the bay was so thick that it hid the existence of the bay from most people. Derrick knew his grandfather always claimed this bay as one of his favorite spots. Thus, immediately upon entering it, he followed the water's edge in search of any recent sign of activity. In some areas, giant cattails and high swamp grass had actually crept far out into the water, making it very difficult to see, much less follow the shoreline, but they moved on as best they could.

Once they reached the southern-most point of the bay, they entered a small, very crooked bayou. They followed it as it snaked its way through a series of smaller bays and crevasses, with each bay having its own maze of lesser bayous called tranauses. These veins of water, some barely three feet wide, stretched deep into the swamp and marshes. Since it was impossible to investigate all of them, Derrick decided to follow only the main ones. Olivia stood up with a pair of binoculars, gazing inland as far as vegetation would allow; however, bay after bay they entered with no signs anyone had ever been there. Moreover, each time she looked at him, shaking her head to signal that she had seen no one, her worry mounted as she thought of the hundreds of tiny bays and waterways where someone could easily become lost. She looked at her watch; it had now been two hours since they had turned off Yankee Canal and entered the first bay.

Once satisfied that they covered the area as thoroughly as possible, Derrick headed back toward Yankee Canal. Seeing the look on Olivia's face, he quickly tried to offer encouragement. "I know it seems pretty hopeless, but remember there are now over sixty boats out looking for him."

Olivia almost lost her composure as she realized just how futile an undertaking it was, considering the vast area they were searching. In a

quivering voice she asked, "How many of these bayous are there leading south from Yankee Canal?"

Derrick answered truthfully, "Quite a few. We'll cover the smaller bayous and let the larger boats get the bigger ones." Still feeling that he had to give her some kind of hope, he went on. "It might not look like it, but believe me, with everyone looking; we'll cover a large area today."

"Well, why haven't we heard anyone on the radio?"

Derrick smiled. "You won't hear anything because the radio's off. It runs on a battery, and I didn't want to run it down so early in the day. I thought we could check in every couple of hours."

"Think we could check in now?" she asked hopefully.

"Sure, I'll call in," answered Derrick as he picked up the radio, turned it on, and then waited a few seconds to make sure that it was clear. "Base, *Miss Teresa*."

After a short pause Ben answered, "This is base. Go ahead, Derrick."

"Just checking in, have you heard anything?"

"Nothing so far, where are you?"

"About five miles east on Yankee Canal, we're checking some of the brackish water south of the canal, over."

"That's a Roger," answered Ben.

"What's happening with the Coast Guard and the air search?"

"The Coast Guard are conducting a full search, but their big cutters can only navigate the deep waters. They also have two rescue choppers in the air with the sheriff's air patrol. I think we'll find him before too much longer, over."

"Roger, Uncle Ben. We'll check back later, *Miss Teresa* clear."

"Roger, Derrick, Base clear."

As Olivia took the radio from Derrick and put it under her seat, he tried to reassure her. "Don't worry, Liv. The day's just begun. You heard Uncle Ben. We'll find Pappy."

Olivia nodded. "Let's just cover as much of this area as we can today, Derrick."

Agreeing, he brought the skiff back through the small cut in the levee and headed once more eastward on Yankee Canal. He knew time was running out for Pappy; he had to be found soon. There was no longer any doubt that his grandfather was in trouble. But was he still alive?

CHAPTER 27

Henry Fuller and Dan Coats, two retired steel workers from New Orleans, had spent the last thirty years working together at the Bondale Ship Yard and were best friends. Henry knew things about Dan that even his wife Hazel knew nothing about, and Dan knew things about Henry that his wife Peggy had better never discover.

Henry and Dan had always shared the usual sporting interests of football, baseball, basketball and especially professional wrestling, but there was one sport they both loved above all others and that was fishing. So it wasn't surprising when Henry suggested "Hey, what you say we go down to the launch an wet a hook!"

"No, I got a better idea, Henry. Let's go fishin'."

"That's what I'm talking about, Dan. Let's go to the launch, while we still have plenty time to fish some," answered Henry, shaking his head in mild irritation that his friend sometimes appeared to be ever so dense about the most obvious things.

Dan, however, was already two steps ahead of Henry this time. "We need to go catch some really big ones. You know, go where the real fishin's done. We gotta go all the way to Grand Isle," said Dan almost reverently.

Henry's mouth opened in awe at the thought and said, "Grand Isle? Man I've always wanted to fish there."

149

Laughing at his buddy, Dan couldn't hold back the thought and said, "Hell, what you say we head out in the morning?"

Henry shouted, "That's the best damn idea I've heard in years!"

"You know, Henry, this retirement ain't half bad, is it?"

"And better'n that, Man, it's only just begun!"

Both Henry and Dan were up early the next morning well before daylight ready to leave New Orleans as planned.

By noon the boys were rolling into Cheniere Caminada and then Grand Isle. By the time they found a marina and a motel the day was spent. That evening, after they had showered and eaten, they found a small Bar in Caminada and were having a great time when a fight suddenly broke out near the entrance to the bar. Complete chaos reigned for a while, and both men wisely sought protection under their table as glass flew everywhere. Neither Henry nor Dan knew how or why it started, but they were well aware that when the fighting subsided the bartender lay dead on the floor from an ugly knife wound to his mid-section. As a result, almost everyone, including Henry and Dan, hurriedly left before the police arrived. In fact, if the truth be known, the pair were likely one of the very first out the door. And though neither ever mentioned it, both were more than anxious to hightail it as far away as possible from the scene of that night's trouble in the Bar.

Very early the next morning – much earlier than a normal "morning after" – Henry and Dan were cruising the shoreline of Caminada Bay searching for just the right fishing spot. They came across a tiny island that looked promising and here they caught a few good fish, such as Dan's six-pound speck, and Henry did have the thrill of his life when he hooked a four-foot hammerhead that completely destroyed his line before escaping. "Damn shark busted my line! Let's find another spot!" said a disgusted Henry

A quarter mile north of the tiny island Dan spotted another hot spot. "Hey, Henry, let's go down that canal!" he urged enthusiastically. "We just might even catch us a few more speckled trout!"

Henry wasted no time and guided their boat into the small canal where he turned the main engine off and allowed their boat to drift effortlessly down the canal. Almost immediately Henry hooked a nice speck and the boys were having a blast. After drifting almost a mile

into the canal, Dan spotted a structure at the end of the canal. "Looks like some old oil well, Henry," remarked Dan, immediately recalling what the marina manager had mentioned about finding good fishing around old oil wells.

"Yeah, and I bet'cha the specks are big around those old pilings," answered Henry using the electric motor to maneuver their boat closer to the pilings surrounding the abandoned well.

Henry took time to look over the marsh. "Look at this place! What a view!" From this vantage point, he could also see over the pilings of the oil well, all the way to the very end of the canal. His eyes suddenly fixed on what looked like a log half in the water and half on land; and although he soon sat down again, the curiosity of the strange-looking log got the best of him. Without a word, he guided the boat around the abandoned well.

"Hey," protested Dan, "where you going? You're taking us out of position to fish the pilings."

"I just wanna check something out at the end of the canal," Henry answered. "So hang on a minute, we can always come back if we don't find something better down there." As soon as he had maneuvered the boat around the oil structure, he realized immediately that what he had seen wasn't a log at the end of that canal. "Look, Dan, a skiff!"

Dan immediately stood to survey the surrounding marsh for the skiff's owner, but saw no one. "Now, what in the world would a skiff be doin' out here without nobody tendin' to it?"

"I don't know, but let's check it out," answered Henry while guiding their boat toward the seemingly abandoned skiff. When they floated within thirty feet of the vessel, Henry stood up; this time with a good view inside the skiff. He shouted in disbelief, "My God, Dan, there's a body in that skiff!"

Though he was still holding his fishing line, Dan quickly set it down and stood up with Henry to get a look for himself. "Is he dead?" he asked.

"Looks like it to me," answered Henry, hardly above a whisper.

CHAPTER 28

Traffic on Yankee Canal was much heavier than usual this Sunday afternoon, just as it had been since early morning due to the massive search for Pappy. After recognizing some of the skiffs and larger shrimp boats that were involved, Derrick stopped to discuss with several of the fishermen primary areas they had already searched and those which still needed probing. He then passed this information on to Ben, who was still coordinating the overall search from the shrimp shed.

Unfortunately, the day was now fast slipping away without the first sign of Pappy, despite their personally having searched more than a dozen bayous and bays along Yankee Canal, all areas Pappy had shown Derrick while he was growing up. The young Cameaux was now drawing on all his expertise while searching for Pappy, but he knew that a man could get lost in the swamp and never found. He also knew that Pappy wasn't lost but sensed something terrible must have happened to him.

Derrick had one more bayou he wanted to explore before the day expired. As he made his turn onto that bayou he noticed another skiff heading toward them in the canal. Since he didn't recognize this other vessel, he didn't stop to talk, but continued initiating his turn for the last bayou he had intended to search. As he entered this bayou, however, he glanced back at that oncoming skiff as it passed the bayou

153

opening. The man at the controls was so low in his seat that he could hardly be seen, much less recognized. Derrick turned his attention away from the skiff and back toward finding Pappy.

While he might not have recognized the man in the skiff, that man certainly recognized him. In fact, Ludvick had recognized the *Miss Teresa* right away. Hence, as the two skiffs were approaching each other, he pulled his hat low over his brow and scrunched farther down in his seat. However, before they could actually pass each other, the *Miss Teresa* had turned south off Yankee Canal, providing some relief to Ludvick that he'd not had to risk a face-to-face encounter after all. Even better, he could hardly believe his luck of recognizing the young Cameaux behind the controls. He had also noticed a woman with him whom, at first, he hadn't recognized until Derrick had made the turn off the canal and the woman had turned and waved.

"O, yeah, I know you well, Ms. Cameaux," he had boasted, now even more intrigued by this unexpected bonus turn of events. Actually, Ludvick had always made it his business to know his enemies. Before now Olivia had never been of any real concern to him, other than being Eric's wife; now, seeing her out here today just might call for reconsideration. Still, the one thing he had always deemed most important about Olivia was that she had borne no sons for Eric Cameaux. Perhaps that was yet the extent of her value; perhaps not.

At any rate Ludvick always kept an open mind to new opportunities, and he now very quickly assessed the situation, wondering exactly why Derrick and Olivia were out on the water. Was it actually possible, after all, that Mato had been telling the truth about his confrontation with Pappy? If so, then that would probably explain Derrick's appearance in the marsh. "He might just be looking for his grandfather," thought Ludvick, "but what about the woman?" True, she was the widow of Eric, one of Olidore's dead grandsons, but could there be more to it than that? After all, for purely practical, useful purposes – which were the only types ever considered by such hardened pragmatists as Ludvick – Eric Cameaux's death severed all prohibitive boundaries which once had stood between Olivia and Derrick. The concept of a genuine bond of love between them had, of course, never entered Ludvick's mind. Then with a grin playing at the

corners of his mouth, he sneered aloud, "Hmmm, then that must explain why I seen so many boats an skiffs all day. They all searching for Olidore Cameaux! Could it be so, Mato, that for once in you damn life you done something right?

Once Ludvick passed the mouth of the bayou that Derrick entered and thus was no longer visible to the couple, he turned his skiff toward the levee and a thicket of cattails and rattlebox that extending profusely into the brackish water. Killing his engine, he drifted toward the thicket which easily provided more than enough cover to completely hide him and his skiff. He then tied up to a stunted palmetto bush and sat motionless on the bow listening for the sounds of the *Miss Teresa* from just beyond the opposite side of the levee.

Ludvick then reached down next to his seat and pulled out his shotgun, which was fully loaded with buckshot. Leaving his skiff, he quietly made his way across the narrow levee, treading carefully through the thick vegetation that made even that short distance difficult. He stopped in the middle of the levee to listen; Derrick was close, very close – so close that Ludvick could almost smell him. If he hurried, perhaps he could actually get a good shot at the young Cameaux and be done with him once and for all. So driven, he moved quickly but cautiously to within ten feet of the edge of the levee; then he stealthily weaved his way through the thick roseau and palmetto, barely rippling a leaf as he passed. He had enough cover ahead to conceal himself, and from this vantage point he could plainly hear the *Miss Teresa's* engine humming not more than thirty yards away and getting closer.

Although the larger bayous generally seemed to plow a much straighter course by sheer force, these lesser ones had to snake their way at the discretion of the marsh, and this marsh had dictated that this bayou flow alongside the levee a quarter mile before resuming its southerly flow. In fact, so snaky was its course that Derrick had to take a sharp turn to starboard soon after entering, thus forcing him closer than usual to the levee. Since this was the last bayou Derrick had intended to search this day, he wanted to follow it as far south as possible until nightfall, regardless of the difficulties involved. It was the perfect set-up for Ludvick.

Completely unaware of the deadly threat just a few yards to their right Derrick and Olivia resumed scanning their surroundings. Well within shotgun range Ludvick's only problem was getting a good shot off because between him and the *Miss Teresa* stood thickets of vegetation standing taller than a man. Straining to see his victim, the old Rabeaux had difficulty at times even seeing the *Miss Teresa*, much less spotting Derrick long enough to ensure a kill. A bit frustrated, Ludvick finally looked beyond the skiff for an opening and found a tiny break in the vegetation just ahead. Though scarcely wide enough and barely within range of his shotgun, he quickly moved to that spot, raised the big gun to his shoulder, and waited for the skiff to come into view.

Maintaining a steady, slow speed Derrick and Olivia conducted the search standing up. The increasingly thick vegetation along the small bayou not only impeded Ludvick's sight, but also made the couple's search much more difficult in terms of both physical passage and visual clearance. Thus, when Olivia noticed a break in the foliage to their right, a natural drainage ditch allowing rain water from the levee to escape into the bayou, her body had tensed for a split second at the sight of a large cottonmouth moccasin swimming in it. She nervously tapped Derrick on the shoulder and pointed to the snake. Nodding, he declared with no uncertainty, "Yeah, that's not something I'd want to fool with, but it does come with the territory."

"I know, but I just hate even seeing one," responded Olivia in a shaky voice, her eyes still glued on the venomous reptile. "Is there any possibility it could just—"

"Hey," Derrick suddenly interrupted her. "Why don't we call Ben?"

"Good idea," she said without taking her eyes off the snake. Just as the bow of the skiff paralleled the drainage ditch, Derrick leaned forward to pick up the radio. Ludvick, on the other hand, still well-hidden in the dense foliage beyond the drainage ditch, remained calm and ready, determined that his aim would be true. However, just as the *Miss Teresa* came into view, only Olivia could be seen.

"Damn you, Cameaux whore!" cursed Ludvick under his breath. For a moment he considered killing Olivia and then possibly getting a second shot at Derrick but that wasn't his way of doing things. He had always maintained a life of patience when it came to killing his enemies;

156

in fact, that's how he managed to nearly wipe them all out. No, he wouldn't take a chance here without a definite kill of the one he intended; he would bide his time as always, making his wait worth his while. In mere seconds, the *Miss Teresa* drifted out of range, thereby reducing him to a mere frustrated spectator grudgingly watching his target drift farther and farther out of his reach. True, they travelled a safe distance from his deadly aim, but not from his piercing, hawkish eyes.

Meanwhile, Derrick turned the radio on and called Ben, but it was Marco Doucet who answered. "*Miss Teresa,* this is base. We been waiting for you call. We have some news."

A feeling of apprehension gripped Derrick as he feared the worst. Derrick and Olivia met each other's gaze "Go ahead, Marco. We're listening."

"Two fishermen found Pappy an he's still alive!"

"Say again," urged Derrick, unprepared for the good news.

"Pappy is alive! Air rescue's taking him to a hospital in New Or'lens now!"

"How hurt is he?" asked Derrick.

"Not sure. We just got word he's alive. Ben an the sheriff are on their way to New Or'lens. They want me to stay by the radio till you call in to give you the message."

"Thanks, Marco! We're on our way in! Over!" With a huge sigh of relief, Derrick put the radio down and then put the *Miss Teresa* in neutral. Never taking his gaze off Olivia, he could see big tears of joy that welled up and spilled onto her cheeks. Immediately feeling deep compassion, Derrick took one step toward her and then stopped, but that one step was all Olivia needed. Instantly she rushed forward and he took her in his arms. "You heard Marco, Liv. Pappy's alive! That old man has cheated death before, and he'll do it again!" As she gently laid her head on his shoulder, tears flowed freely in response to the emotional relief and the comfort of his strong arms.

Ludvick watched the display of affection in amazement from his secluded hiding spot. Although he hadn't heard any of the radio conversation or the words spoken between Derrick and Olivia, that small fact was hardly of importance to him. Instead, he realized just how valuable this unexpected revelation actually meant to his overall

mission; he now knew best how to most effectively get to Derrick. Ever so cold, he whispered aloud, "Oh yeah, Cameaux, I got you figured out now. An I'm gonna use your lust for this woman, boy, to kill you."

After Olivia and Derrick regained their composure he returned to the control panel, turned the skiff around, and pushed the throttle forward. Within seconds the *Miss Teresa* was traveling at top speed as they headed for Golden Meadow as rapidly as she could carry them. Derrick fought against allowing his thoughts to race ahead of him. He was relieved that Pappy was alive, but he knew that could change by the time they reached the shrimp shed.

Remaining well-hidden in the overgrown thicket, the old Rabeaux watched patiently as Olivia and Derrick scurried away. He was convinced that the upcoming round of stealth, wits, and intrigue he was plotting against this most threatening Cameaux enemy would definitely be most enjoyable and satisfying. Oh, yes, and likely the most challenging as well. He now had all the information needed to bring about a final confrontation with Derrick Cameaux, a confrontation that would end in his own favor—no doubt....

CHAPTER 29

Ludvick allowed Derrick and Olivia to get well ahead of him before he followed at a safe distance. He still wanted to find out all he could about Pappy because, deep down, he doubted Mato had killed their old adversary. And, from the way the young Cameaux so hastily departed after the radio message and his obviously romantic encounter with that woman, Ludvick also realized it had to mean either Olidore Cameaux's death or survival. Either way he had to know and that required a trip into town, regardless of how he despised the very thought.

Entering Bayou Lafourche he cautiously followed the waterway southward, avoiding traffic and the prying eyes aboard any vessels he could not evade. Two miles south of town, on the east side of the bayou, stood a small cabin. The Labote family lived here for as long as anyone could remember, for generations in fact. It was now inhabited by Pritch Labote, current head of the family, and his wife Margaret. Along with their seven kids, they made their living working their oyster beds in Bay Palourde. The Labote cabin was Ludvick's destination.

In years past, the Labote family had allied itself with the Rabeaux. However, to his credit, Pritch's father had severed ties with the Rabeaux after losing two of his brothers and several other family members to the endless Rabeaux bloodshed.

Once, Pritch actually worked at the Cameaux Shrimp Shed. At that time it had been many years since the Labotes had fought alongside the Rabeaux, and both Ben and Pappy knew of the family's past alliance with them, as well as of the split between the two families. Ben saw no harm in hiring Pritch and, for a while, things went well. Ben considered Pritch a good employee for the most part, but one day a fellow employee had caught him stealing some equipment from the shed and reported it to Ben. Both Ben and Pappy then confronted Pritch about the theft, having little doubt about the truthfulness of the accusations despite Pritch's vehement denial. Ben fired Pritch and though Ben didn't press charges and didn't tell anyone the cause of the firing, the episode branded Pritch Labote as a thief. Thus the small Cajun community treated Pritch the thief as they always treated thieves in the past and avoided him. From that time on, the Labote family was rarely seen in town.

Ludvick, aware of Pritch's run-in with the Cameaux, had taken advantage of the situation by offering him an opportunity to strike back at his enemies, an opportunity Pritch jumped at. Pritch became a major source of information for Ludvick concerning the activities and movements of the Cameaux family, especially Derrick Cameaux. Revenge was the driving force behind his alliance with the Rabeaux, but Ludvick didn't rely entirely on Pritch's hatred to maintain a valuable ally; he regularly gave him cash which, of course, Pritch never turned down. As Ludvick now neared the wharf in front of the cabin, one of the Labote boys who had been painting an old pirogue in the front yard hurriedly left his work and entered the cabin through a side door. As Ludvick tied up his skiff and stepped out onto the wharf, Pritch emerged from his cabin with a big smile. "Well, if it's not my ole friend Ludvick," he exclaimed, clearly hoping that this visit included more monetary benefits.

Ludvick, however, didn't display any sign of the enthusiasm shown by Pritch when he asked, "How's the family?" In fact, it really wasn't even a polite greeting on his part, but was definitely "typical Ludvick," dripping with all its characteristic caustic sarcasm. Hence, it was intended as a slight barb in Pritch's side, for ever since their renewed alliance, Pritch had never invited Ludvick inside the cabin or

introduced him to any family member. Credit that to Mrs. Labote; she, unlike her husband, had a little decency left. She determined that none of her children would ever have any dealings with Ludvick or any other Rabeaux.

Whether due to worldly wisdom or simple obtuseness, Pritch's eager response revealed absolutely no comprehension or even slight awareness of the old Rabeaux's acidic remark.

"Oh, the family's all good, all good. An cause I thought you just might be coming, I got some gossip for you. Follow me." Pritch then led Ludvick to the rear of the cabin out of sight of any traffic on the bayou, where they sat down on crude wooden chairs under the branches of an old willow tree.

Though the sun had rather uncomfortably warmed the afternoon air even under the shade of the tree, comfort was of no concern to Ludvick, and he wasted no time in addressing the point of his visit. "What you know about Olidore Cameaux?"

"I thought you'd be worried about our ole friend, Pappy. So, when I hear that something happened to him, I made it my business to fine out all I can. That way, I can tell all I know to my friend Ludvick," smiled Pritch, trying to read the blank expression on Ludvick's face.

Truth is, Pritch was much better off not knowing this visitor's thoughts. Ludvick simply looked away, shaking his head slowly. Then, still unwilling to look at Pritch eye-to-eye, his gaze next moved to the willow tree and finally to the ground, lingering there as he shrugged his shoulders and said slowly, "Well, our families go back a long way."

Pritch ignored the meager bone tossed to him and, instead, reveled in the momentary discomfort the old Rabeaux was feeling. He cleared his throat and continued, "It seems that Pappy got himself lost, at least that's what some people say. So, the sheriff an the Coast Guard, they all go looking for him. I hear just before you come that some fishermans by Caminada Bay found him alive."

"You say he was alive?"

"Yeah, alive, but almost dead, at least that's what I hear.

"What about Derrick Cameaux? Tell me what you know about him," insisted Ludvick.

161

"Well, he's been on the bayou a lot since his cousins died. Sometimes I see him every day, an then sometimes I don't see him for a while."

"Tell me what you know about that woman of his?"

"Woman?" asked Pritch uncertainly. "What woman? The only woman I ever see him with is his dead cousin's wife."

"Anything between them?"

Smiling, Pritch answered, "Well, I'm sure if he could, he would. I sure know I—"

Before Pritch could continue Ludvick abruptly changed the subject. "Where did they bring Olidore?"

"I hear some hospital in New Or'lens. That's all I know, an like I said, I hear he was almost dead. It don't look good for you ole enemy," declared Pritch with a gleam in his shifty eyes and a grin twitching the corners of his tobacco-stained lips.

Ludvick didn't notice, however, because he was already deep in thought, formulating his next move and the big part Pritch would play in it. Suddenly he stood up, signaling the end of his visit, but just as he was about to walk away, he asked Pritch one last question. "If I ax you to do something for my family like the things you papa did in his young days, will you do it?" Then before he could even answer, Ludvick pulled out a roll of bills and handed it to him. Pritch was speechless. Obviously pleased by his reaction, Ludvick added, "You will be paid good for your help."

Pritch knew Ludvick was asking him to get involved in the dirty work of killing that the Rabeaux loved so much. And for a few moments he stared at his cabin, thinking about his wife and how she would never allow the family to get involved in anything illegal or dangerous. He knew well that she could barely stomach having Ludvick sitting under her beloved tree, much less having her husband to become personally involved in his evil schemes. As Pritch hesitated but a few seconds his hand instinctively touched the wad of cash now in his pocket and the feel of easy money outweighed any feelings or objections his wife might have. He answered, "Okay, you can count on me, but only me."

162

"You all I need," Ludvick answered him, knowing that just a little more pressure would also get whatever else he wanted from his smiling money-hungry "friend." He then left Pritch, just as he usually did, with three solemn parting words, "La prochaine fois."

Trying very hard to be as cool, aloof and indifferent as Ludvick, but having a very difficult time of it, Pritch finally managed weakly, "Yeah, the next time."

As soon as Ludvick's skiff was out of sight, though, Pritch pulled out the roll of money and started counting.

CHAPTER 30

When Derrick and Olivia reached the Cameaux Shrimp Shed, Marco Doucet informed them that Ben called from the hospital with bad news. The doctors gave the elderly Cameaux little chance of recovery, given the extent of his wounds and the amount of infection spread throughout his body.

The two-hour trip to the hospital seemed like an eternity, especially to Derrick, perhaps because it provided too much time to think the unthinkable.

It was dark when Derrick pulled into the hospital parking lot. He and Olivia hurried through the emergency entrance to the central nurses' station. Uncharacteristically ignoring the two people ahead of him in line, Derrick asked in a loud, determined voice, "Where is Olidore Cameaux? He was brought here in a chopper!"

The startled nurse wanted to tell the rude young man to wait his turn, but so forceful was his voice that she immediately pointed in the direction of the elevator, answering in an equally strong voice, "Third floor ICU waiting room, that's where the family's to wait!"

"Thanks!" called out Olivia as they raced to a set of elevators where Derrick had already pushed the button at least three times before one opened. They waited politely, but impatiently, as an elderly man exited. As they were rushing in, Derrick was pressing the third-floor button and the close-door button almost simultaneously. So quick

165

was this maneuver that the young nurse waiting to enter the elevator with them was left standing as the door closed before she could enter. Even though she had heard his "Oops, sorry!" apology of sorts, in her frustration she kicked the door. "Bet that hurt," whispered Derrick with a sly smile on his face.

When the elevator door opened, Derrick saw Ben standing in a small lobby talking to a short, stocky man dressed in green surgical scrubs. As soon as they stepped out of the elevator, Ben saw them and motioned them over. "Please excuse me for just a minute, Dr. Hebert," said Ben as he turned to them.

Wrapping her arms around him as soon as she reached him, Olivia asked, "Oh, Ben, how's Pappy?"

Ben answered cautiously as he shook Derrick's hand, "I'm glad you two made it so soon. It just don't look good right now. Here's the doctor, so he can tell you all they know so far."

Turning toward Dr. Hebert, Ben introduced Derrick and Olivia. "Dr. Hebert was just starting to fill me in when you arrive, so go ahead, Doctor."

Without hesitation Dr. Hebert replied, "First of all, Mr. Cameaux is alive."

"Thank God," whispered Olivia.

Dr. Hebert then pointed toward a set of chairs. "Please have a seat and I'll explain everything we know up to this point." When they were seated, he continued, "The main thing I want to do is caution you not to get your hopes up too high. Mr. Cameaux is in very critical condition."

Looking up at Dr. Hebert, who hadn't yet had time to sit down with them, Derrick asked, "Can you tell us what kind of injuries he has?"

Nodding, the surgeon pulled up another chair and positioned it so they could all hear him clearly. "Yes, as I said before, I can tell you what we know right now. Of course, that might change as we run more tests. First, he has a broken right arm that's severely infected. I'm not even sure right now that we can save it. Next, he has a nasty bump on the head. So far there doesn't appear to be any hemorrhaging in the cranial area or any swelling of the brain, and that's good. Perhaps no

166

brain damage has been done, but it's actually a little too early for us to worry about that at this point. Now, even if that were all that was wrong with Mr. Cameaux, he would still have a tough time recovering. However, our biggest concern is the large infected wound in his lower chest area. This is a very ugly cut, and he's running a very high fever. Obviously, he has suffered an extreme trauma, and even if he were a young man, I'd still have to say his chances of survival aren't good. If you have any questions now, I'll try to answer them."

Dr. Hebert had minced no words, but rather had tried to prepare the family for the worst. Now, as they sat there trying to assimilate all they just heard, Ben finally asked, "Well, where is he now? Can we see him?"

"He's just coming out of surgery and will be in ICU for a while so that we can keep a close eye on him. As soon as we get him settled in a room, a nurse will let you see him, but I don't want you to stay more than five minutes. We still have much work to do on him and the next twenty-four hours are critical."

"Dr. Hebert, you said that he had a cut. Can you say what caused it?" asked Derrick

The doctor was shaking his head even before Derrick had finished the question. "I can't be sure."

Not satisfied, Derrick persisted somewhat impatiently, "Well, in your best judgment then, Doctor, what caused the cut?"

Dr. Hebert hesitated because he knew better than to speculate on such an important matter, especially when he didn't have to. However, the cause of this cut was actually no mystery to him; he had seen that type many times and to differing degrees of seriousness. He had often treated such wounds in victims of fights common to the offshore oil industry, not to mention the many patients he'd seen from countless Bar brawls. "Knife wound would be my guess. I'd say Mr. Cameaux was cut with a razor or knife."

Olivia, shocked by the doctor's answer, turned in horror to Ben and Derrick. "Who in the world would do such a terrible thing!" Though neither responded, they looked at each other, both knowing the "who," but sincerely hoping Olivia would never have to know.

167

Confused, yet ignoring their silence, she immediately turned back to Dr. Hebert, "Is he conscious?"

"No," came the response, "but if he makes it through the night, perhaps later he'll come out of it."

"I see," said Olivia in a whisper.

"If there aren't any more questions, I'll look in on Mr. Cameaux," Dr. Hebert said as he glanced at his watch before excusing himself.

"Sure, Dr. Hebert," said Ben, "thanks for all your help."

Olivia was confused. All she knew was that she now wished she had been more inquisitive about Pappy's so-called fishing trip. She just couldn't help wondering if she might have been able to do something to have prevented this whole scenario.

No one had all the facts, but both Ben and Derrick could easily put the pieces together enough to know that Pappy tried to deal with the Rabeaux on his own terms. Whereas Ben felt pangs of guilt for not being there with his father, he also felt angry at his father for trying such a foolish plan.

Suddenly all these self-incriminating introspections were interrupted by the appearance of a nurse who had emerged from the ICU. Both Ben and Derrick stood up, catching the nurse's attention and she asked expectantly, "Cameaux family?"

"Yes Ma'am" answered Ben.

The nurse smiled. "I'm Mildred Cox and I'll be taking care of Mr. Cameaux while he's in ICU. Normally we allow only one visitor at a time in a patient's room, but Dr. Hebert said all three of you can go in together. Follow me please."

Derrick saw Pappy through the glass wall even before Nurse Cox ushered them into his room. And although Dr. Hebert warned them of his critical condition, it was still shocking to see all the electrical devices with their accompanying tubes and wires attached to his body. Reading their troubled expressions, Nurse Cox explained, "This equipment is basically standard for most ICU patients, especially the respirator which is usually critical for some to survive."

"Thank you, Nurse Cox," said Olivia as she tiptoed to the bedside to kiss Pappy's forehead and hold his hand. She gently called his name and bravely declared, "Pappy, it'll be okay," despite the sickly fear of

the unknown she really felt. Ben and Derrick also gathered closer to Pappy's bedside, each one silent and feeling more than uneasy. In fact, all Derrick could do was to stand there and stare at his grandfather, for never had he seen him so helpless. Always before, he was the one who needed help and Pappy had always been the strong one, the rock of the family. When Derrick was younger and suffered with measles, mumps, colds, flu and whatever else, Pappy doctored him back to health with his home remedies. This man now lying so helpless before him always gave the help, but now the old gravely ill patriarch needed help of his own. And that was the most difficult and frustrating part of it all— there was nothing Derrick could do to help, and he felt useless.

Derrick then tried to shed a little light and hope as he said, "Pappy's made it this far and he's the toughest man I know. He'll pull through this. Just wait and see."

Ben and Olivia immediately nodded in agreement. "That's right," said Ben with as much enthusiasm as possible. "He's gonna be mighty upset if we tell him about all this worrin'."

At that very moment Nurse Cox approached and stood next to Olivia. "Are you folks all right?" she asked looking directly at Ben.

"We're good, thank you," replied Ben.

"Then perhaps we'd better let Mr. Cameaux get some rest now, don't you think?" Obviously a veteran of diplomacy, her way of saying that it was time to go reminded them of the undeniable seriousness of Pappy' s condition.

As they made their way back to the waiting area, Olivia announced, "I need a cup of coffee, how about you two?" Both Ben and Derrick agreed as she hurried past them and the elevator toward the vending machines.

No sooner had she walked away than Ben growled fiercely, "It was those bastard Rabeaux that did this to Pappy."

"There's no doubt about that. I just wish he would have let us know what he was up to," answered Derrick as he shook his head with regret.

"I just should have been there. I should have been there with him, Derrick. I should have known he'd try something like this!" exclaimed Ben.

"You had no way of knowing what Pappy was up to, Uncle Ben. And even if you had known, you couldn't have stopped him. You know better than anyone that when Pappy makes up his mind to do something, he'll do it regardless. You can't blame yourself for this. Besides, I think it's time I settle the score with the Rabeaux myself," Derrick declared emphatically.

Realizing that he had no time to argue because he could see Olivia returning with the coffee, Ben whispered, "We'll do it together, Derrick, just the two of us."

Handing them their cups of coffee, Olivia said, "Some lady at the vending machine said we're in for some stormy weather."

CHAPTER 31

Not only did Pappy survive the first twenty-four hours in ICU, but after two weeks he progressed well enough to be placed in a private room. Though still comatose – a condition of some concern to Dr. Hebert – his overall strength was actually improving by the day. Derrick stayed near his bedside day and night when he was allowed in the ICU; otherwise, he slept and passed the time sitting out in the waiting room. Once assigned a private room, Derrick stayed virtually around the clock at his grandfather's side. Rarely did he ever allow anyone else to tend to Pappy, but when he occasionally did agree, it was his Aunt Camellia whom he chose to take his place during those necessary trips to Golden Meadow to check on Ben, Olivia and the girls. As important as these visits were to Derrick to see the special people in his life, however, he also had another very important reason and that was to ascertain the current whereabouts of the Rabeaux family. Though he never missed an opportunity to casually make subtle inquiries, the answers were all the same. Not only had the Rabeaux not been seen or heard from since Pappy's near-death encounter, but no one had any clue as to their whereabouts.

With each trip to Golden Meadow, Derrick spent more and more time with Olivia and the girls. He was pleased to see Teresa and Toni laughing and playing almost like old times when Eric played with them. During these visits Derrick, Olivia and the girls grew even closer. He

171

and Olivia genuinely enjoyed each other's company, and both looked forward to their time together. Derrick devoted his full time and attention to them, and there was little doubt in his mind that it would not have been very difficult to tell Olivia how deeply he loved her.

As the long days of Pappy's recuperation turned into weeks, Derrick used his time to begin moving toward accomplishing his goal. One particular trip to Golden Meadow proved very satisfying because through it he felt as if he had taken the first step necessary in his handling of the Rabeaux problem. It happened on the first night he spent alone at Pappy's house after his grandfather's hospitalization. He found exactly what he was looking for – in the small hall closet next to the kitchen, old and outdated maps of South Louisiana. He even found a few old maps under Pappy's bed. Then, in the quiet late-night hours of his vigilance at Pappy's bedside, he studied map after map and set aside those he thought of benefit to him, especially those of the swamps and marshlands east of Bayou Lafourche. Some of the maps were more than a hundred years old, having been hand-drawn with great detail, and he was shocked when he compared them with more recent ones. He felt that uneasy feeling in the pit of his stomach when he noticed the extent that the wetlands had changed over such a relatively short period of time. The old maps had shown islands, bayous, levees and marshlands to the south near Grand Isle and Caminada Bay that no longer existed. Through erosion from great hurricanes and the lack of much-needed sediment deposits from the Mississippi River, these vast areas were now consumed by the tidal waters of the Gulf. Derrick also noticed how great bayous, like Bayou Lafourche, had been dammed at the mouth to prevent the flooding of towns and settlements to the south. He then saw with remorse the cruel irony in it all as he looked at the most recent maps. The very towns and settlements men tried to protect from the flood waters to the north were now being devoured by the tidal waters of the Gulf from the south.

Although fascinated by this intensive study of the maps, it was from the old maps detailing the Cameaux Swamps that he concentrated his search because he knew the area was virtually untouched by the ravages of both nature and man. The Cameaux Swamp and its vast

surrounding area were still out of the casual fisherman's field of interest because it consisted primarily of an endless maze of small mud islands enveloped in thick, almost impenetrable vegetation.

Though remembering much, especially the areas he duck hunted every year, there were still vast areas of this swamp that had never been woven into his memory. Doubtless, detailed memorization of the more familiar, immediate swamp area would be tough enough without adding that unfamiliar, more extensive portion surrounding the Cameaux Swamp, but Derrick knew he must at least become highly familiar with the entire terrain. After sorting through all the piles of maps, he chose about a dozen he could use to focus his efforts on locating Ludvick. He then spent his time memorizing the snake-like shapes of major bayous and bays and the wooded levees that bordered them, some of which were very familiar to him, as well as others he had never seen before. He always waited until late night before he brought out his maps, not wanting to be disturbed or have his mission disclosed either by his being discovered or by the odor of the musty old maps. He would close his eyes after studying a particular map and picture himself paddling his pirogue through and around its main features. As he moved, he committed to memory only the main islands and bays of some maps, but absorbed every detail of entire areas of others.

One night while lost in one of his memory exercises, he heard a slight noise in the hospital room. Because only he and a still-comatose Pappy were in the room, the noise startled him. Immediately opening his eyes, he turned toward Pappy's bed. The IV bottle, which hung above the bed and was attached by the small plastic tubing to Pappy's left arm, was swinging slightly from side to side. Derrick stood up and slowly walked to Pappy's side, hopeful but unsure of what had caused the IV bottle's movement. As he leaned over his grandfather, he softly spoke directly into his ear. "Pappy, can you hear me?" After no immediate response, he was about to return to his maps when Pappy slowly moved his left arm from his side to his chest, again causing the IV bottle to swing gently. Elated, Derrick quickly pressed the call button on the side of the bed.

"Yes," came a voice through the small speaker.

"Can somebody please check on my grandfather?"

"We'll be right there." Within moments, Nurse Cox and a younger nurse entered the room.

Unable to contain his excitement, Derrick exclaimed, "Nurse Cox, he moved! Pappy moved!"

Both nurses rushed to the bedside and began manually checking their patient's vital signs, as well as all the wiring on the equipment that electrically monitored his vital signs. After a thorough inspection Nurse Cox concluded, "Everything seems to be in order, Derrick. It was probably just an involuntary muscle spasm."

"No, it was more like a slow, deliberate move and it was the second time it happened!" insisted Derrick.

Nurse Cox knew and understood the importance of what just happened to Derrick, but she also didn't want to offer false hope. Thus, she answered cautiously, "Well, this could mean your grandfather is ready to regain consciousness."

"I sure hope so. Is there anything I can do to help him?" asked Derrick as he stood by the left side of his grandfather's bed.

Nurse Cox, who stood next to the opposite side of Pappy's bed straightening his pillow, reached forth both her hands, using the right to check his pulse and the left to gently lift Pappy's hair from his forehead and carefully arrange it in a more normal appearance before she looked up at Derrick with a smile. "No, not a thing other than just keep on praying that he'll continue to wake up. But, he's just going to have to do it all on his own."

The younger nurse then pulled down the blanket and sheet that covered Pappy, and Nurse Cox opened his hospital gown to remove the bandage from his midsection. Both nurses touched the wound, looked at each other, and nodded. Though the cut still looked ugly, being very red with blue-black bruises along its entire length, Derrick wondered whether it might actually have begun healing despite its appearance. To confirm his thoughts, the younger nurse said, "It does look much better, doesn't it?"

Nurse Cox nodded in agreement. "Now, let's get out of here so that, hopefully, Mr. Cameaux can get a peaceful night's rest and wake up in the morning to rejoin the rest of our world!"

174

Long after the nurses left the room, Derrick remained next to Pappy's bedside waiting and watching for some movement of any kind, but none came. As the night dragged on, he knew he should get some sleep himself, but he began feeling so helpless that sleep seemed impossible.

Tears welled up in his eyes as he looked at Pappy's frail body. He just couldn't bear the thought of never hearing that voice again. Spontaneously, he picked up Pappy's hand and held it securely in his own two strong hands as he knelt beside the narrow bed. Wiping his eyes on his sleeve, he spoke softly, "Pappy, it's Derrick. I'm right here beside you. You're gonna be fine, I just know you are. Can you hear me? Oh, Pappy, Pappy, please move again, please wake up. Please wake up and talk to me. I just need you to wake up!" This time, the strong young Cajun made no attempt to stifle or wipe away the warm rush of tears that coursed down his cheeks, spilling even onto the wrinkled, sun-burned forearm of the weak old Cajun whose beloved hand he had so yearned to see move once more.

Derrick stayed at Pappy's bedside until he could no longer hold his eyes open. Exhausted and weary, he finally gave in and stretched out on his cot to get some rest. His eyes grew heavier and heavier until he drifted into a deep, but fitful, sleep.

CHAPTER 32

Derrick was up early the next morning and though still somewhat tense, felt fairly well rested despite the late hour he fell asleep and the number of times he awakened to check on Pappy. After downing the hot cup of coffee one of the nurses brought him, he then took a long, relaxing shower and had just finished dressing when there was a soft knock at the door. Before he could even respond, Uncle Ben opened the door slightly and stepped quietly into the room.

"Uncle Ben, come on in,"

Ben was quickly followed by Aunt Camellia and Olivia. "Bonjour, Derrick," said a smiling Aunt Camellia as she walked over to hug his neck.

"And a good morning to all of you," replied Derrick . Then turning his attention toward Olivia, he added, "Well, what a pleasant surprise."

She smiled as she embraced him and said, "And we also have two additional surprises downstairs."

"Teresa and Toni are downstairs?" asked Derrick.

"Oh yes, they just had to come with us to see their Pappy and you."

"That's great!"

With a noticeable tone of disgust, Ben said, "There's this sign downstairs saying something about how kids under twelve can't go to a patients' rooms. I tell you, I never saw that sign before today!"

"That's a bunch of bull!" Derrick said.

177

"Bull or not, the lady at the front desk says that's the hospital policy. An, since she looks tough enough to enforce it, we wasn't about to fight with her," said Ben.

Derrick looked at Olivia, who had an unmistakable look of amusement on her face. She shrugged her shoulders, smiled, and said, "No big deal. They'll be fine for a few minutes until we get back downstairs."

"How is he today?" asked Aunt Camellia as she walked over to Pappy's bed and began re-straightening the already-straight covers.

Derrick quickly answered, "He's getting stronger every day. Last night he even moved his left arm, and it wasn't just a little twitch either."

"That's great!" said Olivia.

"Have you seen Dr. Hebert today?" asked Ben.

"No, not since yesterday, I don't think he's on duty today."

"Well, Aunt Camellia an I want to spend the day with Pappy an give you a break."

Even before he could say a word, Olivia asserted, "That's right, and the girls and I want you to take us to the zoo."

Derrick, nodding in agreement, replied "Who am I to turn down such a gracious offer!"

"Good," said Ben, "Now run along. We can handle this end."

For extra emphasis Aunt Camellia added, "An don't come back till the end of the day. Just be sure an pass a real good time."

Looking at Derrick, Olivia suggested, "Now that you've received your orders, Soldier, you'd better carry them out."

"Don't worry, that's one set of orders I'm looking forward to obeying."

Aunt Camellia smiled and waved the two of them away; then she went right to work straightening the small room. Ben settled into a padded chair near the bed to watch Pappy and pray silently that today would be the day his elderly father would awaken.

As he and Olivia left the room and headed for the elevator, Derrick asked, "Who's watching the girls?"

"Hospital day-care, but I promised them we wouldn't be long."

178

"Good, I can't tell you how glad I am that all of you came today," he said with a smile as they reached the elevator doors.

As he pressed the down button Olivia's hand gently clasped his. Leaning closer toward him she whispered, "We've missed you, Derrick, and we wanted to see you."

"Thanks Liv, you and the girls are the brightest part of my life. Thanks for coming." Olivia didn't release his hand as they entered the elevator. They had so much more to say, but neither one said another word until they reached the daycare.

As soon as the girls saw them they came running and shouting, "Uncle Derrick! Mommeee!"

Derrick picked up both girls and asked teasingly, "Ok, girls, what will it be today? Where are we going?"

Both girls screamed at the same time, "THE Z00000!"

"All right, that sounds good to me. Let's go visit your cousins."

"Our cousins?" asked Teresa with a perplexed look on her face.

"Yes," answered Derrick laughing, "the monkeys!" The girls giggled and pointed to each other as he set them down.

Teresa said, "We have a new friend! His name is Anderson!"

That gave Olivia an opportunity she hoped for. "Girls, play with Anderson a little longer while Uncle Derrick and I talk. We'll leave in a few minutes." The girls needed no further prompting as they ran back to play with their new friend. Pointing to a nearby bench, Olivia asked, "Derrick, do you mind if we sit awhile?"

"Of course not, Liv."

"Derrick, maybe this isn't the right time to ask, but I was wondering about something."

By the tone of her voice he sensed that something weighed heavily on her mind. "What is it, Liv?"

"Well, it's probably nothing, but I was wondering whether there could possibly be any connection between Pappy's injury and Eric's murder?"

The question caught him so totally off guard that his discomfort could hardly be concealed. He couldn't tell her anything he knew about Eric's death, yet he couldn't just outright lie to her either. "I suppose it's not entirely out of the question," he stammered.

179

"Well, the sheriff stopped by the house the other day to assure me they're still working hard to solve Eric's and Jon's murders. Then he asked me whether I knew of anyone who wanted to harm the Cameaux family. Of course I told him no, but why would he even think there could be someone wanting to deliberately hurt us?"

Having had time to gather his thoughts, Derrick tried to allay her concerns, "Oh, Liv, I'm sure the sheriff is just doing his job. He's got to ask all kinds of questions just in hopes of coming up with something concrete to follow. I really don't think you should worry 'cause those questions sound pretty routine to me. By the way, did he say or imply that he had any suspects?"

"He said he has a couple of leads, but I got the feeling it wasn't anything very promising," she answered.

He could see both relief and disappointment, not to mention frustration, written on her face, and he wondered whether she had really accepted his attempts to downplay her conversation with Sheriff Lebeouf. Was she expecting him to say something more? Since he really couldn't tell, he just slowly shook his head and looked down momentarily. Then he looked up, gazed directly into her eyes and asserted, "Don't worry, Liv. Eric's and Jon's killers will be caught. They won't get away with it! I promise you, they won't get away with it!"

Olivia, moving closer to him on the small bench, reached out and took his hand and placed it in her lap. "Derrick, I don't want anything to happen to you! That's what I need you to promise me, that you'll stay out of harm's way. What would the girls and I do without you?"

Still looking directly into her beautiful brown eyes, he softly replied, "Nothing's going to happen to me. I'm afraid you'll be stuck with me for a long, long time." Squeezing his hand she was about to speak when they were interrupted by the daycare attendant.

"Excuse me, Mr. Cameaux?"

A bit startled by the sudden interruption both Derrick and Olivia stood as Derrick responded, "Yes,"

I just received a call from your grandfather's nurses station and they wanted to see you as soon as possible."

"Did they say why?" asked a concerned Derrick.

"No, they said if you were still here to please have you return to your grandfather's room immediately."

As both Derrick and Olivia rushed for the elevator, Olivia asked of the attendant, "Please watch my girls?"

"Don't worry, they'll be safe with me!"

When the doors opened on the sixth floor they heard a commotion coming from down the hall, and they soon realized the commotion was coming from Pappy's room.

"Something's not right!" insisted Derrick as they picked up their pace, only to encounter a new "No Visitors" sign on the door of Pappy's room. Hesitating only momentarily, he quickly opened the door to find a room filled with nurses busily working around his grandfather's bed. "What's happened? What's wrong with Pappy?" he demanded.

Hearing his distress, Ben quickly came to his side. "Derrick, calm down. Everything's fine. Pappy's waking up."

"What!" exclaimed Derrick as he rushed toward the bed to get as close as possible.

Nurse Cox looked at Derrick and smiled. "It seems your grandfather's finally ready to wake up!" One of the nurses stepped aside, allowing him to move closer to Pappy's side.

As he looked down at his grandfather, he could see the old man moving his head from side to side. He was even trying to raise his arms, but the nurses were holding him steady. Then Derrick leaned closer and asked in a loud voice, "Pappy, Pappy, it's Derrick. Can you hear me?"

Slowly Pappy opened his eyes and said in a weak voice, "Course I hear you, Boy! What's all the fuss about?"

CHAPTER 33

For the next two weeks Pappy continued to regain his strength. Physically, he was making remarkable progress; mentally, it was a little slower for the old man. And the nights were always his worst times, for he commonly experienced violent nightmares from which he always awoke shouting, exhausted and literally confused. It was evident to Derrick that even while Pappy's frayed and battered body fitfully slept, his deeply burdened mind actively replayed his fight with the Rabeaux; and though Derrick tried to calm him, often only a sedative would do. Then, with each new dawn came fresh light that seemed to fade all traces of the previous night's terrors. Whether he truly never remembered his torturous dreams or simply refused to expose them, all his daytime conversations centered only on positive thoughts and happy memories of Derrick's boyhood days spent growing up under Pappy's tutelage and in his care. Such reminiscing seemed to provide the old Cajun a deep sense of peace, and Derrick benefited as well from all the personal memory refreshing, as well as all the new pieces of history he learned for the first time. He didn't press his grandfather for answers about what happened in the dead-end canal because he knew there would be time enough for that in the days ahead.

One morning, Derrick left the room and walked down the hall toward the nurses' station, where he saw Dr. Hebert looking at patients' charts. "Mornin', Doc."

"Hello, Derrick, you're just the one I need to see. If you have a few moments, I'd like to talk to you about your grandfather."

"Sure, is everything okay?"

"Everything with your grandfather is fine. Fact is, he's improving every day, and I think it's about time to let him go home."

"That's great, how soon?"

"I'm starting him on physical therapy tomorrow. Then as soon as he's up and walking, he can leave."

"Well, he's been after me to get him up, so I think he's ready."

"Oh, we don't want to rush things. We'll take it easy with him, especially the first few days. If he were a younger man, however, I would have gotten him up sooner. Of course, a younger man might not have survived what that old man experienced. Derrick, your grandfather has the distinction of being the toughest man I've ever had the honor of tending to. By all rights, he should have died the very first day he arrived here, or even more accurately, I don't know how he made it here alive! I really have to admit I still don't know how he survived, especially before he was brought to us. It's as if he just had this incredible will and sheer determination to live despite all obstacles – almost like he's a man on a mission."

"If you only knew," thought Derrick before he voiced the only response he could really to offer. "Yes, there's no doubt he's tough, not to mention a little hard-headed. I just hope he hasn't exhibited his contrary nature too much toward you or your staff."

"Well, I'll have to admit that at first we really didn't know what to make of him. But now that he's getting close to leaving us, I've heard more than one nurse say she'll miss his sharp tongue," laughed Dr. Hebert.

Derrick smiled, "So, if all goes well then, how soon will you let him go home?" Dr. Hebert thought for a moment. "If he does well today and gets up tomorrow and the rest of the week, I'll probably let him go Saturday morning. Just remember, he's still a weak man and will need much rest at home for some time to come.

"I'll see that he gets it. And, Dr. Hebert thanks for saving my grandfather's life."

"Derrick, as I said before, there's something in your grandfather that kept him alive. I have to honestly say that I really didn't have much to do with it."

At that time a nurse walked over and stood at Dr. Hebert's side, awaiting her turn to speak with him. Derrick said, "Thanks, Doc, I'll tell the family and Pappy.

Derrick returned to the room to find Pappy awake and rested. He immediately told him what the doctor said about his going home. Naturally, the self-willed Pappy insisted on getting up that very minute but Derrick answered sharply, "The doctor's orders will be followed to the letter and that means the first attempt at getting up would be tomorrow, not today." Pappy wanted to protest, but he just sighed deeply and muttered, "Okay, if you just have to insist."

True to his nature, Pappy willed his body to perform well enough in physical therapy that by Friday evening, everything was in place for his departure from the hospital on Saturday morning, just as Dr Hebert had said.

Before turning in for the night, Derrick started packing their belongings so as not to be rushed in the morning. Watching his grandson, Pappy knew that the time had come to begin sharing a few things with Derrick. So in his simple, direct, no-nonsense manner, he declared abruptly, "Derrick, first I want to thank you for staying with me through this whole hospital thing, I know how hard this is on you."

Derrick halted his packing and gave his full attention to his grandfather. "It was the Rabeaux boys I run into in that oil-well canal." Barely pausing to take a breath and keeping his eyes diverted from Derrick, Pappy continued matter-of-factly, "I tried to only talk with them boys, but things went the bad way. I think I killed one of them an the other one got away. Main thing is that Ludvick was not with them, an if I killed one of the grand boys, you can bet that devil will be even more crazy now. He'll be after you, Derrick, an he won't never stop till he's killed you. Now, I know you a brave young man, an you know the swamp an marsh more better than most Cajuns, but—"

"I had a good teacher," interrupted Derrick with pride.

185

"Sure, sure," answered Pappy as he hurried on before he could again be interrupted. "Son, this is serious. I got a question to you an need you to answer this for me. Are you staying in Golden Meadow?"

"Yes sir, I'm staying with my family!" answered a determined Derrick.

"Well, guess I should of never expected you to be any less the hard-head than your Papa. I want you to call Valdore Gisclair an Ben tonight. Tell them to meet us at my house tomorrow night for supper. Then call your Aunt Camellia an ax her to have some food ready.

Derrick wanted to protest calling a meeting so soon, but knowing that he wouldn't change Pappy's mind, he agreed hesitantly. "Okay, I'll call them tonight." He hurriedly finished packing and loaded his Jeep with most of their belongings.

Early Saturday morning, just as promised, Pappy was discharged from the hospital. Dr. Herbert and all the nursing staff were there to wish "that real piece of Cajun work," as they often fondly referred to him, and "his devoted grandson" well. Nurse Cox even had tears in her eyes when she bid them good-bye. Both Derrick and his grandfather thanked everyone for all the hard work, dedication, and special attention and assured them they would always be remembered for helping give Pappy another chance at life.

The skies were clear and bright as they left that day, and just leaving the hospital seemed to strengthen Pappy even more. In fact, he talked all the way home as Derrick just enjoyed listening. Whatever the near future threw their way, including life or death, both men knew that from now on, they would face the days ahead with a new perspective: remembering yesterday, hoping for tomorrow, but living life to the fullest today.

CHAPTER 34

Valdore accepted Derrick's supper invitation for Saturday night after he learned that Pappy needed to see him. The meal, as expected, had definitely been worthy of a Cajun cook of Camellia Cameaux's caliber. When they walked into the kitchen the aroma of seasonings and cooked foods embraced their senses. The first course she served was an appetizer of shrimp dip and crackers with a cup of oyster soup on the side. "It's just a taste," commented Camellia, warning them that it was not meant to fill the belly of a hungry man.

When the time was right, she pulled out of the oven a freshly baked cap French bread and set it in the middle of the table, where she cut it into pieces about the size of a man's hand. The aroma of the cap bread was mouth-watering. Next to the bread Camellia set a large platter of fried stuffed crabs along with fresh fried okra. Then, ever so carefully she placed on the table the last two containers of food, a huge bowl of rice and an even larger pot of shrimp fricassee. To top it off, she set a gallon of blackberry wine on the table to be used as needed.

"Well Sista, that's quite a spread," smiled Pappy.

"It's nuttin'. Just hope it's good," answered Camellia.

Once they finished eating the men moved to the living room, where the small talk of supper was soon replaced by more serious issues. Pappy led most of the conversation. He reminded Valdore of the old days when men respected each other's families; he also

187

reminded him of the consequences for those who crossed these lines of respect.

During all this preliminary talk, Valdore knew Pappy was building up to something important. Thus, he sat patiently and listened carefully, responding in kind as the bonds of friendship were recounted. Finally, the old Cameaux looked him directly in the eye and implored, "Friend, I need your help."

With absolutely no hint of reservation, Valdore responded immediately. "Olidore, if I can help you or your family, I will."

And then Pappy dropped an awful bombshell in his lap. "We know who kill my boys, an we need your help to find them." Pappy paused briefly to let him absorb the news.

Valdore sat up a little straighter then urged, "Go on, I'm listening."

Pappy's expression became grave as he continued. "For a long time now we been in this fight to the death with Ludvick Rabeaux, an we gonna just keep on fighting each other till there's not nothing but just one family. Valdore, it was Ludvick an his dogs that killed my boys."

Valdore realized that it wasn't a total shock to him that Pappy knew who had killed Eric and Jon. After all, there were many things Olidore Cameaux knew that no other man knew.

"Ludvick Rabeaux? That family? Olidore, of all the men I know, that Ludvick is the worst! An I know him good, an not nothing of what I know is good! You better not never turn your back on him! Olidore, is there no other way? That Ludvick is a demon!"

"There's no other way, my friend. We have to end this an there's not but just one way—death to the Rabeaux or—"

Pappy hadn't finished that sentence, but there was really no need: if the Rabeaux family didn't die, the Cameaux family would.

"What you want me to do?" Valdore said.

Pappy's answer had been specific. "Firs, I don't want you to fight none of the Rabeaux. All I want for you to do is locate Ludvick an his boys. I need to know if they're in the southland marsh or in the swamps. An unless I'm bad wrong, they'll be east of Bayou Lafourche. Now, I trust you to stay out of their way, Valdore. I don't never want no more innocent blood spilt."

Valdore realized that Pappy had made a very dangerous request of him. All things considered, though, he knew this was really the best and safest way of finding Ludvick. After all, he reminded himself, if Derrick or Ben happened to encounter any of the Rabeaux in the marsh or swamp, the outcome would be unpredictable at best. Pappy was wisely trying to gain an advantage by knowing in advance exactly where their enemies were camped so that he could formulate a workable plan. Thus, when Valdore heard all that he needed to hear, he immediately assured Pappy, "I'll fine Ludvick for you an I'll help you kill him."

Pappy was gentle, but firm. "No killing from you. No, my friend, all I need of you is what I axed. Just find them."

Valdore accepted this response, but wanted to make sure his friend knew he was available for whatever was needed. "When you want me to go?"

"Monday!" Answered Pappy.

CHAPTER 35

Valdore loaded enough provisions for his mission to last three days, knowing that if he needed more, he could live off the land. As he always did when setting out for possibly uncharted regions, he had included his pirogue to ensure access to areas where the skiff couldn't navigate and his shotgun, just in case he got a little too close to any of the Rabeaux.

He stayed on an easterly course until he came to Bayou Janis, a small, lazy waterway of no importance to this trip's mission, except to him. Relatives of his lived in a camp along this bayou, and it was here that he would gather information to begin his search. As he followed the small bayou the almost four miles toward his destination, he kept a close eye for the unexpected because he knew that the Rabeaux were not the only danger out here. The extremely thick vegetation on either side of the bayou, though picturesque, also provided the perfect habitat for numerous animals and reptiles that were always threats to a man's life.

In this particular area it seemed that the normally huge, dominant live-oak trees had been somewhat stunted and were now barely visible because they had been overpowered by thick clusters of rattlebox, cat-tails, elephant-ears and various other plants. Not only that, but in some sections blackberry thickets shot up to more than ten feet, covering everything with an impenetrable barrier of sharp thorns.

Valdore continued his passage through the winding bayou until he came upon a small bay, an opening perhaps three hundred feet wide and five hundred feet long. He could see a narrow opening at the other end where Bayou Janis entered and gently, but ever so deliberately, tried to be the sole water supply for this tiny crevice. He wouldn't follow the bayou beyond this point because the camp he sought was nestled in a thick set of palmetto about half-way across the bay on the west bank. The camp was constructed from this same palmetto from top to bottom. An untrained eye might not see the camp at all, so well did it blend into the scenery. This modest dwelling was home to his cousin Thomas Blanchard, his wife Bridgett and their two young sons aged ten and twelve.

Approaching the covered wharf, Valdore saw the two boys spreading shrimp to dry on the roof. Drying had always been a favorite Cajun way of preserving shrimp without the use of a refrigerator. Once dried, the shrimp could later be used in cooking or eaten as is. Having a special fondness for the delicacy himself, Valdore made a mental note to get some before he left. When the boys noticed him entering the small bay they called to their father, who was busy hanging rabbit and squirrel meat in the smoke house. Valdore waved to the boys, and they quickly climbed down from the wharf roof on simple makeshift ladders.

At the same time, the screen door of the camp opened and out walked the boys' mother Bridgett. She couldn't be labeled as simply cute or attractive, for those were just words used to describe the average good-looking lady. Bridgett Blanchard was definitely a good cut above the average; she was stunningly beautiful. Her waist-length auburn hair fell in ringlets of seemingly endless spirals around her classic face and down her straight back. Her body, even after having borne two sons, was still girlish at the waist and all-woman everywhere else. Her intellect and standards were high and she fully expected her sons to meet those standards as well.

She recognized Valdore from her kitchen window and hurried out of the camp to greet him just as he eased his skiff next to their wharf. As one of the boys secured the bow line he had thrown him, Bridgett

waved and smiled a warm welcome. "Valdore, what a lovely surprise, I hope all is well with your family!"

Climbing out of his skiff, Valdore answered with a big smile, "Everything is fine at the house. I just come by to see my best cousins." Bridgett gave him a big hug and then the two boys shook his hand. "AWWW, boys!" screamed Valdore, holding his hand in mock pain. "That hurt! You boys learn to shake a hand like that from your dad?"

The boys laughed. They always looked forward to visits from their old cousin, whom they had grown up calling Uncle Valdore. The older boy spoke first, "Dad said I could get my very own set of traps for this winter and run my own line."

Bridgett coughed ever so slightly, but it was enough to get her first-born's attention. He quickly looked down and then back to Valdore as he continued, "That is, if I pass geography with at least a high B average."

"No way!" shouted the younger boy, with a laugh intended to goad his big brother.

"Bet I can too!" exclaimed the irritated older son.

"Boys, stop it now! Go play!" It was the voice of their father Thomas and all that was needed for them to immediately cease their banter. Without a backward glance they obeyed, running off behind the camp to enjoy this rare opportunity of freedom from chores and studies. "Hey, Cousin, long time no see," said Thomas as he extended his hand. Grabbing that hand, Valdore squeezed it as hard as he could. Because this young cousin was known to have a viselike grip, he was determined not to be caught giving a limp, token handshake. Thomas continued, "I hope nothing is wrong on the bayou."

"No, everything is good."

"You are going to stay with us awhile, aren't you?" Bridgett asked expectantly.

Valdore recognized the question as a sincere invitation, but knew his priorities for this trip. "No, can't stay long this time, Bridgett. I just stop by to say bonjour."

"Well, at least stay and have some lunch with us. Thomas caught a fat turtle this morning and I've made my special spicy soup."

Valdore grinned. "Boy, Bridgett, you sure know how to keep a man. If you just stop cookin' so good, you could get rid of this husband of yours."

He hadn't been able to resist that last little teasing bite at Thomas, who now jumped into the conversation with an air of mock arrogance. "Well, she can't cook it if I don't catch it. Now, come inside and let's talk."

"Okay, but first, I got something for you," answered Valdore as he knelt down on the wharf next to his boat. He then reached behind the passenger seat and pulled out a large bag of groceries, which he promptly handed to Bridgett. As always, she was moved by his kindness shown her tiny family. She and Thomas weren't destitute, but neither were they blessed with an over-abundance.

Also deeply touched, Thomas asked, "Cousin, why bring us something every time you come here?"

Without hesitation Valdore responded in like manner. "Well, Thomas, why every time I come here, you give me something?" Thomas nodded, but said nothing and then Valdore looked at Bridgett and smiled broadly. "I got you some sugar, coffee, flour, syrup, fresh file an a few other things. Oh, an there's a big bag of candy in there for the boys."

"Thank you so much. You're such a good man, Valdore. Now I better put this up," replied Bridgett as she quickly turned and walked toward the camp, discreetly brushing away the little tears that moistened her eyes. Though the boys hadn't heard Valdore mention what he brought, they remembered well what he always brought them before, so they came running when they saw their mother carrying the large sack. While one came to relieve her of the load, the other rushed up the steps to open the door. Knowing exactly what was on their minds, Bridgett thanked them for their help, but agreed to only one piece of candy before lunch.

Meanwhile, Valdore nonchalantly waited until they closed the door behind them before he motioned for Thomas to stay outside. "What's up?" asked the observant young Cajun, having immediately become aware of his cousin's obvious, caution.

Wishing he could have approached it even more matter-of-factly, Valdore still acted and spoke calmly so as not to draw any more suspicion about his mission. "Nothing much, Thomas, I just know you been fishing plenty lately, an I was just wondering if you saw some people I was looking for."

"Who?" asked Thomas.

Valdore couldn't look him in the eye, but glanced to the side as he replied, "Ludvick Rabeaux."

With genuine concern Thomas asked, "What do you want with him?"

"Believe me, I don't want nothing to do with him or his boys. I'm just wondering where he's at. I'm thinking that if I know the place he's at, then I can stay out of the way of that trouble!".

"Yes," agreed Thomas, who knew Ludvick as well as anyone could, though not because he had ever spoken to him or even come within speaking range of any Rabeaux. No, his knowledge of them came from personal experiences of missing crab traps and other things that tended to vanish whenever these thieves invaded the area. "I saw Ludvick and one of his boys about a month ago in Bay Merci. It was almost dark and I could barely see, but I know it was them."

Valdore rubbed his neck and thought for a second before responding as casually as possible. "That's fifteen miles south of here. Wonder where was he headed?"

"Northeast, or at least he took Bayou Tete in that direction."

"About a month ago?" queried Valdore.

"Yes, and his skiff was loaded down. With what, I can't say, but he had a heavy load."

"Thanks, Thomas. That helps me."

"Now, Cousin, you don't need to be fooling around with people like that," insisted Thomas, always hesitant to offer advice, but feeling compelled in this case.

Valdore was eager to end this topic of conversation since he now possessed the information he needed, and quickly replied, "Like I said before, I don't never plan on fooling around with them. Look, Thomas, you don't have to say too much to Bridgett bout this. I just don't want her to ax me too many things or worry for me."

"What we say between us stays between us, just like always." Thomas was equally ready to drop the discussion, though not thoroughly convinced that his cousin's questions about the Rabeaux were as innocent as he claimed.

At that very moment, almost as if to provide them both an easy way out, Bridgett called, "Hey, you two, I thought you were coming inside for lunch."

"On our way," answered Thomas as he led Valdore toward the camp. Then, just before they reached the steps, he drew close and said almost in a whisper, "If you need some help, just say so and you got it."

Valdore put his arm around his young cousin's neck and insisted, "Thanks, but you just take care of this family you got. I can take care for myself. Now, let me get inside an thank Bridgett for the offered lunch, but I just got to be on my way."

Both Bridgett and the boys were disappointed that he couldn't stay with them overnight or even for a meal, but they understood. Bridgett did prepare a big container of the turtle soup for him to take, and the boys gave him a generous portion of dried shrimp. Although the visit with Thomas and his family had lasted less than an hour, as his skiff left the tiny wharf Valdore promised he would stay longer next time.

"See you later, Cousin. Stay safe," called Thomas.

Cupping her hands around her mouth to be heard above the skiff's idling motor, Bridgett added, "Next time you come, I'll cook your favorite shrimp spaghetti!"

"That's a deal!" shouted Valdore as he brought the bow of the skiff around and waved good-bye, as did everyone on the wharf. He throttled up and his skiff moved quickly forward. As he headed for the narrow opening by which he first entered the small bay, he looked back one last time and waved a final good-bye. Just as he knew they would, Thomas and Bridgett, as well as the boys, were still waving from the wharf. And then he smiled because he knew they would remain there until he totally disappeared into that background of thick vegetation.

Valdore set out in a southward course, remembering a small shack the Rabeaux used many years ago. Though it was possible for them to still be there, the main problem was that Thomas caught sight of them

196

heading northeast in that loaded skiff a month before. Nevertheless, the shack on Bay Merci would serve as a good place to start looking.

Valdore traveled nonstop from his cousin's camp to Bay Merci and then onward to the small bayou where the Rabeaux shack was located. It was late afternoon and the sun was sinking in the western sky when he finally spotted the meager structure, but even from half a mile away he could tell it was vacant. After setting the throttle on his skiff to idle forward, he stood and scanned the area, seeing absolutely no sign of life nor any indication that Ludvick or his boys had recently been in the area. He headed straight for the Rabeaux wharf but kept his eyes searching in every direction.

He secured his skiff to the wharf and turned the engine off. The silence seemed almost unnatural, and he shivered involuntarily as he stood for a few seconds on the wharf just taking in his surroundings. Valdore had never before set foot on Rabeaux property or venture into Ludvick's habitat. Many times he passed near the area, but always felt it wise to avoid a den of thieves. He was not surprised by what he had found; the whole place was filthy. Corroding, smelly old crab traps were strewn everywhere, some still containing the crumbling bones of bait fish; empty beer, whiskey and wine bottles were so numerous on the ground surrounding the shack that it was impossible to walk any distance without stepping over or stumbling on one. And, as if that were not enough, garbage of every other imaginable description filled what little ground was left.

Shaking his head in amazement, Valdore walked to the front door and slowly turned the knob, not really surprised to find the door unlocked. In fact, as it creaked open on its two hinges, he smiled as he realized that the Rabeaux men actually had no need for locked doors because most everything they possessed had likely been stolen and could easily be re-stolen if necessary. The one-room shack was empty, completely stripped: The bunk beds in the corner held no mattresses and there were no chairs or table in the room. However, plenty of dirt and even more garbage filled the sagging wooden floor, and Valdore almost turned his head in sick disgust at the putrid odor that assaulted him. Something rested on the floor in an active state of rotting decomposition. He could see the back of what appeared to be a dead

197

dog; he could only wonder at the pitiful existence the unfortunate creature must have endured.

Valdore turned abruptly and walked out of the shack, closing the door just as he found it. As he headed back to his skiff, he was consumed in a horde of mosquitoes, a sure sign that darkness wasn't far. Definitely not wanting to tarry on cursed property after nightfall, he rushed aboard his skiff and hurriedly maneuvered it northward, away from the Rabeaux wharf. A few miles later, visibility now almost zero, Valdore turned off the bayou he had been following and slowly entered a narrow, shallow tranause. Here, with his skiff well concealed by thick vegetation, he would spend the night. Since time was of the essence, he quickly found a spot and tied up to a small overhanging branch. Then, not a minute too soon, he unpacked and set up his mosquito net which virtually covered his entire skiff. After turning on a low-watt light on the dash next to his control panel, Valdore pulled out his gas cooker and a small iron pot. As he poured the entire contents of Bridget's thick turtle soup into the iron pot and turned up the heat, he remembered with delight the last bowl of her soup he had eaten. Immediately the rich, spicy aroma filled the air and the hungry man uttered a thankful prayer for his meal. While he ate he was serenaded by the harsh, primitive music of the marsh as its indigenous creatures vocally came alive around him just as they did every night. In addition, a humming multitude of hungry mosquitoes assaulted the netting in vain attempts to bring misery to the elderly Cajun, but this old man felt only his exhausted body and ravenous appetite. At least the problem of how best to store left-over turtle soup was solved. In fact, within a few minutes nothing was left of that delicious soup but the bottom of his black pot. He sighed in deep satisfaction and leaned back quietly in his skiff as he recalled the events of the day. And though the day hadn't actually produced the Rabeaux as he had hoped, neither had he realistically expected Ludvick to be in such exposed areas as these southland marshes. North, he thought. Those Rabeaux are in the swamps to the north, better protection there, so they could stay out of sight forever. Then he smiled to himself, that is, if I wasn't the one looking for them!

True, finding the Rabeaux might take a while, but that was all right with Valdore; he was a patient man. Reaching into a brown paper bag next to his cooker, he pulled out a handful of dried shrimp and slowly popped one after another into his mouth. "This is the life, the best there is," he thought as he felt his old body relaxing in that unique way it always did when he found himself surrounded by the awesome sights and sounds of his beloved marshland. Such a lonely, dangerous place to most people, but to Valdore it felt like home, as much his home as that of any of the creatures whose native songs filled the dark night air.

CHAPTER 36

By mid-morning on Monday Derrick had decided to visit the Cameaux Shrimp Shed, especially since Pappy kept insisting that he get out and get some fresh air and maybe even pick up a pound of shrimp for cooking. That, of course, he knew was the real reason his grandfather insisted on his "getting some fresh air." With Pappy, as with most Cajuns, shrimp was a primary mainstay, and Derrick hoped his grandfather's hunger for it declared that the real Olidore Cameaux was truly back among them at last.

When Derrick pulled into the parking lot of the shrimp shed, he discovered that available spaces were at a premium. Pickup trucks with empty boat trailers were parked everywhere because both sport and commercial fisherman used these Cameaux docks to launch their boats. Finally finding a spot next to the main highway, he made his way to the central shed on the bayou's edge. As he approached, the odor of raw seafood was strong; though repulsive to some, Derrick barely noticed it.

Inside the shed things were bustling in order to accommodate all the outside activity. Shrimp boats were continually unloading their catches onto large dock-side conveyers which moved the shrimp into the shed to be weighed and sized. It was crucial to both the fishermen and the shed to get a fair count per pound, and that responsibility fell to Marco Doucet. Derrick watched as Marco, in the presence of a

201

fisherman, poured the shrimp onto a scale until it measured exactly one pound. Then both men would carefully count how many shrimp made up that weight. It was simple; the bigger the shrimp, the less it took to make a pound and the more money per pound the fisherman got for his catch. Nothing progressed further until both Marco and the fisherman agreed on the count and the price. The Cameaux Shrimp Shed had a reputation for both fairness and giving the best price, and Ben Cameaux saw to it personally.

Derrick began making his way toward the shed's main office to speak with Ben. He could see Ben at his desk, obviously writing checks to the fishermen. Choosing not to interrupt him just yet, Derrick decided to help around the shed, but before he could do anything, Marco caught his attention, motioning for Derrick to follow him. Marco headed toward the shed's main entrance facing the highway. Once outside they noticed long lines of still more fishermen in pickup trucks, some there to launch boats and others in place to retrieve them. Marco lit a cigarette, inhaled a deep drag of smoke and then exhaled slowly, savoring every moment. Derrick was still watching the activity at the boat launch when Marco suddenly tapped him on the arm and pointed toward the main highway. With excitement in his voice and smoke billowing from his nostrils and mouth, he exclaimed, "Here they come, Derrick!"

Quickly looking in the direction Marco was pointing, Derrick saw a police car leading a convoy of tractor-trailers. As the first truck passed, he read the logo printed in big red letters on its side:

"BIG JOE'S AMUSEMENTS"

PRESENTS

FUN AND ENTERTAINMENT FOR ALL!

RIDES, GAMES, CLOWNS, FOOD AND MUCH, MUCH, MORE

"That's the carnival rides for the Shrimp Festival," said Marco, as they watched the line of huge trucks pass, loudly blowing their horns

in front of the shrimp shed. Naturally, just as intended, the kids in the boats and pickup trucks pointed and waved at the truck drivers.

"Where are they going?" asked Derrick.

"This year the festival's right there on the church grounds."

"I thought the festival was always held later in the year."

"That's true, but I hear that this year the committee wanted to get the jump on all those other festivals around the parish," Marco explained with a grin. "An that's just right with me! Let the good times roll!"

Impressed by the number of trucks in the carnival convoy, Derrick suddenly remembered just how big an event the annual Shrimp Festival was to the area. "You know, Marco, I haven't been to one of these things in years. When I was a kid, though, I couldn't wait for it every year."

"Then, you just have to make this one. It's gonna be great! Best one yet, some say. Anyway, all I know is how excited the wife an kids are cause it's all they been talking about for weeks!"

"Well, sounds to me like dad just might be looking forward to it a little bit too."

Unapologetic for his enthusiasm, Marco laughed. "Man, you're right! I can't wait either! It starts this Friday, you know. The kids just love all those rides an games, an they eat all that cotton candy an candy apples till they puke. Then they just eat some more! Me an the wife, well, we go for two main tings. First, we get there early to eat. The women from the church do all the cooking an, man, you never saw no better jambalaya, seafood gumbo, chicken gumbo, etouffee, sauce piquante, po-boys of every kind, an the best bread an sweets that you ever did taste! Then, just when we feel good an full like two ole fat bullfrogs, we get out on that dance floor an stay there till our feets fall off! Course, that's not never till almost daybreak. Man, that's just the best! But you know all that. We'll see you there, won't we?"

Derrick knew that Marco spoke the truth, and he certainly had nothing against having a good time. He just didn't know when Valdore would come back with the information they needed about Ludvick. Since he couldn't explain this, he simply assured his friend, "Sounds

like a good time to me, and I know I'd enjoy it. I already have something planned for this weekend, but you just might see me there."

Marco stared at him with a puzzled look on his face. "Derrick, this is the Shrimp Festival! You have to be there!" He viewed his sacred Shrimp Festival on a par with the birth of a child, a wife's operation, or the opening day of duck season. "Man, you can't have no other plans. You just gotta be there!" But Derrick suspected there was an even more important event that he could not miss.

The parade of carnival trucks was followed by numerous RVs belonging to the carnival crew. As they stood there watching, they heard a familiar voice behind them. "I see the carnival made it here on time."

"Hey, Uncle Ben, I came by earlier to see you, but you were so busy I didn't want to bother you."

"You're never a bother, Derrick. Did you need to see me about something?"

"No, I just need some small shrimp for Pappy."

"I'll get it for you," offered Marco. "How much you want?"

"About a couple pounds, I guess. Thanks."

"Be right back," said Marco as he vanished into the shrimp shed.

Still watching the carnival procession as it moved down the road, and almost as if he were thinking aloud, Ben said, "I remember how you, Eric an Jon loved the Shrimp Festival. A great time of mischief, if I recall."

"Yes Sir, we did have more than our share of fun back then," answered Derrick, not really knowing what to say. For some reason, he was feeling very uncomfortable talking to Ben about the boys. He quickly changed the subject. "You have any idea when Valdore will get back?"

"Valdore will be back when he gets all the information we need. Just let him do what he's good at doin'. Then, if he gets us all what we need, the wait will be worth it. Besides, the more time that passes, maybe Ludvick will let his guard down just a little."

Derrick relaxed, realizing that Ben was right. In fact, his uncle was more like a father, and always had a soothing effect on him. "I know, but I just hate to wait. I feel in my gut that now's the time to act."

"I feel the same way, but a few days more won't hurt."

So engrossed were they in the gravity of their conversation that they were unaware of Marco's return until he interrupted them. "Here you go, Derrick. Tell Pappy that me an my wife say hello."

"I sure will, thanks Marco."

"I got him some 50-60 shrimp to the pound. That's what he usually likes to cook wit."

"Well, I guess I'd better get going or he'll call to see about his shrimp! See you later, Uncle Ben and Marco."

"Okay, tell Pappy I might come by later on, just in case he does happen to cook up a gumbo or a shrimp spaghetti," laughed Ben.

On his way back to the Jeep, Derrick spotted Valdore's truck parked near one of the launching sites. He hoped Pappy's old friend would stay safe.

CHAPTER 37

As soon as Derrick returned, he handed the shrimp to a smiling Pappy, who immediately started cooking his gumbo. Derrick retreated to his room to further inspect some of the maps he had selected at the hospital. Studying each map took a considerable amount of time. He scanned map after map, committing to memory even the slightest detail the musty old maps revealed. Deep in thought after an hour of study, he thought he heard a slight knock at the front door then a second knock, this one a little louder. "Okay, I'm coming!" he yelled, more than just a little irritated to have been interrupted.

When he got to the double French doors he pulled the curtain aside just enough to remain unseen, but to be able to see the visitor. There stood Olivia. And Derrick's heart began beating a little faster, an undeniable fact that didn't go unnoticed by him. He quickly opened the door and tried to act cool, but it didn't work. His boyish eagerness and the expression on his face clearly showed his excitement at seeing her.

"Now, you know you don't have to knock, Liv. Just come on in."

"Hi, Derrick, Pappy invited me to have supper with you two. I hope I'm not too early."

"No, you're right on time, come in, come in." He had been caught off-guard, and he was sure she had noticed. Pappy hadn't said a thing about her coming to dinner. As they entered the living room, he motioned

to the couch and invited her to sit down. Once settled and relaxed in trivial conversation, he realized he couldn't take his eyes off her.

"Pappy didn't tell you I was coming for supper, did he?"

Derrick smiled, "Well, no. He must have forgotten."

Then, as though he had been cued, Pappy hollered from the kitchen, "Hey, Derrick, I almost forget to say that I invited Olivia an the girls for supper."

They looked at each other and burst into laughter as Olivia said, "Well, I guess you know now."

"Where are the girls anyway? Aren't they coming?"

"No, they're at a sleep-over at the Terrebonnes. I dropped them off on my way here."

"You mean they're old enough for that sort of stuff already? Boy, they're growing up so fast."

"Don't remind me. For every birthday they have, I'm sure I must be having two or three."

"Nonsense, you're just a kid yourself," insisted Derrick.

Olivia smiled and rolled her eyes at him as she said, "Speaking of kids, why are all these maps scattered all over the coffee table?"

Grinning and then deliberately speaking loudly for Pappy's benefit, Derrick apologized. "Well, I'm sure you weren't supposed to see this mess, but, after all, someone did forget to mention you were coming. Here, let me clean it up. It'll only take a minute." As he hastened to scoop up the maps she suddenly realized that her eyes were glued to him and her thoughts were once again embarrassing her.

"Hey, Olivia, glad you made it," said Pappy, entering the living room with a mischievous smile.

Her face, she feared, surely revealed the look of a kid caught with her hand in the cookie jar, but she stood to give him a hug. "How are you doing, Pappy? Are you sure you're up to all this cooking and having company? Let me help you in the kitchen."

"No, I don't need no help in the kitchen, thanks just the same. You know there's not much of anything I like more better than cooking for my family. Where's the girls?"

"They're at a friend's house to spend the night. They really hated missing this, but they planned the sleep-over a while back. Both of them said to tell you and Derrick they love you."

"Well, I'll see them in a couple days," said a still smiling Pappy. "Now, you just sit back down an relax, an see if you can get that grandson of mine to loosen up." Then, pretending suddenly to notice Derrick and his efforts to clear the messy coffee table, he teased, "Son, you know, if you'd just keep the place clean, you won't never have to worry about company, expected or otherwise."

Derrick threw his hands into the air in mock surrender, then with a perplexed look on his face asked, "Is that burnt gumbo I smell?"

"Better not be!" declared Pappy as he turned quickly and disappeared back down the hallway.

Olivia and Derrick laughed softly as she finally sat once more on the sofa. She smiled to herself, realizing thankfully that no one had access to her earlier thoughts, which even now rushed upon her again, much to her dismay.

Wondering about her obvious momentary introspection, Derrick paused a moment before asking, "Would you like something to drink?"

"Oh, no thanks, I'm fine."

Without hesitation, he smiled. "Yes, you surely are!"

She could feel her face flush again. Surely he couldn't have known what she was thinking, but what did he mean? "Derrick Cameaux, are you making fun of me?"

"No, my lady, I meant every word I said. You are a beautiful woman, indeed!"

"Well thanks," she said before adding almost in a whisper, "I just don't feel very pretty lately."

Gently moving closer, he placed his hand over hers and looked straight into her beautiful brown eyes. "You're the most beautiful woman I've ever known, Liv."

She blushed again, this time even more than before, especially as she gazed into his eyes and sensed his sincerity. Before either spoke another word, they were interrupted by a knock at the door. Neither moved, however, because their eyes were communicating what no

209

words could. In fact, it was only with the insistent second and third knocks that Derrick finally rose to his feet and slowly let her hand slip away from his. She couldn't see the man at the door, but she heard the rather strange exchange as Derrick declared, "We don't want anything you're selling."

The man at the door said, "Well, Mister, could you at least spare a dime to buy me a bowl of soup?"

Derrick quickly stepped back to allow Scott Armont entrance. They laughed at each other as they exchanged back slaps. Now turning back to Olivia, he presented his old friend. "Liv, you remember Scott Armont."

"Hi Scott, are you still doing Cajun music?"

Smiling, Derrick answered, "Well, now let's just say he's a first-class wanna-be Cajun singer who's still trying to do Cajun music."

"Now, Derrick, you know that Scott is the best on the bayou," interrupted Pappy as he entered the room to greet the young man who had grown up with Derrick and had spent so many nights in his home.

Extending his hand, Scott replied, "I hope you're doing well, Mr. Cameaux."

"Thanks, I'm better, Scott. Would you like to join us for some supper?"

"I'd love to, but my wife is cooking up a casserole or something like that. I can't stay long. I just stopped by to invite everyone to the fais-dodo dance at the Shrimp Festival this Friday night. Me and my band are gonna be playing all night." Then turning to Derrick he asked, "Can you make it, old friend?"

He was just about to decline when Pappy jumped ahead of him, saying, "Sure, he can make it. He's done been hanging around here looking after me long enough. In fact, Olivia, why don't you just go with him to the fais-dodo?"

Olivia responded quickly, "Oh, I'd love to go, if that's all right with you, Derrick."

He was outnumbered and out-voted. Of course, he had the same problem as before: he knew that he'd enjoy the festivities, but he just couldn't say with certainty he would still be there on Friday. Thus, once again he responded cautiously, "I'm actually waiting for a call

210

that might put me out of town this weekend, but if it doesn't come and if Olivia doesn't mind escorting me, we'll be there."

"Great!" exclaimed Scott. "Now, let me get myself home or Pam will be trackin' me down. I'll tell her you'll be there. Nice to see you, Olivia, and I hope you're doin' better every day, Mr. Cameaux."

Derrick followed his old friend to the door and just as he opened it, Scott turned and whispered, "Man, she's a keeper! You'd better hang on to this one." Then in an even lower voice, he added, "By the way, I heard how you let Bonnie get away."

"She's just a good friend," was Derrick's only response as he gave Scott a friendly shove out the door.

Pappy excused himself to add the finishing touches to his gumbo while Derrick and Olivia sat back down on the sofa. Olivia said, "I think you got suckered into that one."

"Suckered, nothing!" insisted Derrick. "I'm looking forward to dancing the night away with you."

Olivia smiled, suddenly aware that she hadn't felt so content in a long, long time.

CHAPTER 38

Early Tuesday morning Valdore was up just before daybreak. Still needing the protection of his mosquito net, he made a small pot of coffee, lit a cigarette and sat back to wait for full daylight before resuming his search for Ludvick.

As the sun rose above the horizon, Valdore packed away the mosquito net, coffee pot and butane burner. Since he had already eaten all the turtle soup, he leaned over the side of his skiff and washed the pot, using only his big rough hands as ample scrubbing pads. Smiling to himself, he pulled a clean rag from his back pocket to dry the battered pot for storage until next time.

When it was light enough to see clearly, he started the skiff's engine and untied from the branch. This small tranause served as a perfect hiding place. As Valdore kept his slow search to the northeast for a short distance, following Bayou Tete, he recalled the grousing of other Cajuns about the times Ludvick and his boys stayed in an old abandoned camp along Lost Bay. Their complaints hadn't been so much that the Rabeaux were using the sagging camp; the problem was that when they moved into an area, they just took over everything. No crab traps were safe, and no fishing nets could be left unattended. Everyone knew the Rabeaux were thieves; but unless a man was willing to die in confronting them, he didn't complain directly to Ludvick or any other Rabeaux.

Valdore decided to explore the Lost Bay area, intending to carefully check every camp to be certain that none of his prey was living there now. With that in mind, he turned off Bayou Tete and followed a series of lesser bayous and bays. His meticulous, cautious nature ensured that he would progress in a slow, thorough, but not obvious search. Therefore, as a diversion he set a couple of crab traps on the fantail of his skiff just in case he unexpectedly ran across the Rabeaux. That way, it would at least look as if he were merely a fisherman in search of a good crabbing spot to set his traps.

As he traveled he passed a few people in small skiffs in some of the larger bays; some he recognized and others he was seeing for the first time, but still no sign of the Rabeaux. "If I could just know that they not even in this Lost Bay area, I wouldn't never waste my day!" he grumbled aloud. Yet he continued because he knew that was precisely the reason he was there: It was virtually impossible to know their exact location without searching each of the many possibilities, no matter how many days it took—wasted or otherwise. Besides, he had a workable plan and was determined to follow it through to the end. Valdore chastised himself: "So, just settle yourself, ole man, an keep your mine on the work."

By noon he was near Lost Bay; sensing growing hunger, he decided to eat before continuing his journey. Scanning the shoreline of the small bayou, he noticed that the low tide had provided the perfect setting for small marsh hens which now ran along the exposed mud on both sides of the bayou. What a delicious meal! he thought, but he knew he didn't have time to prepare such a succulent feast. Besides, the only way to get one of these birds would be to shoot it, and he simply wasn't willing to risk exposing his position, which he hoped was now near the Rabeaux. Disappointed but resigned to the wisdom and necessity of delayed gratification, his eyes nevertheless fastened on the birds. He slowed his skiff to a crawl and headed toward two marsh hens that had moved apart from the others and were fighting over a minnow. Suddenly the two almost flightless birds, sensing danger from Valdore's approaching skiff, raced inland and disappeared into the dense salt-water grass. "No need to be scared of this ole Cajun," he chuckled as he shifted his engine into neutral and

let the momentum carry his skiff to the bank of the bayou. Ten feet before the water's edge, the skiff ran aground with an awful grinding sound, like a car being driven too fast over a freshly graveled road, but this was welcome music to Valdore's ears.

He smiled as he opened a small wooden box next to his seat and removed an oyster knife and a pair of thick cotton gloves that he quickly donned as he set the knife to the side. Then, while his grounded skiff sat motionless in the shallow water of the bayou's edge, he leaned over the starboard side and plunged both arms into the water. His gloved hands carefully skimmed the muddy bottom until they encountered something sharp and hard. "Ah, that's it," he sighed as he gently grasped the rock-like objects and pulled them free of the muddy bottom. He rinsed them as he lifted them from the water and placed them in the empty bushel basket next to him in the skiff. Then, again and again, he plunged his arms into the now murky water until his collection was completed. The determination in gathering these tiny crustaceans could be matched only by the intensity of his opening the stubborn shells to savor the delicacies hidden within. Almost everyone has a favorite food, and for Valdore Gisclair, his was the beloved raw oyster. Even for most Cajuns, oysters can at times prove difficult to open, but Valdore surpassed typical; he used his oyster knife like a skilled surgeon.

"Let's see if you fat an salty today," he murmured. Setting the knife point exactly where it needed to be and applying just enough pressure at just the right moment, he expertly twisted the knife. The repeated familiar sound of the tell-tale "pop" signaled success. "Fat like I want you," he said. Once he had popped open the oyster, he slipped his knife further inside, deftly severing the slippery muscle from its once-protective shell. As always, he laid open a dozen oysters on the half shell before ever thinking of eating one and then peeled off his wet cotton gloves to air dry. Then again reaching down into the open wooden box that held so many of his necessities, he pulled out that special little bottle of his own homemade hot sauce and a small package of fresh crackers. He sprinkled the hot sauce liberally over every bared oyster, making sure to coat each one equally. Next, he picked up one cracker and held it high in his right hand while, with his

left hand, he chose the largest, plumpest oyster. With one quick motion he picked up the oyster shell and tilted it toward his open lips. The slippery treat slid across the old Cajun's taste buds to rest, albeit for just a short second, at the rear of his watering mouth. Just before chewing, however, he shoved the crisp cracker inside his mouth with the tender oyster, and only then did he begin to sink his teeth into the salty muscle. Valdore felt so blessed that he even closed his eyes and offered up a quick prayer of thanks for such a delicacy. "Hmm, boy, that's good. Tank you Lord." One at a time, he sucked the oysters from the remaining eleven half shells, performing the same selection ritual each time. When he had finished, he rubbed his lean, firm belly and murmured, "There's no better eatin', nowhere." He easily could have eaten another dozen, but decided to save the rest for another time. Just as his ancestors had enjoyed the marshlands of these bayous for the past two hundred years, so also did Valdore appreciate their bounty.

From the time that Valdore decided to eat until he had taken his push pole and shoved his skiff off the oyster bed, barely thirty minutes passed. He quickly restarted his engine and resumed his search for the Rabeaux. No sooner had he left the oyster bed than a marsh hen, perhaps the very one he frightened away earlier, emerged from the thick grass and ran to the water's edge in search of another minnow. When an uninvited second hen joined the first, another battle ensued. It was as though no man had ever intruded.

Meanwhile, as his skiff glided effortlessly in the tiny bayou, Valdore couldn't help wondering whether his efforts were really helping the Cameaux family. After all, if he did find Ludvick Rabeaux and his boys and the Cameaux family headed into the marsh to fight against them, he could be partly responsible for his friends' deaths. Valdore knew well the sometimes harsh realities of living in South Louisiana; in fact, it was these very conditions that had carved out a people of such a dramatically different breed—the Cajun. Perhaps it was merely the seclusion of the land or the annual threats of killer hurricanes that had driven these unique people to live life with a fervor unrivaled and unseen anywhere else in the world.

For sure, major hurricanes of the past and certainly those yet to come have always been and still remain a constant reminder of the

216

frailty of life on the bayou. In fact, at times death has seemed to strike more often, more quickly and even a bit more viciously in this South Louisiana homeland. Add to that a situation such as faced the Cameaux family—a blood oath having been taken by the Rabeaux against them—understanding each family's urgency and intensity of thoroughly living life becomes more comprehensible. The fun times and good days were unequaled in height and pure enjoyment; the bad days and sad times were heart-wrenching and the despair complete.

So, Valdore thought, that's just the way things played out in the times past an that's still the way of things now, an that's the way things gonna be as long as there's Cajuns in this marsh. He knew he couldn't change the minds or hearts of other men, and he knew better than to try. He also knew that all he could do was what he thought best with his own life, and at this time, that meant helping the Cameaux family.

Valdore entered Lost Bay from the north shoreline, quickly scanning the half dozen camps along the eastern shore and the three camps on the western shore for any sign of life. He saw no movement in the whole area, except for a small skiff trawling for shrimp in the south end of the bay. As he slowly made his way across this half-mile length of the bay, he could see that these camps had been long abandoned and were now in very poor condition, even to the extent of several roof collapses.

As Valdore approached the skiff trawling for shrimp, he recognized Ozeme Lazard, a young man in his late twenties, stocky in build, and not more than five and a half feet tall. His bright red hair, partially hidden under a faded Saints football cap, framed his heavily freckled, expressionless face. Though busy raising his trawl from the water, he looked up briefly, but neither smiled nor showed any sign of irritation as Valdore maneuvered his skiff to within twenty feet of his own. He simply continued his work, pulling the last of his heavy net from the water to reveal a surprisingly large catch of shrimp.

Valdore watched as the young man strained to lift the tail end of the net over the side of his skiff and then set the huge pouch squarely on the cleaning box just forward of his steering wheel. This one's a real Lazard, thought Valdore. Just like the rest of his family, they all

217

hard-working an honest, but not much for talking an carrying on. Glad that he could depend on Ozeme to get straight to the point, Valdore had waited patiently until the young man finished hauling his net aboard. Now, in his customary friendly manner, he greeted him, "Hello, Lazard. Look like the shrimp is good today."

Until then, Ozeme had not even acknowledged Valdore's presence; now he left his catch on the cleaning board and sat down on the starboard side facing him. By this time both skiffs were slowly moving forward in parallel formation. "Hello, Mr. Gisclair. Sure, the shrimp is plenty, but the size is small."

"Seems like Lost Bay's always had shrimp; my papa used to catch them here even when the other bays didn't have nothing in them." Ozeme looked at him, but said nothing in response, just as the older man had expected. "Well, I know that you an your family shrimp a lot in this area. Does anyone stay in any of those ole run-down camps around here?"

Ozeme answered, "No, not no one with any sense! Just Ludvick Rabeaux an his boys." His tone was especially harsh when he mentioned the Rabeaux.

Then, as casually as possible, Valdore continued. "I haven't seen that snake Ludvick in a long time. Have you seen him lately?"

Picking up on his description of Ludvick as a snake, Ozeme nodded in agreement because for years he detested the Rabeaux for harassing his family. However, neither he nor any of his family had ever confronted them to protect their nets and traps. Filled with contempt for the whole Rabeaux family, Ozeme answered, "No, I haven't seen them lately an if I don't never see them again, that's fine with me. They do sometime stay here at this time of the year, though. They usually around here everywhere just stealing an cheating an then telling the lie about it. I don't know where they at now, but I'm just glad I don't never see them in these six months!"

That's all Valdore wanted to hear. If the Lazard family, who virtually lived year-round in this part of the marsh, hadn't seen the Rabeaux in six months, then that could only mean that neither Ludvick nor his boys were in this area. Encouraged by this bit of information, but not wanting to arouse even the slightest curiosity concerning his

real purpose in the area, the old Cajun quickly changed the subject. "How's the family? Everybody is doing good?"

Everybody is doing good," answered Ozeme, as usual offering no information beyond the bare minimum.

Valdore knew that it was Ozeme's personal hatred for the Rabeaux that had uncharacteristically freed the young man's tongue to unwittingly reveal the information he needed. No more and no less, to be sure, but he was always thankful, even for small favors. "Well, it was good to see you again, Lazard. Tell the family I axed about them." Ozeme simply nodded and immediately went back to work on his catch, seemingly lost once more in his own little world as if he had never been interrupted.

Valdore smiled in deep satisfaction as he eased his skiff away and headed back north toward the small bayou which originally brought him to Lost Bay. As he once more entered that bayou, he felt certain now that Ludvick wasn't in the southland marshes. The Rabeaux in those north swamps for sure! he exclaimed aloud as he reflected on all he had learned. Thomas had seen Ludvick, fully packed, heading northward; now Ozeme had verified it by saying that he hadn't seen Ludvick in months. Actually, it was a rather brilliant idea for someone wanting to hide or even just to lay low this time of year, for the swamps provided perfect hiding places. No one would find the elusive Rabeaux in such thick swamps. Well, almost no one. Valdore was confident that he not only could, but would, find them.

Hence, like a hound hot on their trail, he now set his course northward. With renewed vigor he eagerly retraced his journey through the small bayou loaded with oysters and then back to Bayou Tete, the very bayou where his cousin Thomas had seen Ludvick traveling.

He was making good time when a prickly barb of a mosquito on his neck signaled the first sign of the approaching darkness. As he smashed the nuisance in the midst of its attack, he carefully scanned the north shore of Bayou Tete for a small inlet in which to spend the night. Immediately seeing many good choices, he instinctively selected one that would provide safe concealment and headed there for the night. Once Valdore secured the skiff, he hurriedly pulled out his

mosquito net and again began doing his best to secure the edges against those blasted blood-sucking insects, which were now out in full force as the sun dropped lower and lower in the western sky. If all went well, he mused as he worked, tomorrow he just might find the Rabeaux. Tonight, however, he had to be content to spend the night in these brackish waters. Come sunup, though, he would head into an entirely different world of the northern fresh-water swamps.

Hardly noticed by Valdore, daylight faded very quickly as the old Cajun was busy setting up his mosquito net. Suddenly, to his surprise, he sat in almost total darkness, barely able to discern his own possessions that seemed to take on dark, ominous shapes and cast odd, eerie shadows across his skiff. "Is this an omen of things to come?" he wondered as an involuntary shudder and a cold chill raked his spine. A somewhat religious man, he instinctively reached inside his shirt for the chain that always hung around his neck and pulled out his Saint Christopher medal. Clutching it securely, he fervently prayed the prescribed prayer addressed to the patron saint of mariners for protection and success, not only for himself, but also for the Cameaux family. Leaving the medal within easy reach just in case he needed it again, he wasted no time finding matches and his old lamp.

Once he set up his lamp and relaxed in his newly re-established sense of security, Valdore felt the rumble in his stomach and without hesitation opened the old wooden box next to him. He eagerly pulled out the sturdy pair of cotton gloves, his oyster knife, the hot sauce and another pack of crackers for the second time that day. Smiling, he reached into the bushel of oysters at his feet and hoped that the rest of his family would be eating as well as he tonight.

CHAPTER 39

"**G**et them damn pirogues turn ova, Mato! How many times I got to tell you, don't never leave no pirogue right-side-up over night! If it rains, you dumb Coonass, them damn pirogues gonna just fill with water an bus wide open!" yelled Ludvick, shaking his head and waving his arms in disgust as he cursed Mato. At the familiar abrasive tone of his grandfather's voice, the young man rushed to the water's edge and hurriedly turned the three pirogues bottom-side-up. The Rabeaux hid their two skiffs one mile south of this new camp because the water level closer in was much too shallow to maneuver all the way. Thus, without travel-worthy pirogues always ready for use, they could be endangered. It was just basic common sense, which actually required little more than simple projected thinking and planning ahead. That, of course, had never been Mato's strength; he relied primarily on brawn rather than brain power. Ludvick knew this well, but at least expected Mato to have become much more a creature of habit by now in tending to the pirogues. Their small campsite experienced a real flurry of activity in the last month as they worked tirelessly to transport load after load of provisions to this isolated area that they had carved out for themselves in the swamp. Ludvick had decided long ago to make his final stand against the Cameaux right here in the swamp.

They wasted no time in setting up this camp to meet their needs for as long as necessary. Not only were they determined that their larder be initially well-stocked, but they also intended to guarantee themselves a continuous food supply through the new smokehouse Ludvick built to cure game as they killed it. They also improved the small camp they had built years ago by fixing the leaking roof, strengthening the only door, and adding another thousand-gallon cistern for fresh water. In addition to the smokehouse, Ludvick also built a small shack measuring eight feet by eight feet with solid oak walls, dirt floor, and wooden roof. This tiny hut had no windows and only one heavy wooden door, but on each of its four interior walls hung a sturdy hook about five feet above the floor. This had been his favorite project because it had been designed especially for the sole purpose of being a holding pen for a special member of the Cameaux family.

Ludvick sent Mato on ahead to the camp to help Victor prepare their evening meal. Then with what little daylight remained, he walked to the water's edge and looked out across the wet expanse. As far as he could see, the cypress trees stood tall and silent; nothing moved and nothing made a sound. Ludvick relaxed as he felt a sense of confident pride welling up inside. He knew he had chosen the perfect hiding place for himself and his family, for only rarely did he travel here during winter and never ventured here in the summer. Like most Cajuns, his summers were reserved for shrimping in the southland marshes, and that's where they would normally have been this time of year. But these weren't normal times. Two days earlier he once again spoke with his accomplice, Pritch Labote, who told him that Pappy Cameaux was back home from the hospital. Ludvick expected his old enemy to make a quick recovery; nevertheless, he had used the extra time afforded him by Pappy's hospitalization to advance his plan for killing Derrick Cameaux. Now, however, he would wait no longer. The time to fight was at hand, and he looked forward to ridding himself of his enemies once and for all.

Standing now at the water's edge as he did this evening had become almost a ritualistic experience for this methodical Rabeaux as he watched and listened intently over the expanse of swamp for even

the slightest hint of danger. He was well aware that, thanks to him, the Cameaux family had to a great extent ceased to be a significant threat. Nevertheless, because he knew his old adversary only too well, he also knew that as long as he lived, he need be wary. "Can't never take no chance of getting careless," he reminded himself as he noticed for the first time that it had now grown dark and the night animals had begun roaming. Even now, it never ceased to amaze him how the swamp came alive each night with every imaginable sound.

Then right at that precise moment his reverie was broken when the door of the camp swung opened and Victor shouted, "Food's ready!"

Ludvick turned just in time to see his only surviving son quickly close the camp door, and his first thoughts were of his two older sons now dead at the hands of Cameaux. Yep, he thought, can't never get careless an can't never forget what they done to us an how we damn sure gonna make them pay real soon! In fact, as he now walked slowly toward the camp, he was feeling confident with the way his plan was already unfolding.

CHAPTER 40

Early Wednesday morning Valdore wasted little time in resuming his search for Ludvick. He set his speed at near full throttle as he continued north on Bayou Tete. Few people knew this area as he did.

As Valdore traveled northward the changes in scenery were quite pronounced, but he paid little attention to these familiar surroundings. Of more importance to him was the relief of having left behind the southern saltwater marshes with their endless stretches of salt grass and the multiplied hundreds of bayous, bays, and oyster beds. Too, as much as he missed taking part in this year's first shrimping session, he knew that the opening season would fully consume most shrimpers, thus giving few any reasons to travel these northern muggy fresh-water swamps.

Ahead of Valdore rose towering cypress trees, levees and small islands covered in thick willow, red maple and wax myrtle trees. Some tiny islands consisting of no more than a few square yards of mud grew nothing but wild roses, blackberry and palmetto under the thick canopy afforded by the giant cypresses. The deep, clear salt water gave way to the darker and much shallower fresh water. The terrain wasn't the only thing to change, though. In these northern swamps both marine and animal life was quite different as well. The saltwater speckled trout and red fish of the southern marshes could never have survived in these fresh-water swamps, which were home to large-

225

mouth bass, sack-a-lait, and choupique fish . Valdore had now also crossed the line that divided the saltwater shrimp, crabs, and oysters from the fresh-water world of crawfish, giant gators and deadly water moccasins. In fact, several huge alligators dove well ahead of him, sinking to the bottom to patiently wait as the noisy intruder passed.

Bayou Tete continued in a north to northeasterly direction, but Valdore turned west into a lesser bayou filled with water lilies and flanked on both sides by a low levee covered in vegetation. So thick were the lily pads that he had to slow down in order to safely plow through the water. Another four or five miles would take him close to other favorite old trapping sites in the Cameaux Swamp.

Lost in thought, Valdore remembered the last time he had seen the Rabeaux in this area years before. Luckily, he spotted them first and was able to conceal himself and his pirogue in a thicket before they could spot him. Then, from his vantage point he watched as Ludvick and his boys passed and turned north, disappearing into a small tranause. Immediately Valdore emerged from his hiding place and moved in the opposite direction to avoid being noticed. A few days later, however, he decided to return to that small tranause he'd seen the Rabeaux take and followed it to find out where they had gone. He followed the tranause to a dead-end, where he noticed under the low-hanging branches of a weeping willow tree solid evidence that Ludvick and the boys had been there and were likely to return. The large old willows drooping branches provided the perfect hiding place for their pirogues and skiffs, as shown by more than a few pieces of tying ropes hanging off some branches. That wasn't all he discovered that day. He also followed the well-worn trail across the low levee, which led to a shallow bayou. He followed the bayou a mile to the east and discovered the hidden Rabeaux campsite.

As he was now reflecting on all the events of that day five years ago, he knew well that his trespassing in Rabeaux territory could have cost his life. He was also fully aware that if not for that earlier chance encounter, he wouldn't have a clue as to the location of this campsite. Now, a confident Valdore suspected that Ludvick was once more hiding here. But there was only one way to be sure.

Valdore recognized his surroundings and carefully guided his skiff forward, straining to relocate that hidden tranause. He was having a very difficult time, because the same massive overhanging thickets of vines and underbrush that covered the bayou banks had also grown across all narrow tranause openings, making the whole area appear almost as one continuous, identical landscape. He mistakenly entered the wrong tranauses twice before finding the right one. Once he was on course, though, he set the bow of his skiff into the slight opening and steadily pushed forward his throttle. The dense, tangled vegetation resisted, but gradually parted to permit only enough access for him to inch his skiff through the thick vegetation, even as it once again swallowed the tranause opening behind him.

Then, because this tranause was barely deep enough to handle a skiff, his was soon scraping bottom as he moved forward. The propeller immediately started kicking up a soupy mix of water, mud-rotted vegetation and nauseous gases, which Valdore ignored in his determination to reach his destination. After inching almost a quarter mile up the tranause, the vegetation thinned considerably and he began noticing huge cypress trees dominating the scenery ahead. He also recognized that same willow tree to his left that had marked the end of the tranause and the tie-up spot for the Rabeaux skiffs. To his relief, it appeared that Ludvick had widened the very end of the tranause enough for a small skiff to be turned around. Now approaching cautiously to within fifty feet of the circular opening, Valdore looked intently, but could see no sign of pirogues or skiffs. It wasn't until he had entered the area shrouded in the overhanging branches of the willow that he discovered exactly what he had hoped to find. In fact, his skiff literally bumped into two others that were well hidden under the canopy of the willow tree. He quickly cut his engine and crawled forward to his skiff's bow to get a better view. He realized immediately that they were Rabeaux skiffs, one slightly larger than his own and the other about the same size.

Canvassing the thick surroundings, he wasn't surprised to see next to the willow tree the worn path used by the Rabeaux to drag their pirogues across the levee. As he sat there motionless in his skiff studying the path, he concluded from the dried boot imprints in the

mud that no more than two days had passed since anyone had walked on the path. To Valdore, that meant Ludvick often trekked outside his camp area, possibly to check on his skiffs or perhaps even on other more sinister missions. With that thought in mind, he felt the familiar feeling in his gut telling him it was time to go. Ludvick and his boys were in the swamp camp; that much was certain. He didn't need a face-to-face encounter. It was time to return home and deliver this information to the Cameaux. Quickly turning his skiff around, he started the engine and headed away from the Rabeaux skiffs.

Once out of the tranause, Valdore paused to mark the location of the opening so that he could tell Pappy exactly where to enter. How to do that without Ludvick's noticing presented a problem. As it turned out, though, he was relieved to discover the marker didn't have to be man-made. As his keen eyes hurriedly searched the area, he suddenly focused on something he hadn't previously noticed. Just to the right of the tranause opening stood a tall cedar tree. Most unlike this area to have that kinda tree in these swamps, thought Valdore. That's perfect for the marker!

Finally satisfied that he accomplished everything Pappy asked of him, Valdore headed back toward the security of the Cameaux Swamp not far away. Since he had to spend one more night in the area, he knew this was where he would find the best protection. Tomorrow he would report to Pappy, Ben and Derrick everything he knew about Ludvick's swamp camp.

CHAPTER 41

Olivia sat at her dressing table nervously fussing with her hair, denouncing it as "totally uncooperative." Never mind that she'd been enjoying it this way for the past year; this morning it simply wasn't suiting her.

Ooooo, she fumed, slamming her brush down hard, "it's just not right!" Then looking critically at her face in the mirror, she wondered aloud. Do I have on too much makeup, or do I need more blush? Just look at you, Olivia Cameaux, you should be ashamed. There you are, standing there like some kind of dazed teenager getting ready for her first date. Better calm down, girl, and get control of yourself. After all, it's just breakfast with Derrick.

Yeah, only breakfast with Derrick, that's the whole point! she argued back at herself. And now it's already almost seven o'clock! And he'll be here any minute, and I'm not ready!

Through her frustration Olivia could no longer deny the obvious: She knew perfectly well what was going on and it had nothing to do with being ready or not. Right or wrong, she was in love. What immediate relief she felt now that she admitted it to herself without feeling condemned! Actually, she had known for quite a while that she loved Derrick; she just couldn't allow herself to think about it seriously until she was absolutely sure that he felt the same about her. Well, now, she was sure. True, he hadn't actually spoken those three

229

magical words, but she knew in her heart he loved her. "After all," she whispered aloud, "a woman just knows these things!"

Suddenly no longer concerned about or even aware of the time, Olivia stared boldly at the accusing figure in the mirror and realized for the first time that her thinking about enjoying Derrick's company no longer made her feel guilty because of Eric. Besides, she reminded herself again, Eric always loved Derrick like a brother, and she knew Eric would approve of their being together. Pappy and even Ben had suggested on numerous occasions and in many different ways their support of a serious relationship between them. And, most importantly of all, the girls would have no objections.

"So, what is there to feel guilty about kid?" she demanded of the woman still challenging her from the mirror. "Not one thing!" she declared with newfound conviction. The sudden chiming of the doorbell brought her back to reality. Then, with a shrug of her shoulders and a quick "Oh well," she threw on her robe and hurried to open the front door. "Derrick, come in. I'm so sorry, but you caught me right in the middle of getting dressed. Please have a seat."

Derrick laughed and raised his right hand in understanding, "I'm early, Liv, and in no rush at all. Take all the time you need. After all, I guess seven o'clock is pretty early to invite a lady to breakfast."

She only smiled over her shoulder as she said, "I'll be right back," and walked quickly back to her dressing area.

The expression on Derrick's face when she re-entered the room told Olivia that, indeed, she really was every bit as sexy as she secretly hoped. As he stood up, he grabbed her hand and said, "Well, that didn't take long. Hope you're as hungry as I am."

"Starved!" she replied as he led her out the door.

Arriving at Lee's Restaurant and entering the wide double doors Derrick leaned close to Olivia and whispered, "You sure look pretty this morning, Liv."

A slight blush crossed her smiling face as she answered softly, "I just threw myself together. I hope I don't embarrass you."

Smiling in return, he assured her, "You can embarrass me like this any day."

As soon as they sat down, a young waitress hurried to their table. "Good morning, folks. What'll it be, the breakfast bar?"

Derrick and Olivia nodded and even before the young woman could inquire further, he was asking, "Liv, how about a cup of coffee?"

"Yes, please that's just what I need right now."

"Two cups coming right up; help yourselves to the breakfast bar," said the waitress as she left.

As soon as she was out of range, Derrick smiled at Olivia again and said with a wink, "Thanks for having breakfast with me this morning. I really do hope it wasn't too early. As you can tell, I'm not really used to making breakfast dates."

"Too early?" answered Olivia. "Oh, my, no, what could possibly make you think it might have been too early!" she exclaimed, rolling her eyes, giving both of them a good laugh.

Then, in a low, somewhat more serious voice, he said, "I know it's too early, but I just really wanted us to have some time together."

Sensing immediately that something wasn't quite right, Olivia asked, "Is anything wrong?"

Wrong? Oh yes, wrong indeed! thought Derrick, but he knew he couldn't tell her that soon he'd be tracking their common enemy Ludvick Rabeaux, whom she didn't even know existed. He could imagine her reaction if she knew that this Rabeaux family were the ones responsible for murdering Eric and Jon and that now they were after him. So, he put on his best poker face and lied. "No, of course not, Liv. Relax, nothing's wrong, I just enjoy being with you." Then changing the subject, he grinned, rose from the table and reached for her chair as he suggested, "Let's get some breakfast."

She didn't protest but instead smiled and nodded in agreement as she also stood. Olivia saw right through his attempt to ease her mind, and this was very unsettling.

A steaming pot of coffee was at their table when they returned, and both were more than ready for a good hot cup. Olivia smiled and said, "I want you to know that Toni and Teresa are really looking forward to the festival this weekend."

"Well, won't they come with us to the fais-dodo dance tomorrow night?" asked Derrick in surprise.

"No, they'll be staying with Mom and Dad till Saturday morning. I told them I'd pick them up about noon and then we'd spend the rest of the day riding rides and eating hot dogs, cotton candy, or whatever else they want," she answered, pausing only briefly before she continued. "The girls begged me to ask you if you'd come with us. That is, if you're not too busy or don't have something else planned."

Once again Derrick didn't quite know what to say since he had no idea when Valdore would get back or what his news would be. At the same time, he certainly didn't want to miss an opportunity for another outing with Olivia and the girls. Thus, hoping that he'd have plenty of time, he answered with a smile. "That sounds like a good time. You're sure I wouldn't be intruding?"

She declared emphatically and perhaps even somewhat impatiently, "Oh, Derrick, you do know how much those little girls love you! Surely you must realize by now that both they and I always love to have your company!"

"Thanks, Liv, I really appreciate you saying that, and I'm looking forward to being with all you Cameaux girls again. Now, what about this breakfast—we can't let it get cold!" Then he picked up his knife and fork and added with a wink, "Dig in, Ma'am. Dig in!"

Olivia warmed his heart and he couldn't help reflecting on her words about how much her girls loved him. He felt Olivia's love for him as well, and he knew how simple and natural it would be to just tell her right now how very much he loved her. In fact, he desperately wanted her to know she was the most important part of his life and that he longed to spend the rest of his days with her. He was well aware that all he had to do would be to reach across the small table and take her hand in his and then just say those special words he'd never before said to her or to anyone else. It would all be so easy. He silently chastised himself. *You can't tell her how much you love her. You can't promise anything you might not even be here to prove in person! After all, what do you have to offer? Absolutely nothing! Not before this family business with the Rabeaux has been settled.* Then, with that

awful, but undeniable reality echoing through his mind and heart, he winced involuntarily.

To his relief, she seemed oblivious to his distress and certainly had no idea of the task that lay ahead.

However, Olivia was not unaware of his subtle mood swings and subsequent lapses into brief periods of reticence. Her woman's intuition warned her that now was not the time for an interrogation.

During their remaining time in the cafe, Derrick finally relaxed and soon they were once more laughing, talking and enjoying each other's company. When he eventually noticed that the waitresses were removing the breakfast food to prepare for the lunch crowd, he whispered, "We'd better get out of here, or we'll have to eat again."

"Oh my, I didn't realize we'd been here so long!" she exclaimed as they got up to leave. She excused herself to go to the ladies' room, and Derrick headed toward the cashier. Just as he was about to pay, in walked Ben through the nearby entrance. He didn't approach, but simply stood waiting close to the door. His curiosity and concern naturally aroused, Derrick quickly paid his bill and hurried over to Ben. "Morning, Uncle Ben. What's up?"

Unable to completely hide a trace of excitement, Ben answered just above a whisper. "Valdore's back. He's on his way to Pappy's house now, so I came to get you for the meeting."

Just then Olivia walked out of the ladies' room and, as always, was very happy to see Ben. She was all smiles as she asked, "Ben, how are you?"

"Oh, I'm doing good, Honey. The girls still up the bayou?"

"Yes, but they'll be back Saturday for the festival."

"Good, I'll see them when they get back. Tell them their Grandpa's been missing them!"

Then quickly turning his attention to Derrick as they left the restaurant together, Ben casually said, "See ya in a little bit." However, to avoid arousing concern or even the slightest hint of rudeness since he had mentioned seeing only Derrick, he added with a special smile just for Olivia, "How about you two coming over for some supper tonight bout seven o'clock?"

233

"Hmmm, that sounds good to me," she smiled and nodded expectantly at Derrick.

"Thanks, we'll be there, Uncle Ben," answered Derrick.

"Good! See you two then," said Ben, walking toward his truck.

Then came the question Derrick had been dreading. "What did Ben want?"

"Oh, he just stopped by to tell me about a meeting at Pappy's house. Said they wanted me to be there too. That's all."

With her intuition aroused, Olivia asked, "A meeting about what?"

The walk from the restaurant to his vehicle seemed endless as Derrick searched for a way to answer her questions as cautiously as possible. "Just a meeting with Mr. Valdore Gisclair who's been looking over some marsh areas for Uncle Ben and Pappy. He thinks he might have found exactly what they've been looking for. Anyway, they want me there, so I feel like I ought to go. You know how it is with family, and I'm really glad they're including me," answered Derrick, hoping that this plausible explanation would prevent further questions.

As they entered the Jeep Olivia said, "Oh, I hope you do take an active role in the family business, Derrick."

As he backed out of the parking lot, Derrick continued, "I'm seriously thinking about it, getting involved in the family business, that is. Both Uncle Ben and Pappy want me to start running the shrimp shed and some other things related to the family."

"That would be great," said Olivia with a big smile of encouragement. "And now I guess you'd better get me home so you can get to your meeting."

Derrick, thankful that Olivia had not pursued questioning him and relieved that she was unaware of the events unfolding before her, knew that had she known what he and the others were planning, she would have tried to stop it. He also realized, though, that the things she didn't know now, she would soon enough find out. "Perhaps even sooner than later," he reminded himself.

On the drive back to Pappy's house, Derrick reflected on the many months since the deaths of Eric and Jon. He burned with an even more intense anger deep within his soul toward the Rabeaux family. Now

his only consolation was this final opportunity to avenge his own family. Could he do it? He had full confidence in his abilities and skills; he was physically tough and mentally sharp. Perhaps most necessary of all, he was willing and eager; he would hunt the Rabeaux non-stop until they paid for their transgressions. No matter what else, this was a vow that could never be broken, for now it was all left up to him. There was no one else.

CHAPTER 42

As Derrick approached Pappy's house, he recognized Ben's pickup and an older truck that he knew belonged to Valdore. Entering the living room, he was really not surprised that it was empty because he knew exactly where they would be. Following the sound of voices, he found Pappy, Ben, and Valdore sitting around the breakfast table drinking coffee. With a wave of greeting, his grandfather immediately rose and headed toward the coffee pot to pour him a cup of the steaming hot brew while he and Valdore exchanged a strong handshake.

"Mr. Valdore, I'm really glad to see you safe."

"Nothing to it, Derrick, matter of fact, the biggest fight I got into was wit dose damn mosquitoes."

Derrick sat down next to Ben while Pappy set a cup of strong black coffee before him. The old Cajun then refilled the cups of the other men, as well as his own for the third time. Eager to get started, Ben said, "Derrick, we have waited for you to get here before Valdore fills us in on his trip. Before he starts, let me say that he did fine Ludvick's camp."

"That's right. I found Ludvick an all his boys in the swamps," declared Valdore with great satisfaction.

"Isn't that unusual for him this time of the year?" asked Derrick.

By that time Pappy had put the coffee pot back on the stove over a low setting, and it was he who answered Derrick's question as he joined the men at the table. "It is, but Ludvick will do the unusual. You got to always keep that in mine. To beat the Rabeaux, you have to think like the Rabeaux."

Derrick, of course, knew Pappy's answer was born of experience and needed no explanation. Turning to Valdore, he asked, "Mr. Valdore, I've got maps. Do you think you can locate the Rabeaux camp on one?"

"I think so, Derrick. Ludvick's camp sits east-northeast of the Cameaux Swamp, maybe about five miles away. An on the right map, I can show you exactly where it is," answered Valdore.

Derrick disappeared down the hallway and into his room as Pappy and Ben cleared the table of all the coffee cups. Pulling out all the maps he had been studying, he wasted no time selecting several relevant to the area Valdore had mentioned. Quickly returning to the kitchen, he unfolded one of the latest state maps depicting the area from the Cameaux Swamp eastward.

Valdore immediately leaned over the map, studying it intensely as the other men sat quietly nearby, their eyes also riveted on the map. Pappy watched as patiently as possible while his old friend took his time to carefully trace with his fingers the many bayous and bays he had passed on his way to finding the exact spot of the Rabeaux camp. Finally, never looking up, Valdore firmly set his finger squarely on the map and announced, "Right there; that's the location of Ludvick's camp."

Derrick immediately handed the older Cajun a pencil and Valdore marked the spot with an X but frowned and continued looking hard at the map. With the pencil in his right hand, Valdore tapped the end of it on the map and said in a worried tone, "Where I got this mark is the site of the Rabeaux camp, but this map don't show none of the smaller bayous an tranauses I need to show you. Fact is, the location of that Rabeaux camp is on some ole bayou that I don't even know the name of. But I do know you can't use no skiff of any size in it because it's too shallow an full of them cypress knees!"

Derrick needed only a moment to refresh his memory before unfolding another map in front of the now clearly agitated Valdore. This one featured the same area, but was a map more than seventy-five years old.

As Valdore looked at it, he relaxed and said with a smile, "Now, this is the more detailed map. Yeah, on this one I think I can see just what I have to show you."

Once again the old Cajun began slowly retracing his journey while the Cameaux continued their silent waiting and watching. That is, Ben and Derrick waited and watched; Pappy appeared strangely detached and even lost in some deep thought or memory known only to him. "There it is!" Valdore exclaimed a second time as he pointed out an old bayou on the map. "The Rabeaux camp is on this ole bayou right here. I don't never remember nobody ever talking about this ole bayou, an I didn't even know it was there until a few years back when I happen to see the Rabeaux when I was in that area trapping an follow them down that bayou to their camp."

When Pappy saw the bayou Valdore was pointing to and talking about, he nodded his head and calmly added, "That's the one I thought you was talking about. Bayou Bernard, the name of that bayou is Bayou Bernard."

"Bayou Bernard," repeated Valdore, now deep in thought. Then he suddenly recognized the name. "Pappy, is that the swamp the Bernard family first settled?"

Pappy nodded. "That's it. Many, many years ago the Bernard family first set foot there. They even lived there for a time, an that's why it's called Bayou Bernard. But, then before I was born, they moved to Golden Meadow. Not many people know the history behind that bayou since it's so hard to get to."

Ben asked, "Well, Valdore, how did you get to this Rabeaux camp?"

Looking back at the map and with pencil still in hand, Valdore began tracing directly on the map the exact route he had followed, starting from Bayou Tete. "I turn off Bayou Tete on this small bayou right here."

Derrick watched every move Valdore made with the pencil and listened intently to all the old Cajun had to say. He also recognized the

area Valdore was pinpointing because he and Eric had actually explored it several times when they were just kids. "This small bayou, doesn't it flow back into Bayou Tete?"

Surprised that the younger man knew so much about such an obscure waterway, Valdore answered, "That's correct an it's got plenty of twist an turns on the way. I can't begin to tell you how many of those tranauses cut through the levees on both sides of this bayou. But, if you do stay in the main body of water an don't never turn off none, you will finally get back to Bayou Tete."

Though never wandering that far east of the Cameaux Swamp, Derrick was confident he wouldn't have any trouble following Valdore's directions.

Then almost as if in response to some unheard request, there was a brief pause while each man studied the map carefully. In a moment, Valdore resumed his account. "Now, I want everyone to pay close attention. There's this narrow tranause that cuts through the levee of this small bayou." He immediately pointed to the small bayou's location on the map while he spoke and then marked it with the pencil before continuing. "Even on this ole map, I don't see that tranause I'm talking about, so maybe that means Ludvick just cut this himself. I don't know, but look right here," said Valdore as he pointed to the Cameaux Swamp. "About five miles up this bayou, east of the Cameaux Swamp, I saw a cedar tree."

To eliminate any confusion, he looked directly at the men as he repeated, "Now, I said a cedar tree, not a cypress tree, okay?" After receiving a nod from each of them, he turned his eyes back to the map. "I looked hard, an as far as I can tell, this is the only cedar tree in that whole bayou. An that tranause you want is just to the left of this cedar tree. Follow that tranause to the dead-end an then cross the levee with a pirogue. Once over that levee, the ole bayou to the camp is only a hundred feet away. Go east on this bayou an you fine the Rabeaux camp just a mile, maybe a little more."

Although Valdore gave further detailed instructions, Derrick had already formulated his plan. Later, he and Ben would work out a strategy. Finally, at the end of the meeting, Valdore looked each one of

the Cameaux men squarely in the eye as he reminded them of what they all already knew so well.

"Ludvick Rabeaux don't have no conscience. That devil will sacrifice his own family an even his own life to kill you. He knows the swamp an how to use it to his advantage. I ax you, as a friend, to turn over all this that I'm giving you to the sheriff. Let him deal with Ludvick."

The Cameaux men simply nodded and continued sitting in silence for a few seconds, with no sign of emotion. Their loyal friend was expressing his genuine concern and friendship toward the family, and everyone knew it. They also knew that all he said was true and made good sense; nevertheless, his plea was impossible. Valdore expected the reply he got and was not surprised by it.

Derrick answered for the family, "We must and will take care of our own problem with the Rabeaux. No one else need die." His words were direct and Valdore understood them well.

All four men stood and Pappy took a step toward Valdore, extending his hand in appreciative friendship. When his old friend's firm handshake met his with equal force, Pappy's voice almost broke as he spoke with genuine sincerity. "You are my friend an a friend to this family. You done what I axed of you an I won't never forget this day."

As he heard those words, Valdore nodded his acceptance and immediately left Pappy's house. He never asked for any payment; nor was any ever offered. Both men knew without speaking the words that Valdore would never tell a soul about the Cameaux-Rabeaux blood feud.

241

CHAPTER 43

Derrick and Ben left Pappy's house a few minutes after Valdore. They had work to do. First they traveled to the Cameaux docks, where they decided to use the *Miss Teresa* as their skiff for transporting them into the swamp. Derrick made certain that the fuel tanks were topped off while Ben filled two five-gallon plastic containers with fresh water and set them into the bow of the skiff. Then he turned to Derrick. "You know, we need to make a quick list of supplies we'll need."

"Uncle Ben, we'd better travel as light as possible, don't you think?"

"That's for sure. Only the bare needs!"

Then, with all the increased adrenaline flowing, Ben's heart raced a little faster. Immediately noticing his pale face, Derrick asked, "Uncle Ben, you all right?"

"Yeah, It's jus. . . " his voice trailed off. He looked down because he couldn't continue. He wasn't having another heart attack; he was simply overcome with grief. Tears began to well up in his eyes.

Derrick understood. "Is it Eric and Jon?"

Ben nodded. "Yeah, an your mama an papa."

"We'll get them, Uncle Ben. I promise you, we'll get every last one of the Rabeaux! We're almost there!"

243

With renewed hope and faith in his nephew to fulfill his promise, Ben pulled himself together enough to speak. "Derrick, I might not be much help to you on this trip. I'll be the first to admit that, 'cause we both know I'm not feeling good. But, with my last breath, I got to fight these dogs!"

"Uncle Ben, I don't know what I'd do without your help. We're a team, and I can't think of anyone I'd rather have with me." It was true that he really did want to ease Ben's mind, but not all his words were meant solely for the elder Cameaux's comfort. Derrick was aware of the vast amount of knowledge this man would bring with them into the swamps, and he knew he needed all the help he could get.

"Thanks. That really means a lot to me," said Ben, pleased to be wanted and needed.

"Okay, so now let's see what all we'll need to carry with us. We'll obviously have to load our pirogues, push poles and paddles. What about food?"

"Well, we gotta have food for at least two or three days. An if everything goes like I think it will, that'll be enough."

"Good. So that's settled. When do you think we should leave? Tomorrow morning?"

Ben hesitated for a moment. "We'll talk to Pappy about making a plan of attack. An if Ludvick feels safe in his hide-out, then he won't never be expecting us to show up at all. So we have a little time. Let's see, today is Thursday, let's leave Sunday."

"Sounds good to me," said Derrick, relieved that he would not have to lie to Olivia about why he wouldn't be able to take her to the festival on Saturday.

"Okay, tomorrow we can finish loading the skiff. Oh, an don't forget supper tonight. I'll pick up Pappy if you'll bring Olivia."

"OK, Uncle Ben. I'm looking forward to it, and I know Olivia's excited about us getting together too." Then he added with a smile, "Well, it looks like we're about finished here. So, why don't you head on home and start cooking?"

"You don't have to tell me again," said Ben as he climbed out of the skiff.

By the time his uncle left the parking lot, Derrick secured the extra fuel tanks, but he was not finished yet. Just as he always did before any trip, he hooked the fuel line to the engine and cranked it. Relieved that the engine started right away, he let it run while he checked the supply boxes that always stayed on board. These contained all the necessities: life vests, extra rope, a small battery-operated radio, a flare gun and numerous other odds and ends. Only when he was fully satisfied with his inspection did he turn off the skiff's engine and remove the fuel line. And then, even after he climbed out of the skiff, he stood on the wharf for a final once-over scrutiny. The *Miss Teresa* was ready; in fact, the only things missing were their food, personal gear, and the pirogues, which they would load tomorrow. It was now early evening when Derrick finally left the Cameaux docks but before he drove to Pappy's house, he had one more stop to make at Bayou Hardware for some last-minute supplies

CHAPTER 44

A stickler about promptness, Derrick rushed home to shower and dress in double time so that he could arrive at Olivia's house early. To his surprise, she was already dressed and actually had been waiting for him when she answered the door. Immediately recognizing that look on his face, she smiled and said in mock defense, "Well, I'm usually on time when I don't have to get up with the chickens."

Breaking out in laughter, Derrick insisted, "Oh, Liv, I knew you'd be ready. Really, I had no doubt at all."

"Right, well, since you're early, come on in and have a cup of coffee." She had made the strong brew only a few minutes before he arrived, just in case he was early again. As they sat on the living room sofa with their coffee, she asked, "How'd the meeting go?"

"It went fine. Oh, you know, just some boring stuff." Then, since he knew he couldn't discuss details with her, he said, "Liv, you sure have a fine home here."

"Thanks, we always enjoyed it. I guess it would have been hard to move out."

He knew that she was referring to the new house that she and Eric had intended to build. "Might as well talk about it now," he thought. "I suppose you could still build your new house as planned. I'm sure the girls could use the extra room now that they're growing up."

Olivia took a sip of coffee before answering quietly. "Actually, I think it would be hard for me to build a new house now. Maybe I'll just add a room or two to this one."

"Sure, I understand. Besides, adding a few rooms would give you plenty of space and, like I said, you've got a fine home in this one." Then hoping to dispel that unwelcome melancholy mood, he changed the subject. "Hey, guess who I met today?"

"I can't imagine anyone you haven't met in this town," answered Olivia.

"Would you believe Julie Brasseaux?"

"Is that right? Isn't she pretty?"

"Very pretty, and I think she and Jon would have made one good-looking couple."

"I agree. I hope she's getting her life back in order. She took Jon's loss very hard, Derrick. Maybe we could get to know her better. Somehow, it seems only natural since she and Jon were so special to each other."

"I thought the same thing," he answered, taking another sip of coffee. "And, you know, she seems to be adjusting almost as well as could be expected. She even told me she was dating some, and that's a good sign."

Nodding in agreement, Olivia then began laughing and ever so lightly touched Derrick on the left arm as she said, "I remember the first time Jon even mentioned her to us. We were all having supper at Pappy's and were so surprised to hear him volunteer any information at all about someone he was dating. Of course, we still couldn't tell anything for sure about the status of their relationship. You know how Jon was about women, but, this night something seemed different. He almost seemed shy and self-conscious. He didn't quite know what or how to say it, but finally just mumbled something about meeting a sweet girl." Both Olivia and Derrick were now laughing at this simple story. Ordinarily it wouldn't have been funny, except that each of them could picture the ever confident, world-conquering Jon Cameaux's squirming at the mere possibility that any woman could ever harness him.

In fact, it was so comical that somehow during the laughter, Derrick and Olivia ended up holding hands as she continued. "If Jon hadn't always made such a big deal in the past about staying single and never getting serious with a woman, it wouldn't have been nearly so amusing to watch him fidget and stutter as he told us about her. Derrick, it was hilarious. I just wish you could have witnessed for yourself." They both laughed harder than they had in a long time. Olivia was having a hard time even finishing the story. Finally catching her breath, she continued with as straight a face as possible. "Eric and I didn't let him off the hook, though. We made him tell us all about her, how they met, and how long they'd been dating. I think he actually got a little upset with us for that, but it was still worth it."

Regaining his composure, Derrick added, "I just wish I could've been there to help ya'll rub it in. No one deserved it more than Jon!"

"Except maybe you," suggested Olivia under her breath, but he wasn't hearing a word she'd said. Fact is, at that very moment neither was really much aware of anything but each other after his leg had touched hers. She blushed as a tingling sensation reverberated throughout her body, but she was powerless to stop her natural response to his touch.

He too felt the effects of their unexpected contact as deeply as she since he also seemed unable to move away. Each was looking longingly at the other. So close were they now that Derrick could hear her breathe. Furthermore, as she stared deeply into his intense brown eyes, neither felt anything but the powerful force of love that held them captive. And, in that irresistible gentle touch of his lips upon hers, he knew he had never before experienced real love, nor had he ever dreamed that it could be so possessing and controlling.

As their lips melded, both Derrick and Olivia relaxed and slipped into an almost semi-conscious state of bliss, from which they had no strength or resolve to emerge. His touch sent shivers up and down her neck and back, and her kiss brought him to the precipice of internal melt-down. How could they possibly restrain or control the passionate demands of this long-denied love, and that's what it was – real love, of which most people only dream. How they made it from the living room to her bedroom neither would remember. A trail of clothing

249

revealed their strong passion for the inevitable. Leading him by the hand, Olivia stopped at the foot of her bed. Turning slowly to face Derrick the two of them came together, two warm bodies in a tight embrace falling to the bed as one. Their gasps and moans of pleasure grew louder as he took charge and loved her to that blissful place of fulfillment. It took only a matter of minutes till the final climactic push. It had provided an all-too-fleeting glimpse into the awesome love that would bind them forever and from which neither could nor would retreat. Furthermore, their passion left them both wishing they'd never been invited to tonight's family dinner!

Alas, is there no more demanding taskmaster than the ticking of a clock which surely deprives us of precious moments and offers no promise of lost opportunity restored. . . .

CHAPTER 45

Ben Cameaux's choke spaghetti was famous from Thibodaux to Grand Isle. In fact, it was the envy of many a Cajun woman who wished she could cook half as tasty a meal. Pappy was recognized as master of the gumbo; Derrick, on the other hand, wasn't quite the chef his grandfather and uncle were. Having lived alone most of his adult life, he had usually found it much more convenient to stop for burgers rather than go through the trouble of cooking a gourmet meal– or any other kind, for that matter. Perhaps the main difference among the three men was that Ben and Pappy considered cooking a serious part of everyday life, whereas Derrick regarded it as an interruption in his busy schedule.

Olivia and Derrick arrived at Ben's house a little late, but not late enough for anyone to mention—to notice, perhaps, but not to mention. Considering the circumstances, however, it's surprising they weren't much later and emotionally flustered. As composed as always, though, Olivia helped Ben set the kitchen table while Pappy, especially careful not to be overheard, barely spoke above a whisper. "Son, Ben says that you fueled up the skiff?"

"That and checked out the engine and equipment," answered Derrick.

"Good, an you'll finish loading up tomorrow?" continued Pappy.

"Yes Sir, we'll load our personal gear, the food and a pirogue.

251

"Which one you plan to take?"

Without hesitation Derrick answered, "The smaller green one."

Nodding his approval, Pappy said, "That's the one I would use, too. You need to go quick through the swamp, an that small one's the best for that. Now, what about the weapons?

"Knife, hand gun and, of course, my shotgun, all ready." Derrick assured his grandfather.

"Good, make sure you don't never carry too much supplies, Derrick. Remember to hit them first an hard, an make it count!" Pappy had placed the emphasis on "make it count."

Unfortunately, neither man had seen Olivia walking toward them until she had spoken. "Make what count, Pappy?"

Not missing a beat and showing no sign of surprise, Pappy answered nonchalantly, "I was just telling Derrick to make sure that all the shots in life count."

"Well, sounds like good advice. Uncle Ben says supper's ready, so you two come on."

"I'm starved," said Derrick rubbing his hands together.

Deliberately avoiding Derrick's sparkling eyes for fear she'd never stifle the giggle she was struggling so hard to control, Olivia turned abruptly and led the two men to the supper table.

Ben was pleased with the taste of his choke spaghetti and the special oyster salad with his own homemade dressing. Nevertheless, as if that famous piping hot spaghetti and fresh cap French bread were not enough, Ben also served a delicious sweet potato casserole and fresh fried crab claws. Then, topping off this feast, he offered a choice of either strawberry short cake or bread pudding for dessert. Everyone ate until they were full and then ate some more. Ben and Pappy actually cooked this way almost every day. Meals such as Ben spread before them weren't just food but works of art, every bit as much masterpieces as the finest artist could put to canvas.

To complete their evening in true Cajun style, they all retired to the living room for a final cup of strong black coffee. Olivia and Pappy sat on the sofa while Ben and Derrick settled in the recliners. "Ben, that was the finest meal I've ever eaten," declared Olivia as she slipped off her shoes and curled up on one end of the old overstuffed sofa.

Derrick challenged good-naturedly, "I believe you said that the last time we ate here."

"Oh, well, what can I say? He just has a way in the kitchen," laughed Olivia.

Always humble, but deeply appreciative, Ben replied, "Thanks, but I owe it all to Pappy. He taught me everything I know." Laughing and slapping his hand upon his knee, Pappy responded with his usual good-natured, "An don't you never forget that, Son!"

The company was fine and the conversation meaningful, but by ten o'clock everyone, including Olivia, was ready to call it quits. "Derrick, I hate to break up the party, but I've just about had it for one day."

"Me too an I can't hardly hold my eyes open no more," yawned Pappy

"I'll bring you home, Pappy," offered Ben as he motioned to Olivia to just leave the cups on the coffee table.

"No," protested Derrick, "I'll take him. You've done enough already.

Pappy jumped in, "Okay, now that we got that taken care of, let's go."

"Not till I help Ben with the clean-up!" insisted stern Olivia.

"Oh no, young lady, I made the mess an I can clean it up. Besides, it don't take me long," smiled Ben.

Knowing that it was useless to argue, she thanked him again for the delicious meal, gave him a big hug, and they left to take Pappy home. The old Cajun was obviously tired and even though he claimed to be fine, Olivia was concerned that he had been over-doing it since being released from the hospital. Reaching between the front bucket seats into the back, she patted his hand, which rested on his knee. No words were needed; her touch warmed his heart and he smiled. To him, she would always be the daughter he never had.

After dropping Pappy off at his back door, Derrick and Olivia drove the rest of the way to her house in silence. She had no regret for the love she and Derrick shared earlier, for she felt it was pure, though ill-timed. Derrick felt nothing but love for Olivia, though he had concerns that she would have second thoughts. Then at that very moment, as though Olivia read his mind, she reached out for his hand.

253

Enfolding it gently in both her own, she slowly raised it to her lips, kissed it softly, and cradled it in her lap.

Relief flooded Derrick as he realized for certain that their feelings for each other were mutual. When they reached her home, he walked her to the door where they kissed tenderly and said good night. Before leaving, though, he put his hands on her shoulders and looked deeply into her eyes. "Liv, I want you to know that today was the best day of my life."

Without hesitation she responded, "It was for me too, Derrick Cameaux. Of that you can be sure."

As he drove back to Pappy's he reflected on the day. Two important, potentially life-altering issues had been settled for him: the location of the Rabeaux camp and the way he and Olivia loved each other. He knew he couldn't wait for his return from the encounter with Ludvick and his boys to tell her how he felt about her. In fact, he knew he should already have told her. "It has to be tomorrow night," he thought, "either during or after the dance. I've got to tell her exactly how I feel about her and ask her to marry me."

CHAPTER 46

Well before daybreak on that Friday morning Ben, Pappy and Derrick stood around Pappy's kitchen table drinking coffee and going over Derrick's maps.

"I'm sure we can find the tranause Valdore was talking about. Is the bayou leading up to it deep enough for the *Miss Teresa?"* asked Derrick.

"Yep," Pappy answered. "If that's the way you go there."

"What do you mean if that's the way we go there? Isn't that the way Valdore said he went?" questioned Derrick, clearly puzzled.

Before explaining, Pappy slowly took a sip from his cup and then pointed on the map to an area close to the Cameaux Swamp. "I been thinking about this all night long an I don't like the idea of you going in that tranause the way Valdore did. Look at this ole bayou Ludvick's camp is on. See how close it passes to the northeast corner of our swamp? I'm thinking that maybe after you an Ben get as close as you can in the *Miss Teresa*, you just hide her in our swamp an go on in your pirogue the rest of the way."

'That's going to leave us a long paddle to Ludvick," said Ben, shaking his head as if he were not so sure of this suggestion.

Derrick, however, listened carefully as Pappy tried to explain his reasoning for a different route from the one Valdore had used.

255

Pappy pulled out a chair and sat down at the table, followed by the other two men. Derrick could see the deep concern on the old Cajun's face. He knew he was trying to make it as simple as possible, but at the same time there was just so much he had to say. Derrick also realized it would be far better to be led on this expedition by his grandfather so he could just follow his commands as necessary. That's exactly what would have happened with a younger Pappy, but not now. This amazing man at the table with all the knowledge and skill to stay alive for so many years was really a very weak old man in the twilight of his years. Furthermore, his last fight against the Rabeaux almost killed him and could yet prove to be something from which he would never fully recover.

"I know it's longer the way I tell you to go, but listen careful, both of you. I'm not saying that Ludvick spotted Valdore. All I want to say is that it's possible. An, if Ludvick saw Valdore, you can be sure the Rabeaux will be waiting for you in ambush round the tranause. Remember, when you fight Ludvick expect the unexpected, an the only way to kill him is to do the unexpected. He's been through many fights an have always come out the winner. Believe me, the man don't never miss a trick."

Derrick listened to Pappy's advice. The old bayou route seemed the best approach, albeit the longer one. He also knew that the element of surprise would be their greatest chance of success.

Ben asked, "How many Rabeaux do you think will be there?"

"At the most four, but most likely I killed one of the boys, so that just leaves three. But don't never be surprised to see a couple more men with them. Ludvick, on rare times, will hook up with other vermin. The Rabeaux have done that in the past. If you surprise them, though, maybe that one or two more you'll be able to handle."

Derrick caught the word "surprise" again. Pappy keeps saying surprise the Rabeaux, thought Derrick. But my idea of surprise is called ambush. That's what I'll do. I'll give them the same kind of surprise they gave Jon and Eric—a good old-fashioned ambush!

Finally, looking first at Derrick and then at Ben, Pappy asked, "One more thing, when you planning to go after them?"

"We were thinking maybe tomorrow afternoon or Sunday morning," answered Ben.

Pappy nodded in agreement. He knew that the sooner this was all over, the better for everyone. By mid-morning he had finished giving Ben and Derrick all the warnings and instructions he thought pertinent. To his chagrin, however, he wasn't in good health on this Friday morning and it showed, especially in the extended silences which now followed his initial advice for his son and grandson. Of course, they understood that his being unable to go with them to fight the Rabeaux was weighing heavily upon him. Nor did anyone mention the strong possibility that neither Ben nor Derrick would return alive. The old Cajun didn't need to remind himself that if his only grandson didn't kill Ludvick in this encounter, then Ludvick would surely one day kill this last Cameaux seed. That's why, in Pappy's opinion, Derrick and Ben had to strike first and gain the advantage.

At morning's end, Derrick and Ben went into the shed behind Pappy's house, pulled out the two pirogues, paddles and push poles needed for the trip, and loaded them onto Ben's truck. "Derrick, I'll meet you at the shrimp shed in a couple hours to unload the pirogues. I got to pick up a few things at the hardware store. I already put my shotgun an my clothes in the cab of my truck. Are you packed an ready to go?"

"Yes, most of my clothes are packed and ready."

"Good, then I'll meet you at the skiff," said Ben as he got into his truck and drove away.

Derrick walked back to the house and into his room where he could hear Pappy in the kitchen cleaning up after their morning breakfast. From his closet he pulled out his weapons of choice: the Bowie knife, the 7mm semi-automatic handgun, and the 12-gauge pump shotgun.

These weapons had proved reliable in the past. Being well versed in their destructive powers, Derrick felt confident they would again meet his needs. However, as he carefully picked up each one and turned it over in his hands for one final scrutiny, he wondered aloud, "Can I do it? Can I actually kill a man? Mulling the question in his mind he answered his own question, "Yes!" Even though survival had

always been Pappy's main reason in sanctioning hunting the Rabeaux, vengeance was Derrick's driving force.

Satisfied that all his weapons were in top condition, Derrick loaded them. He also packed three extra ammo clips for his handgun, as well as extra boxes of shotgun shells. He was returning the weapons to his closet when Pappy knocked on the door. As Derrick looked up, he saw his beloved grandfather standing in the doorway with a small brown paper bag in his hand. "Come on in, Pappy."

"I just brought something for you that might come in handy. It's some fresh deer jerky."

Opening the bag, Derrick took a deep whiff and smiled broadly. "Sure smells good."

"Just thought it might be a good idea to carry it with you in case you get separated from your supplies," suggested Pappy.

Derrick remembered the small pouch he bought at the hardware store to carry on his new leather belt. It would be perfect for holding the jerky. "Thanks, Pappy. I'm sure it'll come in handy."

Pappy smiled. "Well, are you packed an ready?"

"Just about, all I have left is my shotgun."

"Keep it next to you at all times, Son."

"Don't worry, it won't leave my side."

Derrick read the anguish written on Pappy's face. He loved his grandfather and if it came down to it, he would gladly sacrifice his own life to save him. After all, Pappy had proved his love for him many times over the years, not the least of which was his recently fighting Mato and Toby and almost losing his own life.

Suddenly Pappy turned to leave the room, but stopped abruptly at the door to look back. Neither man said a word for an awkward moment; then barely in control of his emotions, Pappy managed in a soft voice, "Son, I love you an I'm sorry for getting you in this mess."

Before Derrick could respond, the old man walked away. He desperately wanted to follow the elder Cameaux to ease his mind, but what could he say to his grandfather? "Don't worry! Nothing bad will happen?" No, Derrick knew the only way to ease Pappy's mind was for him to come back in one piece, with the threat from the

Rabeaux nothing more than a bad memory. And that's exactly what he intended to do.

Just as they had planned, Derrick and Ben met later at the Cameaux docks. After loading the pirogues, they stacked all the nonessential supplies in the bow of the *Miss Teresa* and placed their readied shotguns within easy reach of their seats. Derrick would be behind the steering wheel, and Ben would ride on the passenger side.

"Looks like we're ready to go, Uncle Ben, but I'm just a little concerned about leaving a fully loaded skiff out overnight."

"I've already taken care of that. Got one of the shrimp workers here on guard duty tonight, an I told him to specially watch over this skiff."

"Good," said a smiling Derrick. "I'd sure hate to lose my shotgun to a thief."

Just then a car pulled into the parking lot and stopped next to their skiff. Derrick recognized his friend Scott Armont, who said as he jumped out of his car, "Your grandfather said I'd find you here."

"Hey Scott, "Thought you'd be practicing for tonight's big dance." said Derrick.

With a grin on his face, Scott responded, "Well, that's just what I came to see you about, ole friend."

Derrick turned to Ben and winked. "You have to really watch this man, especially when he calls you ole friend. That always means he wants something."

"Well, now that you offered, I do need a little help," smiled Scott.

"See, Uncle Ben, I told you," laughed Derrick. "Just what kinda help does my ole friend need?"

"Well, it seems that my band members won't get here till late this afternoon. Now that'll probably be enough time to take care of everything, but I just don't like cutting it that close. So, if you want to help me set up all the equipment on stage I would have no objections." Scott's smile grew broader as he added, "And, as an incentive for helping me, I'll even let you sing a song with us tonight right there in front of everybody, how's that?"

Derrick looked at Ben, not really sure whether he should leave him to go with Scott, but Ben assured him. "Go on, Derrick, We're finished

259

here. I have a few things to take care of at the shed, anyway. I'll see you an Olivia later tonight at the festival."

Derrick nodded before turning back to Scott. "Okay, my ole friend. I'll help, but under one condition."

"What's that?"

"That you don't ask me to sing!"

Scott smiled and said, "Deal! "Follow me."

As instructed, Derrick followed Scott to the festival grounds where they parked next to Scott's trailer. Though willing, he actually moaned aloud when Scott opened the trailer door to reveal the load that awaited them, realizing it will take the rest of the day to unload and set up.

"I do appreciate you helping me, Derrick, cause I was really in a bind."

"Glad to, Breaux. After all, what are friends for, you just sing and play your very best!"

"Hey," answered Scott with a puzzled look, "why would you want me to sound my very best? Could it have something to do with you and Olivia dancing in a romantic embrace?"

"Of course not, I just don't want you to make a total fool of yourself on stage, that's all, now come on, let's unload this thing!"

Already the early birds were arriving. Kids were running everywhere trying to be first in line for their favorite rides. A few couples were gathering at the dart-throwing booth, where the men challenged each other to win stuffed dolls or toys for their sweethearts. With everyone busy in their own little world, no one paid much attention to Pritch Labote, not even when he walked within a few yards of the bandstand eating popcorn. He strolled up and down the festival tarmac as if fascinated by all the sights.

Every few minutes he gazed toward the bandstand to watch Derrick help his friend. Shaking his head and making no attempt to conceal the sinister smile that broke across his face, he tossed his half-eaten bag of popcorn aside and slowly walked away from the bandstand.

CHAPTER 47

By the time Derrick and Scott finished setting up the band equipment, people were pouring onto the festival grounds. The rest of Scott's band arrived shortly after work was done.

Derrick still had plenty of time before the dance started, especially since it was only five o'clock and Olivia wasn't expecting him until six-thirty. Nevertheless, he hurried home to get ready, wanting to spend as much time with her as possible. When he arrived at Pappy's house, he found his grandfather in the backyard walking among his orange and fig trees and called to him from the back door. "Pappy, you ready to go?"

"No, Son, I don't think I'll go this year," he answered as he walked toward the house.

"Why not, you feelin' okay?"

"Oh, I guess I'm a little bit tired. Main thing is, I just don't think I want to fight all those people." He was referring to the record crowd expected for tonight's dance.

"Aw, Pappy, come on. You know you'll enjoy it. We'll find a table next to the dance floor where you can sit and rest, but still enjoy everything."

"I just don't feel up to it, Derrick. You an Olivia go on. I'll make it the next time," he said with finality.

261

"Okay, if you're sure. I guess I'd better go ahead and get ready. Anything you need my help with before I go?"

"No, no, you just go an pass a good time," smiled the old Cajun, waving him away with both hands as he sat down on the steps of his back porch.

Derrick left his grandfather sitting there and hurried inside to shower and change. Little did he know the countless hours Pappy spent sitting in that same spot on the steps overlooking his orchard and garden. It had become one of his favorite "memory jogging" spots, and tonight he reflected on both his own life and Derrick's. He remembered well the by-gone days when he and his young wife would never have missed a fais-dodo dance. She sure loved to dance, and so had he. Oh, how he missed his beautiful bride. His mind filled with thoughts of her and of the many hours they spent on these very steps talking and laughing and just plain having fun together. He felt her presence even now and swore he could hear her laughter and smell her perfume. With no doubt in his mind, he knew that he was a lucky man indeed to have known such love. And that thought both gave him a deep sense of satisfaction and saddened him because of the inevitable one that followed: Would Derrick ever know that kind of love? Would his beloved grandson ever love a woman as much as he had and find the happiness that everyone deserves at least once in his life? Pappy knew that the answer depended on the next few days.

When Derrick finished getting dressed, he walked to the back door and was somewhat surprised to find Pappy still sitting on the steps just as he left him a half-hour earlier. When he asked, "Can I bring you back something to eat from the festival?" he could tell he surprised and perhaps even startled him.

Caught day-dreaming and definitely in no mood to answer questions, the old man immediately got up and started up the steps. Derrick quickly moved aside as Pappy rushed past him, his head down and mumbling, "No... thanks, Son. I got some leftovas I'm gonna heat up later on." Then he lifted both hands and again motioned Derrick off as though he were shooing away birds from his grape vine. "Like I already told you, just go on an have yourself a great time."

Derrick smiled as he stood there for a moment watching him hurry down the hall and round the corner into his bedroom. Shaking his head, he thought, Pappy, you're one-of-a-kind, for sure. The hot summer day turned into a warm, muggy night. Derrick wore a short-sleeved tan shirt and a pair of faded jeans. The fais-dodo dance wasn't a formal affair by any stretch of the imagination, and wise Cajuns dressed for comfort. In fact, in the old days these dances had sometimes lasted all night. Thus, endurance garnered respect as much as dancing ability, and the only way to endure the long evening was to dress comfortably.

On his drive to Olivia's house he realized just how nervous he was. He'd decided that tonight was the night he'd tell her exactly how he felt, but the romantic in him knew that both the timing and mood demanded just the right atmosphere. He wanted to tell her when they were alone, but not now, not at the beginning of the evening. "After a night of dancing and holding each other close, that's it," he thought. "I'll wait till I take her home."

Smiling when he pulled into Olivia's driveway, he parked behind her car, and waved when he saw her peer through the living room blinds. "Oops, he caught me," she laughed as she hurried to open the door for him by the time he made his way to her front steps. "What are you smiling about? You're early again, you know."

Looking at his watch, he grinned innocently. "Wasn't this the time I was supposed to pick you up?"

In a soft, butter-melting voice she said, "I just wish you had gotten here earlier. I missed you, so get yourself inside this house!" They both laughed as he assured her he needed no second admonishment and walked through the front door right into her loving arms. He kissed her tenderly as they held each other. Then Olivia buried her head in his shoulder, whispering, "Oh, I'm so looking forward to tonight."

Derrick held her close, not ever wanting the moment to end, and he almost told her right then how much he loved her. In fact, the words were on the tip of his tongue when Olivia asked, "Where's Pappy? I thought he was coming with you."

"No, he said he was tired. Uncle Ben will meet us there, though."

"Yes, I know. I spoke with him earlier, and he said he'd hold us a table." She led Derrick to the sofa and motioned for him to sit while she remained standing before him. "Do you think what I'm wearing is all right? I had on a pair of jeans, but it seemed pretty warm." Olivia now turned from side to side and then completely around in front of him before again facing him with a young, girlish, even somewhat shy smile playing around the corners of her mouth. She was wearing an all-in-one shorts outfit in the style of a pair of farmer's bib coveralls. The two denim straps that held everything together crossed at the back and hooked over her shoulders to the bib in front. Her bright, red-plaid short-sleeved cotton shirt under the coveralls perfectly complemented her dark hair and even darker eyes, which sparkled mischievously.

In response, his own appreciative brown eyes slowly took in and savored the full length, width, and breadth of her, not the least of which included her incredible long, silky-smooth legs. Convinced that she filled that outfit like no farmer possibly could, he was speechless, but finally managed a weak, "Wow, Liv, that sure looks nice."

"Well, I hope it looks okay. I just want to stay as cool as possible." Derrick couldn't help laughing. Smiling, Olivia asked, "What's so funny?"

"Oh, nothing," he lied, still laughing.

She grabbed him by the arm. "You're not getting off this sofa until you tell me the truth. Should I change clothes? Is that why you're in a laughing melt-down?"

"No, not at all, it looks great! In fact, that's why I'm laughing. You put on shorts to stay cool, but when you walk in a room, the temperature rises ten degrees."

Flattered, Olivia insisted in mock alarm, "Then surely we'd better go, before you overheat again! Or was that me doing the overheating?" The "Again" of Olivia's reference to their love-making the night before brought both of them into each other's arms and a long passionate kiss, but before things heated up too much, Olivia led them out of the house and into his Jeep. Knowing that he found her attractive both pleased and comforted her; at the same time, she couldn't help noticing how good he looked. Strong and handsome she thought, fully appreciating the way his tight jeans molded to his sleek

264

muscular physique. Then allowing her mind to drift to the night before, and Derrick's sleek muscular physique without jeans. . .Derrick startled her when he asked, "Have you spoken to your mother and the girls today?"

Olivia hesitated, took a deep breath, and said, "I called them this afternoon. They're really looking forward to the festival tomorrow, and they send you their love."

He had promised to take Olivia and the girls to the fair on Saturday, but that was before Valdore's return. Now, he was racking his brain to figure a way to make the outing happen in spite of the necessity of his leaving Golden Meadow Saturday afternoon. Finally he had an idea. "Liv, I've had a change of plans for tomorrow. Remember that business I told you about that I'd have to handle whenever it came?"

"Yes, I remember."

"Well, I'll probably have to leave town tomorrow afternoon to take care of it.'

"Oh, that's fine. We didn't mean to interfere with anything you had planned."

"Liv, there's nothing I'd rather do than be with you and the girls. How about if we just take the girls to the festival tomorrow morning rather than afternoon? Would that be all right?"

"Derrick, really, it's okay! We can take the girls another time.

"No, I want to take them tomorrow. I can't disappoint my girls. Besides, I honestly want to see them."

Olivia knew he was sincere, and she was deeply touched when he called them his girls. "Okay. I'll call Mom in the morning and we'll pick them up."

"Great! Thanks, Liv."

Olivia didn't question Derrick about his trip or the business, and he was glad of it. He knew he would have been hard-pressed to formulate an acceptable answer. After all, alarming her unnecessarily was the least thing he wanted to do. And of even greater concern was the fact that he found it increasingly more difficult not being totally honest with Olivia at all times.

265

As they approached the festival and the traffic increased, Derrick decided to park on the side of the main road leading to the site rather than on the festival grounds. He learned from past experience that parking on the grounds usually created problems leaving because other cars were almost always blocking the way. Thus, he carefully selected a spot near a light pole and parked the Jeep along the main road but still within an easy walk to the festivities.

CHAPTER 48

T he last of the day's natural light quickly gave way to the powerful floodlights of the midway. A welcome breeze blew from the south as Derrick and Olivia walked holding hands toward the main entrance. They could already hear music filtering their way. Jazz, country, rock, and Cajun music each blended flawlessly. The organizers planned well and the festivities were spread over a large area, easily handling the record crowd.

Derrick bought two passes upon entering, and they stepped into the crowd.

All the lights from the rides and the numerous games and food stands brightened the night sky as though it were noon once more, and the noise was almost deafening. The sweet scents of dark red candied apples, delectable pastries of every imaginable flavor, and light, fluffy cotton candy filled the air. They also caught a welcome whiff of hot dogs, hamburgers, barbecue, and the unmistakable aroma of the finest of Cajun jambalayas, gumbos, and fricassee, not to mention the countless other unique bayou specialties.

The lighthearted, jolly festival atmosphere was contagious, Olivia's electrifying smile and exuberance were absolutely irresistible, and Derrick responded in kind. Suddenly, like a child, Olivia exclaimed, "Oh, Derrick, look there's the Ferris wheel! I always loved riding on one as a kid."

No sooner had the words left her lips than Derrick promptly had her by the hand and leading her to the Ferris wheel line. "No, no, no, Derrick, I didn't mean. . . ."

"Don't back down now, young lady," he interrupted with a determined grin. "We are definitely riding this big wheel right now!"

Olivia looked up at that enormous wheel going round and round and said rather sheepishly, "Well, now that I'm older, it sure seems a lot higher than I remember it. Actually, I'm sure I could enjoy it just as much from here."

"Oh no, you don't," laughed Derrick as he grasped her hand tighter while he showed their passes to the gentleman collecting tickets. Immediately the pressing crowd swept them into the group gathering at the base of the wheel. Those already riding were a show in and of themselves. Some of the most adventurous rode without holding on at all, while others clutched their safety bars in death vise-grips, fear written across their faces. Still others deliberately rocked their swinging seats and screamed with excitement in high-pitched voices as tortured fellow passengers sat ashen-faced, mute beside them. Then, all too soon for her, she watched the huge machine grind to a halt to be unloaded and then restocked with new riders, or victims, from Olivia's point of view. Slowly they inched forward, the line growing shorter with each step.

Olivia's mind raced a mile a minute, as she calculated the available seats and the riders waiting to fill those spaces. The way she figured it, there were four people ahead of them, but only two seats left. Thus, two people per seat meant she and Derrick should just miss having a spot, especially if she could stall just a little longer. Great! she thought, this means we'll have to wait another complete turn of the wheel, and that'll give me time to convince Derrick I'd rather jump off the highest Mississippi River bridge than ride this overgrown training wheel! But to her horror, as the next-to-last seat was ready for loading, all four people ahead of them walked together in that direction. Olivia wanted to shout to them that there was still one more seat available. She stood there with her mouth open.

"Come on, Liv, it's our turn," coaxed Derrick as he gently guided her into the one remaining seat – their seat. Olivia was convinced that

268

she had seen the ride master wink at Derrick as he swung shut the thin security bar.

When the ride began moving, she laughed nervously and whispered, "You know, Derrick, I was never a very brave little girl, and now I think I've even grown a few more chicken feathers over the years."

"Relax, Liv, you're with me. Would I let anything happen to you?" insisted a confident Derrick while he draped his left arm around her shoulders and drew her close to his side.

As she clutched the safety bar with all her might, she realized she was actually beginning to have fun. Nevertheless, she couldn't resist declaring, "From now on, I'll watch what I say to you." Then, as they both started laughing, Olivia put both her arms around his neck and buried her head in his chest. Instinctively he wrapped his protecting arm more securely around her, pulling her even closer, and his strong right hand increased its grip on the safety bar. As the giant wheel continued its revolutions, Derrick looked across the festival toward the pavilion where Scott and his band would be performing. Already he could see people gathering around the dance floor.

Meanwhile, Olivia thought about the dance and how comfortable she would feel dancing with Derrick even though it would be their first official public outing. She was also relieved that despite all her misgivings at the beginning of the ride, she now ended it laughing and carrying on, just as that little girl had done so many years earlier. Besides, and perhaps most importantly, she liked feeling safe in Derrick's arms.

When they got off the Ferris wheel they casually strolled toward a row of game booths because Derrick had an idea. He steered her closer to the booths and they walked slowly down the row. Then it happened. Pointing to the high back wall shelves of one booth, she exclaimed, "Oh, Derrick, look at that beautiful stuffed puppy!"

"It worked," thought Derrick with a grin. "Now, all I have to do is win it!" As he led her by the hand to the booth counter, he saw to his delight that the featured game was a knife-throwing feat, but they would have to stand in line. Two tough-looking young men were already at the counter challenging each other about being the best at

269

winning their sweethearts something special, and now they were about to come to blows over who would go first. Finally at the insistence of the booth manager, they flipped a coin and the older of the two men won the toss. The short, slender, toothless fellow smiled broadly as he pushed his long dark hair out of his eyes and proceeded to throw. The game was simple: for a dollar each player received three knives for three throws, but there was a catch. The three targets, which were silhouettes of masked bandits, would each be moving across the game board at virtually the same time on three-tiered tracks. Bandit number one would emerge at a normal pace on the first level, just about a foot above the game board base; then the second bandit would appear about two feet above him walking at a much quicker pace; finally the last bandit would come out running on the top track about two feet above the second. The object of the game was to throw all three knives at the moving targets before they crossed the width of the booth, securely burying each knife into its intended mark. Accomplishing this not-so-easy task would then entitle the winner to the largest prize of all, a four-foot tall stuffed rabbit, Of course, hitting only one or two bandits netted a consolation prize worth almost nothing.

The eager player stood ready with the three knives in hand as his sweetheart encouraged him. "Come on, Honey, you can do it for me! You're the best!" In response, the young man flexed his muscles and his confident, toothless smile said it all.

Also eager to begin, the game master counted, "ONE!—TWO!—THREE!" Immediately the mechanical bandits marched forward as if by command. The young man took careful aim at the lowest, slowest bandit and threw his knife. To his surprise, however, just before his knife found its mark, the figure stopped momentarily and the knife flew by unimpeded. The second throw aimed at bandit number two wasn't much better because, like the first, this figure also jerked to a brief halt before resuming its flight. The final throw intended for the third bandit was the most pitiful, for not only was this target on the highest level, but also moved at the most erratic speed. Spitting, slamming his fist on the counter, and obviously embarrassed as well, he bellowed in frustration, "Damn, that's not fair!"

270

The young man standing next to him suddenly broke out in laughter at his older friend. "Aw, shut up an watch a real man throw a knife, you idiot," he taunted, laying down his dollar.

The game master gave him three knives and started the count: 'ONE!—TWO!—THREE!'" Again, right on cue, the mechanical bandits began their well-worn treks. Derrick watched closely the stop-and-go tactics so cleverly programmed into the game. Just as his friend before him, this second young man was now trying his best to accomplish the unlikely. The first knife flew and missed its target, as did the second; but then the young man momentarily froze in a stupor of indecision, apparently not knowing where or when to throw his last knife. Suddenly a loud bell rang as the last of the bandits made it home safely, thus signaling the end of the game.

So upset was this second frustrated player that he threw his last knife directly at the prized rabbit, hitting the bunny in the belly with the butt end of the knife. Loud, derisive laughter immediately erupted from the growing crowd of on-lookers. Angrily the young man looked around and shouted, "That damn game is fixed! I'm not gonna give anudder dollar to it!"

The game master noticed Derrick still standing there, he called to him above the noise. "You there, young fellow!"

"I think he's pointing at you," suggested an amused Olivia.

Surprised, Derrick pointed to himself. "Me?"

The game master shouted, "I'll give you two free runs, six shots all together. If you stick a knife in just one bandit, you win your choice of prizes, excluding the bunny rabbit. For that, you'll have to hit and stick all three. What do you say?"

The crowd answered for Derrick with a rousing round of applause and shouts of encouragement. Derrick looked at Olivia. "The stuffed puppy or rabbit?"

"Oh, the puppy," answered Olivia as she clapped her hands.

"Yes Ma'am, you got it," Derrick assured her as he walked to the counter, and the game master handed him three knives. Holding two in his left hand and one in his right hand just to get the feel of it, he was surprised that the knife felt well balanced. Looking up at the game

master he nodded that he was ready. It suddenly became very quiet around the booth, as all eyes were on Derrick.

"ONE!—TWO!—THREE!" Out came the bandits just as before, but all that could be seen or remembered of Derrick's first set of throws was the first one. He had very slowly brought the first blade high and a little to the rear of his head. Then, with a sudden flash of metal, the blade flew at blinding speed and was immediately followed in quick succession by the other two. It was over before the first bandit had gotten even half-way across the booth. The crowd was stunned for a second before a cheering roar exploded from around the booth as they realized Derrick not only had hit the bandits, but had sunk a knife into each bandit's head.

A stunned game master said in a low voice which no one heard, "Ain't nobody ever done that before." The look on his face was readable as one of both sadness and sorrow, almost as if he were losing a personal friend. The rabbit, after all, lived in his booth for four years without ever coming close to being won. In fact, he never really even considered the possibility. Now that it had actually happened, though, his sudden emotional reaction surprised and embarrassed him. Dropping his head, he sighed and reached for the beloved prize, only to be startled by the unexpected sound of Derrick's voice.

"No sir, I don't want that one!"

The man stopped and looked at him strangely. "You don't want Peter?"

"No, I want that stuffed puppy up there," answered Derrick, pointing in the direction of the front shelf.

A smile spread across the game master's face as he realized that his loss would be minimal, for surely the three hits couldn't be repeated. Handing Derrick the stuffed puppy, he reminded him, "You have three additional throws, Sir."

Derrick looked around and spotted the first man who had thrown before him. "Give it to him."

The toothless man smiled from ear to ear. "Thanks, Man," he said as he reached for the knives.

Derrick stepped back, turned toward Olivia and gently placed the cuddly toy in her extended hands as the crowd clapped its approval. "I believe this is for you, Madam."

The beaming Olivia wrapped her arms around the puppy. "Thanks, Derrick." Then she added, almost in laughter though clearly with pride, "Man, you're bad with a knife!"

Although he didn't respond to her compliment, he smiled and whispered, "Anything for you, Liv. I just hope you enjoy your stuffed puppy. Now, let's get out of here."

"Oh, I will," she whispered back. "He's handsome like you."

"Boy, that makes me feel good," he laughed as he escorted her away from the booth.

Once again they joined hands and continued walking among the crowd. Just like everyone else around them, they were well aware of the great time they were having. Kids were laughing and dragging their parents from ride to ride, and clowns were busy making balloon figures. In time they passed a large tent where older folks were playing bingo, and everywhere there was music. Making their way toward the pavilion, they approached a long row of tables set up by the local women's club for serving food. Olivia asked, "Are you hungry?"

Smiling, Derrick responded, "I've been looking for these ladies since we got here. I never gave up hope, though, cause I knew we'd eventually find them if I just kept following my nose."

Small signs displaying prices stood next to each of the food items. Olivia and Derrick eagerly scanned the tables for just the right dish, but the decision was very difficult, if not almost impossible. One table featured choices of shrimp gumbo, chicken gumbo, and okra gumbo. Another offered jambalaya, stuffed crabs, shrimp bouletts, and bouillabaisse over baked fish. Yet another table boasted boudin, cracklings and pickled pig's feet. And definitely not to be outdone, there were also numerous black iron pots boiling shrimp and crabs in a special nearby roped-off area.

Olivia chose a shrimp casserole, tasty crab patties, and a small bowl of oyster soup. Derrick finally decided on one of his favorites, shrimp jambalaya. He also tried fried soft-shell crabs and a small bowl of chicken gumbo. Though numerous tables and chairs were laid out in

long rows set up around the food court, they were still lucky to find two vacant seats.

"With so much food, this whole place smells good, Derrick," said Olivia, settling down next to him.

"Yeah, I had a hard time choosing. Guess I'll just have to go back for seconds since I couldn't get any more on this plate!" He picked up his spoon to sample the gumbo.

Then just as they began eating, Derrick heard a familiar voice. "Well, I see that you did make it, my friend."

Turning around with his spoon still in his hand, Derrick said, "Hey, Marco, I see you made it too. Hi, Miss Lovina." He stood quickly to greet Marco's wife with the traditional Cajun hug.

"Aw, keep you seat an don't let us interrupt the meal. I'm just so glad to see you two here tonight," she replied as she embraced Olivia, who was also standing.

Looking at Derrick, Marco smiled and pointed to his wife. "See, I told you I wouldn't miss this fais-dodo for nuttin'. She'd never forgive me!"

Lovina, a rather large lady who looked as if she could easily put Marco in his place anytime, laughed and turned to Olivia. "Don't let Marco fool you. It's him that loves to dance all the night long."

Derrick nodded wholeheartedly. "Don't worry, Miss Lovina. Marco doesn't fool us a bit. Have you two eaten yet?"

"Oh yes," answered Marco. "We just finished. When I saw you an Olivia, though, we wanted to come by an say hello. By the way, you know that Ben has a table for you to sit at?"

"He had told us he'd hold a couple of seats for us. Do you know where he's sitting?" asked Olivia.

"Next to the bandstand; we're headed that way now." Then looking at his wife, Marco continued with a wink, "Woman, I'm in the dancin' mood, so let's go an let these two enjoy the food! See you ova there!"

"You bet," answered Derrick as he and Olivia resumed their seats and their meal. "You know, Liv, this really is a fine festival and this food is great!" Olivia nodded her complete agreement.

274

As much as they were enjoying the delicious food, though, they were enjoying each other's company far more. "Derrick, thanks for a wonderful night. The food's great, but the company's the best. I'm having the time of my life!"

Derrick felt the same. To him, Olivia was beautiful inside and out. She would make him a fine wife. "I'm having a great time too, Liv, but the night is far from over. Think you're up for a little dancin'?"

"Better believe it!" smiled Olivia. Derrick returned her smile, knowing that tonight was indeed going to be the perfect night to ask this woman he loved to marry him.

Above the background noise of the crowd they were suddenly aware of Scott Armont's voice ringing over the p.a. system as he introduced his band. Derrick and Olivia then, along with most of the crowd, got up and made their way to the pavilion just as the fais-dodo was about to begin.

CHAPTER 49

V ictor Rabeaux patiently stood at the end of the small wharf overlooking the swamp while awaiting Mato's return from hunting. As Ludvick's only surviving son, he knew that in time he would reign as leader of the Rabeaux family or at least what was left of it. Having been fathered and reared solely by Ludvick, he had adopted many of the elder Rabeaux's characteristics.

Growing up in the marsh and swamp, Victor and his two brothers lived a tough life from the beginning. Barely weaned, all three boys actually witnessed Ludvick's viciously murdering their mother in a fit of rage. Then, he made Victor and his brothers dig their mother's grave, though Victor could barely hold a shovel. And, as if that were not enough, from that time on their father preached that women were nothing more than men's toys to satisfy their lust and make babies. Consequently, standing next to his mother's grave at a very young age, Victor shed his last tear of remorse.

On that fateful day Ludvick had taken a giant leap forward in turning his sons into cold-blooded killers. Over the many years since, he had deliberately molded and transformed all the Rabeaux men into replicas of himself: heartless and devoid of normal human emotion and feeling, with one clear exception. In fact, the common bond that always glued them together was their intense anger and hatred of their historical enemy – the Cameaux family. As flawlessly as Ludvick

277

learned from those before him, in the same way he shaped his sons and grandsons.

So it had raged for more than a hundred years, and Victor was proof of Ludvick's excellent tutelage. The elder Rabeaux successfully multiplied and directed Victor's rage and hate toward the Cameaux. Now, Victor's only regret about losing his brothers and his younger son Toby was that they wouldn't be around to see the end of the Cameaux family.

Finally Victor could see Mato in the distance, and he watched proudly as his one remaining son steadily push-poled his pirogue toward the camp. This son was definitely one-of-a-kind, a powerful man whom no one had ever beaten in a fight or any other man-to-man encounter. His violent temper was easily and instantly ignited. Mato, the epitome of all muscle and no brains, was a deadly combination of manhood that certainly didn't lend itself to a long and prosperous life. And whereas Toby's face had always been rather plain, Mato's facial features had become truly frightful because of his many fights. Victor often wondered whether part of Mato's consistently doing and saying so many mindless things might be related to the batterings he endured in his fights, or at the very hands of his grandfather.

Victor continued watching as Mato drew closer, and for a brief moment he thought of his son's mother. She was a barmaid from Des Allemands whom Ludvick had brought to the marsh and given him. They kept her a virtual slave for three years, just long enough to bear Victor two sons, but even that had been almost intolerable for Ludvick. She was lucky to have lasted as long as she did. It didn't take long until Ludvick tired of her, and he often made that clear with both verbal and physical abuse. Sometimes Victor had considered stepping in to halt the attacks, but he knew better and ignored it, as well as her tears, which always followed.

Finally one day the inevitable happened. When Victor returned from running his trap lines, she didn't show up at the dock to help him tie up and unload as usual. Because she knew better than simply not to show up, regardless of whatever reason she might offer, he knew she was gone. Ludvick claimed that he carried her back to the bar where he'd found her, but Victor knew she was dead. Nevertheless, he said

278

nothing, especially not in protest to his father. In fact, it didn't even bother him much, since he had never felt an emotional bond with the woman. Besides, things were much quieter without her, except for the cries of his young sons for their mother. Ludvick soon cured them of that. "Makes them tough," he had snarled, just as he always did down through the years when they displeased him.

As Mato eased his pirogue next to the wharf, he grumbled, "Got two rails an a turtle. I almost got me a gator too, but he got away."

"Then clean them up so I can cook them," ordered a disgusted Victor, cursing him under his breath because Mato had missed the gator.

The big man climbed out of the pirogue and quickly pulled it onto the bank of the levee. Victor turned and walked back toward the camp, but before he reached the doorway, he looked back over his shoulder to see whether Mato had turned his pirogue over. As usual, he hadn't; but Victor pondered but only a moment before deciding to let Ludvick remind him about the pirogue. Just as he opened the cabin door, he heard Mato's petulant whine as he walked toward him.

"Why I couldn't go with Gramps?"

"If you wasn't such a dumb ass all the time, he'd take you with him more!" answered Victor.

That sounded reasonable to Mato, but he continued the conversation anyway. "I'd sure like to meet those pretty girls from Bayou Lafourche. When is Gramps comin back?"

"Maybe tonight, maybe tomorrow, that's none of your business, Boy, so quit axing stupid things like that an do what I tell you." Needless to say, Victor was just as curious about his father's expected time of return, but even more so about the current status and results of his trip.

CHAPTER 50

Derrick and Olivia made their way through the crowd to the church pavilion. Over the years this large structure served many functions, but none was as popular as a fais-dodo. The high metal roof was supported by large metal beams at the perimeter, and all four sides were open to the elements, allowing welcomed air to flow freely through the crowd. Because the interior of the pavilion was free of obstacles, it was perfect for the construction of a fine wooden dance floor in the center. The bands were always set up high on a platform at one end, virtually taking up one whole side, and tables and chairs were everywhere else surrounding the dance floor.

Just as Derrick and Olivia were walking around the edge of the dance floor to reach Ben's table next to the bandstand, Scott and his band struck up the familiar cords of the old Cajun favorite "Jolie Blonde." Immediately the floor was crowded with eager dancers, completely preventing Derrick and Olivia from proceeding. Oh well, he thought, we'll just dance our way to Ben's table, and he promptly led Olivia toward the middle of the dance floor. "If you would do me the honor, Madam, may I have this dance?"

"Well, Sir, I thought you'd never ask."

There among the other dancers Derrick pulled Olivia close and led her into the Cajun waltz. Before long the two of them almost seemed to have melted into one, so natural was their combined rhythm. Olivia

281

was both surprised and amazed that Derrick was so light on his feet, and he was certainly relaxed and in a dancing mood tonight. Olivia, known for her dancing skills, easily followed close to him at every twist and turn so that by the end of the song, they had made a complete circle of the dance floor.

Just as the next song began and before the crowd cut them off again, Derrick said, "Let's find Uncle Ben's table," Scanning the tables he caught sight of Marco and his wife in the crowd and shouted, "Hey, Breaux!"

Marco saw him and motioned them toward their saved seats at the very first table next to the band stand. Everyone waved and a broad smile crossed Ben's face as soon as he saw them coming. Standing to hug them, he teased, "Man, I was thinking you two got lost!"

"No, just delayed a little," laughed Olivia. "Look what Derrick won for me," she added, proudly holding up her stuffed puppy. Needless to say, Derrick could have done without all the good-natured ribbing that followed, but he just grinned and shook his head as they greeted everyone including Valdore and his wife. As soon as they sat down next to Ben, Olivia immediately leaned over and whispered protectively, "You'd better take it easy tonight."

Ben loved the way Olivia always fussed over him and replied with a wink, "Thanks, Beb, I feel fine. I know how much I can handle."

Scott next played a slow Cajun tune and Ben asked Olivia to dance. She immediately got up and waved to Derrick, but he didn't sit alone for long. Scott's wife Pam came over and asked, "How about dancin' with a married woman?"

"Only if we dance in front of your jealous husband," laughed Derrick. Then, true to his word, he led Pam to the dance floor right in front of Scott, but stayed there only long enough for his friend to see them. Then, with a big smile on his face, he whirled her around and they disappeared into the crowd.

Looking up at him to be certain to catch his eye, but speaking very matter-of-factly, Pam said, "Derrick, Olivia sure is a fine girl. You know, she'd make you a good wife."

Derrick answered, "I think you're right. She would make a fine wife, but I'm not so sure I'd make a good husband."

282

"Oh, come on, you've got to be kidding. You're a good man, Derrick Cameaux, and any woman would be lucky to have you. Don't sell yourself short."

Derrick was pleased to hear Pam's approval of Olivia, especially since he had always been such close friends with both her and Scott. He also felt certain that, in time, Olivia would become good friends with them as well. Oh, Pam, he thought, if you only knew of my plans later tonight to ask Olivia to marry me.

For the rest of the evening Olivia and Derrick danced almost every dance, often with each other, but sticking to the Cajun tradition, with other partners as well. Then, on one of the rare occasions they were resting between songs, Olivia noticed someone approaching them.

Dressed in a skin-tight, very short, red, man-killer dress, it was none other than Bonnie Sladder sauntering their way. Bonnie's reputation was well known to Olivia, especially the fact that she and Derrick had dated in high school. Olivia prayed a quick prayer to divert the diva, but to no avail. She was pretty sure if Bonnie could, she would definitely sink her claws into Derrick. Oh well, here it comes, Olivia thought with some reservation, but she simply took a deep breath and remained cool and collected, not giving Derrick the slightest warning of what was coming.

Meanwhile, he was so busy talking to Valdore that he didn't even notice when Bonnie stopped at their table. Fact is, she just stood there a few seconds smiling coyly at Olivia before completely turning her back to her and facing Derrick, clearing her throat and saying, "Why, Derrick Cameaux, what a pleasant surprise." By this time Olivia was irritated, and the thoughts that flooded her mind were better left unspoken. She clenched her jaw and rolled her eyes, but remained silent and wisely avoided revealing the nagging feelings of insecurity plaguing her.

Derrick turned quickly, almost falling off his chair, to see Bonnie standing only a couple of feet in front of him. Olivia could see his face turning red, but in as calm a voice as he could muster, heard him ask, "Hi, Bonnie, how are you?" Then, almost as an after-thought or perhaps out of guilt, he added, "You know Olivia, don't you?"

Everything probably would have worked out fine, except for the way Bonnie had already acknowledged and then ignored Olivia. Now, her coy, fake smile and her sarcastic reply was much too loud. "Oh,

283

yes, hello Olivia. My, you're looking cute tonight in that nice little farmer's suit you're wearing. You know, my mother has one just like it. She says she loves it because it hides all her little fat spots!" Bonnie started laughing, but then realized she was the only one laughing. Olivia was coming out of her chair until Derrick grabbed her arm to restrain and calm her.

Clearly alarmed and surprised by her own reaction to Bonnie's insult, but not taking more than a couple of seconds to catch her breath, Olivia remained seated while she looked at Bonnie from head to toe. Then, shaking her head as if in disbelief, she declared most convincingly, "Bonnie Sladder, why, the last time I saw a woman dressed like you, she was standing on Bourbon Street in front of a female impersonator bar. In fact, with your big feet, you look just like him!" Others at the table couldn't hide their laughter.

Admittedly, Bonnie had been seeking attention, but not this kind, Insulted, she turned and stormed away as all eyes focused on her retreat. Among those enjoying this little drama was Marco, but from his wife's point of view, he was enjoying just a little too much too long. When Lovina slapped him on the back of the head, he cried out, "Hey, why you do that, Honey!"

Derrick and Olivia looked at each other and then at Marco and Lovina as she replied, "That's for what you was thinking!" Everyone at the table erupted into laughter again, and then, not a moment too soon, Scott and his band began another song. Derrick and Olivia were relieved that everyone else got up to dance, but they were both even more relieved that neither mentioned Bonnie Sladder. Since they couldn't just sit there pretending that nothing happened, Derrick eased the tension by suggesting another dance and Olivia readily agreed. Turns out it was a good idea because they quickly relaxed in each other's arms and were soon talking and laughing as if nothing happened. While it was well and good for them to dismiss the whole exchange, it had obviously not gone unnoticed by those around them and especially by one particular observer of whom they were not even aware.

Always maintaining a safe distance, Pritch Labote kept his eyes trained on Derrick and Olivia because he knew that timing would be all important.

CHAPTER 51

It was almost midnight, but the dance showed no signs of winding down. Most of the men at Ben's table were drinking beer, except for Derrick, who drank colas because he wanted to be completely clear-headed both for tomorrow's challenges and also for his proposal to Olivia later on this special night. The ladies were drinking either beer or wine, depending on their taste, and each man was taking turns buying rounds for the table. When it was Derrick's turn once again to buy, Olivia leaned over and whispered, "I'm going to the ladies' room. I'll be right back."

Smiling, Derrick replied, "Take your time cause when you get back, we're dancin' till this thing ends!"

"You're on, tough guy," she replied, gathered her stuffed puppy in her arms, and headed for the row of portable toilets north of the pavilion. The church wanted to build nicer facilities for the festival, including indoor restrooms, but once again finances just weren't available in this year's budget. Thus, in typical Cajun good-natured humor, most folks tried to make the best of the three dozen portable toilets, though they really had been set up in a rather poorly lighted area and more than a few ladies complained about that. Numerous signs posted around the festival grounds reminded everyone that the toilets were separated into two groups: men on the right and ladies on

the left. Hmm, thought Olivia, seems like it was just the opposite last year. Sure hope nobody gets confused.

When Ben noticed where Olivia was going, he got up to escort her, but more out of personal necessity than from concern for her safety. He had to pick up his step to catch up with her, but when he finally did, he asked as he led the way, "Having a good time?"

"Oh yes, a wonderful time." smiled Olivia.

"Honey, the best times are yet to come," he assured her.

"Ben, I'm lost. Do you know where we're going?" asked Olivia, finding it amusing to be led to the bathroom by her father-in-law.

Ben smiled and pointed straight ahead. "Sure, Beb, there they are!"

Now seeing the shadowy rows of toilets ahead of them, Olivia laughed as she quipped, "Guess you just haven't lived till you've sat in one of these little jewels, huh?"

Ben laughed in return. "Well, now, I'm not so sure I'd advise you to actually sit!" With that choice piece of wisdom, Ben left Olivia at the ladies' section while he looked for a vacancy on the men's side. He found one right away near the pavilion, but Olivia had to walk to the end of the ladies' row before she found an available one.

Derrick, in the meantime, carried the drinks back in two cardboard boxes, setting them in the middle of the table and distributing them as directed. He set Ben's and Olivia's on the table in front of their empty seats and sat down to wait for their return.

Since Ben assumed that he had gotten out of the facility before Olivia, he took a few steps toward the pavilion and waited there for her. With so many people coming and going in the dim light, he thought nothing of not recognizing many of the people he saw, including the man passing in front of him at that very moment.

Pritch, however, deliberately turned his head away from Ben to remain unrecognizable. He watched Olivia walk to the far-end of the portable toilets, and that is exactly where he was heading.

Before opening the door to her unit Olivia unbuttoned the top pouch of her bib coveralls and safely stored her stuffed puppy.

Being this far down the row, Pritch was alone until a lady unexpectedly came out of a unit and bumped into him. She quickly left him behind, hurrying back toward the pavilion, muttering aloud

something about a man who would dare to be found wandering among the women's toilets. Unaffected by this woman's thoughts and opinions of him, Pritch hurried to within five feet of Olivia's unit, his heart pumping a little harder and his mouth dry. Waiting for Olivia to exit, Pritch took one last look in the direction of Ben and was relieved to see how difficult it was to recognize anyone at this distance.

Olivia opened the door of the unit and stepped out. As she removed her stuffed puppy from her pouch she assumed the dark figure in front of her was another woman waiting her turn, and she naturally stepped to the side to let her pass. However, much to her surprise, the dark figure suddenly blocked her path; only then did Olivia see that the person before her was a man. Before she could speak, Pritch cried in a frantic voice, "Miss Cameaux, something terrible have happen! Ben just caught another heart attack! I work at the shed an they want me to bring you to the hospital!"

Olivia was stunned. "Ben, another heart attack?"

"Yeah, now come on! We got to hurry" Then Pritch quickly grabbed her by the arm and began leading her away from the festival area toward his truck.

Five steps later, Olivia stopped and jerked free. "Just a minute – I don't remember you ever working at the shed! Who are you?"

Meanwhile, Ben glanced again toward the woman's toilets. Starting to wonder what was taking Olivia so long, was relieved when he saw her in the distance talking to a man. Then he became confused because he thought he saw them running away, or was it just Olivia who was running from the man? Ben wasn't sure, and not knowing what to make of it, he stood there for a moment pondering the situation playing out before his eyes.

By this time, Olivia had backed away from Pritch. "I'm not going anywhere with you!" She strongly suspected the man was lying. Alarmed, she turned to run in the direction of the pavilion.

Pritch couldn't let her get away, but he had hoped at least to get her to the truck without force. Now he realized that it wouldn't happen without a fight, and he immediately pulled a small-caliber handgun out of his back pocket. Even though she had gained a few steps on him, he quickly caught her and pushed her to her knees. Struggling to get up,

she felt the sharp blow to the side of her head, and collapsed in a heap, unconscious. Pritch hoped he hadn't hit her too hard because she was certainly worth more to him alive than dead. Nevertheless, he figured he had no choice, so he scooped her up.

Ben couldn't believe his eyes. Now, with no thought at all for his own fragile health, he ran toward her as fast as he could. Frantically, he looked for Olivia and her attacker, but he couldn't find them. Finally, just as he reached the end row of toilets, he saw a man running between cars with what could only be Olivia over his shoulders. Ben's adrenaline was flowing and he ran hard toward the shadowy figure. The closer he got, however, the more he realized that Olivia was either unconscious or dead. Then he saw the old pickup, now barely visible in the dim streetlight, and instinctively knew where the man was heading. And despite the distance between them, Ben knew that he could at least reach the truck before the man had time to drive away. With renewed vigor, Ben shouted, "Olivia, Olivia!"

Pritch, in fact, reached the truck when he first heard Ben calling out, and he quickly opened the door and shoved his still-limp bundle inside. Realizing that Ben was now almost to the truck – just another ten feet and he would be on him – the desperate Pritch turned and aimed his gun. Ben never even saw the weapon until it flashed just three feet in front of him. Pain ripped through his right side, but that didn't stop him from crashing into his target. In the fleeting moment before the second shot, Ben recognized Pritch Labote; but too late. The second bullet caught Ben in the upper chest just below the collar bone, and the two men fell hard in a heap, with Ben on top. Pritch automatically began fighting when he suddenly noticed that Ben wasn't moving. In one swift movement he rolled Ben aside, leaped to his feet, jumped into the truck, and sped away. Ben lay dying on the grass.

Derrick and the others waited patiently for Olivia and Ben. Although he didn't want to seem concerned, it had been quite some time since he had returned with the drinks. Finally Derrick turned to Valdore. "I'm ready to dance. What's keeping Ben and Olivia so long?"

"I been wondering the same thing myself," answered Valdore as he stood up. "Let's find out." Marco and the other men at the table nodded in agreement and pushed back their chairs to accompany them.

Though Derrick walked briskly, he fully expected Ben and Olivia to meet them at any moment. However, when they didn't, he became concerned. The men then split into two groups so that Marco and the others could check out the men's units while he and Valdore walked down the ladies' row.

Derrick called out Olivia's name every couple of units he passed, but there was no response. Then, as he and Valdore got to the end of the row and were about to turn around, he spotted something on the ground a short distance from the last unit. As he and Valdore hurried toward that object, Derrick recognized the stuffed puppy, and shouted in a panic, "Olivia!"

They immediately began a frantic search beyond the units, but the farther they ventured, the darker it became until Valdore spotted a dim street light in the distance. As he hurried forward he could see something lying in the shadowy fringes of the light. "There's something here!"

Derrick caught up with him just as he reached the lighted area, "Uncle Ben!" cried Derrick as he saw his uncle lying in a pool of blood.

Valdore knelt down and gently rolled him from his side to his back. Feeling a faint pulse, he said, "He's still alive!"

Derrick immediately dropped to his knees next to his uncle and gently slid his arms under Ben's head. Though weak Ben managed to open his eyes and stammer, "I, I couldn't stop him. He took Olivia, Derrick." He was close to losing consciousness, but was fighting hard to stay awake.

Derrick spoke softly to his uncle, "Take it easy, Uncle Ben. You're going to be all right. Just hang in there and don't try to talk."

Despite their protest, however, Ben still had more to say and both Derrick and Valdore understood him clearly. "Pritch Labote took Olivia. He's one of..." Ben was fighting hard to finish. "One of Ludvick's...men," he whispered just before slipping into unconsciousness.

"We need some help! I'll be right back. You stay here with Ben!" declared Valdore as he left to find Marco and the others.

There, sitting alone with Ben, Derrick suddenly had a crushing thought: Olivia was in the hands of the Rabeaux. He had told her she was safe with him. But he had failed her!

CHAPTER 52

Dazed and veiled in darkness, Olivia drifted in and out of consciousness for what seemed like hours. Could I be blind? was her first horrifying thought as she strained to see. All she knew was that when she tried to move her head a fraction, the pain was too intense and the effort too great; when she tried to move her hands to her head, that didn't work either. And though sleepier than ever before in her life, her body screamed at her to re-position, move, stretch, revive the numbness in her legs, and rub the pain in her head. Nevertheless, her overpowering need to sleep was so much stronger than the awful pain or anything else she felt. Thus, as she drifted off, she was hoping that this would end up being just a bad dream. If it hadn't been for the voices, that is. . . .

"Everything went just like I plan it. I think I even killed Ben Cameaux," bragged Pritch. Ludvick stared out across the bow of his skiff as he navigated through Yankee Canal and listened to Pritch's boasting of how he stole Olivia Cameaux right from under the noses of the Cameaux men. "Yeah, an if that boy Derrick Cameaux woulda come after the girl instead of Ben, I'd have killed him for you."

Even in the darkness Pritch felt Ludvick's fierce eyes upon him. Realizing immediately that he had over played his hand, he quickly fumbled for words to correct himself. "I mean, you know, I plan things to happen just like they happen. Wasn't no harm done to Derrick

Cameaux. You know I wouldn't never done him that, cause I know he's yours to do with what you want." Ludvick quickly turned his head in disgust. Pritch breathed a sigh of relief, mistakenly assuming that his answer appeased his taskmaster and that not being able to see his face directly was a good sign.

Ludvick had much more on his mind than Pritch's babblings, however, and was intent on reaching his hide-out where he would eventually lure Derrick Cameaux into the swamps to kill him. Ludvick didn't doubt he possessed the right choice for bait, especially after Pritch told him how the young Cameaux had been all over her at the fais-dodo. Now, completely ignoring Pritch, Ludvick silently stared straight ahead into the night and amused himself by occasionally peering under the bow of his skiff. Uttering his deeply self-satisfying chuckle, his lips curled in sneering, perverse pleasure as his hawk-like eyes feasted on Olivia's motionless form.

When Pritch brought her to him, Ludvick immediately tied her up and shoved her into the bow of his skiff. In the back of his mind, Ludvick had big plans for this girl and after he used her for his primary task of drawing Derrick into the swamp, then he would give her to Mato. According to his line of reasoning, Olivia could birth another son or two, and he figured they could at least put up with her for that long. The kidnappers traveled the remainder of the night in continued and welcomed silence. Just as Ludvick remained lost in his own thoughts and schemes for the days ahead, so also did Pritch, though he knew that his would never amount to anything more than figments of his own private fantasies.

Toward daybreak Olivia awoke once more. Although she still felt as if someone were pounding her head with a two-by-four, she revived somewhat even though she was not fully alert. She reminded herself to remain calm even in spite of the mounting tension of fear and uncertainty, and forced herself to listen and visualize. Soon she recognized the sound of a motor and comprehended that someone had stuffed her into the bow of a fast-moving skiff with her hands and her feet tied together as if she were a sack of garbage. Then with great difficulty and pain, but with equally strong-willed determination, she managed to bend her head enough to get a glimpse toward the rear of

the skiff, where there was just enough daylight to make out two figures facing her. She couldn't see them clearly because of the low bow, but she was certain that one of the two had hit her at the festival. Questions of why anyone would want to kidnap her and where they could possibly be taking her, not to mention their identities, filled her mind.

She was thankful to gain more awareness of her surroundings, but the down-side of it was that the more she regained her senses, the more overwhelming became the scent of rancid seafood that began assaulting her nostrils. She struggled in vain to lift her head off the deck of the skiff to somehow move away from the sickening odor emanating from the keel just a few inches away from her face. It wasn't at all uncommon for bits and pieces of raw seafood to become wedged between the deck boards and rot over the course of time. Most fishermen would simply remove the deck boards, clean out the rot, and replace the boards until the whole procedure needed to be repeated. The nauseous filth never bothered Ludvick enough to do any cleaning. For Olivia, though, the repugnant odor was so unbearable that she gagged repeatedly, fighting hard not to heave and thus add to the mess. Finally, after biting her lips to stifle cries of pain and again mustering all the feeble strength she could summon, she managed to slowly lift her head enough to place it on a nearby pile of empty oyster sacks.

Though Olivia desperately tried to make some sense of what had happened to her, she simply could find no good reason for any of it. Then panic suddenly gripped her as she thought of her girls. Were they all right, would she ever see them again? What about Derrick? Tears flowed freely as overwhelming feelings of hopelessness enveloped her.

Well after daybreak Ludvick tied his skiff under the well-worn, low branches of the giant willow tree at the end of the long, narrow tranause. When strong hands tightened around her ankles and pulled her from the bow, it was the first real look she had of her captors, and the fact that they didn't bother to hide their identities was not a good sign.

Pritch spoke first, sarcastically mocking her. "Well, if it's not that spoiled Cameaux queen. How do you do, Mizzz Cameaux?"

"What do you want with me?" asked Olivia, barely able to speak above a whisper.

293

Pritch laughed and motioned toward the man next to him. "You just shut up. This Mr. Ludvick will take good care of you.

Then, without saying a word to her, Ludvick scooped her up and carried her from the skiff to his pirogue waiting just where he left it on the opposite side of the levee. Dumping her on the ground, he quickly cut the connecting rope which had secured her bound hands and feet. Though she didn't dare, her first impulse was to stretch her stiff limbs as soon as she experienced the limited freedom of no longer being bent double. She watched his every move as he abruptly picked her up again, stepped into the pirogue and thrust her down hard on the front seat. Speaking for the first time, he growled, "Don't move!"

She sat there motionless, saying not a word, but frantically dredging her memory for any recollection of these men. Try as hard as she could, though, she just couldn't place them or ever remember having seen them. The older one called Ludvick had especially frightened her, not with words but by his very presence and manner. In fact, he didn't speak again to her, yet his dreadful, piercing glare contained sufficient warning to tread lightly around him. The younger man also scared her, but in a different way. Thus, she made a point of not looking directly at him because the way he eyed her body alerted her to be on guard.

They paddled for what seemed to Olivia to be at least an hour. She was still aching from head to toe, but refused to give in to it and, instead, did her best to concentrate. She listened closely to every word the two men spoke, hoping to discover a morsel of information, but nothing they said revealed anything that would explain her captivity. The younger one did most of the talking, but clearly the older man was in charge. Too frightened to observe her surroundings as they traveled along an old bayou, Olivia became even more unnerved as she realized that, just as they never concealed their faces, neither did they appear to be concerned about whether she watched or even memorized every detail of the journey. Do they think I could never find my way out of here anyway, or do they not intend that I'll ever live long enough to find out? The alarming questions bombarded her weary, confused mind, and it was all she could do to keep from falling apart on the

spot. Her thoughts were suddenly interrupted as they came upon a clearing on a low levee. Olivia hadn't a clue as to where they were.

"I just got to hand it to you, Ludvick. This is the best hide-out. No one won't never fine you here. Thanks for taking me with you. You know I'm always ready to help a good friend." This younger man's continuous and obvious attempts to impress Ludvick convinced Olivia that, whatever else she would ever find out about these two, she now knew it had been this Ludvick's idea to kidnap her.

"Pritch, shut up. You just talk too damn much an that's not good," snapped Ludvick as he reminded himself that insurance against Pritch's big mouth was the reason he'd taken him in the first place. Besides, he knew Pritch was only helping him for the money, and he also knew that once Derrick Cameaux met his end, this fool wouldn't be far behind. Ludvick would never leave a loose end like Pritch untied.

The sun rising ever higher beat down mercilessly on the trio. Olivia was the one most affected, since the men were more hardened to it. Sweat soaked through her clothes and ran freely down her face, its brine searing her eyes. And in spite of her determination to show no weakness, the time had come to ask her captives for some relief. By this time her head sagged upon her chest until she lifted it to voice her protest. However, before she could say a word, she saw a camp a few yards ahead of them, and it was obvious they were headed straight for it. Just the thought of getting out of the pirogue and beyond reach of the sun's scorching heat revived her resolve to survive and she remained silent.

As they approached the small wharf Olivia watched two men emerge from the camp and walk toward them. Both looked rough, but the first was unassuming and of average height and appearance; the second, on the other hand, definitely caught her attention. He was a huge man, at least a head taller than the first, as well as considerably larger. He was also undoubtedly younger and much more powerful. Neither man was in the least attractive, but the younger one was downright ugly, if not repulsive.

In place of any formal greeting, Ludvick hurled insults and curses at the two men waiting on the wharf. Olivia was now convinced that

this man called Ludvick was, not only the one responsible for her kidnapping, but also the head of this band of misfits. As his pirogue touched the wharf, he shouted, 'Mato, get over here an help with this Chienne." Olivia winced as she caught the reference to a female dog. She then watched helplessly as Mato walked to her side, stopped and just stood there staring at her. Cursing him again, Ludvick then shouted, "You gonna just stan there all day? Pick her up an set her on the land!"

As ordered, Mato bent down and effortlessly lifted Olivia to remove her from the pirogue. She gasped as they came face to face, for he was even more difficult to view at close range. He had severely distorted facial features, including an almost unrecognizable structure of an oft-broken nose. So preoccupied was she, in fact, by her own personal pain, fear and uncertainty that she could do little more than shudder and look away. She couldn't avoid the assault of a variety of stale odors on the big man's clothes when he pressed her face to his shoulder while carrying her from the wharf. Once on land he tried to set her on her feet, but she collapsed, not so much because her feet and hands were still tied, but because she was so weak. Mato stood there staring at her as she lay on her side on the ground.

"Cut her feet free, Stupid," shouted Ludvick as he shook his head in disgust.

Mato reached for the sheath at his side, and Olivia drew a deep breath as he pulled out his long-bladed knife. Smiling at her fear and watching her closely, he slowly bent down and set the blade between the calves of her legs, deliberately lingering there for a moment before moving the blade downward. So sharp was this knife that her legs were freed the moment the blade touched the rope around her ankles. Her hands remained tied, but she was still able to reach down to rub her red, chaffed ankles, which burned intensely because the rope had been tied so tightly. Her respite from torment lasted only briefly, though, because soon Ludvick was standing over her. Without a word he reached down, grabbed the back of her coveralls and jerked her up. This time she remained standing, despite the uncontrollable shaking of her legs.

"Put her in the shack!" growled Ludvick to Mato, who promptly nudged Olivia forward. When she looked around after two or three steps, he quickly grabbed her arm and walked her toward the solid oak shack Ludvick constructed especially for her. Olivia wondered what lay ahead.

"Everything went good?" asked Victor.

"Good enough," snapped Ludvick.

"What about the Cameaux boy?" Hearing Derrick's name, Olivia strained to listen, but was out of clear hearing range by now.

Pritch viewed the question as a perfect opportunity to enhance his position with Victor and answered with a smile. "He's still alive like Ludvick wanted, but I killed Ben Cameaux."

Immediately looking directly at Ludvick for confirmation, Victor asked, "Is that true what he said?"

That Ludvick doubted whether Pritch had actually killed Ben showed in his sarcastic answer. "That's what he said."

Olivia almost stopped in her tracks. She wasn't sure she'd heard correctly, but had they said that Ben was dead? Surely that wasn't so. It can't be! screamed her thoughts.

When she and Mato reached the shack, he jerked open the door and shoved her inside. Immediately losing her balance, she fell hard to the dirt floor, adding more bruises to her battered body, especially her knees. Mato followed her into the shack and grabbed the back straps of her coveralls just as he had seen Ludvick do. He also jerked her upward, but with much less force and thus set her on her knees rather than her feet. She immediately winced in pain as the dirt from the floor pressed into the open wounds, but that was minor compared to what happened next. When she opened her eyes, she realized that Mato knelt in front of her. With unbridled fear in her voice, she stammered, "What...what are...what are you...doing? Get away from me!"

Mato smiled as he leaned forward to kiss her. Olivia could see his yellow, half-rotten teeth coming nearer, and when he blew his stinking breath into her nostrils, she gagged. She tried to block him with her still-tied hands, but fell backward instead. Stimulated even more by her resistance, Mato simply grabbed her and pulled her toward him, knocking her hands aside and holding them down effortlessly with one hand. She tried to scream, but it was useless, as his mouth completely covered hers and his tongue hungrily probed her lips for an opening. With a strength even she hadn't known she had left, she held her mouth shut, thereby forcing herself to breathe only through her nose. Trying to solve one problem, though, only served to heighten another one: the overwhelming stench of his breath, now even more intense because of its increasingly rapid rate. It was clear that Mato saw her refusal to open her mouth as just another challenge, like all the others on which he, of course, had always thrived.

Mato now stopped kissing her and began licking the sweat off her face as if the salty droplets were sweet nectar. Olivia started to cry uncontrollably, especially when he placed his free hand on her stomach and started moving it lower on her body. Then, like music to her ears, she heard someone yell, "Mato, get out here!" He stopped instantly, but pulled away from her slowly before rising and standing over her momentarily. She could hear his labored breathing, but dared not look up at him. Then he abruptly turned and stormed past his grandfather who was standing just inside the doorway of the shack. Mato was angry, but was familiar with Ludvick's deadly threatening voice and well-enough trained to obey it unconditionally.

Olivia, her eyes still closed, feared that either that beast of a man would return and finish what he started or the older one would ravage her even more savagely. Not until she'd heard Ludvick leave, close, and lock the door did she open her eyes. Suddenly the lingering odor of Mato's unwashed body and the stench of his foul breath prompted a sickening sensation from deep within. Unable any longer to stifle the involuntary retching of her tormented abdominal muscles, she fell forward, vomiting up the putrid, bitter bile that had been threatening her for hours. Completely spent, Olivia at last forced herself to a sitting position and then pushed her protesting body backward until she felt a wall behind her. Crying softly now, she wished for death while wondering what she had done to deserve this abuse. And although her heart and body were aching to see Derrick and to be held securely in his strong arms, she whispered in a barely audible voice, "Derrick my love, don't come here. Please, please, please don't come."

298

CHAPTER 53

Though it seemed like hours, it actually had been only a little over thirty minutes since Olivia's abduction and Ben was loaded onto the ambulance. Suddenly realizing that Derrick wasn't following him back to the pavilion, Valdore hurriedly returned to where Ben had been shot and found Derrick standing alone in the darkness.

"I'm goin' with you an take Ben's place," he declared.

"No! I'm going alone! I need you here to take care of Pappy and see after Ben! I gotta go!"

As Derrick turned to leave, Valdore grabbed his right arm. "Son, I'll do my part, but you better calm down an think with your head, or you're a dead man too!"

"I'm thinking clearly! Clearer than I ever have! I should have done this a long time ago! Listen carefully, don't let Pappy or the sheriff near the Rabeaux until I've had a chance to get to Olivia first, understand? They'll kill her and you know it if they even think someone's headed their way!" Turning suddenly, he then ran to his Jeep without waiting for the older Cajun's response.

As he drove Derrick slammed his hand again and again on the steering wheel. "Who the hell is Pritch Labote? That damn Ludvick Rabeaux has his hand everywhere!"

When he arrived at the docks, he parked as close to the skiff as possible and ran the rest of the way, clearly startling the man Ben had

299

posted to guard the *Miss Teresa*. "Hey, Derrick, man, you the last person I expect to see here tonight, how's the dance?"

Derrick waved, but didn't answer; instead, as he jumped into the skiff he shouted, "Untie me!"

Realizing at once that something was very wrong, the guard moved quickly to obey the order. As the skiff came alive under the roar of her engine, Derrick called out, "Have you seen any other skiff around here tonight?"

Almost at a run, the guard followed Derrick along the length of the dock, shouting excitedly, "I didn't see none round here, but I heard one about an hour ago going into Yankee Canal!"

Derrick gave full throttle to the *Miss Teresa*, quickly leaving the guard and the Cameaux docks far behind. An hour was a big head-start and he knew it. Furthermore, as he traveled eastward into Yankee Canal, he was also well aware that he wouldn't catch Ludvick tonight. Thanks to Valdore's locating the Rabeaux camp, however, he was confident in the one thing he did have going for him: the element of surprise. He knew not only where they were hiding, but also that they had no idea of having been discovered. That would be essential in his saving Olivia. He commanded himself aloud, "Get hold of yourself. This is about life and death – yours and hers. And now, it's all up to you. It's in your hands. You're the only one, just like you said you wanted it. Now, take care of it and get it done!"

His first major decision was choosing the best route to the Rabeaux camp, which in his judgment happened to be through the Cameaux Swamp. A mile into Yankee Canal he turned northeast onto a small bayou he and Eric had discovered as boys; it snaked its way almost directly to their family campsite. This was the route Pappy had encouraged him and Ben to take, despite the fact that it required twice as much traveling time as the well-traveled route through Yankee Canal. Regardless of the time factor, Derrick decided on this unlikely passage for the same reason Pappy suggested it: self-preservation, in case Ludvick had a "surprise" waiting for him along the more commonly traveled Yankee Canal.

Even in the darkness Derrick skillfully navigated the endless twists and turns of the little bayou as though traveling in daylight. Still, it

took him until daybreak to emerge on Bayou Raphael, the southeastern boundary of the Cameaux Swamp, where once more he was able to travel at full speed. Wasting no time at all, now he headed directly toward the Cameaux camp; but just a half mile before reaching it, he turned off Bayou Raphael and into the swamp itself. Although weaned here and right at home, he was amazed that navigating these waters was proving as natural as ever. It was all coming back to him as if it had been only yesterday; his confidence level soared. Nevertheless, though secure in his skill and ability, he was no fool; he knew the dangers of this swamp. With all the cypress knees and hidden logs just at or below the water's surface, it would be courting disaster to blindly steer a skiff through this swamp.

Thus, his successful maneuvering up to this point had definitely not been by chance. Rather, he had deliberately entered this familiar channel of the Cameaux Swamp because it ran its winding course through the midst of the surrounding shallower swamp. Appearing indistinguishable from the swamp-at-large, it was actually anything but that; Pappy had shown him when he was a boy this unmarked bayou. And now for that reason, Derrick felt he could almost relax since he was certain that the skiff's keel wouldn't drag bottom to hinder her progress.

Derrick patiently followed this bayou, which ran on a slight northeasterly course until he reached the very northeast corner of the Cameaux Swamp. There the bayou took a sharp turn to the northwest, but that wasn't the direction Derrick headed. Instead, throttling down the motor until the skiff was barely moving forward, he continued in a northeasterly direction by leaving the deeper waters of the bayou and entering the much shallower swamp. Now in less familiar surroundings, since even as a youth he rarely ventured this deep into the Cameaux Swamp, he had to be very careful. The sudden slight thump under Derrick's feet from the skiff's keel confirmed the shallowness of the water. Turning toward the stern, he saw the thick muck being kicked up by the propeller, but reminded himself as he looked back over the bow, "That levee can't be too far ahead."

The levee he remembered as a young boy lay on the northeast corner of the swamp and ran a couple miles in an east-west direction.

As the skiff plowed slowly through the swamp, Derrick scanned the landscape ahead of him for the levee he was looking for. Visibility, however, was limited because of the numerous cypress trees and the many small islands covered in thick vegetation. Not only that, but most of the morning sunlight was blocked by a thick canopy of cypress trees, although it did little to relieve the extremely high humidity that kept him sweating through his already-soaked clothing. This thick canopy also cast ghoulish shadows everywhere, making it even more difficult to see any distance ahead. Nevertheless, his persistence finally paid off when he spotted the levee that he had not seen since his youth. He adjusted his course to a more direct approach, but as he neared the narrow strip of land the waters became increasingly shallow; consequently, the skiff's engine was severely strained as the propeller dug deeper and deeper into the soupy muck. Eventually Derrick spotted a narrow opening relatively free of vegetation near the levee's edge and steered toward it. When the vessel seemed to hesitate slightly before reaching this opening, Derrick throttled up the engine enough to push the skiff onto the muddy bank. Immediately he turned off the engine and for the umpteenth time swatted at the pesky mosquitoes and wiped his sweaty forehead with his wet sleeve which at least felt cool on his brow.

For a while he just sat there staring at the opening before him and allowing his ears to acclimate to the silence of his surroundings. He could plainly see a well-worn pathway which likely had been created by some animal, perhaps a nutria or an otter. Then as the ringing in his ears from the engine subsided, Derrick stood in his skiff to listen to the familiar sounds of the swamp. He watched a pair of black ducks flying lazily overhead, their ceaseless chatter keeping them in constant communication, seemingly oblivious to his presence. However, the lone otter he spotted nearby definitely did appear to be offended by his intrusion as the fury creature busily churned up water and mud in his effortless gliding to and fro. Within moments Derrick could hear the calls of hidden marsh hens, amazingly as much at home in the swamp as in the marsh. But for all the sounds he did hear, it was what he didn't hear that most caught his attention. Nowhere were there sounds

of cars or trucks or even boat engines in the distance; such was this wilderness that both man and his man-made sounds were rare here.

Derrick tied the *Miss Teresa* to a young cypress tree off the starboard bow and unloaded his pirogue, tying it loosely alongside the skiff. He would travel lightly, very lightly indeed, since speed and mobility were so critical to his plans. On his way to the levee he had exchanged the light-colored shirt he wore at the fais-dodo for a dark green camouflaged one. He kept his jeans, though, preferring the denim toughness over the lighter, cooler cotton camouflage pants. He placed in the pirogue only his push pole, paddle, and shotgun. Then he strapped around his waist the new leather belt which now held his Bowie knife and two small pouches, one filled with extra ammo for both his shotgun and handgun and the other with the jerky Pappy had given him. Not having Ben with him made it possible to leave behind some supplies he would have otherwise taken, but one necessity he never would have omitted was the gallon of fresh water, which he now set next to his seat. He then strapped on his shoulder- holstered gun. He double-checked to make sure both his shotgun and handgun were ready for use. Nodding in satisfaction, he next slipped off his shoes and put on absolutely essential heavy rubber hip boots. Even as bulky and cumbersome as they were, he would never have ventured into the swamp without them. Finally, Derrick untied the pirogue and pushed it as far up the low levee as possible from where he was standing in the skiff. Then with one last look around the *Miss Teresa* to make sure she was safe, he climbed over her bow and jumped onto the levee next to the pirogue. Quickly he sank to his knees in the gooey mud banking the water part-way up the levee. Then, as if they hadn't been bad enough already, in an immediate, swirling frenzy which almost engulfed him, mosquitoes by the hundreds renewed their relentless, blood-thirsty attack upon him.

With no time to waste, however, Derrick tried to ignore the mosquitoes, grabbed hold of the front end of his pirogue, and began pulling it as best he could across the lower part of the levee. Although the thick mud seemed determined to devour, not only him but also his pirogue, it wasn't this sticky mess which stopped him dead in his tracks little more than five steps from the water's edge. He clearly

303

heard a low, deep grunt less than twenty feet in front of him. And even though he couldn't see more than half that distance because the trail twisted so and the vegetation on either side was extremely thick, the sound was unmistakable. Thus, when he heard that low grunt again, he forgot the pirogue and all its carefully packed provisions and began looking frantically around for a life-saving escape route. Completely oblivious to the mosquitoes still assaulting his neck and face, he knew that the greater threat ahead could definitely ruin his day. Once more he looked to his right and had barely glanced back in front of him when a low-to-the-ground, dark, shadowy figure came charging down the very path he had been taking. Derrick reacted instinctively, diving into the vegetation to avoid the very powerful jaws of a large female alligator. No sooner had he dived to his right than the gator snapped at his left leg, missing it by inches. With the sound of her snapping jaw echoing in his ears like the firing of a small-caliber rifle, Derrick immediately scrambled up on all fours and turned to stand firmly in the face of the formidable beast. With gun in hand, he aimed carefully for a fatal shot to the gator's head, for he knew that trying to outrun her on this muddy levee was futile. As his grip on the gun tightened however, he realized he couldn't fire because of the risk that the Rabeaux might hear the shot, thereby ending his chance of saving Olivia. Now as she crouched there not more than a couple of feet away, she glared and hissed at him through huge open jaws. Knowing he had no real choice, Derrick took a deep breath, eased his grip on the gun, and waited for her final attack. Within a couple of seconds, though, he was surprised by sounds of soft, rustling grass behind him. The real shock came, though, when he looked down to see baby gators slither between his feet and through the thick vegetation, converging at their mother's side briefly before rushing for the water ahead of her. Not until the last of her leathery offspring entered the water did that fierce mama close her life-threatening jaws and slither away to join her young for a morning swim. Derrick felt a chill up his spine as he took another, even deeper breath and looked around once more time before replacing his gun in its holster. He trudged back to his pirogue to resume hauling it across the levee. Only then did it occur to him that he now knew very well exactly what had created that path where he

was trespassing, and he certainly had no intention of tarrying there any longer than necessary.

Once on the north side of the levee, Derrick carefully scanned the whole area for additional surprises before pushing his pirogue into the water and climbing aboard. The swamp on either side of the levee was virtually the same, with endless cypress trees surrounding countless islands of thick vegetation and boundless animal activity. With push pole in hand, the young Cameaux now stood straddling the rear seat and forcefully shoving the pirogue forward with each stabbing and subsequent push-off motion of the pole against the muddy swamp bottom. Like riding a bike, standing in a pirogue and push-poling was a little tricky at first; but once mastered, it was a skill never to be forgotten. Thus, Derrick gave no thought to these second-nature movements, and his every stabbing push on the pole made the pirogue surge effortlessly through the shallow water.

CHAPTER 54

Time, thought Derrick, it's already been over twelve hours since they kidnapped Olivia. I can't waste a minute more! He knew he'd sacrificed the quickest route to the Rabeaux hide-out for the sake of stealth. He only hoped that he hadn't made yet another error in a long line of mistakes since the deaths of Eric and Jon. "No time or energy for second-guessing, Cameaux," he chided himself aloud. Then he heard in his head, "You know, boy, you gotta keep you focus on you mission an save you strength for what's ahead. You gonna need it!" This bit of Cajun wisdom flashed into his mind as clearly as if Pappy himself had voiced the words again. And, in spite of himself, Derrick smiled as he remembered many occasions when his grandfather settled his boyish anxiety and calmed his frustrations with that apt advice. It worked again. Even as he continued his swift pace in a northeasterly direction, guided only by the sun and instinct, it had enabled him to settle into a comfortable, relaxed push-poling rhythm, thereby eliminating undue stress on his body.

Now almost three miles from the levee where he had left the *Miss Teresa* tied, Derrick slowed his pace to about half-speed. Pushing slowly and focusing his intense gaze ahead and to his right, he searched the swamp for its channel into Bayou Bernard, which Valdore had said was near the northeast corner of Cameaux Swamp. Also concentrating on listening as well as watching, he strained to

307

detect even faint sounds of humanity which would help him judge his distance from the Rabeaux camp. Within a few more minutes he caught sight of the bayou exactly where Valdore had located it. Barely distinguishable from its surroundings, it was at least virtually free of cypress trees.

Then as Derrick pushed his pirogue on toward the bayou he could see that it was more well-defined in shape and wider than he had originally thought. He also noted, though, that it was actually even more shallow than he had first realized, thus making it impossible for most skiffs to navigate. Pirogues, however, were a different matter. Compared to the swamp which surrounded it, this bayou ran practically obstacle free. Derrick allowed his pirogue to glide within ten feet of the bayou's edge, but dared not enter so as not to risk being spotted if anyone were in the area. Not only that, but after seeing how relatively straight the waterway ran he formulated his plan to involve the bayou, but not directly use it as his final water route to the Rabeaux camp. Instead, he would use it only as a map into enemy territory, preferring the swamp and its potential hiding places as his safer approach.

Now withdrawing the push pole from the water and securing it under the front seat of his pirogue, he sat down and pulled out his paddle. From now on he would proceed with extreme caution and personally stay low to the water. Next he paddled away from the bayou until he drifted at least five hundred feet north of it. Then, still in the swamp, he began making his own water route basically parallel to the bayou, weaving around giant cypress trees as though he were in an obstacle course. Actually the trees gave him little trouble, but the plethora of tiny islands of thick vegetation was more difficult to maneuver. Sometimes he found himself over a thousand feet away from the bayou he was supposed to be following, while at other times he was uncomfortably close, often merely feet away. Though he still felt it necessary to remain in the swamp rather than travel the bayou, he also knew he had to be very careful, especially since he didn't know the exact location of the Rabeaux campsite. Whatever the risks, though, he was satisfied that he chose the best course because he still figured that Ludvick would be looking to the south for his enemy.

Derrick couldn't shake the thought of Ludvick and the Rabeaux possessing Olivia. He knew why they took her but he had no idea that the old Rabeaux was so well informed as to his personal relationship with Olivia. Perhaps it was just as well that he was unaware of the extent of Ludvick's knowledge because it would have served only to heighten his fear for her safety.

On and on he paddled, constantly alert to all potential danger from both man and the native swamp dwellers, primarily the many gators with their young that he watched swimming all around his pirogue. He was now doing his best to be as unnoticeable as any human could be under the circumstances. This demanded only slow-motion movement to avoid calling attention to himself. As nerve-racking as the situation was, Derrick endured the endless assault from hordes of mosquitoes, not to mention the miserable, steamy weather. This experience would try a man's patience, if not also his very sanity and will to survive. But what else could he do there in the middle of the swamp with not even a whisper of a breeze crossing his path? Continually sweat-soaking his clothes, the oppressive heat and high humidity engulfed him like a suffocating blanket. And though he longed to quench his thirst, only once did he stop to take a swallow of fresh water. Derrick knew his own endurance, and he would push his body to the limit or beyond to rescue Olivia.

He began running into even more serious difficulties farther into his journey because the group of increasingly larger islands he was approaching forced him to draw nearer and nearer the bayou to avoid becoming lost. Amazed at just how really well the Rabeaux camp was hidden, he had no doubt that if not for Valdore's chance stumbling upon it, Ludvick could have remained hidden forever. But as he carefully moved forward, Derrick noticed the beginnings of a low levee that separated him from the bayou. "Getting close," he muttered. He intentionally paddled next to the islands, using the vegetation as cover and at times even losing sight of the levee altogether, especially when he circled the larger islands. Always deliberate, and acutely aware of his surroundings, he weaved his way from island to island, never exposing himself for long and then only when absolutely necessary. The continued absence of any wind not only added to the

unbearable heat, but it also made the swamp deathly quiet. Even the slightest move seemed amplified and echoed across the water.

Eventually he began working his way back toward the levee when he came upon a small island which completely separated him from it. Realizing that the island was no more than twenty feet wide and perhaps twice as long, he eased his pirogue under a low hanging bush and tied her there. Quietly stepping from the pirogue onto the island, he automatically crouched as low to the ground as possible and made his way to the side of the island facing the levee. Stopping at the water's edge behind a young palmetto bush, he spotted the levee less than a quarter mile in front of him. He thoroughly scanned its thick tree line for any sign of the Rabeaux camp, but saw nothing. Then under his breath in a barely audible whisper, he reasoned, "Surely the camp can't be much farther. I know I've got to be close!" From this short distance he had a perfect view of the oak, chinaberry, willow, swamp maple and many other tall trees which covered the levee. In fact, so thick were the trees on this narrow strip that their dense foliage virtually blocked all but faint slivers of light shining through from the bayou side.

Derrick would have remained longer behind the young palmetto bush had he thought it worthwhile. However, since one last look at the levee's dark undergrowth revealed nothing so far, he figured the camp had to be just a little farther. Nevertheless, just before he turned away, something to his left and high atop the tree canopy caught his attention. Perched high on her nest atop a giant cypress tree, a huge bald eagle was peering curiously at him before taking flight. Momentarily spellbound by such an awesome, rare sight, he watched the beautiful, majestic bird effortlessly clear the tops of the trees and follow the levee to his left. Staring intently as the eagle slowly disappeared in the distance, he unexpectedly caught sight of something else. Since this was his first time he had cast his eyes skyward because of his preoccupation with his immediate surroundings, he quickly stood to his full height and moved closer to the water's edge to get a better view. He had no choice but to validate or discount what he thought he had seen. At first it was difficult spotting it again because of all the thick vegetation; when he finally did locate it this time there

was no doubt as he gazed upon a thin spiral of smoke. Derrick's shoulders relaxed slightly and he exhaled in a sigh of relief. "The Rabeaux camp!" Making a mental note of the smoke's distance from the small island, he slowly retraced his way to the pirogue.

Even as he settled into his seat, he grabbed his paddle to back away from the small island, but he wasn't paying enough attention to the sedia bush where he had tied his pirogue for cover. Suddenly he saw it. Stretched out on the lowest branch of that nondescript bush was a huge water moccasin, and though he tried frantically to stop the front of his pirogue from bumping the bush, he was too late. The resulting hard lick dislodged the poisonous cottonmouth, and it fell with a thud into the bottom of the pirogue. Then with speed that surprised even Derrick, the snake raced directly toward him and he gasped as the diamond-shaped head brushed against his left thigh. As though frozen in time, he could do nothing more than watch the viper slither onto the seat next to him, coil its supple length for striking, and open wide its white venomous mouth in anticipation of sinking its deadly fangs into him. With desperate speed, Derrick drew his Bowie knife and swung the broad blade, expertly pinning the base of the threatening head to the seat. Instantly from the serpent's open mouth spewed the vile, deadly venom just as Derrick severed the head from its body, setting off a series of convulsive, wild twists. The headless body whipped madly against his leg until he could finally grab and fling it into the water. Then using his knife, he flipped the head overboard as well. On more than one occasion he barely escaped being bitten by an aggressive cottonmouth, but this by far was the closest he'd ever come to being stung by one. Without moving from his seat he took a deep breath, closed his eyes and leaned forward, propping his elbows on his knees and resting his head in his cupped hands. He let the involuntary shivers run their course throughout his body as he listened to his heartbeat pulsating loudly in his ears. Generally fear was not an emotion familiar to Derrick, but if there was one thing on earth which unnerved him, it was a snake.

Regaining his composure within minutes, he once again scanned the skies for that trace of smoke and pointed his pirogue in that direction. Night was fast approaching.

CHAPTER 55

As he did at the end of every day at this campsite, Ludvick once again stood on the tiny wharf. Facing southwest he listened and watched intently, satisfied at hearing and seeing nothing. He always welcomed the dependable cloak of darkness which would soon be cast upon the swamp and his secret hiding place. He almost, but not quite, even allowed a visible smile to cross his face as he pictured the Cameaux out in force looking for the girl. The fact that almost twenty-four hours had passed since he took Olivia and no one had yet arrived at his campsite satisfied him and confirmed that he planned well and he was safe. In fact, he was very confident that no Cameaux would ever find him until he chose to make his presence known. Ludvick gazed one last time down the bayou as full darkness was slowly settling, and then he turned to face his camp. Using the sun's very last hint of daylight, he now carefully surveyed the area to be certain that nothing was amiss. Four pirogues turned bottom-sides-up rested high and dry on the levee with push poles and paddles beside them. The makeshift stockade which held Olivia was locked with a heavy wooden bar across the door and not a sound from within could be heard. Only as an afterthought did he even glance toward the rear of the camp at that dark abyss of the swamp, that most formidable defensive barrier which he was sure his enemy neither would nor could possibly breach to reach him.

Content with how well the day had gone, the single-minded Rabeaux eventually made his way to the camp door. He felt a great sense of joy at the prospect of finally obliterating the family he hated above all else in his world. First he would kill Derrick to eliminate the chance of any more offspring; then he planned to kill Ben – just for revenge, of course, and also because he doubted Pritch's earlier boasting. Last, but certainly not least, he would savor his long-awaited opportunity of killing the old man. At the very thought of Pappy, he instinctively reached into his back pocket and pulled out a well-worn, brown-leather pouch about the size and shape of a man's wallet. Halting his steps just short of the closed camp door, he stared at the pouch for a few seconds, lost in thought. Never had he gone anywhere without this leather pouch. Suddenly hearing someone turn the inside doorknob jolted him back to reality, and he quickly stuffed the pouch into his pocket. Just as if nothing had happened, he calmly stood face to face with his grandson. Side-stepping the older Rabeaux without a word, Mato now walked past him to the spot where the hip boots hung at the corner of the camp and relieved himself.

As Ludvick entered the camp and walked toward the small table where his son and Pritch were sitting, Victor said, "Food's ready. I cooked some black duck."

"Bout time!" spouted Ludvick as he headed for his bunk which rested at the far corner of the camp next to a large chest of drawers. There he exchanged his camouflage shirt for a light green undershirt before sitting on the corner of the bunk to remove his socks and boots. Before getting back up, he again pulled that small leather pouch from his back pocket. Turning it over in his hands, he pushed it under his pillow. Then he walked bare-footed to the pots of food on the stove and served himself a large portion of rice and roux-soaked duck.

About that time Mato re-entered the camp and said in hopeful expectation, "The girl is still there. Maybe I feed her after while."

Pritch responded excitedly, "Boy, Mato, you sure gonna have youself one fine woman there!"

Mato smiled. "I think she likes me. Her an me, we gonna have a lota fun." Everyone laughed except Ludvick.

"Les eat," suggested Victor. "I'm starved!" The others heartily agreed.

Each man then served himself and sat at the table with Ludvick, who had already begun eating without them. As usual, the meal was void of manners and proper etiquette. Slurps and belches were considered compliments to the cook. Forks and spoons were available, but hands were much more convenient, and having no napkins, not a problem. Whatever couldn't be licked off the fingers was simply wiped on pants or a good long-sleeved shirt, which also serviced both mouth and nose in one swipe. This was normal for these men; they knew no other way. So self-absorbed were they in stuffing themselves, that it wasn't until the end of the second serving that any conversation occurred at all.

Finally finished, Pritch pushed his chair away from the table and stretched like a satiated fat cat. He clasped his hands behind his head, leaned his chair back on two legs and looked directly at Ludvick. "Well, now that we got the girl, you got a plan?"

Victor found humor in Pritch's always asking Ludvick stupid questions, and he had to look away to avoid laughing out loud. If Pritch kept it up, he would surely find himself in serious trouble soon.

Without so much as even a glance toward Pritch, Ludvick answered sharply, "The plan is to kill Derrick Cameaux. The plan don't never change, Stupid. If we kill him tomorrow, or we kill him next year, or we kill him in a hundred years, the plan is always the same. So don't ax me no more cooyon questions." Pritch was slow, but even he felt the sting in Ludvick's voice. Mato got up from the table and took his plate to the stove, where he managed to salvage three small pieces of meat from the meager remains in the black iron pot. Dumping these on one side of his plate, he briskly scraped the sides and bottom of the rice pot and plopped about a tablespoon's worth of scorched rice down next to the meat fragments. Adding a little tepid water to stretch what was left of the roux, he thoroughly mixed the rice with this now cold, rather greasy mixture.

Watching his son, Victor couldn't help asking in a rather needling tone, "Boy, you still hungry?"

With obvious irritation Mato answered, "This fricassee is for the girl." He then quickly filled a cup with water and started out the door, but not before Ludvick stopped him.

"Hold up, Boy. Be sure, when she's finish, you tie her up for the night." Mato nodded as he closed the camp door, mumbling under his breath what he would never have dared say aloud to his grandfather.

In sheer torment since sunset, the mosquitoes by the hundreds attacked and bit Olivia without mercy. She spent all her time swatting and scratching. She heard the door to the camp open and she braced herself as best she could as to what that meant for her. She was seated on the dirt floor when the door to her prison opened and Mato stepped in. "I brung you something to eat," he said as he thrust the plate toward her. Olivia certainly had not wanted to eat anything her captors might have given her, but now she was in a desperate situation. Thus, as Mato stood before her with the plate of food in his outstretched hand, she could smell the duck and her hunger drove her to reach up to accept the food. Barely able to see in the dark, she felt around the plate for a fork, but finding none, used her fingers to explore the food on the plate. Recognizing the rice, she cautiously lifted some to her mouth, and was surprised and relieved that she not only ate it, but also kept it down. She decided to eat as much as she could, knowing she needed whatever nourishment it could provide. Mato watched with fascination as she ate all the food on the plate and then he said, "Here, some water." Olivia quickly grabbed the cup from his hand and drank every last drop, and though still thirsty, she stubbornly refused to ask for more.

Once she finished the meager meal, Mato stepped to within inches of her and she thought, "Well, this is it. Now I get raped!" However, to her surprise, while she remained seated with her back to the wall, Mato raised her arms and tied both her right and left hands to the wall by looping the ropes through steel rings Ludvick had placed there for just this purpose. She remained seated and helpless in stunned silence until she suddenly became aware of immediate danger. Overwhelmed by the foul odor of Mato's breath, Olivia gagged as he bent over and kissed her, harshly jarring her back to her senses. She then bravely braced herself for what she was certain would follow, but he backed away from her instead. Then just before he closed and re-locked the

door he boasted confidently, "My name Mato Rabeaux. I killed your husband an I'm gonna kill Derrick Cameaux too. Then me an you gonna get tied up together!"

The next sounds the stunned Olivia heard were the slamming door and Mato's satisfied laughter. "They killed Eric?" It had never crossed her mind that these vile men had any connection to Eric's murder. And as if that weren't bad enough, now they were planning to kill Derrick too. Unable to control herself, she shouted, "You filthy animal!" Whether or not he heard her, she winced as the sound of his laughter echoing through the darkness. Although she'd surely cried all she was able, yet more tears streamed down her face as her now limp body shook with uncontrollable sobbing. The mosquitoes resumed their fierce attacks, and now hogtied and unable to swat at them or even scratch the unbearable itching, it was all unbelievably tormenting. To Olivia at that moment, everything else appeared useless and hopeless—so much so that dying actually seemed far more welcome than living.

CHAPTER 56

Long after midnight Pritch was still awake. Ludvick, Victor, and Mato slept in their bunks, but his bedding consisted of an old filthy blanket on the floor next to the kitchen table. But that wasn't the reason he couldn't sleep. From the first moment he laid eyes on Olivia, he knew he had to have her and that's all he'd thought of that whole day. Pritch burned with lust.

Now, at last under the cover of darkness and waiting as patiently as possible for everyone in the camp to fall asleep, Pritch listened carefully for any wakeful movement. Much to his relief he heard only the loud, unmelodic sounds of heavy breathing and snoring. Slowly and quietly he arose from his rumpled blanket, pulled on his pants, and silently walked bare-chested and barefooted to the door. Deliberately grabbing the knob with both hands in hopes of somehow lessening any possible noise, he carefully turned it until he heard a slight click. To his delight, he pulled the door open without a squeak and stepped outside. The rough wooden planks of the makeshift porch felt cool to his bare feet as he closed the door behind him and sighed deeply. Cautiously, he waited on the porch a few seconds to be certain that no one was aware of his excursion. Sensing no sounds of movement from within, he relaxed and smiled to himself, assuming he had disturbed no one. Now hardly able to control his anticipation for what awaited him, he quickly pulled from his back pocket the two old sweat rags he intended using to ensure

Olivia's silence. He then hurried across the yard to the shed and quietly lifted the bar which had held the door shut.

Olivia was startled to hear someone at the shed door because she neither heard the camp door open nor the footsteps that would have warned her of someone's presence. Not surprisingly she couldn't fall asleep because of the constant buzzing and biting of the mosquitoes, as well as the numbness in her hands and arms and the burning sensations in her shoulders from the way Mato had secured her to the wall.

When the door opened, the man who stepped inside whispered teasingly, "Mizz Cameaux, I just bet you got pretty lonesome out here all by yourself."

Olivia immediately recognized his voice and cried out, "What do you want?" However, before she could utter another word or scream for help, Pritch stuffed one rag into her mouth and then quickly secured it with the other dirty cloth that he tied at the back of her head. She screamed, but only a faint, muffled sound came through the thick cloth.

When he then stood up again in the open doorway of the shed, she could easily see his dark frame silhouetted against the lighter background of the night sky. She watched in horror as he unbuckled his pants, and then she closed her eyes for just a second to say a quick prayer. When she opened her eyes again she realized that he was bending over to remove his pants, but at first she thought the night was playing tricks on her. Just as clearly as she could see Pritch's bent torso, at the very same time it appeared that his silhouette was still standing. It didn't take her long to realize that someone else was behind him, and her immediate thought was, are all of them outside waiting to have their way with me?

Pritch stood once more, now kicking aside his crumpled pants and blocking her view of the other man. Almost drooling he boasted, "I'm gonna teach you what a real Cajun can–OOOFF!!!" Pritch instinctively grabbed at the knife blade which had sliced through his back and was now protruding from his lower chest. But the blade was withdrawn before he could touch it.

She was terrified as the body before her slowly slid to the dirt floor; however, she felt no comfort at all in still seeing the silhouette of that

second man at the door. Even his sudden, low whisper, "Liv, you alright?" didn't register immediately. Sure her mind was playing the cruelest of jokes on her, it was only after that whispered voice had spoken a second time, "Liv, I've come for you!" that she realized she was neither crazy nor delirious. She cried out his name, but luckily, this time the gag did stop her cry just as Derrick reached her. He quickly cut her hands free, removed the rags from her mouth, and cradled her in his arms. "Liv, I love you. I've always loved you, only you."

As she clung tightly to him, she cried so hard she couldn't say a word. Clearly feeling the awful intensity of her uncontrollable tremors as she welcomed his tender embrace, Derrick gently caressed her weak and battered body, constantly reassuring her of his love. Finally Olivia softly spoke between sobs. "Oh, Derrick, Derrick, we have to get out of here! These men, these men..." She drew on all her reserves to finish. "These men, they killed Eric and Jon!"

"Yes, I know, but we'll make it out. Can you walk?"

"Yes," she answered, though not at all sure she could.

"We have to be very quiet," Derrick reminded her as he helped her to her feet. Though every part of her body was screaming pain, she stood strong and held tightly to his arm as they stepped over Pritch's lifeless body. Once outside her prison, he led her eastward, following the levee in the direction where he left his pirogue. They walked slowly at first because just putting one foot in front of the other hurt her; however, every step she took brought new vigor to her legs and a renewed determination to live. In fact, before long, Olivia surprised both of them by keeping up to the demanding pace Derrick set.

Ludvick heard Pritch get up and leave the camp, but assumed he went to relieve himself. However, when he didn't returned within the few minutes he had allowed him, Ludvick cursed angrily under his breath and got up to dress. He automatically glanced at Victor and Mato, noting that they were still sleeping; he turned away, shrugging his shoulders as if to give credence to his feeling of nothing but disgust for his offspring. "Good thing I don't never depend on them for nothing much!" he growled under his breath as he left the camp to look for Pritch. Seeing nothing nearby, he looked at the dark shadow of the shed and began walking toward it. Remembering the way Pritch

stared at the girl, Ludvick already made up his mind that if Pritch were raping her, he'd kill him without question. His intent, of course, was not to protect the honor of the girl, but to preserve and use her for the procreation of his own family through Mato. He certainly wouldn't allow her to carry a child seeded by Pritch Labote!

Ludvick's anger intensified with each step toward the darkened shed because he could see the door standing wide open. Not only that, but just before reaching the open door, he spotted a pair of feet protruding from the doorway. Sensing the inevitable, he ran the last few feet to the shed and looked inside. Banging his fist against the open door, Ludvick's anger immediately turned to rage when he realized that Olivia was gone. Aimed at her, he spewed forth through his clenched teeth, "Damn! Cameaux putain! Dog!" Then with a fierce jerk, he dragged Pritch's naked body from the shed, noticing at once the dark blood oozing from the deep knife wound on his back. As Ludvick stood there gazing at the pathetic sight before him, at that very moment he wished Pritch were still alive so that he could have the pleasure of the kill himself.

As soon as Ludvick walked into the shed he could see and feel that the ropes which held Olivia were cut. He came to the realization that he and Pritch had been followed, but the aggravating question was "By whom?" Storming out of the shed, he now stood motionless just outside the door listening intently in the dark silence for any sound to indicate the direction he should follow.

Derrick and Olivia were less than a hundred yards from the shed when Ludvick found Pritch's body. And despite his leading her away as quickly as possible, there was really no such thing as a rapid escape through the maze-like thickness of underbrush that choked the levee. In reality, the best he could do to keep the distance growing between them and the Rabeaux was to hope they wouldn't find Pritch's body before daylight.

Derrick constantly dodged low-hanging tree limbs and huge thorny blackberry thickets for both of them because he couldn't let go of Olivia's hand. In fact, she followed him so closely that once she stumbled on his feet, and they both ended up in a heap on the ground. Trying to maintain sanity and composure in such trying circumstances

proved extremely frustrating, but they knew they had to keep moving, no matter what.

Common sense demanded that he hide his pirogue, not only as close as possible to the Rabeaux campsite, but also in the area least expected by Ludvick. Now, just as the pirogue was almost within reach, Derrick suddenly side-stepped a thin tree directly in his path. Olivia, however, because she followed so closely behind him, never saw the tree. Had he only realized what tree it was, he would have seen to it that she safely bypassed it as well. Cajuns know this menace as a devil tree: Because its trunk and limbs are blanketed by a multitude of needle-sharp barbs; it's almost impossible to touch without great risk of being pierced by its four-inch spikes. Derrick safely avoided the tree without a scratch, but Olivia's attempted side-stepping didn't work.

At first she'd felt only the tug on her clothes as two barbs ripped holes in her short overalls; within moments, however, Olivia was very much aware of the third barb which caught her just below the hem of her shorts. Her momentum carried her right thigh full force into the very bark of the tree and the entire four-inch length of that barb penetrated her exposed skin. It then broke free of the tree, leaving the stinging shaft deeply buried in her tender thigh. Like a hot branding iron set to bare flesh, the searing pain was instantaneous; she grabbed her leg with her free hand and screamed. Derrick turned just in time to catch her as she fell headlong into him, knocking both of them to the ground again.

"Olivia, what's wrong!"

She moaned barely above a whisper, "On that tree, Derrick, something on that tree stuck into my leg. Oh Derrick, it feels like fire! It feels like fire!"

He crawled back to the tree and carefully extended his hand until he lightly touched one of the sharp barbs of the devil tree; he knew exactly what he had to do. Quickly returning to her side, he wrapped his left arm around her shoulders and pulled her close to his side as he asked the question. "Where did it stick you?" Olivia placed his hand on her thigh where he could feel about a half inch of the barb above her skin. Then, without explaining his action, he suddenly braced himself, laid his right leg securely over hers, and placed his left hand

over her mouth while his right thumb and forefinger grabbed tightly around the shaft of the barb and pulled hard. Olivia screamed again but this time Derrick pressed his hand hard over her mouth to muffle the sound. But it was too late. With her first scream, a sensation of near panic gripped him as he realized just how close they still were to the Rabeaux camp

Pulling her even closer he whispered, "Sorry, Liv, but I had to do it that way! It had to come out, and I couldn't let your scream lead the Rabeaux to us. We have to stay hidden and stay as far ahead of them as possible." He deliberately didn't mention her first scream of only moments before. In spite of his best attempts, though, the sudden realization of how she unintentionally might have jeopardized their chances of escape registered clearly on her face. As she opened her mouth to chastise herself, Derrick laid his fingertips lightly on her quivering lips and whispered, "No, my love, it's all right. But we must keep moving. The pirogue isn't far. Can you make it?" Olivia nodded. Then while she rested her weary head against his chest and continued crying softly, he picked her up and carried her the rest of the way to the pirogue. Once they reached the pirogue he set her down gently on the front seat, kissed her forehead and without a word moved to the rear, scooped up his push pole, and quickly pushed the pirogue away from the levee.

Over and over in his mind he was lamenting that he had not gotten to her much earlier in the night. At this point he was hardly more than a stone's throw away from the levee and the Rabeaux camp, but the first sign of daybreak was already at hand. Almost as if he thought he could outrun the sun, he pushed harder and harder on the pole to force the pirogue to surge forward. Again and again he pushed with all he had in him, but the added weight of Olivia, no matter how slight that might be, was making the pirogue less maneuverable and much slower. Nevertheless, knowing that they could be caught if the Rabeaux were already on their trail drove him to do whatever one man could to put distance between them.

Because they were still too close to the Rabeaux camp, Olivia and Derrick dared not speak a word which would carry like a shout in the stillness. Still, she did turn every few minutes to encourage him with

her loving smile of trust and confidence, despite her awareness that their chances of escape weren't that promising. And in light of that stark reality, her heart ached with each thought of Teresa and Toni, but she also found great comfort in knowing that, at least, they were safe. Then she thought of Eric and their shared dream of so long ago, a dream shattered by what had once been her nightmare's evil shadows of something beyond her imagination and grasp. Now, though, the evil shadowy men in her nightmare had faces and a name—Rabeaux, and she thought, "You turned my life and the lives of those I love up-side-down. I hate you!"

CHAPTER 57

Not only had Ludvick heard Olivia's first scream, but he also heard another voice in response and immediately realized it had to be Derrick Cameaux with her. The leader of the Rabeaux stood motionless, straining to detect the exact location of his enemy, which within moments he knew to be the swamp side of the levee. Almost as a reflex reaction, that smoldering vengeful bitterness burned anew in the old Rabeaux. His body trembled with the fierce hatred he longed to unleash on his enemy. In seconds Ludvick assessed the situation and decided not to follow Derrick and Olivia on the levee; instead, he would launch his pirogues directly into the swamp at the rear of the camp. Propelled by pure demonic rage, he ran back to the camp yelling, "REVEILLER!! REVEILLER!!"

So rudely startled from sleep, Victor immediately jumped to his feet in a state of dazed confusion. Giving Mato a violent shake and shouting, "Get up, Boy!" he headed for the front door in his underwear.

At that very instant the door flew open and in rushed Ludvick, unleashing an endless, almost unintelligible babble of curses. Though well accustomed to Ludvick's outbursts of insanity at seemingly insignificant matters, this time was different. They finally heard and understood a single sentence in all of Ludvick's madness: "THAT DAMN BATARD DERRICK CAMEAUX GOT DA GIRLL!!" No

further explanation was necessary, and without another word, Victor and Mato scrambled into their clothes. Mato strapped his long knife to his side, and both men grabbed their shotguns and ammo on their way out the door.

Ludvick jerked on his camouflage shirt and grabbed his shotgun and ammo box. All three men put on their hip boots, and under Ludvick's direction, they pulled their pirogues to the swamp side of the levee. Neither Victor nor Mato had even given Pritch a thought until they noticed his body lying in a pool of blood next to the shed door. "What happen to Pritch?" asked Mato.

"That Cameaux kill him!" snapped Ludvick, as if it were not obvious. When they reached the water's edge, he quickly motioned for Mato to take the lead. "That damn Cameaux boy is gonna try an circle us an head back to the Cameaux Swamp. We can cut him off. Mato, you head yourself in that way." The elder Rabeaux pointed in the direction he was certain Mato could intersect Derrick and Olivia.

All the commotion at the Rabeaux camp had clearly carried across the water to them. In fact, real panic momentarily seized Derrick as he realized to his horror that the Rabeaux were on his trail far quicker than he expected. Especially now with the night cover gone and the sun shining brightly, he knew they were vulnerable. Once again he could no longer stand in the pirogue to push-pole because he couldn't take the chance of being spotted. His only option was to sit and paddle, and the reduction in his forward speed was immediate. The Rabeaux were standing in their pirogues and push-poling at a feverish pace, completely unconcerned about sacrificing silence for speed. In fact, he could plainly hear the Rabeaux clan drawing nearer his position by the minute. The only reason he couldn't see them now or, more importantly, why they couldn't see him and Olivia, was due to the maze of heavily vegetated mini-islands he had determined to use to his advantage.

Meanwhile, Mato push-poled with the fervor of an unleashed demon on his way to torment an unsuspecting soul, his powerful body meshed as one with the pirogue as each thrust of the pole sent the vessel skimming swiftly atop the water. He had been taught the fine art of controlling a pirogue since he was little more than a babe, and it

was one of the two things he could do about as well as any Cajun anywhere. In Mato's mind Olivia was his woman and Derrick Cameaux had stolen her from him. Over and over he growled, "Damn you, Cameaux, I'm, gonna cut you open an eat you heart!"

Ludvick encouraged Mato to get well ahead of him because he hoped Mato's blindly barreling his way in the direction he sent him into the swamp would flush Derrick and Olivia out into the open. There he and Victor could trap and kill this troublesome Cameaux who, despite Ludvick's angry, bitter hatred of all Cameaux, he now recognized as more difficult prey. It irritated him as he begrudgingly recognized Derrick's enormous courage. Many years had passed since a Cameaux had directly challenged him in such a personal way. He mumbled, "You gonna come an steal from me? You come to my camp! My swamp!!" Derrick Cameaux invaded his private domain and rescued the girl right from under his nose. This was not only unthinkable, but also unbearable and a definite cause for revenge, even if there had been no other. Thus, his fight with the Cameaux now became even more focused against this brash upstart, this young, impudent Cajun. Why, just like an interloper, he'd suddenly now appeared on the scene to take over and single-handedly end a Rabeaux-Cameaux war which had raged for more than a century. NO! NO! NO! thought Ludvick. THIS IS NOT HIS WAR! THIS IS MY WAR! I'M IN CONTROL!! And the more he thought about Derrick and what he was doing, the more incensed he became until he finally hissed aloud between clinched teeth: "NOT NO MAN ALIVE HAVE NEVER OUTSMART LUDVICK RABEAUX, AN NOT NO MAN ALIVE WILL EVER OUTSMART LUDVICK RABEAUX!"

Derrick could hear the rapid approach of at least one Rabeaux who seemed very close, and he could also hear the others in the background. Not only Derrick, but Olivia as well, knew the situation was perilous. And more than just a hint of guilt stabbed at her now as she realized that without her, Derrick would have a far greater chance of survival. She glanced at her prince's handsome face and could see the determination and strength it projected. In reality, though, she knew they couldn't count on a fairy-tale ending to this dire situation.

The Rabeaux were quickly closing in on them, and any advantage they might have had earlier was all but gone. The swamp devil pursuing them had his own version of how this prince and princess were to spend their final moments together, and it surely didn't include living happily ever after.

CHAPTER 58

L udvick suddenly yelled at Mato to wait for him and Victor. Since the small islands they were approaching were so numerous, he'd reasoned that a more coordinated search would now be more effective in achieving his desired results.

The sun, now out in full blistering force on another cloudless day of extremely high humidity, was an almost lethal combination that guaranteed physical exertion to be torturous and painful. The only solace was the occasional shaded area provided by the canopy-like top of the great trees surrounding them. Even the thick, steamy air seemed almost stagnant, making lungs work twice as hard for any trace of fresh air; but none would be found, not on this day. Amidst such circumstances Derrick paid special attention not to knock his paddle against the side of the pirogue because the resulting thump would certainly travel straight to the Rabeaux, immediately exposing their position.

As the islets surrounding them grew more numerous, Derrick took advantage of the natural shield they provided against the Rabeaux. A short distance ahead he spotted an islet that was clearly one of the largest in the area. Because he already knew that trying to outrun these hounds was pointless, he remembered Pappy's advice to always be alert and innovative in his dealings with them: "Always do what they don't never expect, Boy!" So without hesitation, Derrick decided to

make a stand on land rather than allowing the Rabeaux to run him down on the water.

To reach this larger islet, however, he must first leave the relative shelter and safety of the smaller bits of land and cross an open body of water. While the distance didn't appear too great initially, he felt exposed and vulnerable as he plowed into that unprotected water. He knew that if he had misjudged the location of the Rabeaux to his rear, it could be over for him and Olivia within minutes. But Derrick never looked back in the enemy's direction once he'd made his decision. His gaze was fixed on that larger islet's watery edge in hopes of identifying the best location to hide the pirogue and get ashore. As quietly as he could, but with powerful strokes to his paddle, he crossed the open expanse to the islet, without the Rabeaux any wiser.

On the contrary, they still seemed unconcerned with any noise they made. Mato even called out to Derrick and Olivia from time to time, mocking both them and their family. They could plainly hear his loud ranting in the distance, but were unable to understand any of the babble. One thing Derrick did gather from Mato's chatter was the distance they still were from his location, a distance which he estimated to be three to four hundred feet and closing fast.Precious little time remained for Derrick to reach the islet and hide the pirogue and Olivia. But as they neared the land, he immediately noticed a well-worn path leading from the water's edge and disappearing into the thick vegetation. Wary of such well-worn paths, considering the incident near the *Miss Teresa* twenty-four hours earlier, he looked for another route. He found it no more than twenty feet away, in an area of thick cattails. Derrick headed straight for it.

Ludvick revised his plan and split the three Rabeaux men up to maximize their search area. As they searched, they were never to stray far from each other and were always to stay within shouting distance. At this time, Ludvick and Mato were busy circling a group of small islets while Victor found himself in an open body of water facing one islet much larger than the rest. From his standing position in his pirogue, he had a good view of this large islet and eased his way ever closer. He noticed that on the far side large oaks and swamp maples

dominated, but the portion closest to him was blanketed with roseau, cattail and blackberry.

Within a few yards of the islet's watery edge, Victor actually caught sight of movement in one patch of cattails. He watched as a few of the plant heads rippled and leaned ever slightly. To be sure, he would have paid little attention if the slightest breeze crossed his path but the air surrounding him was stagnant. "Hmm, what we got here?" He thought of calling out to Ludvick and Mato for help but wanted desperately to be the one to kill the last of the Cameaux seed. Thus, he just continued watching quietly as the slight movement worked its way from the center of the cattails further onto the islet until at last he lost sight of it altogether. The adrenaline was pumping throughout his body as he eased his pirogue closer to this patch of cattails that extended several feet into the water. He even spotted an area freshly parted; the water there was still quite muddy. Certain now that Derrick had made his way onto the island, Victor decided to follow his prey. Suddenly he noticed a well-worn path leading from the water's edge to the interior of the islet. "What luck!" he thought, figuring the path would give him quick, clear and unobstructed access through the thick vegetation. "May, yeah!" he said aloud with a self-satisfied chuckle. "In no time at all I'll be the Rabeaux to end this! ME! Not Ludvick! Not Mato! No One But ME!" Hastily, he guided his pirogue to the base of the path, and just as it touched land he glanced in the direction he'd last seen Ludvick and Mato. Relieved to see neither, he smiled to himself and stood motionless in his pirogue for a few moments. He helped kill Eric and Jon Cameaux, as well as others over his lifetime, but still he'd always lived his life in his father's shadow. Now everything would be different, for today was the day he would establish himself as his own man. From now on he would make his name rank at the top of the list when it came to great men in the Rabeaux line. So with an unmistakable sense of destiny waiting to be grasped, the confident Victor stepped out of his pirogue and onto that well-worn path.

After leaving the pirogue hidden in the cattails, Derrick and Olivia struggled in vain to reach the center of the islet. They found the trek especially formidable when they ran headlong into an impenetrable blockade of thorny blackberry bushes. He knew they had to get beyond

that prickly barrier somehow, but their options were poor. To their right was the well-worn path, and to their left the thick wall of thorns seemed to surround the cattails and finally end only at the water's edge. Before he could choose their best course of action, however, he heard someone approaching the islet by pirogue, and he quickly motioned to Olivia to get down. Because they hadn't yet gone far enough onto the islet to reach dry land, they stood in ankle-deep mucky slop, a half-water and half-mud combination that smelled worse than rotten eggs. Nevertheless, Olivia followed Derrick's instructions without hesitation and knelt next to him in the soupy mess. They were close enough to the water to hear the pirogue's approach and landing as it slid part way up the muddy trail.

Careful not to let his shotgun touch the muddy floor while he knelt in that slop, Derrick decided to sit in it so that he could better support himself and his weapon. Derrick leaned forward as far as possible, his eyes straining to see both the man and that old worn trail he was taking.

Victor was trying to quietly walk up the path, but his boots were making a loud sucking sound every time he lifted them from the mud to advance another step. It was a slow go, but he continued walking, meticulously inching his way closer and closer to Derrick and Olivia. They weren't sure whether or not he knew they were there. It was this very uncertainty that kept Derrick holding his shotgun tightly to his chest and leaning even closer to the putrid mud, trying his best to see through the thick vegetation to the path which lay only a few feet away. With visibility limited, still Derrick never took his eyes from the direction of the path because his ears were confirming the man's approach. In fact, he held his face so close to the mire that he could feel his hot breath deflecting off the mud and back into his face. By this time Olivia followed Derrick's lead and remained motionless in the foul muck. Never before had she ever experienced such tension, and she was more than convinced that this Rabeaux would find them simply by following the thunderous beating of her pounding heart.

The footing on the path was becoming easier now for Victor since he reached its more defined areas of use. It was still sloppy, but far better than the slime Derrick and Olivia were experiencing.

Derrick still could see only a short distance onto the path. Meanwhile, Victor knew that Derrick and Olivia couldn't be far. He listened for any sound in the direction of the cattail patch where he earlier viewed the movement, but he heard nothing there. Instead, he heard a slight rumble a short distance ahead and continued walking cautiously forward.

Derrick eventually spotted him coming up the path, or at least he was getting glimpses of Victor's boots and legs through the blackberry bushes. Finally Victor appeared close enough for Derrick to see him clearly through the brush. In fact, only a few more steps would put him within ten feet of them. Close, thought Derrick, too close. He'd always known that he had little choice other than killing Victor before he discovered them, and it looked as if that time had come for sure. Suddenly without warning, Victor stopped dead in his tracks. Derrick assumed they'd been spotted and aimed his shotgun at Victor when he heard a low grunt. A chill ran down Derrick's back as he recognized the sound, as did Victor. Derrick dared not move and hoped Olivia would remain still and silent as well.

Victor froze when he heard the low grunt, and the color drained from his face while his stomach grew weak. He looked to his left and then to his right for an escape route, but the vegetation was too thick to make a run in either direction. His mouth became uncomfortably dry; he realized he was standing on the path of death. He had to get back to his pirogue if he were to have any chance at all.

Derrick and Olivia heard more of the ferocious attack than they actually saw, which was definitely just as well, especially for Olivia. Nevertheless, with his eyes glued to whatever he could see of the worn path to his left, Derrick did catch sight of the giant gator, a massive reptile at least twelve feet long with a body so thick that it easily parted the thick vegetation as it raced toward Victor. This time it wasn't a female gator protecting her young, though that would certainly have been deadly enough. Derrick had seen many large gators before but this huge male had no equal. And whether that giant gator sought to actively protect his territory from Victor's intrusion or simply was seeking his own escape down the only path on the islet was of little importance. Either way, Victor stood in the way of an incensed, vicious animal.

Victor heard the rush of the beast coming fast toward him, and he turned and ran for his life. The giant gator was directly behind him. As long as he remained on dry land the beast lumbered forward using his beam-like legs as propulsion. However, as the ground beneath him became softer and muddier, the reptile began skimming atop the mud much as a bobsled sliding down a steep, snowy slope. The gator made expert use of his thick tail, which slithered powerfully from side to side to aid his forward motion.

Victor thought he could make it to his pirogue and threw down his shotgun to lighten his load. He wasn't thinking clearly now because fear controlled his actions, but obviously his only real and practical defense against such an awesome threat was his shotgun which now lay in the thick mud. As he neared the pirogue his footing became softer, and he sank deeper and deeper into the mud with each step. The sucking sounds of his boots as he pulled first one and then the other foot out of the sticky mire could be heard clearly once again by Derrick and Olivia. Victor strained to keep his footing, stumbling once and almost falling head-first into the mud, but managing at the last second to stay upright. Victor had two steps to go before reaching his pirogue. Straining again, this time with all his might, he thrust his body forward, but his momentum propelled him faster than his legs could carry him under the circumstances. When he tried to lift his left leg for the last step of his life-saving run, it wouldn't budge. That thick black mud held his foot like a steel trap refusing to free its quarry, and down he went head-first into the muck. The beast was so close to him now that he heard it slither atop the mud only a few feet away. Victor finally freed his foot and frantically crawled for his pirogue. Just as he reached it, he grabbed one side and pulled hard to upright himself, but the great gator lunged forward to prevent his escape.

Victor's piercing scream could be heard across the swamp. The gator's powerful jaws clamped onto his right leg, crushing bones as if they were twigs. Derrick and Olivia heard him scream so loudly that it seemed as though he were right next to them and, in fact, he was no more than a few short yards away. Olivia instinctively covered her ears

with her hands to shield herself against the sounds of the horrible attack.

Victor was being ripped to pieces; yet even in excruciating pain, he still tried desperately to cling to the side of his pirogue. But the giant beast wasn't finished; he swung his grotesque head so violently to the right that the pirogue instantly dislodged from Victor's grasp. At the same time the defenseless Rabeaux fell once more into the muddy bog which now consisted of more water than mud. The gator wasted little time in adjusting its grip on him and released his leg only to clamp down on his soft belly. Victor's screams grew even louder until the gator began a series of barrel rolls with the hapless Victor in its mouth. Bones popped as water and blood churned with mud to form a pinkish dirty froth atop the water.

Derrick and Olivia endured the awful attack and Victor's screams until silence once again enveloped them. The great gator then pulled Victor Rabeaux's lifeless body away from the islet into deeper water and slowly dragged him below the surface. Both Derrick and Olivia knew that those screams were heard by the remaining Rabeaux and they would be on their way to the islet shortly. Once again facing a no-other-choice situation, Derrick simply looked at Olivia and asked, "Are you ready?"

"Yes, which way?"

"Let's crawl through these blackberry bushes onto the path. It isn't far," answered Derrick in a low whisper.

"Do you think it's safe?" asked Olivia.

"I'm not sure, but we have to get to the middle of this island before the Rabeaux find us." He took her by the hand again and while they were still on their knees, led her through the blackberry bushes to the worn path. As they stood up Olivia felt the pain grow worse in her leg, and as they walked up the trail she limped more and more. Although Derrick was concerned for her, he knew they couldn't spare the time to treat or even look at her wound from the devil tree. If the Rabeaux were to catch them, the wound would be the least of their worries. Thus, he led her farther up the path to an area not quite so overgrown with brush, and from there they headed for the larger trees at the end of the islet.

337

All this time Ludvick and Mato push-poled toward the islet to help Victor. Mato reached the empty pirogue first and began looking for his father, but it was Ludvick who spotted the bloody froth and bits of clothing in the water and recognized its source. Both men knew that Victor was gone and made no further attempt to locate a body. Mato was so angry that he shook in uncontrollable rage and screamed at the top of his lungs, "I'll kill you, Cameaux! I'll kill you!"

Ludvick stood in his pirogue thinking how stupid Victor was to get himself killed that way. He then eased his pirogue forward until he came to the thick patch of cattails and saw the parted vegetation just as Victor had. But unlike his son, Ludvick followed the trail and discovered Derrick's pirogue. He then pulled out of the cattails and started to circle the islet. Mato was still so consumed by his anger that he was unaware that Ludvick had moved on, and his grandfather called to him just to get his attention. "Mato! Bring youself over here, you batard" After he finally heard, he obeyed and pulled alongside Ludvick's pirogue.

Times like this were made for Ludvick. He thrived on anarchy and chaos. While other men such as Mato lost control, Ludvick remained calm and in total control. He knew how to manipulate people to achieve his desired ends, and he intended to use Mato as his instrument to reach this goal. He would exploit Mato's weaknesses and use them to his full advantage. After all, that was the only reason he had crafted his grandson into the Rabeaux he was.

Ludvick spoke first. "You know that Cameaux boy killed you Pop!"

"An I'm gonna kill him!" replied the obsessed Mato. "I see to it!"

Deliberately adding fuel to that rage, Ludvick continued, "An he got your woman too!"

Mato's anger was peaking to a feverish pitch, having been expertly stoked by the master himself, and now he was a rabid dog straining against the leash to get at its tormentor. Ludvick wasted no time at all in releasing his mad dog and yelled harshly, "Go then, Boy! Go fine that Cameaux batard an kill him like those Cameaux killed your pop an brother!!" Needing no other prodding, Mato pushed hard on his pole and the pirogue lunged forward. He would follow along the shoreline for a while and then if he didn't see signs of Derrick and

Olivia, he'd get out of his pirogue and hunt them down on land. It made no difference to him; he was simply hell bent to get at them.

The fact that Ludvick used him like a blood-thirsty cur released on a hot trail had never occurred to Mato. Not only that, it probably wouldn't have mattered, since he'd never really known any other relationship with his grandfather anyway.

Sacrificing his last grandson to kill Derrick Cameaux was a card Ludvick played without remorse. Truth of the matter, Ludvick never had any positive feelings about Victor or Mato and Toby, much less any stirrings of love and compassion. Simply put, he'd only been tolerating them for the sake of expediency, merely as tools to achieve his own personal goal: Killing the Cameaux line was all that mattered, all he ever lived to accomplish and this was the day he would make that happen. Ludvick loved the hunt and soon he would satisfy his blood lust. Under his breath he whispered, "Cameaux boy, now you a dead man!"

CHAPTER 59

Olivia and Derrick heard voices in the distance as they made their way toward the end of the islet to the cover of the larger oaks and swamp maple. Derrick knew Ludvick wouldn't be far behind, so he had to find a safe place for Olivia to hide. Locating such a spot would be a challenge even though this islet was larger than most in the area, but their main obstacles were time and Olivia's physical condition.

Walking became increasingly difficult as her leg began to swell. Derrick held her close to his side, half carrying her with one arm while holding his shotgun in the other. "Hang in there, Liv. Don't worry, we'll make it," consoled Derrick as convincingly as possible.

"I'm worried about you, Derrick. If you didn't have to deal with me, you could just...I mean, you could just leave me and..."

"Stop it, Liv. That won't happen," answered Derrick sharply in a whisper. "Just a few steps farther now," he coaxed as he led her toward a large oak tree with a huge root system standing almost a foot above ground. Tightening his arm around her for better support, he helped her to the base of the tree where they both sat down for a moment to rest. He immediately felt her sag against him and he watched her smile fade as she began to sob quietly. He quickly wrapped both arms around her and rocked slowly as he tenderly caressed her weary body.

"Derrick, I want you to leave me here and save yourself. I just can't go much farther." The tears fell gently down her face as she continued, "One of us has to survive to take care of Teresa and Toni. I love you so much, Derrick. Please go and save yourself both for them and for me." He admired her courage, but knew very well he would never leave her here to face the Rabeaux alone.

"Liv, it's out of the question and I've already told you that once. I love you. I was a fool not to tell you before how much you mean to me. We're both gonna make it out of here alive to raise our children together. Believe me, we're not done yet, so just hold on a little longer."

Glad he'd finally shared his heart, she thought she might at last understand why he hadn't said anything sooner. She asked, "You knew all along who'd killed Eric and Jon, didn't you?"

"Yeah, shortly after they were murdered, Pappy told me. And ever since then I've been planning to avenge them but one thing after another got in the way."

"Like me?" asked Olivia.

Derrick removed his arms from around her and gently laid his hands on her shoulders, holding her just far enough away to be able to look into her tear-stained eyes. "No, like me! I've learned a lot about myself since Eric's and Jon's deaths. You see, I'm Cajun, no matter where I go, no matter where I live. For a while, I forgot that and tried to be something I'm not. I've let the Rabeaux and circumstances dictate my fate. I've been just reacting to choices other people instigated instead of making decisions to guide my own way. I've underestimated my enemies and because of that, I've endangered your life. I love you, Liv. I want to grow old with you, and I want to raise Teresa and Toni as my own."

Olivia was at a loss as to how she should respond, but she did manage to ask with a smile, "Why Derrick, is that a proposal?" Immediately he slipped from sitting to kneeling and held both her hands in his. "Oh yes, my love, and now I'm on my knees asking you officially to please be my wife."

There was no question in her mind about her response as she playfully grabbed him by the front of his shirt and drew him closer.

She smiled once more and said, "I love you, Derrick Cameaux, and if you figure out a way to get us out of here alive, I'll marry you for sure." He cradled her in his arms as she leaned over and they passionately kissed. Then, without a word, Derrick abruptly stood and began pulling moss from the lower limbs of the oak tree.

"What are you doing?" whispered a puzzled Olivia who was still absorbed in the joy of the previous moment despite the gravity of their situation.

"You'll see," answered Derrick as he carefully placed and packed the soft gray moss between two large oak roots next to where Olivia was sitting. Then he gently and lovingly picked her up and set her down on the bed of moss. Next he unsnapped the strap that held his gun in its shoulder holster and removed the gun. Then he handed it to her and whispered, "Take this and keep it close at hand."

"What for?"

He hesitated for a moment before replying, "Just in case that old gator comes back."

Olivia knew the gun wasn't for the gator, at least not the four-legged kind, but she nodded with a knowing smile and reached out to him as he knelt beside her once more. "Derrick, I'll be fine," she whispered. "Do whatever you have to do."

"I love you, Liv. Now lie down here and try to shield your head while I cover you with the moss. I'm fixing you an air passage, so please be still and don't move. I'll be back for you as soon as I can. Just always know that I love you no matter what happens."

Leaving her here now was difficult. He piled on the moss until she was completely covered, except for an inconspicuous air tunnel which he made to travel the length of one of the oak tree roots.

As he was finishing he whispered, "It'll all be over in a short while. I'll see you soon, my love." And with that, he turned and walked away, remembering yet again the words of Pappy that the only way to beat Ludvick and the other Rabeaux was to do the unexpected. So far, that was exactly what he'd been doing, and it was definitely the reason he and Olivia were still alive. "And doing the unexpected like Pappy said is just what I'm gonna keep right on doing, thought Derrick. Especially now, cause the time has come for me to be the

hunter, not the hunted!" That personal declaration gave him confidence as he walked toward the end of the islet, which he reached a couple hundred feet from where he'd left Olivia. This end had higher, drier ground and different vegetation from the place where he'd hidden his pirogue and the vegetation fit in perfectly with the first stage of his new offensive. The palmetto growing here weren't as plentiful as it could have been, but it would certainly be enough to hide behind, especially since it grew all the way to the water's edge. Thus, with his shotgun in hand and his Bowie knife at his side, he hid behind one of the bushes close to the water's edge and waited.

Between the palmetto palms Derrick could see the open water and anyone who might be approaching by pirogue. Derrick guessed right in that he expected Ludvick to circle the islet at least once before setting foot on it. As patiently as possible while longing to strike at his enemies, he waited in the quiet serenity of the swamp. He reflected on all that had been going on, but still could make no sense of it or even come close to understanding Ludvick and his unfathomable hatred for the Cameaux family. He had no answer for the nagging question he'd asked himself a thousand times: Why did Ludvick hate to such a depth of evil that no humanity seemed to remain in him? How was such hatred even possible? The answer, he was sure, would never be known, and he was deep in these thoughts when he heard someone approaching.

Mato was push-poling his pirogue harder than he had ever pushed before. He scanned the islet to get a glimpse of the girl he wanted so badly and the man he hungered to kill. His shotgun rested at his feet, ready to be fired at a moment's notice, and his killing knife hung from his hip within easy reach. Derrick listened carefully to discern whether he heard the sounds from one or two pirogues, but he was unaware that Ludvick was following Mato from a distance. In fact, Ludvick held so far back that sometimes he would lose sight of Mato entirely.

As Derrick continued waiting and listening, he made up his mind that he would kill both Ludvick and Mato the same way they'd killed Eric and Jon – with a wicked shotgun blast.

Mato had been following the islet close to its shoreline, continually searching its interior as far as he could see, which wasn't very far at

times. He was now getting restless and decided that it wouldn't be long before he jumped on dry land and hunted Derrick Cameaux down like a common animal. He was now approaching the end of the islet where the palmetto bushes with their wide fan-shaped leaves obstructed his view, but not entirely. He could even see bare spots every now and then just to the rear of the palmetto bushes where the tree line began.

By now Derrick caught glimpses of Mato, but not Ludvick. Thus, only one Rabeaux presented an immediate problem for Derrick: Should he use his shotgun and reveal his position to Ludvick before he really wanted to do that? No, he decided not to fire the shotgun and instead placed it on the ground at his feet and drew his Bowie knife from its sheath. The weighty knife felt good in his hands, and he was confident in his ability to use it. Derrick knew he had the advantage of surprise. He had to strike first and hit hard. And with this somber resolve, he continued waiting and watching.

Mato traveled at a careless pace, with no concern at all for his safety because he was so sure he could kill Derrick Cameaux. After all, many men before Derrick had fallen victim to him. He'd never lost a fight.

The big Rabeaux was now rounding the tip of the islet and coming closer to Derrick's position. Derrick could clearly see both Mato and his pirogue and it appeared that he was alone. Derrick had to time his run at the water's edge exactly or he would miss Mato altogether. Thus, eager, ready and feeling the adrenaline flowing freely, he chose a narrow path leading from his position to his chosen point of contact. Then as soon as the nose of Mato's pirogue reached the narrow opening, Derrick rose to his feet and charged. Every muscle in his body worked in unison to propel him as though he'd been shot from a cannon. Timing was everything, so much so that even when he reached the water's edge and jumped forward, he still was seeing only the front of the pirogue, but not the big man himself yet.

Mato heard the rush toward him and dove forward for his shotgun, but it was too late. All he saw was a blur coming from his left. With knife in hand, Derrick was in mid-air when his target came into view, and Mato was still leaning forward reaching for his shotgun when they

345

met with stunning impact. Derrick's knees hit the surprised Rabeaux hard in the ribs, and the force sent both men flying out of the pirogue into the waist-deep water in a fight-to-the-death struggle. Mato came up first, knife in hand and looking for his enemy. Derrick emerged also with his knife drawn and facing Mato from not more than three feet away. It was a miracle that he'd held on to his knife after that initial contact with Mato, so jarring was the collision. This, of course, was his first close contact with any Rabeaux and what a man he faced. All that Ludvick's grandson lacked in looks and wisdom was twice made up for in physique and strength. He was a powerful killer looking for his next victim. And the big man wasted no time in showing the Cameaux his power as he swung his killing knife at his head. Derrick met and blocked the blow, but the deadly weapon came within a hair's breath of his face. In response Derrick immediately swung his knife at Mato's belly, but the Rabeaux moved quickly and watched the blade cut only air. This momentary diversion proved costly, however, because Derrick caught him off guard and punched him full force in the face with his free hand, drawing instant blood from the multi-scarred mouth and nose. Shocked and enraged, Mato countered with a series of frenzied knife blows, swiftly advancing on Derrick until he was close enough for the young Cameaux to catch his flailing knife hand. Instantly Mato also grabbed Derrick's hand, and the two men stood there face-to-face with their knives pointed at each other in a deadly game of strength. Derrick held his own for a while, but the much larger Mato was winning the test of strength as his knife inched its way ever closer to his opponent's chest. Suddenly Derrick sent a knee to the Rabeaux's midsection, sending Mato staggering backward. As soon as he regained his balance, Mato backed away until he stood facing Derrick in knee-deep water closer to the shoreline. Derrick quickly followed, feigning a direct blow to Mato's stomach until the huge man lowered his knife to block the blow. Then with lightning speed he went for Mato's neck, forcing him to jerk back and thereby leave his chest unprotected. Derrick's knife then cut deeply into Mato's exposed chest, sending a look of genuine pain and shock to his face as he looked down at the bloody, gaping wound. That fleeting

expression, though, was secondary to the one of insane madness that instantly replaced it.

Mato sensed his opportunity was now or never, and he determined to put all he had into one last powerful blow. So he lunged forward with a speed that temporarily caught Derrick off guard until he realized that even in this unexpected movement, Mato had left himself vulnerable. Now each man lunged forward in a final thrust to kill the other. Derrick moaned in pain as Mato's knife found its mark just to the left of center below his ribs. But at the same instant, Derrick's Bowie knife pierced Mato's body at a slight angle upward just below the breast bone. For the next moment each man stood there, staring into the other's face. Then Mato's hands dropped heavily to his sides, and with his eyes wide open the big Rabeaux fell backward dead, with Derrick's knife embedded in his heart. Likewise, Mato's knife remained buried in Derrick's side; he reached for the handle and pulled out the long blade. He then fell forward onto Mato's body which now lay half in the water and half out. Suddenly he heard the sounds of another pirogue approaching.

Ludvick had heard the fight ahead of him, but couldn't get there in time to help Mato. Within two hundred feet he found Derrick alive, but sprawled across his grandson's dead body. The two men spotted each other at the same time; but before Derrick could react, Ludvick turned his pirogue around and fled from the islet into open water. Derrick couldn't believe his eyes – Ludvick Rabeaux was running away like a coward! As he pushed himself upon all-fours and then to his feet, Derrick was weary but paid little attention to the blood flowing down his torso and his left leg. Instead, he took a deep breath and retrieved his shotgun from where he'd left it next to the palmetto bush. The old Rabeaux was on the run and he had to stop him because even though the body of the snake was dead, the head was still very much alive and would strike again if not stopped. And it was Derrick's destiny to make sure that this nightmare ended today. Derrick found Mato's push pole and pirogue and climbed inside as he watched Ludvick head toward a series of small islets to the north.

Derrick didn't know for certain just how badly he'd been wounded because the area around the wound was numb and he was still running

347

on adrenaline, which allowed him to stand in the pirogue and push pole without much pain. He was pleased to discover right away that Mato's pirogue was every bit as swift in the shallow swamp waters as his own. Now as he moved into the open waters in pursuit of the old Rabeaux, he could see him in plain view just a few hundred feet away, headed toward the smaller islets. Derrick had to get much closer to Ludvick before using his shotgun, and he also knew he was pushing both the pirogue and his body to the limit for that end. He was made especially aware of that fact when he unconsciously brushed his hand over his left thigh and felt wet, sticky blood. Ignoring the blood and sweat, he continued concentrating on Ludvick and thought he actually gained a few yards on the old Rabeaux. In reality, however, Ludvick kept his distance exactly the same as when Derrick began chasing him. Realizing that did nothing to discourage Derrick, but what really irritated him was the slight feeling of light-headedness he experienced. He still pushed hard on the pole, but he could tell his power was waning. Nevertheless he persisted, doggedly seeking to maintain the feverish rhythm he'd set for himself.

Meanwhile, Ludvick seemed unconcerned and only occasionally glanced back toward Derrick. There was absolutely no expression on his face—no smile, no smirk, no sense of urgency, simply nothing. His only visible indication of any exertion whatsoever was the strong, steady stroke after stoke after stroke he gave to his push pole.

Derrick recognized a survivor when he saw one, and he had no doubt the old Rabeaux would do anything in his power to stay alive. Still, he was perplexed to see him run like a coward. Pappy taught him many things about this character, but never used words like coward or fearful when describing his old enemy. Something about this just doesn't make sense, thought Derrick, suddenly feeling the shocking heat of the day beating down on him.

When Ludvick finally reached the small islands, his puzzling behavior was even more annoying because he immediately began weaving in and around them. Derrick stayed with him, not losing any ground, but not able to gain on the Rabeaux, either. At times it even seemed that the slippery Cajun had vanished behind one island only to reappear next to another. In fact, Ludvick led Derrick almost two miles

away from the islet where Olivia hid. And try as hard as he might, he was simply unable to get any closer to the man; to make matters worse, as critical minutes passed, all glimpses of him now were getting fewer and fewer. It seemed as though his adversary were actually playing hide-and-seek, but what else could he do other than to follow. Also, he had noticed that the old devil was leading him more to the east where the islets were larger and provided much thicker cover, both features that benefited Ludvick at this stage.

Derrick saw the Rabeaux's pirogue round an islet just ahead; but when he reached that same spot, neither the pirogue nor the man were anywhere in sight. He stopped for a moment to listen for any sound that would point him in the right direction, but he heard nothing. Finally he decided to move on, albeit at a much slower pace, in the same northeasterly direction. Critical minutes were now passing, and there was still no sign of the elusive renegade. More than once Derrick growled under his breath, "Where are you, Rabeaux?" Yet he saw and heard nothing. Suddenly he stopped his pirogue again.

Then it happened. At first he thought his mind was playing tricks on him because he could have sworn he'd heard a voice in the distance. He knew he wasn't crazy, but he was no longer minimizing his physical weakness either, and he wondered whether the voice were real or just the result of his continuing loss of blood. Then suddenly he heard it again, clearly this time. "Cameaux, you lost? Follow me to hell, Boy! I'm gonna take you to the DEVIL hisself!"

To his horror, Ludvick shouted to him from a long distance. In fact, that deceiver was now heading back to the south. Derrick suddenly felt sick to his stomach, but not only from his now painfully throbbing wound. Ludvick Rabeaux headed back to where Olivia was hiding. Derrick's head sagged as he realized Ludvick had outsmarted him. With whatever strength he could muster, Derrick immediately turned his pirogue around in pursuit. He knew he couldn't allow that snake to reach the islet because he would surely find Olivia, given enough time. Unable to contain himself any longer, he yelled in frustration, "DAMN YOU, RABEAUX!!! DAMN YOU!!!"

349

A vexing, devilish laughter and bone-chilling "COME JOIN ME CAMEAUX, COME JOIN ME!!!" erupted and reverberated maddeningly throughout the stillness.

Derrick realized his opponent was the master of the swamp and that he, at best, was a novice by comparison. He stared for a moment in the direction of his destiny: One way or another, whatever it would be—life or death—there was no alternative. With a sigh of resignation, and as much determined strength as he could muster, he headed back for the islet and Olivia.

CHAPTER 60

O livia had no way of knowing what was happening. Quite a bit earlier she'd heard what she assumed was a fight somewhere in the distance, but she couldn't be sure. Derrick packed her in moss so securely that she knew she couldn't trust any sounds that drifted her way. What worried her was that if Derrick won the fight, then why hadn't he returned for her?

Meanwhile, Ludvick steadily push-poled his way to where he knew he'd eventually find Olivia. Since the old Rabeaux acknowledged Derrick a worthy opponent, he knew that killing him would be gratifying, but simply killing the young Cameaux wouldn't satisfy his sadistic soul. He wanted Derrick to suffer, to see the one thing he loved most in life die right before him. The treacherous old Rabeaux, now far ahead of Derrick, crossed the last hundred feet of open water and reached the islet of Olivia's hiding place.

Though he didn't see Ludvick land, Derrick knew by this time that he'd never be able to overtake his enemy before he reached his destination. Weakening by the minute, Derrick continued to propel his pirogue forward as before but struggled with every push. He hoped Olivia would remain hidden long enough to at least give them both a fair chance against Ludvick. The crafty trickster led Derrick on such a wild run that he had wondered whether he'd ever work his way out of that maze of islets. But as always, his perseverance prevailed, and he

351

finally saw the large islet he sought just ahead. With as much strength as he dared to expend at this stage, he pushed his pirogue onward. Despite the pain in his weakening body, Derrick recoiled when the silence of the swamp was suddenly shattered by two quick gunshots. Immediately recognizing these shots as coming from his nine-millimeter hand gun he'd left as protection for Olivia, he could only hope they meant she'd surprised and killed the old Rabeaux.

By now unable to trust his balance, Derrick could no longer stand in his pirogue. Sweat poured out of him in the stifling heat. He longed for a breeze to give him some slight relief but none came. Finally, he had no option other than sitting and using his push pole as a double-handed paddle. Within moments he spotted Ludvick's pirogue pulled half on land and beached next to Mato's body. As he continued his slow but steady paddling, his left arm unexpectedly brushed down across his blood soaked wound. All the previous numbness which had allowed him to pursue Ludvick earlier was replaced by pure raw pain.

Derrick let his pirogue drift those last few feet of open water until it slid alongside Ludvick's. Once on land, he pulled the pirogue half out of the water, reached inside and retrieved his shotgun. Then as he rounded the front of the pirogue he noticed that Mato's body was still lying as he'd fallen. Leaning over, he removed his Bowie knife from the big Rabeaux's chest and replaced it in the sheath hanging on his side. With only one driving thought uppermost in his mind, he lurched past the line of palmetto bushes and into the darkness of the thick tree canopy which virtually blocked out all sunlight high above his head. At first he was a bit disoriented by the darkness and paused briefly to get his bearings and allow his eyes to adjust to the dim light. He knew that in his present condition it would be futile to try taking Ludvick by surprise. In fact, he was doing well just to remain standing. Then as from a dark abyss, Ludvick called out to him, "Cameaux! Over here, Cameaux! Come on, Boy! Come see what I got! I think you got interest here!" Derrick pushed on and saw the dark silhouette of Ludvick standing under the giant oak tree where he'd hidden Olivia. "That's it, Boy, that's it! Come closer! Let me see you!" Derrick merely gritted his teeth and walked to within a few feet of Ludvick, where he could see Olivia standing next to him. She had a dirty

handkerchief tied around her mouth so that she couldn't scream or talk, and Ludvick held his gun to her head.

"Let her go, Rabeaux! This is between you and me, just the two of us!"

Ludvick mocked, "Sha, where you learn to talk so good? I bet Pappy teach you how to be a smart boy like a good Cameaux! I bet he even teach you all kine of good things!" Ludvick then shrugged before continuing, "May, so what? Good things, bad things, you still a Cameaux, an I'm gonna still kill you."

Derrick listened patiently as Ludvick continued to belittle him and his family, or at least pretended to listen as he tried to figure his next move. His head was swimming from his loss of blood; he knew that in order to rescue Olivia, he must do it quickly. Once again he remembered those timely words of wisdom from Pappy: "To beat Ludvick, do the unexpected."

Ludvick rattled on, "Yeah, sha, I remember when we killed those two Cameaux boys. You should have been there. Those two didn't never stand no chance against us. An I remember when we killed your mama an papa too. They didn't never know what hit them."

As he kept the gun aimed at Olivia's head, Ludvick never stopped talking. He was plainly savoring the moment he'd looked forward to for a lifetime: seeing the look on Derrick's face the moment he pulled the trigger to kill Olivia. "Hey, Cameaux, you want to know just what I'm gonna do? Could be, I'd just kill you first an then have your woman to myself. Or maybe I just have her right now right here in front of you. How'd you like that, Boy? Sha, you know just to kill you right now would be too easy for the way to end the Cameaux name. No, I'm gonna make you die the double death. I'm gonna kill this girl first an then I'm gonna kill you, Boy, an wipe out the Cameaux name, just like I always said Boy, unto the last seed!"

Derrick decided that talking time was over. Slowly and without a word, he brought his shotgun up waist high and pointed it directly at Ludvick and Olivia. This unexpected, subtle move brought a slight smirk to the old Rabeaux's rugged face. "Say, Boy, you gonna kill your girl if you shoot me."

With the coldest, hardest expression and the most brutal tone he could muster, he answered, "Rabeaux, I plan on killing both you and the girl. What good is she to me now? Why would I even want her after you and your foul family laid your filthy hands all over her and then had your way with her?"

These words caught Ludvick off guard and gave him cause to think. But the old Cajun couldn't rule out the possibility that Derrick would think of killing Olivia because he knew if the roles were reversed he would do the same thing. "Well, then, you an me, we of the same blood, jus the same after all!"

"That's right, both our blood is red and I'm about to draw some out of you!" Then, still maintaining his dead-level aim on the pair in front of him, Derrick firmly braced the shotgun tightly against his right side. And for the first time ever, there was a trace of doubt on Ludvick's evil face and Derrick saw it. The old Rabeaux lived too long and worked too hard to let this brash Cameaux boy kill him now. He wasn't really convinced that Derrick would kill Olivia to get to him; but if he were wrong, he'd shortly be a dead man, and he just couldn't take that chance.

Suddenly, without warning and with startling speed, Ludvick jerked the gun away from Olivia's head and aimed it at Derrick. Surprising even herself, Olivia instinctively lunged for her captor's hand, but not in time, as the gun jerked. The noise was deafening.

Instantly the bullet hit the wooden stock of Derrick's shotgun just in front of his left hand, shattering the wood into a thousand pieces and knocking the gun out of his hands. Derrick could feel the combination of wood and metal rip his body as fragments flew everywhere. Undaunted by fear for her personal safety, Olivia continued pulling Ludvick's arm downward as he fired two more rounds at Derrick, sending these bullets into the ground just in front of him. With what little energy he had left and in one fluid motion, Derrick pulled his Bowie knife out of its sheath.

Though he was trying to shake her off, Olivia held tightly to Ludvick's arm as he frantically tried again to shoot Derrick, but to no avail. He watched in horror as the young Cameaux raised his knife high above his head and in a split second hurled the weapon at him.

Ludvick moved quickly enough to prevent the knife from killing him, but still the razor-sharp blade cut flesh. From the left corner of his mouth to his left ear, the blade sliced deeply, causing him to release the gun and claw at his face.

No longer able to stand on his own, Derrick stumbled, toppling almost unconscious onto the ground before him. Ludvick staggered forward in an attempt to retrieve the gun, but Olivia beat him to it. Dropping to the ground as soon as he'd released it, she quickly scooped it up at his feet, sprawled on the ground and rolled over on her back just as the old Rabeaux was leaning forward to wrestle the gun from her. Immediately she thrust the barrel into his stomach as he reached for both the gun and her neck. His hands never touched her, though, because the gun leaped in her hands. Ludvick flew violently backward and slammed into the giant oak tree where he crumpled motionless to the ground. As the smoke cleared, Olivia sighed in relief when she saw Ludvick's body lying still at the foot of the oak tree.

Struggling to maintain consciousness, Derrick managed to prop himself up on one elbow and whisper, "Nice shooting, Liv. Remind me to never piss you off." His words brought her back to reality and she sat up, removed the handkerchief Ludvick had tied across her mouth, and eagerly crawled to Derrick. As they embraced, Olivia noticed that he was seriously injured. She was horrified by his condition. "What now?" was the unspoken question that burned in their hearts, and demanded an answer. Either she would do whatever necessary to get them to the fringes of civilization or they would, indeed, perish in this God-forsaken swamp.

CHAPTER 61

O livia helped Derrick to his feet as both of them looked upon the motionless body of Ludvick as Derrick said, "It's over Liv, it's over."

Olivia knew that it wasn't over. She said, "We have to get you some help, Derrick." Under Derrick's direction, Olivia half carried him as they walked slowly toward the pirogue. When they finally arrived she turned aside at the sight of Mato's body, and asked no question. Instead, she helped Derrick into the pirogue and situated him on the deck just in front of where she sat on the rear seat so that he could rest against her. "Okay, now what?" she asked with as much enthusiasm as possible. "Just point me in the right direction."

"Back to the Rabeaux camp for starters," he whispered as he weakly pointed south. "If you head in that general direction, you'll eventually reach the levee leading to the Rabeaux camp. Just take your time and try not to knock me on the head with the paddle."

That bit of humor brought a slight smile to her face as she patted his shoulder and replied, "Sure, but remember, if I hit you on the head, Derrick Cameaux, it won't be by accident." He smiled back, but said nothing as she wasted no time and headed directly where he'd pointed.

Olivia never claimed she could handle a pirogue in the swamp, but under their present circumstances she was determined to make it back to the campsite so that she could see after his wounds. The swamp

cooked under its hundred-degree temperature and high humidity even though it was getting late and the sun was casting long shadows all around them. Sticky sweat saturated her body and made her clothes cling uncomfortably, especially over her wounded thigh, but she just kept closing her mind to the pain and hoped for the best. Her first concern was for Derrick and his increasingly laborious breathing, which now confirmed her earlier fears of his critical condition. So she set her gaze firmly ahead and powered the pirogue forward by pulling on the paddle even harder.

At first Derrick tried not to lean too heavily against her legs, but by now he was practically lying slumped at her feet and had to strain to see when she asked for directions. Thankfully, those times were few, but they were facing one now because the Rabeaux campsite levee appeared dead ahead. She knew it was the right levee, but she just didn't know whether to follow it to the left or right. Almost as if he'd been reading her mind and having barely moved a muscle until that point, Derrick now slightly raised his shaking hand and pointed to the right. "Thanks," Olivia responded as she brought the bow of the pirogue around and headed in that direction. Within a few minutes she saw the opening of the campsite, and when she finally touched the bow of the pirogue to the levee, she noticed for the first time the fading light. Helping him out of the pirogue they struggled toward the porch. Twice she had to bear his full weight as he fell to his knees.

Olivia cringed when she pushed opened the door of the smelly, filthy camp, but she knew it had to be better than spending the night outside in the swamp, and she knew first hand that it beat her holding pen. Once inside, Derrick mustered enough energy to help her get him to a bed located behind a large chest of drawers. She helped him sit and then carefully lie back and prop his head on an old pillow. She then lifted his legs to the bed and elevated them with another pillow, then hurried to find a lantern and some matches. When she returned with the light, she sat next to him on the bed and noticed him struggling to breathe. She then began gently unbuttoning his blood-soaked shirt, and when she opened it and saw the raw wounds for the first time, she involuntarily gasped aloud, "Derrick!"

"I know, Liv. I was hoping it wasn't as bad as it felt, but..." his voice trailed, and he could barely speak even at a whisper.

Visibly shaken, Olivia quickly looked away in fear that he would read her face. "I'd better try to find something to clean your wounds."

Derrick tried to speak, but again it was only a weak whisper. "You'd better take care of your leg first. I know you're in pain." There was so much more he wanted to say, aware that a big part of her pain was the result of continuing neglect and abuse made necessary by his injuries and her efforts to save them both. His eyes filled with tears, but she never saw them, for she was already looking for whatever she could find to help him. In fact, she really hadn't heard anything he'd tried to say because she methodically opened every drawer, tin can, bag, sack and anything else she thought might hide some form of medicine she could use to make him well.

Derrick tried to shift his weary body to find any possible comfortable position, but the bed was so lumpy that he finally gave up. In particular, the pillow felt like a rock under his head. As he slid his hand beneath it to rearrange it his fingertips touched something solid. Puzzled, he pulled out an old leather pouch. Derrick looked at it, turning it over in his hands several times before untying and loosening the worn drawstring. He looked inside and pulled out the contents of the old pouch, two folded pieces of paper. Slowly he unfolded the first and recognized it to be a Louisiana birth certificate, which he immediately thought was a very strange keepsake for any Rabeaux. The certificate was old and had obviously been handled very often over the years. Nevertheless, it was legible and Derrick read it very carefully.

THE GREAT STATE OF LOUISIANA

CERTIFICATE OF BIRTH

LET IT BE KNOWN THAT ON DECEMBER 10, 1940,

A BABY BOY WAS BORN HIS NAME: <u>LUDVICK RABEAUX.</u>

| MOTHER | FATHER |
| ANDREA CAMEAUX | TEMPE RABEAUX |

Derrick was stunned. His hands began shaking, but not because of his injury. He spoke in a whisper, "Andrea Cameaux is my great-grandmother, Pappy's mother." He then opened the second piece of paper, a hand written letter.

"Tempe Rabeaux, I give you your bastard son Ludvick, which for nine months I carried in my womb and despised both you and him for it every day. Why did I despise such an innocent child? Because it reminded me of you and all the filthy Rabeaux! You have made my life a living hell since the day you raped me. I've had to live in shame away from my family because of the abomination in my womb. I never want to see you or that bastard ever again. May you both burn in hell!"

ANDREA CAMEAUX, January 1, 1941

An involuntary shudder which had nothing to do with his wounds ran through Derrick's body as he folded the pieces of paper and replaced them in the pouch. He pushed the pouch deeply into the front right pocket of his pants and lay on the bed in profound silence as he thought, "Could it be? Could Ludvick Rabeaux really be Pappy's half-brother?" Then the old Rabeaux's last words suddenly came flooding back to him: "You an me, we of the same blood, just the same blood after all!" At the time Derrick had assumed the words meant only that they were both Cajun. He never imagined that he and Ludvick were actually related by "the same blood!" "It's true," he whispered weakly, "and now it all makes sense. Did Pappy know Ludvick was his half-brother? And if he did know, then why didn't he tell me!" He didn't know the answer to the second question; but the more he thought about the first one, the more convinced he was that Pappy knew all along.

Just then Olivia came back to his bedside with what she hoped were clean rags and fresh water. Seeing the look of dismay on Derrick's face, she asked, "What's wrong? Are you in more pain than before?"

Yes, great pain and not just from his physical wounds, though he had no intention of burdening her with that now. He simply whispered, "Believe me, Liv, the only pain I'm feeling now is the pain of my love for you. So smile at me, my love, if you share my pain."

Olivia brushed his hair back with her hand and looked deeply into his eyes. "Oh, do I ever share your pain, my love," she whispered with a big smile, not only to reassure him, but also to hide the hurt she felt inside. "I love you, Derrick Cameaux," she said softly as she bent to kiss his forehead.

A slight smile crossed his face and he managed to whisper, "Don't grieve for me, Liv. You're all I've ever needed, and my life is complete now that I know how much you love me. I know—you—wanted—to marry me—as much as-I-wanted—wanted to marry you."

Olivia held his hand and tried to smile again, but this time through her tears. "In my heart you are my husband, Derrick. I've loved you from the first day I met you so many years ago, and my love for you has never diminished, nor will it ever die. You just hold on, my love. We still have too much living ahead of us. Please, please, don't go and leave me here alone. I need you, Derrick!" He couldn't answer, but Olivia saw his faint nod and felt his feeble attempt to squeeze her hand, and she was thankful. She sat quietly next to him, holding his left hand and lovingly stroking his hair with her fingertips. Tears filled her eyes again as she helplessly watched this man she so dearly loved ebb away from her.

In fact, so deep were her thoughts and so complete her remorse that at first she didn't even hear the distant humming sound. Then, a few seconds later when she did notice it, she assumed it was only the wind until she became aware of its uniquely distinct rhythm. Suddenly, as if she'd just been awakened from a heavy stupor, the sound registered! She stood up and hobbled toward the camp door. "That's not wind! That's a motor and it's coming closer!" As soon as she opened the door she recognized the unmistakable sound of a helicopter and limped out to the small wharf to signal for help. The pontoon chopper approached from the west and was flying along the levee just above the tree tops. Olivia waved her arms wildly and shouted repeatedly at the top of her voice, "Here we are! Please hurry!" The

361

men spotted her right away as they hovered over a clearing on the edge of the campsite and set the craft down as soon as possible. The door of the chopper flew open and out stepped Pappy, already almost at a run toward her. As she tried to run to meet him, though, she stumbled and almost fell, but Pappy caught her just in time. And right behind him, with their firearms drawn were Sheriff Lebeouf, Lt. Autin and another deputy.

"Derrick's hurt bad. We've got to get him to a hospital fast!" she cried while she grabbed Pappy's hand and hurried them all to the camp. As they raced inside to his bedside Olivia called out, "Derrick! Derrick! Pappy's here. It'll be all ri—!" The words caught in her throat the moment she realized that his motionless form showed absolutely no signs of consciousness or even of life itself. Shocked and alarmed she stopped abruptly a few feet short of the bed, and Pappy had to quickly step around her to get to Derrick, as well as to avoid a collision.

When the old Cajun reached the bed he knelt beside his grandson and grabbed his hand as he called to him. "Son, my Son, it's Pappy. I'm here, Son." Derrick managed to open his eyes and turn his head slightly toward Pappy. "That's it, Son. You just hang on. We gonna get you to the doctor fast an you gonna soon be back to your ole self again." Pappy then turned and called the officers. "Lebeouf! Autin! Help me get this boy on that choppta!"

The three officers rushed forward to help Pappy, but Olivia was still in the way. And even when she heard Sheriff Lebeouf softly speak her name, she simply couldn't move or respond. Perhaps the whole ordeal had taken its long-awaited toll; whatever the cause or reason, she felt her own strength and awareness slipping away. She teetered ever so slightly and then collapsed into the arms of Lt. Autin, who caught her just before her head hit the hard wooden floor. Now they had two patients to load on board, and that's exactly what they did.

Just after take-off Olivia regained consciousness enough to realize where she sat. Sheriff Lebeouf and Lt. Autin sat on either side of her to help keep her from toppling over. Pappy sat in the seat across from her with his arms wrapped around his beloved grandson. Streams of tears flowed down his old weather-beaten cheeks and he talked

continuously to Derrick. Pappy had seen the look of death on the faces of men many times before, and he knew the endless, awful ways a man could slip into eternity. These very experiences convinced the old Cajun that his grandson would soon join the long list of Cameaux who had died at the hands of the Rabeaux.

Suddenly Pappy felt Derrick's weak body move slightly, and he immediately relaxed his hold a bit and looked longingly into his grandson's face. At first he hadn't noticed that Derrick had moved his hand down to his side, but before long he realized he was trying to retrieve something from his front right pocket.

"What is it, Son? Let me help you," Pappy said as he reached for whatever was in that pocket. Then when he removed the small leather pouch, he knew immediately that it didn't belong to Derrick. Not only that, it didn't take him long to figure out that it must have belonged to one of the Rabeaux, possibly even Ludvick. The old Cajun also realized that his grandson was saying something, and he quickly bent over to get every word.

Barely audible above the roar of the chopper, Derrick whispered, "I know the truth about Ludvick and your momma." Then as his eyes grew heavier and his breathing more shallow, he asked, "Why didn't you tell me?"

Startled, Pappy took a long, deep breath and was about to respond just as he saw Derrick slip into darkness and knew that he couldn't hear him.

There were many things Olidore Cameaux had never revealed to anyone, and heading that list was the fact that Ludvick was, indeed, his half-brother. That secret he'd planned to take with him to his grave. Not that he'd ever wanted to tell the story of how Ludvick's father had raped his mother; on the contrary, he'd often longed to relieve himself of this heavy burden. He just never could bring himself to admit that he and Ludvick had the same blood running through their veins. Not even Ben knew that secret. And now as Pappy looked into the face of his grandson, the last seed of the Cameaux family, he wondered how he could possibly have told Derrick the truth. How could he have explained that this very man who would stop at nothing until he had

killed every last Cameaux male also just happened to be his brother! Pappy simply shook his head at the futility of it all.

Olivia saw the anguish etched on Pappy's face and was sure she was also wearing that same expression. Then as she pondered again what life would be like without Derrick, she quickly tried to dismiss that thought and instead concentrate on her two small daughters who needed her to be strong and happy. Happiness she could reasonably fake, but her strength and, most importantly, her joy lay still and quiet in Pappy's arms.

A rather unexpected thought now suddenly crossed her mind as she sat gazing at Derrick's limp body just a few feet from her. He was the last seed; after him there would be no more Cameaux. She had no knowledge of the curse of Beto Rabeaux to wipe out the Cameaux bloodline "unto the last seed – The curse seemed to have been fulfilled that day. But little did she know of that tiny heart which even now beat steadily in her womb. . . .

EPILOGUE I

I t was a beautiful, bright summer morning as Pappy ambled out onto the back porch of his house, cautiously carrying his three-month-old great-grandson. His mind filled with many thoughts as he looked into the sleeping face of this miracle Cameaux. Then as he sat in his old swing, a big smile covered his face when he gently placed his fingertips on the baby's forehead and ever so softly followed that sweet face to the tip of the tiny chin. His tender touch evidently had a soothing effect because the proud Cameaux patriarch swore that a slight smile had crossed his great-grandson's face. Pappy gazed upon the infant as he whispered, "Hey Little Man, you the one, you a strong Cameaux seed."

At that very moment the screen door opened and out stepped Olivia with two steaming cups of coffee. "Come sit with us, Momma," urged Pappy as he patted the spot next to him. She set the coffee cups on the little table by the swing and sat next to the old Cajun and her new baby boy to watch Pappy enjoy fussing over him.

After a few moments of silence Olivia asked quietly, "Do you know what day it is today?"

Pappy paused a moment before he spoke. "Yeah, an it's hard to think that it's been a year ago already."

"Pappy, I want my son to be brought up in all the old Cajun ways. I don't want him to grow up naive and vulnerable, and I'm asking your

365

help to make sure that doesn't happen. I want him to know all about the family's past, and perhaps more importantly, what will be expected of him in the future."

Pappy looked at her with sadness and replied, "I'll help, I promise, an I'll tell him everything." Just then they heard a horn and both turned to the driveway side of the old house in time to see a Jeep pull in right next to the porch. Out scrambled Teresa and Toni, who both immediately ran up the steps to smother their mother and great-grandfather with hugs and kisses and to wake up their new baby brother. Olivia arose and walked down the steps in time to greet Ben, who now seemed happier than he'd been in a long, long time. Embracing her, he had a certain gleam of pride in his eyes as he asked, "You happy, Hon?"

"O yes, Pop, very happy."

"Hey, you'd better save some of that for me!"

Smiling, Olivia turned to face the love of her life and with outstretched arms hugged him tightly. Then with her head resting on his shoulder she whispered, "Derrick Cameaux, you make me so happy. Promise me you'll always take care of yourself so we can grow old together."

"Aww, Liv, nothing's gonna happen to me or you or any of our family. We didn't come this far to stop now. So don't worry, because the only thing we have to be concerned about is just raising these kids."

Olivia lifted her head and looked deeply into his eyes as she continued, "But they never found his body?"

Derrick's soft chuckle reassured her. "Liv, don't give that old man another thought. And now, my lovely wife, get our son and let's go for a walk around Pappy's garden." Taking that to mean that all was well, she smiled and turned to climb the porch steps to get the baby.

As she left his side, Derrick felt a cold chill run through his body, but quickly whispered under his breath: "Of course that old devil's dead! After all, we killed him, didn't we...?"

EPILOGUE II

It was a horrid, cloudy summer night with flashes of lightning and deep, long rumblings of thunder echoing throughout the darkness as the lone skiff approached Caminada. Its only occupant was an old Cajun wearing camouflage coveralls and a pair of hip boots turned down just below the knees. From under his hunting cap, which was completely encircled by an unbroken string of Mallard curl feathers, a shock of straight white hair flowed down to his shoulders. His aged, leathery skin revealed years of exposure to the elements, but those only accounted for some of the deep crevices that lined his face. Many told the story of brutal conflict, and one particularly devilish feature which almost seemed to shimmer every time lightning flashed around him was the deep scar that ran from the left corner of his mouth to his left ear. Nevertheless, his most haunting feature, without a doubt, was his dark, deep-set eyes that revealed an even darker soul void of anything good. His cold, relentless stare was unnerving, leaving most people feeling not only unclean but also uneasy. Ludvick Rabeaux, the old swamp devil, tied his skiff on the first piling, bow to the open bay. As he climbed onto the catwalk which led to the dimly lit Bar, it was obvious he'd not yet fully recovered from his injuries of the previous year. Despite that, with shotgun in hand he slowly and cautiously made his way to the Bar's only door. His eyes darted left and right in

continuous vigil against an attack from any enemy who would dare come near him.

Gloria was now alone behind the bar since she'd sent home the only help she had an hour earlier. Startled when the door slowly opened, she was determined not to let it show; she knew who it was even before he entered. She had been expecting him every night for the past two weeks and tonight the wait was over. There he stood, filling the whole doorway while distant flashes of lightning produced auras around his dark silhouette. Gloria's mouth dropped open as she froze from fear. It was an unmistakable fear she'd known only once before in her life, the night of her first encounter with a Rabeaux.

Now, without saying a word, Ludvick walked straight to the bar opposite where she stood. She noticed immediately that his eyes were fixed on her in a gaze that seemed to penetrate her very soul. For an awkward moment, the two stood face-to-face staring at each other in what seemed a contest of defiance. It was a contest Gloria could never have won. She actually wanted to recoil from the animal in front of her, for the face she gazed upon appeared non-human. And try as hard as she might not to look away, she quickly turned and hurried from the bar. Ludvick's uncompromising glare followed her and held fast to the narrow door through which she disappeared.

Gloria returned immediately and this time she was crying. In her arms she carried a baby, her baby boy. Every day since the birth of the child she had looked upon the tiny face only to be reminded of how she'd been brutalized by the baby's father. She'd tried to love the child, but something inside had revolted against her every effort and now, without hesitation, she handed the infant to Ludvick. He instantly laid the child on the bar counter and began removing its clothing, including the diaper. Then Gloria thought she almost saw a smile cross the disfigured face as he proved to himself that the baby was, in fact, a boy. And it was then that Ludvick looked down at the child and spoke the only words Gloria ever heard from him: "Yeah, Boy, you look just like Mato!" With that, he reached into his back pocket, pulled out a dirty envelope full of money and tossed it on the bar in front of her. Without wasting another moment he gathered up the boy and his shotgun and walked out the door. Gloria ran from behind the bar and

as quickly as possible slid the dead bolt into place to secure the lock. She felt almost light-headed, but relieved to have survived her second encounter with a Rabeaux, not to mention having rid herself of the child who reminded her of the worst night of her life.

She needn't have worried about locking the door against Ludvick Rabeaux, though, for he had the only thing he'd come for in the first place. As he headed northwest into total darkness, there was a glimmer in his sinister eyes because he was making plans to train this boy to be a Rabeaux. Looking down at the child in the seat next to him he growled, "Yeah, we got a new Cameaux on the bayou, but I'm gonna teach you good an we still gonna kill all the Cameaux – "UNTO THE LAST SEED!"